D1535463

Tales from Southern Africa

Perspectives on Southern Africa

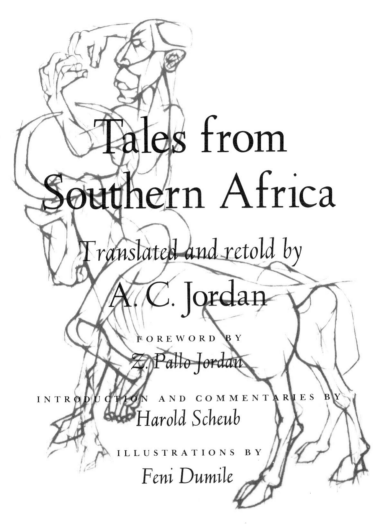

Tales from
Southern Africa

Translated and retold by

A. C. Jordan

FOREWORD BY
Z. Pallo Jordan

INTRODUCTION AND COMMENTARIES BY
Harold Scheub

ILLUSTRATIONS BY
Feni Dumile

UNIVERSITY OF CALIFORNIA PRESS

BERKELEY · LOS ANGELES · LONDON

1973

University of California Press, Berkeley and Los Angeles
University of California Press, Ltd., London
Copyright © 1973
by The Regents of the University of California
ISBN: 0–520–01911–3
Library of Congress Catalog Card Number: 76–145787
Printed in the United States of America
Designed by Dave Comstock

Contents

Foreword

BEFORE THE ADVENT OF MODERN INDUSTRIAL societies
an individual might have no special knowledge of the past of
his community, but by virtue of being brought up in a particular environment, he became the repository of special traditions, turns of speech, and even skills. The disappearance of
the more homogeneous communities of the past and their re-
placement by large urban complexes has, to a large extent, ex-
cluded the majority of the people from access to the traditions
that once shaped their societies. With the exception of those
who choose to specialize in the study of the past, most urban
dwellers have little besides a textbook knowledge of the past
to fall back on.

Hence we find that adults and children in Africa and
Asia have a richer store of folklore and folkways than do their
contemporaries in the metropolitan countries. In South Africa
the urban African has all but lost touch with tradition, while
his rural cousin, who is closer to the traditional mode of life,
still retains it. Before venturing into the material of this collection, it is perhaps fitting that the reader be acquainted with
the societies from which the tales are drawn, and understand
how time has changed these and their people.

The central institution in the traditional societies of
South Africa was the popular assembly. It breathed the spirit
of community life, embracing the economic, political, and eth-
ical outlook of the community. All men participated fully in
the affairs of the assembly, hence there were no paid legisla-
tors, and there was no clear distinction between the political

authority and the citizens of the realm. The king or chief presided over the assembly in council with advisors drawn from among the populace on the basis of merit and experience. Territoriality, rather than kinship, was the basis of the community. In many cases those coincided, but unrelated families might be neighbors, and strangers were often absorbed into a community. Political and kinship ties interlocked and both were expressed and reinforced through ritual. A king combined in his person both political and ritual functions. As the descendant of the founding ancestors of the community and the senior kinsman of the royal clan, he was mediator between ancestral spirits and his people. From this function there arose an insistence on blood ties with the lineage of the ancestors, for the numina of an exclusively personal association were reputed to spurn sacrifices brought by one not related by blood. In his political function the king was mediator between disputants among his people. The main concern of his office was the reconciliation of parties rather than interpretation of points of law. He also symbolized the unity and integrity of the community. As such, any injury done to one of his people was considered an injury against his person.

Traditional society held that there was a mutual dependence between the social and physical universe. Any disharmony in one was bound to have an effect on the other. One of the major functions of the monarch was to maintain the equilibrium between the two in very much the same manner as he served as the link between the living and the dead. The king inaugurated each sowing season with rites and performed sacrifices to the ancestral spirits at each harvest. At each summer solstice a great fete was celebrated during which further sacrifices were offered. This was also the occasion for the reconciliation between the king and his people. All were encouraged to publicly voice their grievances against neighbors, relatives, and the king, without fear of retribution. All debts of a material kind or of honor had to be settled, all quarrels and disagreements admitted, and the disputants reconciled. In this manner the community was sustained by an interlocking system of ritual and a well-reasoned political philosophy.

The religious life of the community was centered around

cults of household gods or ancestral spirits. Kinship was at the core of these cults and rituals and ceremonials were strictly proscribed for members of a lineage, except for those involving the welfare of the whole community, when all other affiliations were submerged in favor of the greater unity, symbolized by the royal household. Each homestead usually had two shrines, one being the gate of the cattle fold, the other, an inner sanctum in the main house. (Among some communities, the first shrine was the center of the courtyard, in which a tree usually stood.) Life was viewed as a cycle passing through a number of phases and finally tapering off in death. Each phase was inaugurated with an initiation ceremony during which the individual assumed certain social responsibilities and obligations. At each level persons were integrated into the social whole and enjoyed the sustenance given them by their fellow men. Mutuality and reciprocity were in command of all social arrangements.

The ethos of traditional society was enshrined in an oral legal, religious, and literary tradition through which the community transmitted from generation to generation its customs, values, and norms. The poet and the storyteller stood at the centre of this tradition, as the community's chroniclers, entertainers, and collective conscience. Their contribution to society was considered of the greatest significance, and they were usually maintained by the community through gifts, fees, and, in the case of exceptional artists, through royal patronage on behalf of the community.

Into this picture, from about the middle of the seventeenth century, intruded a new factor, destined to transform and finally destroy the traditional African community. For the next two hundred years European expansion steadily pounded at the foundations of African societies until they finally collapsed under the weight of the bombardment. The Africans resisted with all the power they could muster, but, through a combination of territorial annexation and forced acculturation, the gun prevailed over the spear. Thus began a new chapter in the history of South Africa, characterized by the total transformation of human relations.

European intervention in Africa was the product of a period of intensive technological and cultural revolution, coinciding with political and economic changes. The new cities were at the middle of this revolution, cities that had grown up as centers of crafts and commerce during the middle ages. The political changes underway conspired to abet the expansion of trade. European monarchs, intent on controlling their often rebellious barons, encouraged commerce as a source of revenue to support themselves in their struggles with their nobility. The fusion of these four currents resulted in the extension of commercial links with the Americas, the East Indies, and Africa.

From the mid-fifteenth century European merchants possessing charters from their kings, had traded and raided along the African coast for slaves, ivory, gold and hides. To secure a favorable trade relationship, the European powers often exerted political influence in the states with which they traded, making and dethroning kings, in order to improve conditions for their business. The technological edge they enjoyed over Africans gave them tremendous leverage in local affairs, until the original equal relation between the trading partners was transformed into one of dependency. These events in the fifteenth century set the pattern for all future contacts between Europe and Africa. What was initially an arrangement of mutual benefit gradually changed into an unequal partnership, with Europe dominant.

European colonization of South Africa began as the appendage of this larger commercial venture directed at the East Indies. With time it developed its own momentum, evolving along lines set by previous conquest. Conflict inevitably broke out between the colonizers and the indigenous peoples, usually involving the attempts of the colonists to dispossess the aborigines of grazing and cultivated lands and turn them into docile servants and dependents. The impact of European expansion on African societies took two forms, (1) military aggression and territorial annexation, and (2) gradual acculturation, proceeding parallel with the former. As white settlement spread outward from the cape, the indigenous Khoisan were either integrated into the colonial economy or were displaced and dispersed. Contact was finally established with the Bantu-speaking peoples further inland, first through trade in skins and ivory. With the settlement by whites of the border regions near the Negroid peoples, interaction between the two groups increased, each influencing the other to some degree. The colonial governments, dominated by what Adam Smith called "the petty spirit of commercial monopoly," controlled both trade with the outside world and internal trade. Such controls were difficult to maintain because of the distance between the administrative capital and the colonists' desire to break the government's monopoly on trade. As trade between the two communities increased, so the needs of both underwent mutation. White settlers wanted ivory, cattle, hides, and sometimes servants, all of which could be had only through trade with Africans. The Africans on the other hand, bought metal, beads, horses and later manufactured goods such as blankets, knives, guns, and brandy from the whites in return for their wares and often their services on white farms. While this trade remained at a relatively low level the fabric of the two societies remained more or less intact. But with increasing interaction, interspersed with wars and cattle raids, the technologically advanced culture began to supersede its partner in the advantages accruing to it.

The missionaries imported from Europe by the colonizing powers were a key element in the transformation of African societies. The Africans often mistook the preachers for seers, rainmakers, and diviners, like the ones they had in their own communities. It would often happen that a missionary would be invited to a local community, primarily for the benefits of his supposed magical powers. Once established, the preachers would proceed with his work of winning souls by learning the language, teaching his own to the new converts, and later attempting to translate the gospels into the language of his prospective parishioners with the aid of the converts. These missionaries brought with them the values of the society from which they came—hard work (indeed the very virtue of work), thrift, temperance, and respect for authority. They pressed their converts to adopt the standards of dress, agriculture, and living of their societies, vilifying the local traditions as savage, pagan, and ungodly. Every convert to Christianity became also a convert to the "Christian way of life." In order to acquire the paraphernalia for his new life style, the convert had to sell his cattle to get money or else enter into employment with a white farmer, if he was not a man of means. Charles Brownlee, native administrator in the Cape, later remarked: "in proportion to the spread of missionary influence, the desire for articles of European manufacture grew and spread. . . . To the missionaries mainly we owe the great revenue derived from native trade." The Christian missionaries thus became a crucial factor in encouraging interaction between the colonists and the African peoples. The influence of their ideas tended to be one-sided, in favor of the settler-community at the expense of the traditional societies. The extent of this estrangement can be judged by the fact that African converts often fled to the white occupied areas during times of war between their own people and the colonists.

Relations between the two societies were aggravated as much by the similarities between them as by the divergences. Both were communities of pastoral farmers and therefore sought grazing land into which to expand and secure water supplies. Each depended on the other to fulfill certain long-standing and newly acquired needs. However, the divergent concepts of property observed by the two groups jeopardized any modus vivendi they temporarily managed to agree on. The Africans knew only usufructuary rights to land, streams, and natural resources. Theirs was a community which knew nothing of fences and boundaries, the symbols of private ownership. Clashes inevitably occurred over the interpretation of boundary agreements, the cession of land, and the use of certain resources. The white settlers became notorious as a people who lacked common humanity, who were opposed to peace, and who were extremely quarrelsome (*makgowa*) and always ready to despoil their neighbors' flocks (*amadlagusha*). These clashes regularly escalated into wars and after each war the settlers annexed land, causing severe congestion, took cattle as an indemnity and destroyed property, impoverishing their victims and doing untold violence to the quality of communal life. This led to the breaking down of the old bonds that had held African communities together. The destitute among the Africans were forced to seek work with white farmers in order to earn a living. This increased dependence on the settler community had the effect of widening the scope for barter between the two societies, which further compounded the problem as local goods of African manufacture were unable to compete with imported European products. The balance between agriculture and crafts was completely overturned, throwing large numbers of Africans into the colonial labor market. The parallel currents of missionary endeavor and military conquest synchronized to force the Africans either to adapt very rapidly to the European presence, or drive the colonizers out by force of arms. Successive attempts to break the back of European expansion failed, owing to the rapid disintegration of traditional society and the technological superiority of the whites. Adaptation thus became the only real alternative, but such adaptation could occur only at the expense of the traditional society.

The Changing Role of The African Artist

One of the most striking features of African art is its anonymity. No works are inscribed with the names of their creators. Africans, like other peoples, distinguished between the charlatan and the savant, the creative genius and the mediocre. In most of the communities of Southern Africa, the names of the great poets and storytellers are still preserved, but, very rarely do we find a particular work attributed to even these. The explanation for this anomaly lies in the collectivist ethic of traditional societies. Artistic creations seem to have been regarded as collective works rather than the product of a particular genius. This applied particularly to the tale. In the traditional society, the tale was performed publicly, with the teller meeting his audience face to face. The setting for such performances varied. The homestead is probably the smallest unit in which such performances occured. Within the homestead the

older women, usually grandmothers or old aunts, were the storytellers. In a local community, each homestead would have
its own favorite storyteller; from among these a few would
emerge as particularly gifted and would come to be regarded
as the literary giants of the locality.

The custom of oral transmission of the literary tradition
lent to it a flexibility and dynamism, which could be utilized
by the teller and the audience to enhance their aesthetic experience. Unlike the written word, which can be removed from
its unique moment, be referred to, and reexperienced as often
as the subject pleases, the spoken word, the tune spontaneously sung, once it has been uttered, is gone and cannot be
recaptured. It has a unique existence, has the flavor of a particular moment and place which cannot be reexperienced.
Thus, though a tale may be repeated over and over again, it
can never be quite the same tale each time. As it is borne by
word of mouth from one teller to another, from one location
to another, its form and sometimes its content, undergo
change. Each individual artist squeezes his brush just that little more or less than the previous one. The colors take on new
hues and, with the additional colors drawn from personal and
community experience mixed in by each artist, often change
completely. As each new situation is colored by each new
imagination, a tale may grow or wither in the hands of different artists. The tale in Southern Africa is susceptible to free
improvization, dramatization and revision, making it possible
for each rendition, even of the same tale, to be excitingly new
and unique. This also gives the tellers, both men and women,
the freedom to adapt and readapt to each new audience they
encounter. In an unpublished paper, entitled: "Tale, Teller
and Audience in Spoken Narrative," A. C. Jordan recounts
what must have been one of the most exciting instances of this
practice:

> While the beer pots were passed around, the men were dis-
> cussing the latest developments in the Qawukeni dispute. At a
> certain stage, one of the younger men made the remark that:
> "if these eagles and vultures of Qawukeni are not careful, the
> grass-warbler will hop on their backs." Most of the men recog-

nised the allusion immediately, but there were a few who did not see the joke at all, and so the story had to be told in full. It was this that occasioned the birth of what I consider the most entertaining version I ever heard. There began the most spontaneous co-operation I have ever seen in story-telling. No less than six of the audience went with the principal narrator. They began "fattening" the narrative with dialogue, mimicry, bird calls, graphic descriptions of the grass-warbler's stunts when left alone in the sky, etc. etc. What was most revealing was the attitude of the original narrator to all this. Far from feeling he was being interrupted, this man was the most delighted of all. He was obviously getting fresh ideas for future occasions of story-telling. [The tale referred to: "The Birds choose a King," is included in this anthology.]

As Jordan tells us this adaptation and readaptation is not one-sided. Audience as well as teller are involved. The assembly of listeners are not passive observers, but are drawn into the tale and become totally involved both in its creation and consumption. There is no clear demarcation between artists and audience. This particular dialectic expresses most vividly the collectivist ethic at the center of the literary tradition and makes it possible to erect towering structures even on the meanest foundations. Although there is a teller who provides the theme and plot around which the narrative is constructed, the men, women, and children in the audience are encouraged to contribute what they can. Because of this instant feedback from the audience, the artists give their best, and in return they have their repertoire of tales enriched both qualitatively and quantitatively, which produces the vitality and dynamism of the tradition.

The Bantu language communities of Southern Africa classify tales into three genre. The first, *iintsomi,* is understood to refer to the fictitious, mythological, and fantastic; the second, *amabali,* refers to the legendary; the third, *imilando,* refers to the historical or events that are considered historically true by the community in question. These categories are themselves subdivided on an age-rank basis, conforming to the intellectual abilities of the audience for which they are intended. There are obviously discrepancies in classification even within

the same community, especially with regard to legend and history. Sometimes within the same tale or cycle, certain events
might be regarded as fictitious, while others are regarded as at
least feasible. It is therefore quite conceivable that a legend or
historical tale may contain elements that are fabulous
(*buntsomi*—literally, fiction-like).

Great significance is attached to these classifications by
the communities in question. We can discern this through the
ritual and taboos pertaining to them. In all civilizations of
scarcity, there is a certain ambivalence towards the arts, rituals, and festivals. The ever present concern with planning and
building for the future consumes so much time that ritual and
artistic creation have to be relegated to spare time. The struggle to create the means of life orients mankind away from the
past towards the future, so the pursuit of immediate pleasure
must be deferred until after the day's tasks have been accomplished. In the traditional societies of South Africa, these controls were reinforced by taboo against telling *iintsomi* during
daytime. It was held that anyone violating this taboo would
grow horns. It is significant that the taboo did not apply to
the legend and the historical tale. This would seem to convey
some functional distinction in the classification of tales. We
may assume on the basis of this differentiation that *iintsomi*
were considered primarily as a form of entertainment, a lei-
sure activity, while *amabali* and *imilando* were regarded as essential for the orientation and adaptation of the individual to
his society. In this manner the traditional society maintained a
dialogue with the past, while retaining a correct pulse of the
present and a perspective of the future through speculative
thought and imagery embodied in tales.

On days when the normal routine of the homestead was
disrupted, the taboo against telling *iintsomi* during the day
was relaxed. A simple ritual was all that was required to avert
the calamity attached to its violation. Both audience and teller
tucked a piece of wood in the hair above the forehead before
the performance began. But, even in respect to this taboo, we
find uneven application. The taboo was very rigidly applied
in the case of tales dealing with human subjects, while it was

liberally interpreted with regard to animal tales. This discrepancy would seem to indicate that human tales were judged to be intellectually and aesthetically of a higher order than animal tales. Animal tales were often told by a group of herd boys in the pasture, among a group of revelers or among a group of travelers on the road to alleviate their boredom. The typical animal tale is an Aesopian allegory commenting on the condition of men by projecting on animals certain human faculties and frailties. Tradition holds that the best exponents of this form were menfolk, which is probably accounted for by the division of labor in the communities. Since men were the cattle herders and hunters, they had an opportunity to study the habits of animals more closely than women. Women, especially the older women, are said to have excelled in the interpretation of tales dealing with human subjects. Human tales had a wide range of subjects. Through them the communities and their artists attempted to define the ideal by reflecting on human life. Then as now (and this is true of all peoples the world over) people were concerned with the answer to the great imponderables: what is truth, what is virtue, and what is beauty.

European colonization and conquest had the most dire effects on the role and position of artists in African societies. What had begun as the steady erosion of the foundations of communal life reached its peak during the 1850s when the British Governor of the Cape changed policy in order to "make the Natives a part of ourselves—useful servants, consumers of our goods, contributors to our revenue; in short a source of strength and wealth for this colony. . . ." By that time numerous Africans were already dependent upon selling their labor to supplement their incomes or make a living. War and annexation of communal lands had caused terrible congestion which brought with it new problems of soil erosion that had been unknown in the past. The growing disharmony between the land and its occupants produced a mass psychological crisis, which erupted in the cataclysm of 1857, when the Xhosa clans, in a desperate attempt to regain their lost lands embarked on mass cattle slaughter, which irrevocably destroyed the economic foundations of their community. The resultant famine drove thirty thousand to seek work on white farms. The decisive wars of 1879–1880 completed this process of disintegration by reducing the independent kingdoms to British tributaries and confiscating the communal lands as crown property.

By destroying the traditional economy, the European conquerors threw the African artists on the tender mercies of the market place, just as they had coerced hundreds of others to adapt to the "civilized" habits of working from dawn till sundown on a white man's farm. Without the requisite audience or traditional patronage, the artists had to adjust to their new condition by acquiring the ability to read and write and had to seek a new audience among the missionary-educated converts. The first African writers from South Africa emerged during this period of adjustment and reintegration. The introduction of the printing press altered the form of the oral tradition. The very act of recording and distributing the tales, epics, and poetry of the old tradition in books, to some degree, robbed them of their vitality. The written work, unlike the spoken narrative, is immutable and stands or falls in its first published version. The portable book, being a uniformly reproducible item, can be read and enjoyed in privacy, and for precisely this reason, deprived the artists of the freedom they had enjoyed in the traditional setting, sapped their work of that unique dynamism and flexibility it owed to collective performance.

Left to fend for himself as an isolated individual in modern industrial society, the writer had to seek out publishers who were willing to invest in him. Among other consequences of this new situation, was the total disappearance of women from the literary scene, in sharp contrast to the past. No African woman writer of note has yet appeared in South Africa. As the dissolution of the old communities proceeded with urbanization and the absorption of the Africans into the modern industrial economy, the literary tradition of the past has begun to disappear. In the urban ghettos where permits are required to hold public meetings, it is no longer possible to assemble to hear a storyteller perform. In white-ruled South Africa where the black man is required to have a permit to travel from one place to another, storytellers can no longer travel freely from village to village to entertain. In the context of gold mines, factories, and dockyards, the symbolism and imagery of the animal tale cannot have the same significance. Portions of it have been preserved in collections, and the traditional epic still survives in distorted form in and around the households of government-appointed chiefs, where some form of "royal" patronage still survives.

Deprived of land ownership by annexation and racist legislation, the African communities have lost control over the economic prerequisites for cultural production in industrial society. The few African publishing houses that were established were short-lived because the successive South African regimes have limited African rights to land-ownership and acquisition of business premises and forbidden financial transactions with other racial groups. As a result the few independent African publishers who survived have had neither the scope to expand, nor could they solicit financial backing from banks. By thus proscribing the mobility of the African middle classes who might have become the sponsors and patrons of indigenous art forms, the South African regime has effectively prevented development and elaboration on the foundations laid in the traditional society.

Industrialization and the proliferation of modern means of communication have brought even the most localized traditions into contact with each other, and researchers have reported instances of excerpts from the Greek classics being retold in Africa as if they were part of the local tradition. This latter is undoubtedly the result of contact with the major European literary traditions through books, journals, radio, and the cinema.

A. C. Jordan had a background typical of many young South Africans of his generation. In and around his home there was never a shortage of adults besides his own parents— great aunts, distant relatives, and dependents. In his village there was a widow in whose house the local men and boys

who tended the flocks gathered on rainy days. It was from
these people that he heard his first tales. On rainy days, together with other boys of the locale, he would sit around the
widow's fire and listen to tales narrated by the widow, Nofali,
and other herders. His father and a great-aunt who lived in
his home and who had a reputation as a good storyteller introduced him to the Greek classics in addition to the tales of
their own and neighboring communities. It was probably during this period that he developed his love for literature. But it
was during his years in college, after he had acquired a firm
grounding in the study of literature, that he began to articu-
late a coherent point of view with regard to African literature.
He and his contemporaries, like others before them, had
begun to question the things they had been taught about Africa and its peoples. They sought to redefine the African past
and the present in the light of both the "official" history and
the oral African tradition, and thus reassert a community with
pride in itself and its past, but looking in the direction of
"modernization." Imbued with this mission, Jordan dedicated
himself to African studies.

Modern African Nationalism in South Africa is the ideo-
logical offspring of this generation of men and women. Nationalism in the arts usually finds expression through music
and literature, both public arts, which can draw on the creative genius of the common people. In colonial societies, where
the majority of the people are, as a matter of policy, kept
semi-literate, the "folk" can be a revolutionary concept em-
ployed for the reaffirmation of a national identity. Jordan,
therefore, chose the Southern African tale—with its oral tradition, and hence not limited to a reading public—as the medium through which to express his protest against the existing
order. He sought to transform the tale into a great collective
symbol around which the African people could be mobilized
for social and political change. Whenever he went into the
rural areas, he sought out the old women who were renowned
as storytellers, to record their tales. While he was in Cape
Town, he would visit the older people in the townships, to
add to his collection of tales. One of his favorite haunts was a

house in Stone Street in that notorious slum, District Six. In this house there lived a number of men from Tsolo and Qumbu districts of the Transkei, where he had spent his childhood. Each Thursday, a woman from Qumbu, who worked in town, visited the house in Stone Street. She had an extensive repertoire of tales and was known as a great narrator. Together with the large audience that gathered for her sessions, she contributed quite a few tales to this collection. Though the atmosphere was perhaps contrived, it was the closest parallel to the traditional setting that could be recreated in the cities. As in the traditional setting, improvizations, dramatizations, additions, and revisions were freely offered by the audience. In this way the collection grew in quality and size. By trying to recreate the collective interaction between teller and audience as far as possible, Jordan recaptured the traditional flavor and atmosphere of tale-telling, thus adding greatly to the authenticity of this collection. It can therefore be said that this anthology is a truly collective effort in the spirit of the traditional society.

Z. PALLO JORDAN

Introduction

THE INTELLECTUAL IN XHOSA ORAL SOCIETIES is also an artist, a nonprofessional artist who communicates the ancient wisdom of the Xhosa peoples by means of artistically attractive and entertaining *ntsomi* performances.[1] The intellectual is an artist because of the special qualities and patterns of thought and the communication of thought in such oral societies, because ideas and customs and values are transmitted through art. There is no system of writing, no arrangement whereby man's thought achieves permanent form in books. It would be incorrect to say that a Xhosa "encyclopedia" exists in these oral narrative forms. Rather, a complex system of remembered clichés from which full performances can be fashioned compose a wide repertory of images and choices for the improvizational creation of a narrative or narrative-cluster. Individually these clichés do little more than communicate broad social ideals, of the "crime does not pay" moral variety. On their surfaces, the narratives of such oral societies as the Xhosa suggest simple "tales" with obvious themes. But the entire system must be considered, the full and rich tradition of narrative-possibilities, along with the vast and deep experience that artist and audience commonly possess of these narratives and their considerable variety in performance.

All children in Xhosa societies create *ntsomi* images, and they develop from hesitant storytellers into accomplished performers. Among adults, it is primarily women who produce

[1] This is discussed at length in my Ph. D. Dissertation, "The Ntsomi: A Xhosa Performing Art" (The University of Wisconsin, 1969).

the *ntsomi* performances. Men compose heroic poems,[2] extolling (or deftly criticizing) in rhythmic and often declamatory fashion important leaders and events of past and present. Men are also the historians in Xhosa oral communities. But there is no rigid division of labor among the sexes as far as these artistic creations are concerned: *ntsomi* performances are not the sole province of women, and poetry and history are not strictly reserved for the male members of the society.

The artist is not a preacher; she does not openly moralize. This is not to say, however, that her performances are not moral and even didactic, but the educational functions are subtly realized and are not evident to the alien. The performer develops her narrative by objectifying images, and it is in the construction of the image before an audience that ideas and social values are communicated. She is a consummate actress, performing, exploiting the poetic qualities of the language, blending the verbal elements of her production with such nonverbal materials as vocal dramatics, body movements and gestures, utilizing the imaginations and bodies and voices of the members of the audience to externalize image-sets which are remarkable in their internal complexity. The artist is more than a storyteller, for she does not merely tell a "tale." She memorizes nothing, she but recalls certain core-clichés. And as she objectifies the ancient clichés, the members of the audience learn, not through an analytical examination of ideas, but through a total emotional and psychological involvement in the performance.[3] The audience fully participates in the development of the *ntsomi;* many tensions exist —between artist and audience, between those involved in the artistic production and their milieu—and the performer seeks to control these tensions and convert them into aesthetic and educational values.

Because it lacks an obviously moral and didactic framework, the *ntsomi* tradition initially appears to have no educational function whatsoever. The performance has as its dynamic center a core-cliché, an easily remembered song or

[2] Called *izibongo* in Xhosa.
[3] Cf. Eric Havelock, *Preface to Plato* (New York, 1967).

chant (which may sometimes be flattened into sayings) around which the narrative-plot is constructed. Implicit in the core-cliché is the plot, but it should be emphasized that the cliché in itself is only a song or chant; the linear plot is not developed until the actual performance takes place. In a very broad and exceedingly complex sense, *meaning* is probably also implicit in the core-cliché, because all of the clichés, when objectified, support the general tenets of the society. It is closer to the truth, however, to say that meaning is really absent until the artist endows the cliché with meaning in performance, that the core-cliché is actually a vehicle for the communication of those ideals deemed of current validity by the artist. The performer (and, equally important, members of her audience) have a repertory of such clichés. When the performer is in the actual process of creating a *ntsomi* image, she mentally scans this repertory. Simultaneously certain cues (from any number of sources—from the image in the process of objectification, for example, or from members of the audience) bring to her mind certain additional clichés which she then adds to the original one. She is thus able, on the spot, to introduce new and perhaps seemingly unrelated clichés, developing them into full images. She can thereby create a longer narrative, objectifying a series of theoretically separate images into full, cohesive, tightly constructed and vividly dramatic performances. But it is not simply a string of clichés that she has linked together: the final clichés are carefully incorporated into the initial clichés, so that the whole has the illusion of unity.[4]

A basic esthetic element of the *ntsomi* tradition is repetition. The movement between conflict and resolution takes place structurally through the continued repetition of the core-cliché.[5] Thus, the cliché and associated details and image-segments, which combine to create the full *ntsomi* image

[4] See the work of Albert Lord and Milman Parry (especially Lord's *The Singer of Tales* [New York, 1965]) for a discussion of formulatic techniques regarding poetic epics.
[5] See my article, "The Technique of the Expansible Image in Xhosa *Ntsomi*-Performances," *Research in African Literatures*, 1, No. 2 (1970), 119–146.

can be called an *expansible image,* because the core-cliché and allied details can be repeated any number of times. But this repetition is never gratuitous. It has a very practical value: it is through repetition that the *ntsomi* plot is developed, that the narrative is moved forward from conflict to climax (or from conflict in one image to conflict in another). It also has esthetic value: repetition creates the very form of the *ntsomi* performance.

The following little *ntsomi* text from my own collection will illustrate this use of the expansible image. The core-cliché is a song:

> *Travel, Ndololwani, hurry!*
> *Travel, Ndololwani, hurry!*
> *Don't you see that we'll be killed,*
> *Ndololwani? Hurry!*

This cliché is used five times in this particular *ntsomi,* but it might have been used twenty times (and the song might not have appeared at all, its use being *implied* only). In the text that follows, this cliché is the structural and narrative keystone. When the plot shifts suddenly from imminent disaster to rescue and safety, it does so through the continued repetition of the cliché.

> *A ntsomi said—*
> *A boy was herding some cattle. Some Zims* [6] *arrived and said,*
> *"Boy, drive these oxen, make them travel!"*
> *The boy simply remained quiet.*
> *They said, "Boy, drive these cattle, make them travel!"*
> *The boy just remained silent.*
> *They said, "We'll kill you!"*
> *The boy said,*
>> *"Travel, Ndololwani, hurry!*
>> *Travel, Ndololwani, hurry!*
>> *Don't you see that we'll be killed,*
>> *Ndololwani? Hurry!"*

---

[6] A Zim is a cannibalistic creature which, though it has but one leg, is capable of great speed. When the Zim is born, its parents pounce on it and eat the infant's one sweet leg (the other leg is bitter).

The cattle travelled. They travelled, they travelled and travelled, and they came to the Zims' home in the fields. Then the ox was put into the cattle-kraal.

Someone said, "This ox must be slaughtered!" They stabbed it—

but the ox would not be stabbed! They stabbed it, it would not be stabbed!

They said, "Boy! speak to this ox!"

He said,

> *"Die, Ndololwani, hurry!*
> *Die, Ndololwani, hurry!*
> *Don't you see that we'll be killed,*
> *Ndololwani? Hurry!"*

The ox died. They skinned it then, they skinned it—but it would not be skinned!

They said, "Boy, speak to this ox!"

He said,

> *"Be skinned, Ndololwani, hurry!*
> *Be skinned, Ndololwani, hurry!*
> *Don't you see that we'll be killed,*
> *Ndololwani? Hurry!"*

The ox was slaughtered, and it was skinned. Then the ox was cooked.

The boy was given some of the meat, but he did not eat it. He continued to pick up the bones, he gathered them together. Then the meat was finished. He took the skin and put it into the kraal. He took the offal and poured it inside. Then he took the bones and put them inside. He collected the skin. Then the Zims left to gather some firewood.

The boy said,

> *"Get up, Ndololwani, hurry!*
> *Get up, Ndololwani, hurry!*
> *Don't you see that we'll be killed,*
> *Ndololwani? Hurry!"*

Then the ox got up. As it got up, it swayed. The boy beat it, and as he beat it, the Zims suddenly came into view!

He said,

> *"Travel on, Ndololwani, hurry!*
> *Travel on, Ndololwani, hurry!*
> *Don't you see that we'll be killed,*
> *Ndololwani? Hurry!"*

Ndololwani hurried out of the kraal.

It said, "Hakiiiiiiiiiiiiiii!"

The other oxen thundered after, together with the boy. The

Zims followed. They appeared here! they appeared there! appeared here! and there! The ox went off with this boy, and then they appeared at home.

The ntsomi is ended, it is ended.[7]

Another relatively uncomplicated *ntsomi* text from my collection will illustrate how a number of such expansible images can be brought together to form a longer production. It should be remembered that each of the three expansible images that make up the following text could be performed singly. The first image has a song as its core-cliché, a song which is used three times:

> *Rock! Rock-of-two-holes!*
> *Open! that I may enter!*

The second image also has a song as its core, and again it is used three times:

> *I'm not a dove to be beaten, kantikintikintiki!*
> *Not a dove to be beaten, kantikintikintiki!*
> *I seek Furujani, kantikintikintiki!*
> *His sister is being eaten, kantikintikintiki!*
> *By an old Zim, kantikintikintiki!*
> *It dismembered, dismembered her, kantikintikintiki!*

Finally, the third image has a *saying* as its core-cliché uttered twice by the Zim with a similar response each time by the heroine:

> *The Zim said, "Demazana! Demazana, what's that always going 'Zzzzzzzzzz'?"*
> *Demazana said, "No, Grandfather, it's just the clouds gathering!"*

The entire text follows:

---

[7] No. 1971 in my collection. The performance took place on November 13, 1967, at about 11:30 A.M., in a home in Nyaniso Location, Matatiele District, the Transkei. The performer was a Hlubi woman, about 65 years old.

A ntsomi said—

Furujani and Demazana travelled, going to their uncle's place. They travelled, they travelled and came to a rock. When they got to the rock, they said,

> "Rock! Rock-of-two-holes!
> Open! that I may enter!"

The rock opened. They went inside, they arrived there. On the inside they found the meat of an ox.

When they discovered this meat, Furujani said, "Demazana, don't eat this meat! I'm going on, I'm travelling on to our uncle's place." And so Furujani went on his way.

A Zim arrived, and it aid,

> "Rock! Rock-of-two-holes!
> Open! that I may enter!"

Demazana said, "Get out, you! You aren't my brother!"

The Zim journeyed on, it went to some other Zims. It said, "Men, what would you do if you found an animal?"

The Zims said, "Heat up an axe until it's red hot! Then swallow it, it'll come out below!"

The Zim heated the axe, it swallowed this red-hot axe. Then, when it came to the rock, it said,

> Rock! Rock-of-two-holes!
> Open! that I may enter!"

The rock opened. The Zim went in, it slashed into the meat and began to eat. Demazana saw it was almost finished, and she called a fowl.

She said, "Fowl, what'll you say if I send you to my brother?"

The fowl said, "I'll say, 'Kukurukuruku!' "

"Pig?"

The pig said, "I'll say, 'Nre!' "

"Goat?"

" 'Meeee!' "

"Donkey?"

The donkey bawled.

Demazana said, "Dove, what'll you say if I send you?"

The dove said, "I'll travel and say,

> 'I'm not a dove to be beaten, kantikintikintiki!
> Not a dove to be beaten, kantikintikintiki!
> I seek Furujani, kantikintikintiki!
> His sister is being eaten, kantikintikintiki!
> By an old Zim, kantikintikintiki!
> It'll dismember, dismember her, kantikintikintiki!' "

This girl, Demazana, said, "Travel! When you get back, I'll give you some kernels of corn!"

The dove travelled on its way. When it had gone, it came to some men who were sitting about. It arrived and perched above the kraal. Then the men tried to beat it. The dove dodged, and disappeared below. It dodged, and then it said,
 "I'm not a dove to be beaten, kantikintikintiki!
 I'm not a dove to be beaten, kantikintikintiki!
 I seek Furujani, kantikintikintiki!
 His sister is being eaten, kantikintikintiki!
 By an old Zim, kantikintikintiki!
 It'll dismember, dismember her, kantikintikintiki!"
Someone said, "There it is! In the yard!"
 The dove flew off, it came to Furujani who was milking. It arrived and perched. A beer party was going on at Furujani's uncle's place, and some men said that they were going to beat the dove.
 "Beat it! Beat it, Men! Here's the dove!"
 They tried to beat it, but the dove dodged out of the way. It said,
 "I'm not a dove to be beaten, kantikintikintiki!
 Not a dove to be beaten, kantikintikintiki!
 I seek Furujani, kantikintikintiki!
 His sister is being eaten, kantikintikintiki!
 By an old Zim, kantikintikintiki!
 It'll dismember, dismember her, kantikintikintiki!"
 Furujani said, "Hey! That's my sister!" He left the milk on the ground. Then he took a pail of paraffin, a gallon of it. He also took some fire along. He said, "I am brave! I am brave! Look at what I'm doing!" Then he travelled, and came to arrive far away at that rock. He arrived and poured the paraffin on top of the rock. The Zim blazed, the hair of the Zim was on fire!
 The Zim said, "Demazana! Demazana! what's that always going 'Zzzzzzzzzz'?"
 Demazana said, "No, Grandfather, it's just the clouds gathering!"
 The Zim ate, the Zim ate. Its hair went on burning, but the girl had said that the sky was just clouding up. The hair of the Zim was burning! and now it was getting near to the skin of the Zim's head!
 The Zim got up. Again it said, "Demazana! Demazana! what's that always going 'Zzzzzzzzzz'?"
 Demazana said, "No, Man! Grandfather, eat that meat! The sky is just clouding up!"
 The Zim got up, it felt the skin of its head already burning! It ran, it went out of the house and threw itself into a marsh.

Its buttocks stuck into the air, its head disappeared in the marsh!

It happened then that some children were wandering about, they had gone to gather some firewood.

One of them said, "Good god! here's a beehive! There's a lot of honey here!" The bees had indeed produced a lot of honey, and she ate it, and called the others. The children ate, they came and ate the honey there in the buttocks of the Zim. They did not know that it was the buttocks of the Zim, because there are its feet sticking up into the air! They ate and ate. Then one of the children scraped around, and her hand disappeared! It stuck tight! she tugged this hand, but her hand stuck tight! It was clear that her hand would not come out of the Zim's buttocks! They despaired, and they cut off that hand there!

And so it is that when people talk about the cutting off of this hand in the hole of this Zim, it is said that it is here where the Zim died.

The ntsomi ends there.[8]

The expansible image is the key structural device of the *ntsomi* narrative-plot. This image can be repeated as many times as desired and brought into any number of combinations. More accomplished artists frequently diminish these obvious structural characteristics of the narrative, perhaps even to the point of omitting the core-cliché altogether. But in most cases, it can be demonstrated through a comparative analysis of *ntsomi* variants that a core-cliché was the originator of the image, whether it is actually uttered or not.

The performer of *ntsomi* images has much freedom to improvise and originate, to bring her images into any number of arrangements and combinations. In fact, she is often judged on the freshness which she brings to the externalization of images that the members of her audiences have heard countless times. But she is always guided by a broad theme that centers about the need for an ordered society, a stable and harmonious community; in negative and positive ways, each *ntsomi* performance reveals some aspect of this ideal society. There is a

[8] No. 1789 in my collection. The performance was created on November 9, 1967, at about 12:30 P.M., in a home in Nyaniso Location, Matatiele District, the Transkei. The performer was a 40 year old Hlubi woman.

thematic movement from an impure society through purification and into a healthy social order. This odyssey is often expressed by means of a dramatic enactment of the male and female initiation rites, and usually finds its metaphorical perfection in symbols of nature. Fantastic creatures and animals are introduced into the realistic milieux created in the narratives as allegorical representations of this dissonance and the efforts to bring about a new equilibrium based on tradition and custom. Taken together then, the images that make up the *ntsomi* tradition indicate the value system of Xhosa society. Such a system cannot be worked out however on the basis of a single performance. It must be discovered through an analysis of the entire tradition. When a performer creates a *ntsomi*, her audience is aware of all other images in the tradition, and members of that audience use their imaginations and memories, first, to fill in any gaps left by the artist, and second, to enrich the image which the artist is in the process of creating. The audience is also intellectually prepared to place the particular performance being presented into the context of the entire tradition, viewing the individual image as an affirmation of the general theme of the *ntsomi* tradition and therefore of the entire Xhosa social system.

The artistic elements of the *ntsomi* performances are closely tied to the theme and thus to the educational function of the entire *ntsomi* tradition. One cannot seperate image from idea, they are the same. Objectification of image means the expression of an idea. The esthetic system developed over the years apparently because that was the most useful method (1) of communicating the basic Xhosa values from one generation to another, and (2) of educating the young of any single generation through a deep psychological involvement in the *ntsomi* performances and thus in the ideal Xhosa society (for the *ntsomi* is an organic extension of the society).

The collection of narratives in this book is based on *ntsomi* performances, but the narratives are not now *ntsomi* performances. They have not been retold by A. C. Jordan so much as recast by him. In the actual performances, for example, the performer seldom provides verbal descriptions of characters. She is herself the character, her body and voice giving the character dimension and detail. There is thus no need to describe the character in words, for the artist becomes that character through the magic of her performance and by virtue of her very presence, her very being. When the text of her performance is written down, however, her body and voice are gone; there are only the words—without intonation, without the music, without vocal and body drama, without the richness created by nonverbal artistic tools. Characters thus became "flat" on the written page, they lack body. But this is not an artistic flaw in the *ntsomi* tradition; it is one of the many problems involved in the translation of an oral art form into a written genre. Such a transference cannot be made without a terrible injustice to the performer and the tradition. The written text becomes a mere outline, a scenario—nothing more. The rhythmic movement of the language is gone; the rhythmic flow of prose into song, the very immediacy of the performance, these are replaced by the written word. The projection of an image kept alive by the artistic machinations of a lively artist is replaced by the written word. The word was never intended to be the only element of *ntsomi* performances: the creation of a *ntsomi* image depends on the many other elements which can never be captured in the written word. The image depends as much on the body and voice of the artist as it does on her spoken words. Moreover, it is an *oral* language that is involved in the expression of the purely verbal aspects of the production, and the qualities of an oral language are untranslatable to the written page. The tensions that exist between artist and audience, and the performer's manipulation and exploitation of those tensions: how can these essential ingredients of a public performance be captured in the privacy and remoteness of a page in a book?

Core-clichés become artificial when they are removed from their oral context. The dynamic movement of the narrative from the familiar milieu which surrounds the performer and her audience to the injection of fantastic creatures and actions loses much of its vividness when translated to another medium. All of this is to say that when the *ntsomi* performance is transferred to the written page, it can no longer be a performance—but it is not a short story either. It is a special genre, a hybrid, which cannot depend on the actual performance for its support. It must stand on its own as an artistic medium, and of course few artists have ever succeeded in giving these remnants of oral productions a life of their own within a context of the written word.

Jordan, himself a Xhosa and a writer of considerable merit and repute (his novel *Ingqumbo Yeminyanya, The Wrath of the Ancestors,* is one of the great African literary works), witnessed many *ntsomi* productions in the Transkei as a child. He has now recast them, and if the result is closer to the short story than to the *ntsomi* in structure, elements of the *ntsomi* nevertheless linger. Repetition has been muted, but that is also the case with the great oral artists' works. Jordan has retained many of the core-clichés, but these have now been diminished as important structural features of the narratives. He has also added descriptive details of character and scene which the Xhosa performer would have found unnecessary, even superfluous. He sometimes interpolates comments of his own, as would any good oral performer, but, because he realized that the readers of this book would be far removed from the South African oral traditions, Jordan also took pains to explain and motivate all actions, something which in actual Xhosa performances would not be necessary because of the familiarity of the members of the audience with the *ntsomi* repertory. There can be no doubt but that the oral flavor of the performances is gone. The personality and unique style of the individual oral performer which characterizes each *ntsomi* production have now been replaced by a more homogeneous, less personal, less vivid and colorful style. The spontaneity, the effect of the audience on the developing performance, the use of nonverbal devices—all have of necessity been sacrificed, as the tools of the short story come into prominence. The author must compensate for the lack of any nonverbal elements in the narratives, and this means works which are wordy and, at times, flat.

Jordan remembered these *ntsomi* images when, as a teacher in South Africa, he was lecturing on Greek mythology. His interests in classical Greek literature led him to his own Xhosa past, to the rich fund of oral traditions among the various peoples of South Africa. He recalled his youthful experiences when he witnessed the productions at the feet of his great aunt and others in his family in the Transkei. The broad span of years did not dull his appreciation of those early dramatic encounters—Jordan himself remained a splendid performer of *ntsomi* images until his death in 1968. But he was nevertheless unable to conquer the towering problems involved in translating not just a few Xhosa words into English, but in translating an entire dramatic experience with nothing but the written word. How does one put the suggestion of hand on paper? the movement of the body? the fleeting indication of sorrow? the tense and productive relations between the performer and members of her audience? How does one suggest the musical qualities of the language? the easy movement from rhythmic narration to song, from narration to a kind of restrained dance? Jordan did not attempt to do this, because he knew it was impossible. Instead, he fleshed out the scenario with words. He used techniques of the short story to bring life to the skeletal outlines, and he thereby moved away from the original *ntsomi* performances into the hybrid art form that exists on the pages of this book. Certain elements of *ntsomi* structure remain in these recast performances, and the themes of the original images are in no way impaired. But these narratives must be appreciated and judged for what they are, and not as *ntsomi* performances.

All of the narratives in this collection are derived from ancient core-clichés, and all support the general theme of the *ntsomi* tradition. I have written commentaries for most of the narratives, hoping thereby to suggest the development of that theme as it is revealed in the several plots.

HAROLD SCHEUB

The Turban

Nyengebule has two wives—one of them, the head wife, fulfills her function as wife, co-wife, and mother in proper traditional fashion, always adhering to custom, never stepping out of her role as the perfect wife. And yet her husband loves the second wife, a young woman who does not satisfy the customary demands placed on a wife. However, she is barren. In addition, her husband has so lavished his love on her that she develops few mature traits; she becomes irresponsible to the point that she neglects him *as well, forgetting to bring him some of the honey that she has found in the forest. This enrages her husband who, in his anger kills her.*

The husband's love of his junior wife is emphasized throughout the story. Though she is barren, he will not take one of her sisters as an additional wife, though his own family and his in-laws urge him to do so. His love is sufficient. And he is happy—he is very popular with his in-laws; he is an expert dancer and singer, and is thus desired at all festivals. The love he has for the girl and the great popularity he enjoys become the frame of the narrative and also do much to heighten through contrast the enormity of the crime. In his passion, he destroys the object he most loves; then, in a stark and horrifying way, he walks straight to his certain death: he goes to the festival and lies about the absence of his wife.

But the husband has committed a crime, he has disrupted the harmony on which the security of his society is based, and nature steps in in the form of the honeybird (and then its wing) to right the disrupted equilibrium. The honeybird in-

forms the in-laws of the crime, and the in-laws do the rest. The hero is ritually killed, and he is buried with the symbols of his status in life, the things he most cherished and which brought him the most happiness: the goat, a symbol of his wealth and, because it was a gift to his in-laws, a symbol of his respect for his wife's family; the bag of gifts, also a symbol of wealth and also a symbol of the affection in which he was held by those for whom the gifts were intended, and the affection he held for them; and the turban, symbol of his intense love for his wife. He goes to the festival and acts as if nothing had happened. When he is called into the council of his in-laws, he seems not yet to know why, though the murder took place just the previous night.

It is his ability to continue with life, almost as if in a stupor, as if nothing had happened, that invests the story with much of its horror, and which simultaneously, strangely underscores the love that he had for his wife. The man has committed a crime, and does not know what to do. He has destroyed the thing he loves most, and in almost automatic fashion, he can only go through the actions of his normal way of life. He has so completely destroyed his happiness that, confronted now with the need to do something, he can only follow the familiar routine.

He has compromised tradition by not taking another wife in addition to the barren wife, but both sides of the family seem to accept this. The love of Nyengebule and his wife is outside the boundaries of custom and tradition: there are no children, the relation is based purely on love, but the woman, because of her thoughtlessness, does not fulfill her own part of the marital contract. She obeys neither the traditional rules established by Xhosa custom, nor does she obey the laws set up by her husband in the special relationship that they enjoy. The murder affirms tradition, for had he loved the girl within the context of the society's tradition, he would have found mechanisms for punishing her for her thoughtlessness. More important, had she been placed properly within the frame of custom, she would have developed those qualities which she now lacks and which lead to the tragedy.

The narrative thus becomes an affirmation of tradition over boundless emotion.

The core-cliché at the center of this narrative is a song, sung twice (with continued repetition implied):

> Nyengebule has killed his favorite wife,
> She discovered bees and gathered the honey,
> She ate and forgot to leave him a share;
> He buried her together with her festival dress,
> And saw not the turban dropping on the way.

In this song is the core of the narrative, tightly compressed. This is the only thing that the performer remembers during an actual ntsomi production. The details, it is obvious, are suggested by the words of the song.

The Turban

IT CAME ABOUT, ACCORDING TO SOME tale, that there was a man named Nyengebule. This man had two wives, and of these two, it was only the head wife who bore him children. But Nyengebule's *ntandanekazi* (favorite wife) was the junior one, because she was younger, livelier and more attractive than the head wife. Nyengebule's in-laws by the junior wife were very fond of him, all of them. He was a warm-hearted and generous man. The women especially—his sisters-in-law including his wife's brothers' wives—used to be delighted when he paid them a visit. They would crowd round him and listen to the amusing stories he had to tell and also to demand the gifts to which they were entitled. These Nyengebule never failed to bring, but because he knew he was the favorite *mkhwenyethu* (brother-in-law), he delighted in teasing the women before producing the gifts, pretending he had not brought them any gifts because he had had to leave home at short notice, or because he had lost the bag that contained them on his way, or because his wife had offended him in one way or another just before he left home, and he had decided to punish her by not bringing her people any gifts. Then he would sit listening and smiling as the women coaxed and cajoled him, calling him by the great praises of his clan and by his personal ones. But in the end the gifts always came out, each one of them accompanied by an appropriate spoken message of flattery to the receiver. Nyengebule was very popular with the friends and neighbors of his in-laws too, because he was a great entertainer, a great leader of song and dance.

Whenever there was a *mgidi* (festival) at his in-laws, the whole neighborhood used to look forward to his coming, because things became lively as soon as he arrived.

Nyengebule's in-laws were sad that their daughter could not bear this man children. In the early years of this marriage, they tried everything they could to doctor her, and when they were convinced that she was barren, they suggested that one of the younger sisters should be taken in marriage by Nyengebule so that she could bear children for her sister. Nyengebule's own people supported this and urged him, reminding him that, by virtue of the *khazi* (bride-tribute) he had already given for the woman who turned out to be barren, he could marry one of the younger sisters without giving any more cattle. But Nyengebule kept on putting this off. To his own people he stated quite openly that he did not desire to do such a thing, that he did not see the need for it because he had enough children by his head wife, and because he loved his junior wife even though she bore him no children. To his senior in-laws he spoke more tactfully, because he knew that it would hurt them if he stated that it made no difference to him whether or not there were children by his marriage with their daughter. So he asked them to give him time. With his brothers-in-law he treated the matter as a joke.

"Oh, get away, you fellows!" he said on one occasion. "I know you will be the first to hate me if I do this, because it will deprive you of the opportunity to extort cattle from some other fellow who would have to give some cattle for the girl you offer me."

Everyone present laughed at this. But one of the senior brothers-in-law pressed him. Then Nyengebule said he wanted time to decide which one of his growing sisters-in-law would get on well with his wife as a co-wife. But when the girls he promised to choose from reached marriageable age, he had some other excuse for his delay. At last there came a time when the in-laws decided never to raise the matter again. Nyengebule was happy with their daughter, and the best thing to do was to leave it to these two to raise the matter, if and when they should desire such an arrangement.

One day, there came an invitation to Nyengebule and his junior wife. There was going to be a great festival at his in-laws, on such and such a day and he was being invited to be present with his wife. With great delight these two made all the necessary preparations. Two days before the day of departure, it occurred to the wife that on her return from these festivities she would be too tired to go gathering firewood, and that it would be wise to gather sufficient wood now, to last her some time after her return. She mentioned this to her co-wife, who decided she might as well go and gather some wood too.

The two women left home early the following morning. When they entered the woods, they separated, each one taking her own direction to find, cut, and pick dry wood and pile it to make her own bundle. But they kept in touch all the time, ever calling to each other to find out if things were going well. The final calls came when each one thought her bundle was big enough, and the two came together to sit and rest before carrying the firewood home. This was early in the afternoon.

While they were sitting there, there was a chirrup! chirrup! The junior wife was the first to hear it and she immediately recognized it as the call of the honeybird. She looked about, and saw this tiny bird fluttering about, now towards her, now away from her, and then towards her and away again.

"The honeybird!" she said and sprang up to follow it.

The honeybird led her on and on, chirruping as it went, until it came to a bees' nest. As soon as she saw this the woman called out to tell her co-wife that she had "discovered." The head wife came immediately, and the two gathered the honeycombs and piled them on a patch of green grass while the honeybird fluttered about hopefully. When they had finished, they picked up all the honey, except one comb that they left for the bird, and returned to the place where they had left their bundles of wood, and they sat down and ate together.

As they ate, the head wife took two pieces at a time, ate one and laid the other aside. She did this until they finished. It was only when she saw the head wife packing together what

Marriage.

she had been laying aside that the junior wife became aware of what had been happening.

"Oh!" she said. "I didn't think of that. Why didn't you tell me to put some aside too?"

In reply the head wife said, "You know why you didn't think of it? It's because you have no children. It's only a woman who has children who remembers that she must lay something aside as she eats."

The junior wife made no reply to this, and the two picked up their bundles and carried them home.

Nyengebule had been busy all day setting things in order. As far as his side of the preparations was concerned, everything that he intended to take with him to this festival was ready. Even the large fat gelded goat he was going to give as a son-in-law's customary contribution to the festival had already been chosen and fastened to the gatepost, so that it should be ready to lead away the following morning. Now he was waiting until his wives returned so that he should announce to his head wife formally that he and the junior wife would leave at cockrow, and also to give orders to his boys as to what had to be done by this one and by that one while he was away.

As soon as his wives had entered their respective houses and seen to the few things that usually need straightening up when a wife has been away from her house the whole day, Nyengebule went to the house of his head wife and made this announcement and gave the orders to the boys. His head wife listened very carefully as he gave orders to the boys, and when he had finished, she went over them all, taking one boy after the other:

"Have you heard then, So-and-so? Your father wants you to do this and that while he is away. And you, So-and-so, have you heard what your father says? He wants you to do this, and this, and that."

After this, she brought out the honey. She took some combs and served them up to her husband in a plate made of clay, and the rest she gave to her children.

"So you women discovered bees today!" said Nyengebule as he gratefully received his share.

"Yes," said his head wife. "It was *Nobani* (So-and-so) who discovered them. She was drawn by the honeybird."

"Well done! said Nyengebule. "But aren't you going to have any yourself?"

"No, thank you. I had enough in the woods."

So Nyengebule ate his share and finished it. Then, thanking his head wife for the honey, he said good-bye to them all and went to the junior house. He was looking forward to a much bigger feast of honey. If his head wife had so much to give him, certainly his *ntandanekazi* must have laid aside much more for him, especially as it was she who had "discovered." There were no children to share the honey with, and he and his *ntandanekazi* would enjoy the honey together, just the two of them.

He found his junior wife busy with her packing. The evening meal was not yet ready. Nyengebule did not say anything about the honey, because he thought his *ntandanekazi* wanted to give him a pleasant surprise. Maybe she would produce the honey just before the evening meal. But when the food was ready, his wife served it up to him and said nothing about the honey. After the meal, she removed the dishes and washed them and put them away. Now, surely, the honey was coming? But the woman resumed her packing, paying particular attention to each ornament before deciding whether to take it with her or not. She would pick this one up and add it to her luggage, and then replace it by another one. Now and again she would find something wrong with the beads of this or that necklace and pull them out and reset them. She would dig out some ornament that she had not worn for a long time and compare it with one that she had acquired recently, taking long to make up her mind which one was more suitable than the other for this occasion. This went on and on until everyone else had gone to sleep and the whole village was quiet.

When at last she was satisfied that her luggage contained everything she would require for the festivities, the woman yawned and looked at her husband.

"I think we had better sleep now if we mean to leave at cockcrow," she said.

"Sleep? Isn't there something you've forgotten to give me?"

Something to give you?"

"Yes! Where's all the honey you brought me?"

"I didn't bring you any honey."

"You're playing!"

"In truth, I didn't bring you any honey. If you think I'm playing, look for yourself. I forgot really."

"You forgot? You forgot *me*? What is it that you remember then, if you forget *me*?"

Before she could reply, Nyengebule grabbed a heavy stick and in his anger he struck her hard. The blow landed on her left temple, and she fell to the ground. Terrified at this sight, Nyengebule flung the stick away and ran across the hut and bent over her body, calling her softly by name. Weakly her eyes opened, and then they closed, never to open again.

Nyengebule burst out of the hut, his first impulse being to shout for help, but no sooner had he run out than he retreated into the hut on tiptoe, frightened by the peace and silence of the night. He knelt by his wife's body and touched her here, here, and there. Dead! His *ntandanekazi* dead? Yes, quite dead! What is he going to do? He cannot call anyone in here now. He must bury her before dawn. Yes, he must bury her alone. He is lucky too that everyone knows that he should be away at cockcrow. He must bury her and leave at cockcrow as arranged. Then his head wife and the children and all the neighbors will think she has gone with him.

He took a shovel and a long digging-rod and crept out to dig the grave. When he had finished he returned to the hut and looked around. That luggage! That luggage of his wife's! That must be buried with her. He carried the woman's body and laid it in the grave. Then he brought the luggage and laid it beside her body. He covered the body with earth and removed every trace he could find of this night's happenings. But there was one thing he had not noticed. The turban his wife had been wearing that evening had dropped on the ground between the house and the grave.

Nyengebule returned to his house, but not to sleep. What must he do now? Can he still go to his in-laws? Yes, that he must, because if he and his wife do not turn up, the in-laws will know there's something wrong and send someone to come and see what it is. But he has never gone to such festivities alone. His wife has always gone with him. How is he going to explain her absence this time? It will not sound good to his in-laws to say their daughter is ill, for how could he leave her alone then? What is more, they might do what they have always done when their daughter was reported ill—send one of her younger sisters to come and look after her and her hus-

band. But go he must, for this is the only way he can find
time to decide what to do. He will leave at cockcrow as arranged. Then he will try to be as he has always been until the
festivities are over. Then what? Then what?

"*Kurukuku-u-u-u-ku*" crowed the cocks. Nyengebule
crept out of bed and picked up his bags. He tiptoed out of the
hut and fastened the door. He spoke softly to the goat as he
approached it, in case it should make a noise and rouse his
dogs as well as those of his neighbors. But the goat did not
give him the least trouble. It was willing to be unfastened and
led away.

Nyengebule travelled fast, like one who was running away
from something. The goat did not handicap him because his
boys had trained it for purposes of riding. Sometimes he led it
by the rope, and sometimes he drove it before him.

Early in the afternoon, he had to leave the straight road
by which he had been travelling most of the time and take a
turn, walking along a path that led straight to his in-laws.
Nyengebule stood for a while at this point, undecided whether
to take the turn to his in-laws or continue along the straight
road, going he knew not where. At last he took the turn. He
had taken only a few paces when a honeybird appeared. It fluttered a little ahead of him and led him the way he was going,
but the calls it made were not those that a honeybird makes
when it leads a person to a bees' nest:

UNyengebul' uyibulel' intanda- *nekazi,*	Nyengebule has killed his favorite wife,
Ibonisel' iinyosi, yaphakula, *Yatya, yalibal' ukumbekela;*	She discovered bees and gath- ered the honey, She ate and forgot to leave him a share;
Uyiselele kunye nezivatho zom- *gidi,*	
Akasibon' isankwane sisiw' en- *dleleni.*	He buried her together with her festival dress, And saw not the turban drop- ping on the way.

Nyengebule was startled. Did these words really come
from that bird? And where had this bird gone to now? It had
vanished. He went on. The bird appeared again and repeated

its actions and song, but before he could do anything about it, it had vanished. But now he made up his mind what to do if it could come again. He would throw a stick at it and kill it. The honeybird appeared a third time and repeated its actions and song. Nyengebule let-fly his stick and hit it, breaking one of its wings. The bird vanished, but the broken wing fluttered a little and then fell at his feet, no longer a honeybird's wing but the turban worn by his wife the time he killed her.

He let it lie there for a while and stood looking at it. His *ntandanekazi's* turban! Can he leave it there? It should have been buried with her. He must keep it until he can find an opportunity to do this. He picked it up and put it into the bag that contained gifts for his in-laws.

As soon as he came in sight of his in-laws', the married women came out to welcome him with the shrills and ululations that announce the arrival of anyone who comes driving an animal for slaughter to such festivals. As soon as Nyengebule reached the *nkundla* (courtyard), his brothers-in-law relieved him of the goat, and their wives continued to sing his people's praises as they led him to the hut set aside for him and his wife. In no time, the sisters-in-law came crowding in this hut.

"But where's our sister?" they asked.

"So she hasn't arrived yet?" asked Nyengebule.

"No, she hasn't arrived. When did she leave home?"

"I left a little earlier than she because of the goat I had to bring with me. But she was almost ready when I left, and I thought she would be here before me because she was going to take a short cut and wasn't handicapped like me. She should be here soon."

They brought him water so that he could wash, and immediately after, some food and beer to make him the jolly *mkhwenyethu* they knew he could be.

The festival was to open on the following day, and therefore the in-laws and their closest friends were busy with the final preparations. The women were straining those quantities of beer that must be ready for the next day, and the men were chopping wood and slaughtering oxen and goats. All the people working at these assignments were already keyed up for the festival. There was plenty of meat and beer for them, and there were far more people than work to do. Therefore most of them were practicing the songs and dances with which they intended to impress the guests expected. Nyengebule's arrival therefore caused a great deal of excitement. Now that he had come, they could be sure that they would more than measure up to the famous expert singers and dancers with whom they would have to compete during these festivities. They were sure that this great singer and dancer had added something to his store since they last met him, and they were eager to learn these new things before "that great day of tomorrow." So, even before Nyengebule had finished eating and drinking, there were loud, impatient calls from his brothers-in-law and their friends to the *mkhwe* to "come to the men." But his sisters-in-law were not prepared to let him go until they had fed him, and until they knew what gifts he had brought them. For some of these gifts might be dainty ornaments that would just be suitable for the festivites.

At last, two of his brothers-in-law went to him.

"On your feet, *mkhwe!*" they said. "These wives and sisters of ours can get their gifts later. Get up and come to the men."

So saying, they lifted him up and carried him away, amid the amused protests of his sisters-in-law, as against the shouts of triumph from the on-lookers to whom Nyengebule was being carried. As soon as he arrived, the men greeted him with his praises and with song and dance, and invited him to join them. Many of the less busy women in the courtyard cheered, and in no time the place was crowded with on-lookers of all ages.

The sisters-in-law, however, remained in the hut, more curious to know what gifts they were getting than to join the admiring crowds. "I wonder what gift he has brought me this time, and what naughty things he is going to say when he gives it to me!" thought each one. After all, he was their favorite *mkhwenyethu,* and if he should discover at some time that while he was dancing in the courtyard they opened the bag of gifts just to have a look, of course he would pretend to be offended, but in fact he would be delighted. So thought the sisters-in-law, and they pulled out the bag of gifts and opened it. When a little bird's wing flew out of the bag and fluttered above their heads towards the roof, there were screams of delight, for everyone thought this was just one of the *mkhweny-ethu's* endless pranks. But the next moment, the women huddled together, horrified by the song of the honeybird:

> *Nyengebule has killed his favorite wife;*
> *She discovered bees and gathered honey,*
> *She ate and forgot to leave him a share;*
> *He buried her together with her festival clothes*
> *And saw not the turban she dropped on the way.*

The women watched the wing speechlessly as it came down, down, down, until it landed on the floor and became a turban that they all knew very well.

Shouts and cheers in the courtyard! Shrills and ululations in the courtyard! Hand-clapping, song and drums in the courtyard! Admiration and praises for Nyengebule in the courtyard! Few of the on-lookers, and none of the dancers, have noticed that the sons of this house—Nyengebule's brothers-in-law and their cousins—are quietly being called away, one by one, from this rejoicing. To the few who have noticed this, nothing is unusual about *imilowo* (those of the family) occasionally withdrawing quietly to hold council about the running of a big festival of this nature.

Nyengebule was just beginning to teach a new song when two of his in-laws' elderly neighbors came to tell him that he was wanted by his in-laws. Up to this moment, he had not met his parents-in-law, and he assumed that he was being requested to go to the great hut and present himself formally. But when he indicated to the two elders that he would have to go to his hut and change his dress before meeting his parents-in-law, one of them said, "There's no need for that. It's over there that you are wanted." The elder was pointing higher up the slope, to an old, high-walled stone building—the most prominent building among the ruins of what used to be the home of the forebears of Nyengebule's in-laws.

Married together.

The elders walked a few paces alongside him, and then they stopped and once again pointed out the building to which he had to go. Who wanted him? he wondered. Maybe his brothers-in-law needed his help about something or other? Maybe they expected so many guests that they thought they could prepare this old building for the overflow? But when he reached the door, the place was so quiet that he did not expect to find anyone inside.

He pushed the door open without knocking, and he felt cold in the stomach when he entered. Here were all his in-laws—his parents-in-law, his wife's father's brothers and their wives, his wife's father's sisters and their husbands, his wife's mother's brothers and their wives, his wife's mother's sisters and their husbands, his brothers-in-law and their wives, his wife's cousins and their wives or husbands, his sisters-in-law—all of them standing, silent, solemn. In the center of the building there was a newly dug grave. On the piles of earth that came out of the grave was the bag containing the gifts he had brought his sisters-in-law. Next to this lay the body of the large fat gelded goat he had brought as his contribution to the festival. No one acknowledged his hoarse, half-whispered greetings. Instead, his father-in-law pointed a finger at the bag of gifts.

"Open that," was all he said.

Nyengebule lifted up the bag and opened it, but he dropped it again, his knees sagging a little. The wing of the honeybird had flown out and was fluttering above the heads of those present, singing its song. When it finished, it dropped at Nyengebule's feet and became his dead wife's turban. Nyengebule gave it one look and then raised his head to look at his father-in-law for the next order. But the father-in-law turned his face away from him and signalled his eldest sister, a married woman. She stepped forward, lifted the bag of gifts, and cast it into the grave. The father-in-law signalled his two eldest sons. They stepped forward, lifted the dead goat, and cast it into the grave. Once more the father-in-law signalled, and this time all his sons and brother's sons stepped forward and closed in on Nyengebule. All the women covered their faces, but the men looked on grimly, noting every little detail of what was happening. They noted with silent admiration that Nyengebule did not shudder when these men laid their hands on him. They noted that he did not struggle or try to resist when they laid him down on the floor, face down. They noted that he did not wince when some of the men bound his feet together and sat on his legs, while others stretched out his arms sideways and sat on them. They noted that he did not groan when his two senior brothers-in-law raised his head and twisted his neck.

Four men jumped into the grave and stood ready to receive his limp body from their kinsmen. Everyone was looking now. As the four men laid him carefully on his back beside his rejected gifts, everyone saw the wing of the honeybird fluttering over the grave. As soon as the four men had done their solemn duty and climbed out of the grave, everyone saw the wing of the honeybird landing on the chest of the dying man and becoming his dead wife's turban. Everyone saw Nyengebule's arms moving weakly and rising slowly, slowly, slowly from his sides to his chest. The women sobbed when they saw his hands closing on the turban and pressing it to his heart.

His brothers-in-law and their cousins brought shovels and took their places round the grave. They lifted their first shovelfuls, but before throwing the earth onto his motionless body, they paused just for one moment and bowed their heads, for they noticed that the turban was still pressed to the heart of the dead man.

Demane and Demazana

*A fantastic element—the milk-producing bird—is intro-
duced into a realistic environment to expose the selfishness of
the children's father. And the realistic element that is introduced
into the fantastic world of magical rocks and speaking birds is
the human children. These two* parallel image-sets *represent
the basic structure of this performance, and it is in this structure that the theme reveals itself. The evil of the children's
home (the selfishness of the father in his refusal to share the
milk of the bird with his starving neighbors) finds its counterpart in the evil of the Zim, and the mediating element between
that evil and the purification of the children is nature—in the
forms of the rock and the bird.*

*A number of core-clichés make up this narrative: First,
there is the bird's injunction to the weeds:* "The weeds of this
field, go scatter! scatter!" *Repetition is implied. The second
core-cliché is the request that the bird produce milk:*

> *Bring it out, my little winged cow!*
> *Bring it out, my little hornless cow!*
> *Cow whose udder has never been seen with eyes,*
> *For truly is it hidden deep in your body,*
> *That we may see by the wonders you perform*
> *That indeed you are the foremost of milk cows.*

*Again, repetition is implied. A shorter demand is repeated a
number of times (*"Bird of our home, please produce amasi"*).
The third cliché involves the quest for the bird, and the query
of the children:* "Aren't you the bird of our home?" *Fourth is
the command that the rock open:*

Rock of Two-holes,
Open to us that we may enter.

The continued attempts of the Zim to enter the rock are a part of this core-cliché. Finally, the Zims' efforts to cut the tree down are a part of a core-cliché, but this cliché is never fully developed in this particular version of the story. It is thus an image-segment. *(Full analyses of four Xhosa versions of this narrative can be found in the article, Scheub, "The Technique of the Expansible Image in Xhosa* Ntsomi-*Performances,"* Research in African Literatures, I *(2): 119–146.)*

Demane and Demazana

IT CAME ABOUT, ACCORDING TO SOME tale, that in a certain family there were twins, a boy named Demane and a girl named Demazana, In the village where the twins lived, the men used to hunt, the boys used to look after the livestock, and the women and girls used to cook at home and, in the proper season, till the lands with hoes, sow the seed, and hoe the ground again to clear away the weeds. Demane and Demazana were yet too young to have such serious duties, and so, while the parents were away during the day, the twins used to play with the children from the neighboring homes.

It happened at one time that there was a terrible drought, and the people lost much of their livestock. There was no milk in the homes, not even for the youngest children. Even when the drought came to an end, there was still no milk because many cows had died during the drought, and those that had survived were so lean that they produced just enough to keep their young calves alive. However, the rains had come in time for the people to till their lands and sow their seed.

When the hoeing season came, the mother of the twins had to go to the lands early every morning and work till late in the afternoon. On returning home, she used to prepare the evening meal.

One evening, after the children had gone to bed, the woman said to her husband, "*So-mawele* (Father-of-the-twins), there's something I've been wanting to tell you since I began weeding this summer, but I have been hesitating because I'm sure you will not believe it."

"And what can this be, *No-mawele* (Mother-of-the-twins)?" asked the man.

"It is this. Ever since I began hoeing, I've worked very hard each day. But if you were to go and inspect our land, you would think I'd never done any work."

"How does that happen?"

"Each day I weed a very large patch, as large as from here to over there, but when I go again the following morning, I find that all the weeds I removed the previous day have gone back to their places, taken root overnight, and grown as tall and thick as they were before I weeded."

"What tale is this you're telling me, woman? How can such a thing happen?"

"I knew you wouldn't believe, So-mawele. I myself find it difficult to believe, even though it happens to me. It's the truth nonetheless."

"Well, the only thing we can do is to watch. You are to go to the lands tomorrow as usual. You are to work as hard as you can until I come. Together we'll look at the work you've done, and then you'll come home and look after the children. As for me, I'll remain there and watch."

The following morning, No-mawele rose earlier than usual and prepared some food for the children, who were still asleep. Then she picked up her hoe and set out for the lands. She fully expected to find the weeds she had removed the previous day back in their places and grown overnight. So, when she found it was truly so, she was not surprised at all. She began to weed the patch again and when she had just covered the same ground as she had covered the previous day, her husband arrived. They looked over the patch together to make sure that not a single weed should be left standing. When they were satisfied that No-mawele had done her work perfectly, the man said, "I've seen, *No-mawele*. You can go home now and look after the children. Before tomorrow's sun rises we'll know who this sorcerer is."

As No-mawele picked up her hoe to go home, the man began to look for a place to hide. On finding one, he lay there quiet till nightfall. Suddenly, a strange little bird appeared

from nowhere and landed exactly on the patch that had been
weeded during the day. The little bird hopped about from
place to place, and as it went, it said repeatedly:

Utyani bale ntsimi, ho chithi! *chithi!*	The weeds of this field, go scatter! scatter!

Thereupon all the weeds began to move. They scattered
all over the weeded patch, each one going back to the spot
whence it had been removed by the woman, and there they all
stood firm again, and as alive as if they had never been removed. From his hiding place the man gazed at this wonder
of wonders for a long time, and when at last he rose to look
for the "sorcerer," the little bird had vanished. He went to inspect the patch. He tried this weed, then that one, and he
found that all were as firm as ever.

"What strange thing is this? So the sorcerer who has been
eating away my wife's strength all this time is a bird, a tiny
bird! Would that No-mawele had told me this the day she discovered it".

He hurried home to tell his wife what he had discovered.
As soon as he entered, No-mawele knew that he had discovered something very unusual. But she remembered that he
must be hungry, and so she gave him some food first, and
when he had finished eating, she cleared the dishes and then
came back to sit down and listen to his report.

When her husband told her what he had seen and heard,
No-mawele found it very difficult to believe. First she thought
he was only playing, but when she realized that he was serious
she asked, "*So-mawele,* you are sure you were not stolen upon
by sleep to dream all this?"

"No-mawele," said the man, "I swear by my mother I
haven't closed my eyes since you left me in that field."

Then his wife believed him, because she knew he would
not have made that sacred oath if he had not spoken the
truth. They sat there for a long time, thinking what to do, but
at last they went to bed without arriving at anything.

Just when she began to feel sleep descending pleasantly

upon her, No-mawele was startled by her husband's voice, and she sat up.

"I've got it, No-mawele!" he was shouting with joy. "I've got it! I know the way to catch that little sorcerer!"

"Say it, So-mawele!" she said, her face brightening with excitement.

"Tomorrow morning we'll both go weeding, and we'll take a handful of millet grains with us. We'll weed as much as we can until it's time for you to return home. But before you go, I'll dig a deep hole in the middle of the weeded patch, deep enough for me to hide in. The only part of my body that'll be outside the hole will be my right hand. You'll put the millet grains in my hand, cover the hole with branches and leave. I'll keep my hand open until the bird comes. As it hops about, it will see the grains. I'll let it stand on my hand and take a few of these, and then I'll close my hand on it and crush it."

"This plan of yours sounds good, So-mawele! I'm sure we'll catch it that way."

Early the next morning, the man picked up an axe and a long digging-rod, and the woman picked up her hoe, took a handful of millet grains, and the parents of the twins set out for the lands. On reaching there, both of them worked with energy, because they were excited about their plan. Before the sun was right above the head, the man stopped hoeing and began to dig the hole, but No-mawele went on hoeing until she had covered the whole of the patch she had weeded on the previous day. When she had finished, she went to rest in the shade of a big tree, waiting for her husband to finish digging. When the man thought the hole was deep enough, he dropped the digging rod, picked up his axe, and cut enough branches to cover the hole. Then he dropped the axe by the hole, jumped in and signalled his wife to bring the millet grains. She brought the grains, placed them in her husband's open hand, and covered the hole with the branches. Then she picked up her hoe and went home.

At nightfall the little bird landed on the weeded patch not far from the man's open hand. Again it hopped about from place to place and said:

Utyani bale ntsimi, ho chithi!   The weeds of this field, go scat-
chithi!   ter! scatter!

Thereupon the weeds began to move, and in no time the
whole patch was covered with them. But in its hopping about
the bird came very near the hole, and as soon as it saw the
grains, it hopped onto the man's hand. Peck! and it swallowed. Peck! and it swallowed. Peck! and it swallowed. Then
the man closed his hand on it.

"You wicked little sorcerer! I'm going to crush you to
death."

"Don't kill me!" pleaded the tiny bird. "I am the bird
that yields *amasi* (fermented milk). If you take me to your
home, I'll yield *amasi* every day, as much as you need for
yourself and your wife and your beautiful little twins."

"So you know everything about my house, you sorcerer!
You even know that I have twins!"

"Yes, I do know that. Believe me, I can help you."

"Ha! Ha," laughed the man. "Do you think I'm such a
fool? Who ever heard of a bird yielding *amasi?*"

"Take me to your home and try me, if you don't believe."

"I'll try you right here—NOW!"

So saying, the man put out his left hand and transferred
the bird to it. Then he threw away the remaining millet
grains, cupped his right hand and held the bird in his left
hand over it.

"Proceed!" he said.

Immediately the bird filled his cupped hand with rich
amasi. Astonished but still suspicious, the man tasted this cautiously with the tip of his tongue and, on finding it very rich,
he swallowed the whole handful at one gulp and asked for
more. The bird filled his hand a second time, and he swallowed this at one gulp and asked for more. The bird filled his
hand a third time, and this too he swallowed at one gulp.
After this third round, he was satisfied that this was the greatest blessing that could ever come to any man, and he climbed
out of the hole and took the bird home.

Mother and children were in the cooking hut when he arrived home. He called out to his wife without stopping, "No-

mawele, *phothula!* (grind some boiled millet)," and he hurried on to the great hut, followed by the twins. His wife noticed that he was greatly excited, but she was puzzled that she should be asked to *phothula* when there was no milk in the house. She followed him to the great hut and asked anxiously, "So-mawele, what's come over you? How can you ask me to *phothula* when you know that we haven't had a drop of milk for moons?"

"What do you mean what's come over me? I told you to *phothula.* I've something here that will surprise you in a way you've never been surprised in your life. Go back to the cooking hut and *phothula.* When you've finished, bring the *mphothulo* here, and then I'll show you."

No-mawele saw that her husband was in earnest, and she became excited and hurried back to the cooking hut. There she knelt at the grindstone to *phothula,* and when she had produced enough for the family, she brought the *mphothulo* to the great hut in three separate basins, one for her husband, one for herself, and one for the twins. She put these on the floor in front of her husband, went to sit down on her mat, and then looked at her husband as if to say, "Now it's your turn. Proceed."

The man smiled and motioned her to bring him a larger basin. As soon as this was put in front of him, the man nodded and produced the bird from under his cloak. He held it in his hand over the large basin and praised it:

Wakhuphe, mazi yam e maphikwazana!	Bring it out, my little winged cow!
Wakhuphe, mazi yam e ngqukuvazana!	Bring it out, my little hornless cow!
Maz' e bele lingazanga labonwa ngamehlo	Cow whose udder has never been seen with eyes,
Kuba kaloku lifihlwe ngaphakath' embilini,	For truly is it hidden deep in your body,
'Kuze sibone ngezimang' o zenzayo	That we may see by the wonders you perform
Ukuba kanti uye phambil' intsengwanekazi.	That indeed you are the foremost of milk cows.

When they saw the bird's response to these praises—the rich curds that flowed out of its body and filled the basin—the mother and her twins were so amazed that they could find no words.

"There you are, No-mawele!" said the man triumphantly. "I know you thought I was mad when I asked you to *pho-thula.*"

"So-mawele!" whispered No-mawele. "Am I dreaming? What wonder is this? What good thing have we done to be rewarded with a gift of such value?"

"This is not the time for such questions," replied the man as he covered the bird under his cloak. "Prepare the food and let's eat."

Mother-of-the-twins prepared the *mvubo* (mixture) of *amasi* and *mphothulo* and the family settled down happily to eat.

After this meal, the parents put the bird into a large clay pot together with a jar of water and plenty of millet grains, and they covered the clay pot with a mat. Before the twins were taken to bed, their parents warned them never to uncover this clay pot, never to tell their playmates about the bird, and never to enter the great hut when the parents were away.

Left alone, the parents began to consider how to conduct the affairs of this house without letting their neighbors discover this great secret. They decided that they had better carry on with the usual duties and not do anything that would make them look better off than their neighbors.

Everything went well for some time. But there came a time when the twins became noticeably stronger and in every way livelier and more active than other children. Their parents too looked much brighter and energetic than any of the other grown-ups in the community. The neighbors began to talk about this. How was it that the grown-ups and the children of this house always looked so well fed when everyone else in the community was starving? What was this that they ate alone and never told anyone else about? The neighbors talked about this everywhere, even in the hearing of the children at their homes.

One day, while the parents of the twins were away, the village children came to play with the twins. After they had been playing for some time, with the twins never getting tired like their playmates, one of the playmates asked the twins, "How is it that you are so fat when the rest of us are so lean? What do you eat?"

"We won't tell you!" said the twins together.

"Please tell us!" begged the other children.

"No! We won't tell you. We were warned never to tell."

"Oh, do tell us, please. We shan't tell that you told us."

Then the twins told them that their father had one evening brought a bird that yielded *amasi*.

"Where is it now?" asked the playmates, excited. "We shan't tell that you told us."

"It's in the great hut."

"Go and show us."

"No! We were warned never to open the great hut when the old people are not at home."

"We shan't tell that you opened it."

Proud of the wonderful bird of their home, the twins ran to the great hut and opened it, and their playmates rushed in and looked about.

"It's in that clay pot," said the twins, pointing.

"Just take off the mat and let's have a look."

"No! We were warned never to uncover the clay pot."

"We shan't tell."

Demane took off the mat and the playmates crowded round the clay pot and looked at the bird.

"Please take it out and ask it to produce a little *amasi* for us."

"No! We can't do that. *Tata* will beat us!"

"We shan't tell."

So Demane took the bird out of the clay pot and said to it, "Bird of our home, please produce *amasi*."

The bird replied and said, "If I am the bird of your home, put me down."

Demane put it down and said, "Bird of our home, please produce *amasi*."

The bird replied and said, "If I am the bird of your

home, pick me up and put me down at the center of the hearth."

Demane picked it up and put it down at the center of the hearth, and said, "Bird of our home, please produce *amasi.*"

"If I am the bird of your home, pick me up and put me down on the doorstep."

Demane picked it up and put it down on the doorstep and said, "Bird of our home, please produce *amasi.*"

"If I am the bird of your home, pick me up and put me on that *xhanti* (forked gatepost) over there."

Demane picked it up and ran to the gate of the pen, followed by all the other children. He climbed up the *xhanti* and put the bird on one of its forks. As soon as he put it there, the bird sang:

Uyise kaDemane undicothele,	The father of Demane crept on
Undicothele ndingamboni	me,
Wandibek' umlandu;	He crept on me when I didn't
Kungoku zihlangene ngam iin-	see him
twana neentwazana.	And indicted me,
Khuza, mntwana! Kuud' eMkho-	And now the little boys and
manzi,	girls have united against me.
UMkhomanz' o negawelwa	Exclaim, child! So far away is
mntu,	the Mkhomanzi (river),
O welwa ziintaka zodwa kuba	The Mkhomanzi that is forded
zinamaphiko.	by birds alone, because
	they have wings.

Then mpr-r-r-r-r-r-r! Away flew the bird.

"Come back, bird of our home! Come back, bird of our home!" cried the twins, and they ran after the bird, trying to catch it.

The bird settled on the branch of a tree, but took off again before they could catch it, and it fluttered away to perch on some other tree. The twins chased it, but it took off again just as Demane was trying to climb the tree. This went on and on until the bird reached a forest and mixed with other birds on a tree. It was a large swarm of birds, and they all looked so much alike that the twins could not say which one of them was the bird of their home. Nevertheless, Demane climbed noiselessly up the tree and managed to catch one bird before the swarm flew away.

"Are you the bird of our home?" he asked.

"No," replied the bird. "I am the bird that produces blood." So saying, it dropped some blood into his hand. He let it go and climbed down and looked around. He saw a bird on some other tree.

"That must be the bird of our home!" he said hopefully as he climbed up the tree. He was even more hopeful when he noticed that the bird had seen him and did not make any attempt to fly away until he caught it.

"Are you the bird of our home?"

"No, I am the bird that produces gall."

And it dropped some gall into his hand. He let it go and climbed down.

He saw another bird on a tree and climbed up and caught it.

"Are you the bird of our home?"

"No, I am the bird that produces spittle."

And it spat into his hand.

Demane let it go, climbed down and sat on the ground, tired. His sister Demazana had not been able to keep up with him, but when she saw him sitting, obviously in despair, she ran up to him, her eyes wide open with fright.

Meanwhile where were their playmates? They had scattered, carrying their feet on their backs as they ran, each one to his or her home. They knew that the twins would be beaten that evening, and everyone of the playmates wanted to be far from the twins when this happened.

"What are we to do, Demazana?" asked Demane. "I can't find the bird of our home, and if we stay here, *tata* will kill us when he comes home. Let's run away and never come back."

So saying, Demane stood up and took his sister by the hand, and they ran, not knowing where they were going. They ran and walked, ran and walked, ran and walked until they were tired. They sat down to rest, and they fell asleep in each other's arms. They were awakened by the songs of the birds of the early morning, and once again they took each other's hand

and moved on. They walked as long as they could, and when
they felt hungry, they plucked some wild fruit from the trees
or dug *nongwe* and *magontsi* from the ground. When they felt
tired, they sat down and rested and slept.

After travelling in this way for some days, they came to a
rock shaped like a hut. Walking round the rock and examining it, they discovered that it had two holes, and they concluded that the inside must be hollow. They wanted to go in,
but they found that the holes were too small to go in by. How
were they going to get in? They sang:

Litye lika Ntunja-mbini,	Rock of Two-holes
Sivulele singene.	Open to us that we may enter.

Thereupon the Rock of Two-holes opened, and the twins
entered. In truth, it was hollow. It had a smooth floor, and
the inside of it was just like the inside of a hut. The two holes
let in the air, so that the inside was dry and fresh. Although
there was no one inside, it was clear that someone had lived
here, because there was fireplace and firewood, a little axe, two
fire-producing pieces of wood, and a calabash full of fresh
water. On exploring the place further, the twins discovered
some buffalo meat and buffalo hides.

It was only after they had seen all these things that the
twins realized that the Rock of Two-holes had closed behind
them. They tried to find the entrance by retracing their steps,
but since the rock was round, they could not say where they
had started. So they sang again:

Litye lika Ntunja-mbini	Rock of Two-holes,
Sivulele.	Open to us.

The rock opened directly in front of them. This delighted
the twins and they embraced each other. The rock closed
again on its own. Now they knew how to get in and out!
They had found a home. They would live in the Rock of
Two-holes, and if their father was looking for them in order
to beat them for what they had done, he would be disappointed because he would never find them. They would roast

and eat the buffalo meat they found here, drink the water they found here, and as bedclothes they would use the buffalo hides they found here. If it became necessary to seek food, Demane would go out and gather wild fruit. He would also bring firewood. If they wanted water, he would take the calabash and go out to find a spring. As for Demazana, she would remain inside the rock and cook. She must never come out of the Rock of Two-holes when her brother was away, and she must never open the rock to anyone except her brother. After making these arrangements, the twins roasted some meat, ate and slept.

The following morning, Demane armed himself with the little axe and went out to gather wild fruit. While collecting, he discovered that, besides the path that had led them straight to the Rock of Two-holes, there were many others in the forest, going in all directions. So he decided to find out who their neighbors could be. Possibly it was some other children who had had to run away from their homes for fear of being beaten by their fathers for disobeying orders. He saw smoke coming out of a cave, and he drew near and listened. But instead of hearing children's voices he heard rumbling noises like thunder, and then he saw a hairy-bodied, fierce-looking *Zim* (cannibal) lying in front of the cave, fast asleep. Then he realized that the rumblings he had heard were the snores of this *Zim*. He turned and crept softly away, and as soon as he thought he was far enough, he ran back to the rock. He stood outside and sang:

Demazana yo! Demazana yo!	Demazana yo! Demazana yo!
Demazana yo ka mama!	Demazana yo, of my mother!
Ndivulele ndingene	Open for me that I may enter
Kweli litye lika Ntunja-mbini.	Into this Rock of Two-holes

Demazana recognized her brother's voice and sang from inside. The rock opened and Demane entered.

"I've been roasting some meat, Demane," said Demazana as soon as her brother entered. Let's sit down and eat, and then you can tell me what you saw."

"No! I can't wait for that," said Demane. "You know what I saw just now? A *Zim!*"

"What!"

"Really! A real *Zim.*"

"Where did you see him? Tell me about him. What does he look like?"

"In front of his cave. He was lying on his back, fast asleep. He has a big stomach, as big as a hut. And his snores are like thunder."

"Wow! Did you speak to him?"

"How could I speak to a *Zim?* I crept away softly, and then I ran back here."

"Has the *Zim* any children? What do they look like?"

"How can I know that, Demazana? After seeing the *Zim* I didn't wait to see anything more. I ran!"

Demazana did not ask her brother about anything else. She prepared the food and they sat down to eat, and all the time her mind was on the *Zim.* Frightened as well as curious, she envied her brother the exciting experience he had had. But when Demane warned her again that she was not to open the rock to anyone except himself, she assured him that she would never open it unless she heard him singing as he had sung that day in his return.

One day, the *Zim* saw Demane from a distance and decided to follow him. But Demane reached the rock in time to be let in before the *Zim* could overtake him. He had not even realized that he was being followed. From a distance the *Zim* saw him entering the rock and wondered how he did this, for, as far as the *Zim* knew, there was no entrance to this rock. So, while the twins were eating and talking inside, the *Zim* went round and round the rock, looking for the entrance. Not finding one, he concluded that there was some trick about this rock that he did not know. He wondered how many people were inside there with this nice morsel of a boy. His mouth watered, and he resolved to catch and eat all those inside. So from that day he watched Demane's comings and goings, followed him unknown from and back to the cave every time he went out. At last he was able to follow the boy so closely that he heard him sing the song. Then he knew that in order to be admitted inside, he would have to learn this song and sing it like Demane. He came a number of times and listened carefully to the song, and each time, on reaching his cave, he sang it over and over again in what he thought was a boy's voice. At last he felt sure that he could sing it just like Demane.

The next time Demane went, the *Zim* came to the Rock of Two-holes. His plan was to enter and eat whoever was inside and then wait inside until the boy came and sang his song. Then he would let the boy in and eat him too. The *Zim* stood outside the rock and started to sing:

Demazana yo! Demazana yo!

But before he had gone far, Demazana interrupted him.

"That's not Demane's voice!" she shouted. "You think I don't know my own brother's voice? Go away, whoever you are!"

The *Zim* went away disappointed.

Demane returned some time after the *Zim* had gone. He found his sister full of the exciting news that someone had tried to deceive her by singing his song in a gruff voice just outside the Rock of Two-holes.

"But I didn't even wait for him to finish the song," said Demazana pleased with herself. "I told him to go away, whoever he was. How could he hope to deceive me with that ugly voice of his?"

The twins laughed. But soon they stopped laughing and began to wonder. Who could it be? Evidently it must be someone who had overheard Demane singing his song. They suspected the *Zim,* for this was the only man-like being Demane had met in the neighborhood of this home of theirs. But if the *Zim* had managed to come so near without being seen, why had he not caught Demane and eaten him?

The *Zim* was still determined to enter this rock. So after his disappointment on the first occasion, he returned to his cave, he sang Demane's song over and over again until he felt sure that his voice was as smooth and sweet as a boy's. The next time Demane went out, the *Zim* watched him until he

was some distance away from the cave, and then he crept to
the rock and sang:

Demazana yo! Demazana yo!

"That ugly voice is not my brother's. Go away!"

Again the *Zim* went away disappointed. He knew that it
was still the voice that betrayed him, and now he made up his
mind to seek advice and have his voice doctored. He went to
see his fellows at some other part of the forest. When he told
them his problem, one of them said, "That's very easy. If you
want your voice to be thin and smooth and sweet like a boy's,
take an axe and roast it in a very hot fire. When the axe itself
becomes red hot, take it out of the fire and swallow it. After
that your voice will deceive the people in the rock."

The *Zim* thanked his fellows and returned to his cave. He
did everything he had been advised to do, and his voice became like Demane's. He went to the rock while Demane was
away and sang the song from beginning to end without being
interrupted, and to his joy, he saw the rock opening.

When Demazana saw the *Zim* instead of her brother, she
uttered a cry of terror and fled to the other end and coiled herself up helplessly against the wall. But the *Zim* paid no attention to this. He was attracted by the fat buffalo meat that was
roasting on the fire, and he grabbed this and swallowed it hot
as it was. Next he devoured the piles of raw meat together
with the bones. Next he devoured the hides. Then he looked
around and saw the girl. But by this time his stomach was so
full that he could not take any more, even though his mouth
watered for human flesh.

"I can't eat you now, because I'm too full, too full," he
said, and he stroked his mountain of a stomach with his large
hairy hands, and he looked down at his stomach as if he was
angry with it for not being larger than it was.

"I'm thirsty," he said after some time. "Where's the
water?"

Demazana pointed at the calabash, too terrified to speak.
The *Zim* picked it up, opened his large mouth very wide,

threw his head back and poured the water down his throat. Then he held the empty calabash before his hideous face for a moment, as if debating in his mind whether to swallow it or not. Again he looked at the girl.

"Come out of there!" he commanded. "Haven't I told you I'm too full to eat you just now? Come and sit down. I'll lie down and rest a little, and then I'll carry you to my home so that I can eat you when I've rested my stomach. As for that singing brother of yours, I'll chase him until I catch him, and eat him too." So saying, the *Zim* threw down the calabash, stretched himself on the floor and yawned, and yawned and yawned, and closed his eyes.

Demazana had partially recovered from terror, and she began to think of a way of escape. She knew that in order to open the rock she would have to sing, and this would at once rouse the *Zim*. She must wait until she heard those thunderous snores Demane told her about. But the snores never came. Evidently the *Zim* was not asleep. Suppose Demane should return now and sing! Oh, how was she going to warn him not to come near the rock? But she must act, and act now. If the *Zim* was going to carry her to his cave alive, then there was still a hope that she and her brother might escape. She crept up to the *Zim*, very very softly, and looked at his face. She could not be sure whether he was asleep or not, so she crept back to the place where she had been sitting. But she must do something NOW, whether the *Zim* was asleep or not. If she just sat there doing nothing, the *Zim's* stomach would deflate and——and ——! In fact, hadn't it deflated a little already? She looked at it with wide-open eyes as it rose and fell, rose and again fell, rose and again fell. She could not be sure whether it had deflated or not, because it never stopped rising and falling. But what about her brother? What if he should come now, while the *Zim* was here? The *Zim* would gladly let him in and lie down again until his stomach deflated, and then he would swallow them both as greedily as he had swallowed the meat and the hides. Would that Demane be delayed by something until—until the *Zim* carried her away! Then Demane would come and sing his song, but there would be no reply. How would he know that she was still alive? And if he thought she was still alive, how would he know where to find her?

Then her face suddenly lit up with hope. She crept softly to the calabash, picked it up and filled it with ashes. Then she covered it with her little mantle and went to sit down again. Her mind was made up now. She must save her brother's life by getting out of here before his return, but she must have a way to make him know which way to go to look for her.

As if he knew her desire, the *Zim* opened his eyes and raised his head. He looked around, and when his eye fell on her, his mouth watered. He felt his great stomach and, finding it still full, he thumped and cursed it, and then he sprang up, seized the girl with one hand and flung her on his shoulder. Then he looked around puzzled. He went around, feeling all along the wall for the door, but there was no door.

"How do you get out of here?" he asked, glancing over his shoulder.

In reply Demazana sang:

Litye lika Ntunja-mbini,   Rock of Two-holes,
Sivulele siphume.   Open that we may go out.

The rock opened, and as soon as they were outside, Demazana turned the calabash upside down, but kept its mouth closed until the *Zim* began to walk towards his cave. Then she removed her hand, and the ashes began to fall out gently behind her, making a track along the route the *Zim* was taking. She held the calabash like that until all the ashes had come out, and then she dropped it behind her. On reaching his cave, the *Zim* brought out a rope and bound her arms and legs so that she would not be able to get up. Then he left her in the cave and went to look for her brother. He knew which way Demane had gone, because he had seen him going out in the morning.

Demane, however, had gathered enough fruit for the day and was on his way back. Before going very near the cave, he took care to look around to make sure that no one was near enough to hear his song. While doing this, he came across the

ashes and noticed that they came from the rock. He ran to the
rock and sang his song. Silence! He sang again. Silence! He
sang for the third time. Silence! He banged the rock and
shouted his sister's name repeatedly, "Demazana! Demazana!
Are you there?" Silence! He turned his back on the rock and
followed the trail of ashes, running most of the time, because
the trail was clear. At the end of the trail he stopped and
looked about, not knowing which way to go. Then he saw the
calabash and recognized it immediately. He grabbed it and examined it. Yes! The ashes he had been following came from
this calabash. There could be no doubt that his sister had
been carried alive to the *Zim's* cave. But now he had to be
careful because the cave was not far, and the *Zim* might see
him before he could rescue his sister. Cautiously Demane approached the cave until he was so close that he was satisfied
that the *Zim* could not be outside. Nearer and nearer he came,
and then he paused to listen. He heard his sister's sobs and,
without waiting another moment, he ran into the cave. There
was his sister twisting and rolling, struggling to free herself.
Demane leapt forward and cut the rope, and the twins took
each other's hand and ran out of the cave.

Meanwhile the *Zim* had been all over the forest and even
to the Rock of Two-holes and, not finding the singing boy, he
had decided to return to his cave. When he found his rope cut
and the girl gone, he concluded that some of his own fellows
had robbed him of his prey, and he ran to their home. They
assured him that they had not been anywhere near his cave
that day, and they offered to help him find both the girl and
her singing brother. The twins knew by a terrible hue and cry
that they were being chased and they climbed a big tall tree.
They stepped on one branch after another and went up, up,
up, until they reached the topmost one.

The *Zim* and his fellows arrived and saw the twins high
up on the tree. They tried to climb up, but each time a *Zim*
put his foot on a branch, the branch broke under his weight.
The only thing to do now was to hew down the tree. But
some of the *Zim's* friends felt this was not worth while. The
tree was too thick to hew down before the end of the day, and

there were so many to share the twins' flesh that each one would get a mere *mvungulo* (particle of food stuck between one's teeth). The cannibals quarreled and fought so much over this matter that it became impossible to work together, and all except the *Zim* who had originally discovered the twins abandoned the whole thing and went back to their caves.

The *Zim* sharpened his long fingernails on the rocks and then proceeded to dig them into the trunk of the tree. It was clear that it would take him some time to hew down the tree this way, but he was determined to have these twins. Every now and then he had to pause and stretch himself, because his stomach was too heavy for this work. Then after some time, he began to yawn, and finally he lay down on his back to rest.

The twins looked at each other, and then down the tree and at the *Zim* lying under it. Then they looked at each other again. How would they ever be able to get down from this tree? Even if the *Zim* were to fall asleep or go away now they would not be able to get down, because, in trying to climb the tree, the cannibals had broken all the lower branches of the tree, and to jump down would be to kill oneself.

Just at this moment, they heard the chirrup! chirrup! of young birds, and they looked about. In their fright, they had not noticed that on the very next branch there was a nest with two pretty little fledglings. The mouths of these fledglings were wide open, because their mother—a beautiful bird with a very long tail—had just arrived with a worm. The mother fluttered about a little and finally settled on the branch on which her nest was suspended. She tore the worm into tiny pieces and dropped these into the mouths of her little ones. The little ones swallowed and became silent again. The twins watched all this with interest. They also watched the mother tidy up her nest by collecting all the scattered feathers and putting them back in their places. They watched her push her little ones until they lay close together. Finally they saw her spread her wings and cover her little ones to keep them warm.

Her little ones now quiet and perhaps asleep, the mother bird spoke to the twins.

"Thank you for looking after my little ones and keeping them happy while I was away. But don't you think you had better go home now. It's getting late, and your parents must be wondering where you are."

"We've been away from home for some time," replied Demane. "Our parents don't want us any more. Our daddy will beat us if he ever sees us again."

"They don't want you? How can parents not want such beautiful twins? I don't believe what you're telling me."

"You see we . . . we . . . we did wrong while they were away from home, and we ran away because we knew we would be beaten."

"And so you think your parents don't want you any more because you did wrong? Parents aren't like that. Your parents must be missing you, especially your mommy. If you go home now, your parents will be so glad to see you again that they won't even ask you about the wrong you did."

"Are you sure?"

"Yes. I'm sure. How do you think I would have felt just now if I had found my little ones gone? I would have wept, and I would still be weeping, and I would continue weeping until they returned. I think I know your mother too. As I was seeking for food for my little ones, I saw a woman standing in the rain at the edge of a forest. She looked very sad. She was gazing at the forest just as a mother does when she doesn't know where her children have gone and hopes she will suddenly see them running out of the forest and throwing themselves into her open arms. I'm sure that was your mother. Your twin sister here looks very much like the woman I saw."

The twins looked at each other and smiled. But they looked down the tree, and their faces clouded.

"I know what you're thinking," said the mother bird. "You're wondering how you're going to get down this tree. But in fact that is no difficulty."

So saying, the mother bird came out of her nest, opened out her wings and fluttered about a little and then lowered her long tail to the twins and said, "Take hold of my tail and cling to it. I'll take you home right now."

The twins took hold of the tail, and the mother bird opened out her wings and lifted the twins to the sky. They flew over mountains, over wide plains, over rivers, over forests, over villages, over cornlands, and everything on the earth was beautiful. The mother bird gradually folded her wings and landed exactly on that spot in the forest where the twins had joined hands to run away from home.

"Wait here," she said. "I'll go and tell your mommy to prepare to receive you, and then I'll return here and pick you up again."

She flew straight to the home of the twins and found No-mawele standing in the yard, looking very sad. The mother bird fluttered low and spoke to the sad mother.

"No-mawele, pick out the most beautiful kaross in your home and spread it out on the green grass in front of your great hut. Your beautiful twins will be home as soon as you have done that."

"Are you laughing at me, mother bird?" asked the mother of the twins sadly.

"How could a mother laugh at a mother in distress? Believe me and do what I tell you." And the mother bird flew back to the twins.

Could this be true? wondered No-mawele as she hurried into the great hut. Should she tell her husband? No! He would think she was mad. So, without explaining anything to him, she brought out the most beautiful kaross and spread it on the grass in front of the great hut. Then she sat down, watching quietly. Then suddenly the mother bird lowered her long tail on the kaross, and, without landing, she dropped the twins safely on it and flew away.

"Mama! Mama!" shouted the twins joyfully as they ran to fling themselves into their mother's open arms.

"So-mawele!" shouted the mother. "Come out and see!"

But the father was already beside her, for he had heard the little voices.

"Oh, my children!" he said.

And the four stood there for a long time, the arms of the parents round the little bodies of their beloved twins.

The Maidens of Bhakubha

The crucial episode here is the princess's willful violation of her society's customs in two important respects: she goes counter to the custom of intonjane *(the female purification rites) by leaving her secluded place, and she further ignores custom by going to the forbidden pool to swim. This show of disrespect and childishness are dramatically underscored by her reaction to the monster which sits on the girls' clothing. In her arrogant reaction to the hallowed traditions of her people, she has become monstrous: poetically, she has become one with the monster. The beast retaliates by biting her so that she becomes as ugly as the monster itself; this is a metaphorical way of equating the girl's behavior to the repulsiveness of the evil creature. That is, the* sinyobolokondwane *is a dramatic manifestations of the girl's attitudes and actions. Only when she and the other maidens of Bhakubha realize the enormity of their act is she cleansed, and this is symbolized in the milk-purification episode of the narrative.*

The princess's experiences, like those of Nomxakazo in the next story, become a symbolic and dramatic fulfilling of the purification ritual, intonjane. *Through her experiences, the princess is cleansed, her beauty is restored, and she is finally prepared to enter the world with the dignity and wisdom of womanhood. Only then can she be married, only then can she be restored to her home and her friends, only then can she become the "mother of the people" of the young prince's kingdom. Her indiscretions are contrasted with and thereby heightened by the prince's selfless and relentless quest.*

Throughout this narrative, gentleness and concern for others are pervasive themes, but these are matched by the princess's arrogance and her disregard of tradition. She dispels the general harmony of the countryside, along with the other maidens, and they must therefore be expelled from the land until they have been purified—they must be secluded (as they are in fact secluded during intonjane). *At the same time, they must be guarded so that their physical beauty is in no way tampered with. The princess's ugly deeds find their reflection in her sudden ugly appearance.*

The Maidens of Bhakubha

It came about, according to some tale, that a certain king had a very beautiful daughter. From early childhood, this girl was very bright and cheerful. In this way she made everyone at the Great Place so happy that the people said she was like a sunbeam to this land. As she grew up, she became so famous for this quality that throughout the land of Bhakubha she was known as *Nomtha-we-Langa* (Mother-of-the-Sunbeam).

Nomtha-we-Langa was greatly loved by the girls of all age groups in her homeland. Those of the villages surrounding the Great Place used to come in large numbers to visit her. Sometimes they would remain at the Great Place the whole day, playing with the princess. Sometimes all the youths of these villages would gather together and come as a group. As they came, they used to sing, inviting the princess to come out and have fun with them in the fresh evening air:

Litshonil' ilanga, Nomtha-we-Langa!	The sun is down, Nomtha-we-Langa!
Kha uphum' usichwayitise ngolo ncumo.	Come out and cheer us with that smile.

This song so delighted the king that every time the young people's voices reached him with the evening air, he would have an ox slaughtered in honor of his daughter's guests. The young men would make great fires that lit the sky, and there would be singing and dancing, roasting and feasting, far into the night.

But what Nomtha-we-Langa enjoyed most was to go bathing with the other girls, far from the Great Place. Bordering her father's land was a big river with many beautiful swimming pools. It was to this river that the girls used to go, at least once every moon in the warm days of spring and summer and autumn. It was pleasant to leave home with the baskets full of food provisions. It was pleasant to bathe and then come out and lie on the rocks like lizards enjoying the sun, and then jump into the water again. It was pleasant to come out of the water and recline on the green grass with all those baskets full of food. It was exciting to see the young men from the other side of the river watching from a distance, high up on the cliffs, and to overhear them commenting on the shapeliness of the bodies of the maidens of Bhakubha. It was amusing to join in the friendly battle that went between the girls and the youth on the cliffs. Sometimes, as the girls reclined to enjoy their midday meal, a young man would call out, "Hey, you girls! Why are you so stingy? Why don't you invite us to come sit and eat with you?" To this Khabazana, the bold leader of the maidens, would reply, "We really pity you, neighbors, if your sisters don't know how to cook. No wonder you're so lean! Do come over and eat. We invite you." Then everyone would laugh, because both groups knew that what was being suggested was just not done.

Familiarity grew between these two groups, and there came a time when the young men would cross the river some time before the girls reached their favorite pool. Then they would walk in the opposite direction and meet the girls as if by chance. Of course, the girls knew this was all planned, but they really enjoyed it. On such occasions, as soon as they saw the youths coming towards them, the girls would laugh and break into two groups and form two lines, one on this side of the path and one on that, and then stand facing each other, as if making way for the youths to pass through. But as soon as all the youths were between the lines, the two girls facing each other at each end would immediately join hands, so that there could be no going forward or retreating. The girls in each line would also join hands quickly so that there would be no es-

cape by the sides either. Then the girls would make the
youths carry out the customary game of *ukwenzisa* whereby
each young man pointed out the girl he considered the prettiest of all. If any young man refused to do this, he had to pay a
fine for insulting the girls. All this was done in a friendly
spirit. The girls who were pointed out were congratulated by
their friends, and the sport was over.

At the early stages of this game, Nomtha-we-Langa hardly
ever won a place, but on every occasion at least one young
man would point at her and say, "She is still young. But the
day she reaches full maidenhood she will sit down everyone of
you girls. She will be the tallest and most beautiful of all the
maidens of Bhakubha." The girl who never failed to be
pointed out, either as first or second, was Khabazana. But all
the girls remembered the occasion when Nomtha-we-Langa
first won. On that day, the girls met only three young men,
one of them the Cub of the Lion (king's son) of the neighboring kingdom. His name was Sidlokolo. He was the last to
make his choice, and when his turn came, he took his time
looking at the girls. His gaze rested a while on Khabazana
who stood directly opposite Nomtha-we-Langa. Then he
turned his face and looked at Nomtha-we-Langa and without
hesitation he walked up to her with dignity, took her right
hand in both of his, and holding it tenderly he said:

"The maidens of Bhakubha are the fresh green stalks in a
fertile field of corn, all bathing in the morning dew. But you,
Nomtha-we-Langa, draw my eye as well as my heart, because
you rise the tallest in the center of the field, your blades out-
spread to receive the purest of the dewdrops that fall silently
from the heavens, and to embrace the first sunbeam that
brings a glitter to the beads that dropped from the heavens
while we slept."

There was a great deal of cheering from the maidens of
Bhakubha as they opened the way to let the young men go,
and Nomtha-we-Langa never forgot that occasion.

When the girls returned from the pool one afternoon,
Nomtha-we-Langa had to be covered up and Khabazana and
some of the other bigger girls had to take turns carrying her

on their backs all the way home. When the mothers saw the girls approaching, they knew at once what had happened. Some quickly cleaned and tidied a secluded chamber, and others brought forth reeds from the riverbank and made a bed in this chamber. Nomtha-we-Langa had reached full maidenhood and would have to lie on this bed of reeds for some moons and undergo custom.

This brought misery to Nomtha-we-Langa. Life to her was the light of day, the river, the company of other girls—and also the "chance meetings" with the youth from the other side of the river. The other girls were allowed to enter her chamber occasionally, and now and again she was left alone with the two or three who were allowed to see her. But such visits made her longing for other young people all the stronger. She revealed none of these feelings to the three elderly women who attended her during this period, for such an attitude would have been a disgrace, if it should be known. Only one person knew how lonely the princess felt. This was a girl who remained with her all the time, running errands for her as well as for the elderly attendants.

One bright morning, while Nomtha-we-Langa was alone with this girl, she heard the song of the maidens of Bhakubha. Knowing that they were going to bathe, and that they would be passing near the Great Place, Nomtha-we-Langa sent this girl to ask Khabazana to come and see her just for a moment. The girl ran out and in a moment she was back to say that Khabazana was coming.

Khabazana entered a little after, accompanied by two other girls of her age group. They were surprised to find Nomtha-we-Langa on her feet, dressed in the clothes of the other girl, and this other girl lying on the bed of reeds, all covered up and pretending to be asleep.

"Sh!" said the princess, before they exclaimed. "Don't say a word! I'm coming with you." And without waiting to hear what they had to say to this, she pulled and pushed Khabazana and her companions to go quickly before any of the elderly attendants returned. Partly horrified and partly infected by the princess's excitement about this daring conspiracy, Khabazana and her companions grouped around her, and the four took a secret path and overtook the other girls. There were now two hundred in all, and infected by the princess's spirit, they giggled and continued their journey.

On the way, it occurred to Nomtha-we-Langa that this ruse would certainly be discovered before they had gone far. So, as soon as they were out of sight of their homes she suggested that they had better change their course and go to the Lulange pool, a deep pool where no one had ever bathed before.

"Go to Lulange?" exclaimed Khabazana. "Haven't you heard people call it 'the Lulange pool whence there's no return?'"

"Oh! that's just a way of talking," replied the princess. "Those are just tales of old that have never been traced to any source. Come girls! Let's go. Of course, if we find the Lulange pool the happiest place to live in, we'll never return."

Thereupon, all the girls laughed and followed the way the princess pointed.

Not one of these girls had ever been anywhere near Lulange, and not one of them knew of any living person who had ever seen it. But they all knew where it was. It was a deep pool in the big river, far to the left of their favorite pool, but about the same distance from their homes. So they went, travelling fast, taking good care to keep away from all beaten paths and highways, in case they met people who might recognize the princess.

To reach the Lulange pool, they had to take a big bend and then climb a ridge. Looking down from the ridge, they saw the pool, the dark deep pool whose length seemed to have no end. From their position, it did not look as wide as they had expected, because there were trees along its banks, and the pliable twigs of some of the trees bent low as if to dip their tips in the still waters. They could see no path leading to any part of the pool from any direction, and this confirmed the story that this pool was very seldom visited, if ever. The girls hesitated and some of the more timid ones seemed to fall back.

"Forward, maidens of Bhakubha!" came the voice of Nomtha-we-Langa. "It must never be said of us that we hesitated and retreated from our resolution just for fear of tales of old. Can't you see that large beautiful patch of green grass along the bank? What is it for, if it's not for us maidens to recline on?"

The girls scrambled down the hill and finally landed on the patch of green grass that the princess was the first to see. Here they laid down their food baskets. They they removed their beautiful ornaments, took off their shawls and skirts and packed them together with great care. They formed a large ring about their bundle of clothes and joined hands. The princess stood next to Khabazana, on the right-hand side. Then Khabazana gave the order to move to the right, and the girls trotted in a ring round the bundle of clothes, the regular beat of their feet on the ground in harmony with the rattling of the bright-colored beads that decorated their waist aprons. They took three rounds, and then Khabazana let go the hands of the girls on either side. She raised her arms high and with a shout, she plunged into the water. Plunge! Plunge! Plunge! followed the other girls, all of them shouting with excitement, and the last was Nomtha-we-Langa.

They swam upstream and downstream, never getting very far from the bank. They came out of the water and ran up and down the green patch of grass along the bank. They plunged into the water again. Some came out of the water and reclined on the grass, while others remained to enjoy the rhythmic *qam,* all abreast. Some played hide-and-seek among the trees on the bank of the river, while others gathered wild fruits—*amaqunube* and *amavilo*—and heaped them on the grass for everyone to take and eat. They all reclined on the grass and enjoyed their midday meal. Some went to sit on the rocks and sang, while others lay fully stretched on the grass to enjoy the sun. And so it went on.

But the bigger girls were watching the sun, and as soon as they saw the afternoon shadows beginning to stretch out, they suggested that the troop must think about going home. To this Nomtha-we-Langa protested.

"Go home?" she asked. "Go home when the sun is still so high? Come, So-and-So! Let's go in again and beat qam."

She was joined by a large number who also thought it was not time to go home yet.

The next time it was Khabazana who spoke. She said quite definitely that it was time to go home. But Nomtha-we-Langa begged the girls for just one more plunge into the water.

"Remember," she said, "that when we get home I am going to be shut in that dark chamber and made to lie on those reeds. Let's go in for the last time."

"All right!" said Khabazana. "Come all of you! Let's make a ring."

They all came and formed a ring, repeating exactly what they had done before their first plunge, and again Khabazana led them into the water. A large number of girls joined Nom-tha-we-Langa in her favorite *qam,* and they delibertely beat the water hard with their feet, laughing and shouting so that they should not readily hear Khabazana's voice the next time she shouted that it was getting late. At last, Khabazana spoke directly to Nomtha-we-Langa.

"But why do you treat us this way, *nkosazana?* Haven't we got ourselves deep in the mud already by encouraging you to violate the custom? And have you thought of the calamity that may befall us all for coming to this pool?"

"Peace, maidens of my homeland," said the princess remorsefully. "I was so carried away that all such considerations became unimportant to me. I've been missing you, girls, and when I think of the loneliness I'm returning to, I find it hard to part with you. But let's go now."

Khabazana stood on the bank and counted the girls as they came out. Nomtha-we-Langa was the last to come out and Khabazana held out her hand and helped her to land. But just as she let go the princess's hand, there were screams of terror and the foremost girls ran back towards Khabazana and the princess.

"What's the matter?" asked Khabazana, retreating and pushing the princess behind her to shield her.

"Come and see!" cried the girls.

The girls all moved cautiously towards the spot where they had packed their clothes. They were horrified to see a huge, ugly-looking slimy monster lying fully stretched on their clothes, warming his back in the sun, his eyes half closed. As soon as the exclamations stopped, the monster opened his eyes and gazed at the girls and smiled. By this time Khabazana had taken her place in the front. She stepped forward and sang:

Sinyobolokondwane! Sinyobolo- *kondwane!* *Zis' iingubo zam.* *Kukud' eBhakubha.*	Slimy One! Slimy One! Give me my clothes. It's far to go to Bhakubha.

The monster smiled and looked at Khabazana, his gaze going up and down her body. Then, without taking his eyes away from her, he moved his slimy hand, pulled out all her clothes and handed them to her. The next girl came forward and sang the same song, and again the Slimy One smiled, gazed, and pulled out the clothes and handed them over. So one after another the girls came forward and recovered their clothes after begging the Slimy One in this manner. Then came Nomtha-we-Langa's turn. She was the last of all.

It was a long distance from the princess to the Slimy One, because while each of the girls in front of her had taken a step forward each time one of their number recovered her clothes, Nomtha-we-Langa had not moved a step. The other girls looked at her, expecting her to come forward and recover her clothes as everyone else had done. But the princess stood there stubborn, tall and proud, looking with defiance and contempt at this loathsome monster.

"Come forward and sing, Nomtha-we-Langa," called the other girls.

"I won't!"

"Oh, do come forward and beg for your clothes, *nkosazana,* even if you don't sing."

Then the princess blazed with anger.

"What! Beg for my clothes from this ugly monster? How dare he lay his loathsome belly on the clothes of the maidens of Bhakubha?"

"Oh, Nomtha-we-Langa! Oh, nkosazana! Do come forward and beg him," implored Khabazana. "How do you think you will recover your clothes unless you do as we all have done?"

Meanwhile the Slimy One was looking coolly at the princess, his eyes going up and down, up and down her body, his face still wearing its smile. This angered the princess beyond bounds.

"All right!" she said to the other girls.

Then she walked forward and came to stand right in front of the monster, her arms akimbo. She screwed her face and so shaped it that it looked as ugly as the monster's. Then she thrust her neck forward and sang the same tune. But she deliberately sang in an ugly, husky voice and showed her defiance and contempt by rejecting the words of persuasion sung by the other girls and substituting:

Nyi-nyi-nyi-nyi!   *Nyi-nyi-nyi-nyi!*
Nyi-nyi-nyi-nyi-nyi!   *Nyi-nyi-nyi-nyi-nyi!*

Thereupon the monster reared his head angrily, bared his long fangs, and bit one of her thighs. The other girls screamed and fled in terror. But before thay had gone far, Khabazana shouted, "Why are we running? Come back, maidens of Bhakubha! Let's die fighting for the princess of our homeland."

At these words the troop rallied. The girls grabbed stones, sticks, and anything else they could find, and they closed together and rushed back. But the Slimy One had vanished and—O, horror of horrors!—there lay the princess in a heaped-up position, alive and conscious, but her face and whole body as ugly and loathsome as that of the monster. One look at her and every girl carried her hands on her head and cried aloud:

O, princess!   O! what will become of us?
O, Nomtha-we-Langa!   O, we're as good as dead!"

"How are we to report a thing like this? How are we going to explain our madness, bringing the princess to this, of all places, in her present condition? We'll be killed, everyone of us."

Afraid to touch the princess, afraid even to look at her again, the girls collected their belongings hurriedly and fled. They took the way towards their homes, but every now and then, one of them asked, "Where are we going?" At last, when they had travelled far enough to feel out of danger from the pool of Lulange, Khabazana bade everybody stop. Then she addressed them:

"Girls! In truth, I don't know where to start. She who asked 'Where are we going?' asked the only question that can be asked. Where, indeed, are we going? Is there one among us who has a home to return to? Is there anyone here among us who has the liver to look her parents in the face and tell them what has happened? Is there anyone here among us who has the heart to remain in this land and look anybody in the face, after we have murdered the princess—the princess whom everybody loved so much? After the evil we've done, won't our parents fear to let us approach their homes, in case we infect everyone with the misfortune we have brought upon ourselves?"

Khabazana broke down and sobbed, and all the maidens wept in silence. Khabazana composed herself and spoke again: "Weeping is not going to help us in the least. Let's do something. Wait here all of you. As for you, So-and-so and So-and-so, remember that it was we three who brought the princess out of her chamber. Before we do anything else, we must enter the Great Place unnoticed and whisper this calamity to the elderly women we betrayed this morning. This we must do; otherwise the whole of this land will believe we murdered the princess deliberately. As to you other girls, all I can say is that if we don't return before cockcrow, you must know that we have been caught, and perhaps killed for our misdeed. And we leave it to you to decide what to do then. Let's go, you two!"

The princess's elderly attendants had discovered the ruse by midday, but, fearing to be killed together with the girl who impersonated the princess, they agreed among themselves not to tell anybody, because they trusted that the princess would return before this was discovered. They were waiting in the chamber anxiously when Khabazana and her companions arrived and knocked at the door. When the girls entered the chamber, the senior attendant drew Khabazana aside and whispered, "Where is she? What have you done with the king's baby?"

"Oh, grandmother!" cried Khabazana. "I don't know what will become of us. The princess has not returned."

"Was she drowned?"

"No. She was bitten by a monster and—she became something else. She changed and became—an ugly thing, a monster whose name we don't even know."

The senior attendant motioned the other women to draw near and listen to this strange thing. Khabazana then started from the beginning and related all the happenings of that day. The three girls expected to be reviled by the elderly women for this misdeed, but when Khabazana finished, the elderly women were so horrified that for a long time they just sat there, unable to utter a word.

At last the senior woman spoke to the girls: "My children, you must understand that the absence of the maidens of these villages from their homes tonight is another crime for us three elderly women. You must go back to them at once. Wait there, all of you, until you get word from us. Now go!"

As soon as the girls had gone, she turned to her younger colleagues and said, "Follow those girls, but don't try to overtake them, for you mustn't be seen by anyone walking or talking with them. When you reach the place where the girls are waiting, sit together, all of you, and decide where to go. One thing you must stress. You must all keep together wherever you decide to go. As for me and this child (pointing to the girl who lay on the bed of reeds), we must wait in this chamber until—I don't know when."

In every home in the villages that night, father and mother sat up late waiting for their daughter or daughters to come home. Early the following morning, it was noticeable to everyone that there was something wrong about every home. There was a great deal of quiet moving about. As no one wanted any and everybody in his village to know that his daughter had not slept home, relative approached closest relative, friend approached most intimate friend and whispered this, only to find that the closest relative or most intimate friend had the same disgrace to whisper about his own house. It was only at the Great Place that people seemed to be going about their normal duties.

Just when the morning dew disappeared, the woodcutter of the Great Place slung his great axe on his shoulder and went to the woods. As soon as he began chopping, he heard a girl's voice singing:

Wa, mf' o gawulayo!	Hey, woodcutter man!
Wa, mf' o gawulayo!	Hey, woodcutter man!
Undibulisele kuma nobawo.	Remember me to my mother and father.

The man paused, looked about, and listened. Silence. He raised his axe and began to work again. Hack! Hack! Hack! Again the girls's voice:

Wa, mf' o gawulayo!	Hey, woodcutter man!
Wa, mf' o gawulayo!	Hey, woodcutter man!
Undibulisele kuma nobawo.	Remember me to my mother and father.

Again the man paused and listened. Silence again. Where did this voice come from? he wondered. From the sky or from the trees? Again he set to work. Hack! Hack! Hack! Again the girls's voice:

Wa, mf' o gawulayo!	Hey, woodcutter man!
Wa, mf' o gawulayo!	Hey, woodcutter man!
Undibulisele kuma nobawo.	Remember me to my mother and father.

The woodcutter put his axe on his shoulder and hastened back to the Great Place to report what he had heard. The king immediately ordered a troop of men to follow the woodcutter back to the wood and find out what this meant. Nomtha-we-Langa's brother, who was only a boy, insisted on going with these men, and his father allowed him. When they reached the place, the leader of the troop ordered the woodcutter to get to work.

Hack! Hack! Hack!

The voice sang:

Wa, mf' o gawulayo!	Hey, woodcutter man!
Wa, mf' o gawulayo!	Hey, woodcutter man!
Undibulisele kuma nobawo.	Remember me to my mother and father.

"That's my sister's voice!" exclaimed the young prince. "What can she be doing here? The singing came from one of those tall trees over there!" And he ran the way he was pointing, followed by all the men.

"There's something up there!" he said, pointing at something that looked like a human figure among the branches of a tall tree.

Two men climbed up quickly and helped each other to bring this thing down from the tree. When they put it on its feet in front of him, the prince was startled.

"Is this you, Nomtha-we-Langa? How did you get here? How did you become like this?"

"It was the Slimy One," said Nomtha-we-Langa, and she pointed at the wound on her thigh and wept.

"Don't ask her any more questions, Child of the King," said one of the men. "Let's carry her home."

The men carried the princess to the Great Place. They made her sit down in the shade of a big tree in the courtyard, and then two men went to tell the king what had been found. When the king came, he looked at her only once and he turned away, his face a mixture of horror and unspeakable grief. The prince followed his father as he walked slowly this way and that, and finally back to the Great Chamber. The king had not realized that he was being followed, and when he noticed his son, he called him be name without looking at him and said, "If your sister is able to speak, tell the men to ask her what happened and come and tell me."

The young prince returned to his sister, and he and the men listened to what she had to say. Nomtha-we-Langa told her story calmly, from the moment when she had heard the other girls singing and decided to join them, to the time when the other girls left her on the bank of the Lulange pool. She put all the blame for what had happened on herself. She went on to relate how she managed to get on her feet just before sunset, how she had walked most of the night, trying to reach home in time and explain everything to save the other girls. But when dawn came and she saw her condition, she felt she would rather die than present herself to her parents in such a condition, and so she went into the wood and climbed up a tree, deciding to die there undiscovered. But when she heard the sound of the axe, she felt such a longing for home that she could not help singing to make her presence known. In conclusion, she repeated that the fault was hers alone, and she pleaded that the other girls be spared.

While the young prince was repeating his sister's story to his parents, the startling news of Nomtha-we-Langa was spreading quickly from house to house, and from village to village, and parents in large and small numbers were to be seen hurrying to the Great Place. The disappearance of the girls ceased to be a secret whispered only to one's relatives and closest friends. It was now a matter for the whole community to know and handle. Everyone was speculating. Some thought the monster must have chased the rest of the girls and swallowed them. Some thought he must have bitten them as he had done the princess and that they were all on trees in the woods. Some put their finger on the monster's lying on their daughter's clothes. This deed must have given him power over their daughters, and in all probability he had used that power to draw them back to the Lulange pool and keep them as his concubines.

When the king became aware of the great gathering of people in the courtyard, he came out to greet them, and to thank them for coming to express their sympathy with him and his wife in the calamity that had befallen them. He had not yet heard that the daughters of these people had disappeared. He had just seated himself on his official stool when the princess's senior attendant fell on her face at his feet:

"Oh, Sun of Suns! Most Beautiful Child of the Beautiful! I beg forgiveness of you and the queen for the unspeakable

Scene by the river.

grief I have brought upon you. I beg the forgiveness of my people for defiling the entire maidenhood of this land. I know that I must die, but I shall be happy if I die knowing that I am forgiven. I shall die happy if I die knowing that you have forgiven the beautiful maidens of this land who have fled to other lands for fear of their terrible misdeed."

The king motioned the old woman to rise from her prostrate position. When she had done so, he spoke with concern and said, "You have mentioned the maidens of this land. Before we decide what to do with you there is something we must know at once. You see all these people here? They want to know where their daughters are. Apparently, you know. Tell me. Are the maidens of this land alive and out of danger? Or have they all been destroyed like this child of mine?"

The old woman related what she had done about the girls the previous night, and she went on to explain, "I did all this, Child of the Beautiful, because I felt that since the princess was not bitten to death, there was still a hope that some day a miracle would happen and she would be cleansed of this curse. If that miracle does happen, and the princess is cleansed of this misfortune, how can she be happy if the girls she has loved so much from early childhood are not here?

"Rise, old woman," said the king with deep respect. "Return to the secluded chamber and guard the girl who impersonated my child until the council of this land summons you to this court to hear what we have decided to do about you two."

"May the Most Beautiful One have mercy on that poor child," pleaded the old woman as she rose. "As it is, she is as good as dead with fear, shame, and grief. She is only a child and did what she did for love of Nomtha-we-Langa."

"Go, old woman," said the king. "The council has heard."

"I thank you, Sun of Suns."

After the old woman had gone, the king consoled the parents of the girls and put all the blame on his own daughter. It was she, he said, who had initiated the whole thing. She knew, he said, that it would be difficult for the other girls to refuse, because they missed her and they knew that she missed them.

When the king had finished, So-Khabazana (father of Khabazana) rose to speak in the name of the parents. He said words of sympathy to the king and queen for the misfortune that had befallen them, and he thanked the king for what he had said to the parents. But he refused to put the blame on the princess.

"It is the other girls who are to blame," he said. "Has the king done wrong to love these children so much, making his home their home? Why did they tempt the princess by telling her with their singing that they were going to bathe? And how could the senior girls not have known that to do a thing of this nature was to defile their maidenhood? No, Child of the Beautiful! The princess is not to blame. She is the youngest of these girls, and it was the duty of the senior girls, my own daughter included, to stop her. If they could not stop her, they could have done one of these two things—report the mat-

ter to the elderly attendants or, if they did not want to tell on
her, give up the idea of going to bathe.

"The old woman asked a question. 'If that miracle should
happen and the princess is cleansed of this misfortune, how
will she be happy if the girls she has loved so much from early
childhood are not here?' I too then have a question, and it is
this. 'If the Most Beautiful One were to forgive these girls and
allow them to come back to their homes, how could they be
happy if the princess who loved them so much from early
childhood had not recovered from the misfortune they
brought upon her? How could we, their parents, be happy
with them at our homes, while the princess remained in this
condition? Could any of us parents have the heart to present
our daughters to the Royal House, knowing as we would that
the very sight of them brought grief to the parents of the princess? So says my question, and now I proceed to answer it myself. My answer is, No! Not until the miracle has happened
and our Nomtha-we-Langa is once again with us, as she was
when they tempted her out of her sacred chamber."

After the parents had shown their full-hearted support of
So-Khabazana's speech by their fierce murmurs and emphatic
nods, the king requested the parents not to leave, and he summoned his inner council to meet in the Great Chamber immediately. The inner council did not take long to arrive at their
decisions. When they returned, the king named ten men, with
So-Khabazana as leader, to take the princess immediately to
the farthest of the royal outposts and look after her. He gave
them five tens of cattle, among these many milk cows, to take
with them as food. As the princess was being led away weeping, the king told So-Khabazana and his subordinates that no
woman, whether old or young, was ever to see or talk to his
daughter while she was at that outpost. As soon as his daughter was out of sight, the king ordered that the princess's elderly attendant be summoned to appear before him. She came
and fell on her face at his feet.

"Old woman," said the king, "Take the girl who impersonated my child and go find the maidens of this land. Tell

them I say to all of you, all of you, I want my child. None of you may ever enter the borders of this land until my child has been restored to her mother, restored as she was when the mother entrusted her to your care."

As the parents murmured their support, the old woman kissed the ground next to the king's feet and, without a word, she rose to go. She returned to the secluded chamber, collected her belongings, took the girl by her hand, and the two left the Great Place. The parents watched them in silence until they passed through the great gate. Then the king called everybody's attention and said, "Parents of the maidens of the maidens of Bhakubha, you have heard the decisions of the inner council. Now I must appeal to you all. As you return to your homes, remember that those who made these decisions weep with you, for the girls they have banished include their own daughters and the daughters of their relatives and friends."

When the news of the calamity of Lulange reached the prince Sidlokolo and the youth of his age group, these young men immediately resolved to get themselves fully involved in this matter. First, they would find the maidens of Bhakubha and take them to a place where no harm of any kind would befall them. They were sure that these girls were hiding somewhere in this land. The next thing would be to hunt the monster Sinyobolokondwane and kill him.

In the beginning, they thought all this could be accomplished without anyone outside their group knowing about it. But even before they started on their search, they realized that at least one senior person would have to be taken into their confidence, for they must find a home for the girls. So Sidlokolo approached the *sothanga* (overseer) of the biggest of the royal outposts and told him what he and his braves had resolved to do. After listening to the story, the *sothanga* immediately raised the question: "Where are you going to find a place for the girls to make sure they will be safe?"

"That's precisely why we are telling you what we haven't told anyone else. Do help us."

"You will be sending some men, of course, to look after them?"

"The most trustworthy of them all, I promise you. My father's brother's son, Mlindazwe, with two tens of men under him."

"If Mlindazwe is in charge, then I have nothing to fear, Child of the King. He's the most trustworthy of all."

Sidlokolo returned to the meeting place, and the braves planned their search carefully. Sidlokolo was stationed at the meeting place with a number of men. Among these were runners. The rest broke into groups and scattered all over the land. The first to be found were the banished old woman and the young girl. These were told what the arrangement was and taken straight to the outpost. The rest were found camping at some sheltered spot, far from any homes.

Sidlokolo called Mlindazwe aside and told him what he and the sothanga had agreed upon. Mlindazwe felt this to be a serious responsibility, but he accepted the decision and proceeded to pick the two tens he considered most reliable for this position. The names were announced, and those who had been chosen collected their things and followed Mlindazwe to the maidens' camp.

Their comrades sat watching them until they disappeared. Then Sidlokolo grabbed his weapons, leaped to his feet and made a signal. Thereupon the braves grabbed their weapons and rose as one. Another signal from Sidlokolo, and the leader of song started a bloodcurdling hunting song, a song that they had been taught to sing only when setting out to hunt dangerous monsters. As soon as the braves took up the song, Sidlokolo raised his spear and shield high, and his powerful voice rose above the virile chorus: *"ELulange!"* ("To Lulange!") and, in defiance of the horrifying tales of old, he led his men away, determined to fight and kill the Sinyobolokondwane alone, on land or in the pool, have him flayed, and have his skin carried home to his father's Great Place.

Before crossing the river, the braves stood on the high cliffs overlooking the pool and looked down on the scene of the calamity, examining the woods and rocks very closely. The waters of the Lulange pool were surprisingly calm. Indeed, the whole place was as calm as if nothing had happened recently. But these braves were used to hunting the most dangerous, most treacherous of beasts of prey. So, in spite of the calm before and around them, it was with extreme caution that they crossed the river and approached the clearing.

The clearing lay between a high rock and the bank of the river. Sidlokolo took his stand alone on this rock and ordered his men to stand in two rows at two edges of the clearing, stretching from the bank of the river towards him. The men took their positions and the two rows faced each other, leaving the clearing quite open between them and all the way from the bank to the high rock on which their leader was standing.

As soon as his comrades were ready, Sidlokolo called out, and in his powerful voice challenged the monster to come out of the water and fight him on the spot where he had wounded the princess. But the waters of Lulange remained as still as ever, and the only sound that reached the braves was the prince's own voice coming back to them in echoes after hitting the high cliffs on the opposite bank. Sidlokolo repeated his challenge a second and a third time, but there was not a sign that the challenge had been heard. He jumped down from the rock and led his comrades up and down the banks of the river. They beat the trees and bushes and bulrushes, ever calling out to "this coward of a monster" to come out and face "other men." Not a sound in the woods other than their own noise, not a stir in the pool. They crossed over to the other bank and repeated this. Still no response. They returned to the clearing, laid all their clothes in a heap. They threw down their shields and jumped into the water, each with his spear in his hand. After swimming for some time they came out and rushed to their clothes, hoping to find the Slimy One lying on them. No Slimy One. Not a sign of him. Not a trail. It occurred to them that "this coward of a monster" was frightened of their weapons. So they picked up their shields and hid behind rocks and bushes, but nothing happened. They gave up and returned to the meeting place.

They came on the next day and on the next. They repeated everything they had done on the first, and still nothing
happened. As from the fourth day, they changed their plans.
Sometimes they came early in the afternoon and remained till
midnight. Sometimes they came in the depths of night and remained till sunrise. Sometimes they spent the whole night
and the whole day at this place, but there was never a trace
of any monster. At last they decided to give up. But before
they left the pool, Sidlokolo climbed on his high rock, and in
his powerful voice he reviled this monster—"this slimy, ugly-
looking, coward of a monster, this monster of loathsome
habits, this coward of a sorcerer who bares his fangs and bites
a defenseless girl but dares not show so much as his ugly nostrils above the water when challenged by another man."

"For the last time I call you to come and fight," he said.
"Look! I throw my shield away, and you are still no match for
me if I have to face you with my spear alone."

Not a stir in the Lulange pool.

Sidlokolo jumped down from the rock, picked up his
shield and led his men away. They crossed the river and hurried to the outpost to see the maidens of Bhakubha. Sidlokolo
was hoping that there might be news that the princess had been
cleansed. But there was no news of her at all. What was
worse, neither the elderly women nor the maidens knew in
what direction he would have to travel in order to reach the
outpost to which she had been taken. But this did not deter
Sidlokolo. He was determined to find her, and he became
angry when the princess's senior attendant tried to advise him
that he had better not insist on seeing the princess in her present condition.

"Son of the king," pleaded the old woman with patience,
"you are looking for the beautiful maiden you used to meet
on the way to the river, the girl you used to watch from the
high cliffs while she bathed in the river or reclined on the
green grass. In a word, you are looking for Nomtha-we-Langa,
the gay young girl who gladdened the hearts of all who met
her. I didn't see her in her present condition, and I am thankful for that, because from the descriptions of those who have

seen her after she was bitten by that monster, she is not the girl I used to know. So be thankful too that you haven't seen her and—be patient."

"Till when, grandmother?"

"Till something happens to restore her beauty."

"When will that be?"

"If I knew, I would tell you, Child of the King."

"But *will* it happen at all?"

"It's difficult to answer that question."

"If you can't answer it, then let me do as I chose."

"May I ask you a question now, son of the king?"

"Proceed."

"If the princess chose to die and dry up on a tree rather than be seen by her parents, *by her parents,* in her present condition, do you think she would like to be seen by *you?*"

"I understand you now, grandmother," said Sidlokolo after thinking deeply.

"If you understand me, Child of the King, then promise me one thing."

"Proceed, grandmother."

"It is good that you don't want to rest until you have found the princess. But promise me this—that when you have found out where she is, you will not have the stubborness to want to see her. You see, Child of the King, you have shown bravery in going to Lulange and offering to fight that monster alone. It is a different kind of bravery that is required of you now, a rare kind, a deeper kind of bravery—the bravery to bear agony. Now, do you promise?"

"Yes, I promise, grandmother."

"I thank you for that promise, Child of the King."

She took his hand and kissed it as she said this. Then she turned to the rest of the young people—for they were all there listening—and she said, "Need I warn those who will be going with the prince not to keep on reminding him not to break his promise? No. For he wouldn't have made it in the presence of all of us if he didn't mean to keep it."

All the young people laughed.

After this conversation, Sidlokolo called all his comrades

to council. All the women set about meanwhile preparing food, for the prince had indicated that he would like to leave as soon as possible after the meeting. All the braves, except those who had been charged to look after the girls, had taken it for granted that they would be going with their leader. They were therefore disappointed when he made it known that he wanted only ten men, and that the rest must return to their homes.

"It's not that I don't trust any of you, young men of my homeland," he said when he saw how disappointed they were. "I think we mustn't all go on this search. The reason is that if such a large number of armed braves enter the land of Bhakubha, such a thing may be taken ill by the braves of that land, for we must remember that, in spite of their parents' decision, they are in all likelihood wandering all over their land, looking for their sisters and their betrothed. They could easily jump to the conclusion that we, on hearing that their girls have been banished, are out on a big hunt, just to amuse ourselves with these unprotected girls."

After listening to this explanation, the braves agreed that his decision was right and they now called upon him to choose the ten he would like to accompany him. But Sidlokolo chose only two, and these were the two companions who were with him the day he named Nomtha-we-Langa as the most beautiful of the maidens of Bhakubha. After requesting the meeting to choose the remaining eight, he took his chosen ones with him to have his last talk with the elderly women. He told the elderly women what the meeting had decided and, commending them for the manner in which they conducted affairs, and the senior one especially for her wise advice, he begged for the road and promised that, as soon as he knew where the princess was, he would let them know. Then they all sat conversing until a messenger came from the meeting to tell the prince that the eight remaining men had been chosen, and he told him their names.

The prince returned to the meeting and closed it formally. Mlindazwe and his band brought meat. Khabazana and the maidens of Bhakubha carried pots and pots of beer to the

meeting and requested Mlindazwe to *landula* (make the customary speech) on their behalf. The girls also took the opportunity to say good-bye to the prince and his comrades and
wished them success. Then Khabazana led the maidens back
to their quarters.

The sun went down and word went 'round that the
prince felt it was time to go. The braves collected their belongings and sat together ready to move as soon as they were
told to do so. The prince meanwhile was conferring with
Mlindazwe and Khabazana, who had brought some food provisions for Sidlokolo and his ten men. The headman of the
outpost had supplied them with meat, some roasted, some
boiled, and some raw, and also with two large calabashes, one
full of *amasi* and the other full of beer. These would last them
some days. The maidens of Bhakubha had prepared them
enough bagsful of *utshongo* (baked corn meal) and baked
amazambane (kind of potato), to last them a moon.

The braves left the establishment as soon as the *mnyele*
(milky-way) brightened in the sky. They all traveled together
as far as the border, those who were going home helping to
carry the food provisions. They all crossed the river that
marked the boundary between the two kingdoms and found a
cave. Here some of the *utshongo* was stored carefully so that it
would not get wet or be destroyed by ants. Then early in the
morning, those who were going home said good-bye to their
comrades and recrossed the river.

Left to themselves, Sidlokolo and his comrades had to
make up their minds in which direction to go. All they knew
was that the princess had been taken to the farthest of the
royal outposts of Bhakubha, and this could be in any direction. But they reckoned that the outpost would not be very far
from the border. They therefore decided to turn towards the
rising sun and keep close to the border all the time until they
reached their cave again. Then they would start again, deeper
in, and go round until they were back at their starting-point.

They started on their first round. They moved cautiously,
trying as much as they could not to meet people in groups.
Mostly it was herdsmen and boys that they met, for these they

could not avoid. Whenever they met these, the travellers put down their luggage and rested, partly because they did not want to be suspected of scouting for cattle raiders, and partly because they wanted to elicit all the information that would help them to find the way to the outpost they were looking for. The herdsmen were elderly men and did not know these youth. They believed all the stories these strangers told about themselves. Some of the herdsmen were free with information, and from them the braves heard many versions of "the calamity of Lulange" and of "the expulsion of the princess." Some knew also that "the Cub of the Lion beyond the river has taken the fugitive girls under his wing," and that "this brave young man and his troop had sworn to hunt this monster and kill it." But there were also those who were very suspicious and would not say just anything to strangers about their land. They would talk on general matters, but as soon as the conversation began to slant towards "the calamity of Lulange", they either closed their mouths completely or stated quite frankly that it was not done to discuss such matters with strangers. In one respect, however, the herdsmen at these outposts were all alike. Even the most suspicious of them were very generous with their food. They shared everything with these strangers, and when the braves had to move on, the herdsmen refilled their calabashes with *amasi* and beer and their leather bags with boiled corn. In this way Sidlokolo and his comrades never went hungry.

The first moon of autumn died before they had finished their first round, and they did not even know how far it was to the cave from which they had started. But they journeyed with hope all the time. Far from being discouraged when they had to climb mountain range after mountain range, they felt their hopes rising, because they thought that if the outpost they were looking for was not on this side of the mountain range before them, then it was on the other side, and so on. It was only when they saw nothing but ever-stretching flat plains on every side that they found their search tiring.

But where, in fact, is the girl they are looking for? What is her condition? She is at the outpost where her father or-

dered her to go. She never sees anyone. The food is prepared
by an old woman she has never seen, and brought to her by
one of the men who came here with her. When he brings it,
he knocks at the door. The door opens ever so little and a
hand and arm, all covered with gloves made of buckskin,
stretches out to receive the food. All he hears is her voice
when she thanks him for the food. The men are very watchful.
If she moves about in her closed chamber, she hears footsteps
just outside, and she knows that one of them has come to listen to what she is doing. This happens often during the day,
and always in the night when she moves things about, tidying
her chamber. She comes out every night when all people are
supposed to be asleep. She walks to and fro, to and fro, to and
fro in the large clearing in the yard, thinking about home,
thinking about the other girls. She knows that she is being
watched all the time, for every now and then she hears a shuf-
fling of feet, she hears a man clearing his throat or sneezing
quite close to her. This used to startle her on the first few
nights, but now she has been here two full moons and is used
to it. When she hears the first cocks crow, she enters a small
secluded hut and finds her bath tub full of clean water. She
takes her bath and returns to her chamber to sleep. The
watchmen go to sleep too. She knows that her tub will be full
and her bathroom tidy when she comes again. This will have
been done early in the afternoon by the only person who ever
enters this hut—the old woman she has never seen. All she
knows about this old woman is her voice. This voice awakens
her from sleep sometimes, and she thinks she is among her
people at the Great Place. It is with a pang that she realizes,
when she is fully awake, that she is still at this outpost and in
this condition. Sometimes she is tempted to look through her
window, if only to have a glimpse of the owner of the only female voice she has heard these two moons, but then she remembers that her father's last order was that no woman was
ever to see or talk to her while she is at this place. She lies
down again. A knock at the door. She jumps out of bed and
quickly puts on her gloves. She opens the door ever so little,
stretches out her hand to receive the food and water. An exchange of greetings with the man, her thanks to the man, and

she closes the door again. She washes and eats, and she sits or lies about in her closed chamber, to wait for her evening meal, and all the time wishing that the sun would go down quickly so that she can go out and drink the air of the evening.

She does get news of home, because So-Khabazana is very kind and considerate. He comes late every afternoon and knocks at the door to greet her and ask if everything is all right. If there is news from home he tells her briefly and then goes.

One afternoon, just after he had been to greet her, she heard a voice that she immediately recognized as that of a runner from the Great Place. She did not hear a word of the conversation between him and the outpost men, but she marked that it was lively and exciting. That night as she was walking to and fro, So-Khabazana's voice greeted her in the dark. She stopped, because she sensed that he had something pleasant to tell her.

"Everything goes well at the Great Place, *nkosazana*", he said. "There's news about the girls too".

"Oh, do tell me! Where are they? Are they well?"

"Yes, they are all well and in safe keeping."

"Where?"

"Nobody knows where exactly. But it is known that they were all picked up by a band sent by the prince Sidlokolo and taken to one of his father's outposts together with the old women who looked after you. They are guarded from all harm by Sidlokolo's comrades."

"Oh, I'm so glad to hear such good news! So the girls of my homeland are safe! So pleasant is that news!"

"Very pleasant, *nkosazana*! Very pleasant indeed!"

It was long before cockcrow when this conversation took place, but after it the princess went to take her bath and returned to her chamber to enjoy the happiness she experienced on hearing this news. The girls! The maidens of Bhakubha! The prince! Where could he be now?

Sidlokolo and his comrades had been trudging it up a slope. It was hot and they were thirsty. They had drunk the last drop of the water they carried in one of the calabashes. The other calabash contained *amasi* that they found too thick to quench their thirst. Besides, in such warm weather *amasi* would make them lethargic and unable to travel. From the ridge they looked in all directions for a river or spring, but saw neither. An old woman appeared. She was approaching a small homestead on the slope, some distance from the travelers. Noticing that she carried a clay pot on her head, the travelers concluded that she must be just returning from a river or spring. Two of them went to ask her where they could find water. She told them that as they came up the slope, they had passed very near a spring of cold water, but that as strangers they could not have seen it because it was half-hidden by rocks.

"But why don't we walk home as we talk?" she said. "We've plenty of cold whey at home. I'll give you a whole potful to bring to your comrades."

The young men accepted this offer joyfully, signalled to tell their friends they would be back soon, and walked beside the old woman to her house. But something puzzled them as they approached this homestead. The old woman had told them there was plenty of whey in her house, and yet there was no sign of cattle or goats or even a pen. They were even more puzzled when they entered the hut into which she admitted them. There were two large calabashes of *amasi,* and it turned out too that the pot she had just brought with her was full of milk.

She brought a bowl of whey and knelt before the strangers. She took the customary sip, and then put the bowl down on the floor and invited them to drink. When they had finished, she asked them the customary questions—who they were, where they were going, and what for. She listened attentively until they had finished one of their invented stories, and then she told them about herself and her old man.

"We live just by ourselves here, my old man and me," she said. "But he is not here now. He is the chief herdsman at the royal outpost just over the ridge—the way you are travelling. He has been serving there since those cattle came two moons ago."

The young men nudged each other.

"I serve there too," continued the old woman. "Every day I go there to tidy the place and also to cook for—there are no women there. Only men. And when I have finished for the day I come home carrying a whole potful of milk, as you saw just now."

"Milk must be very plentiful at that outpost if they give away so much in one day," remarked one of the young men.

"As plentiful as in a dream!" said the old woman. "The men there just don't know what to do with it now. There's more than enough for the men, the calves, and even the dogs."

"You say 'the men'. Are there no women and children?"

"No women and no children, except a girl who is— sickly."

"I see. So that's why you have to go and tidy and cook for those men?"

"Yes, that's why. But it's not for the men I cook. It's for the sick girl. The men cook for themselves."

The young man who had been silent nudged his companion at this point and brought the conversation to an end.

"Grandmother," he said, "news never comes to an end. Our companions must be wondering what has become of us."

"Oh, my children!" she said as she rose to her feet. "You know what we old people are, especially old women. We just go on talking, talking."

She picked up the bowl and washed it. Then she pointed at a large clay pot and said, "That's too heavy for me. Pick it up yourselves and take it to your companions. Oh, wait a little!" and she took off the lid, drew a little whey with the ladle and drank it.

"Now you can take it."

One of the youths lifted the pot and carried it, and the other one carried the bowl they had been drinking from.

"Thank you, grandmother," said the more talkative one as they left the house. "We'll see you again when we return your things."

As these two approached, their comrades noticed that they were in very high spirits.

"What kept you fellows so long" asked one of them.

"You look jolly too!" remarked another. "Is there a beer-drinking party at that old woman's?"

"Just stop asking questions!" said the talkative youth as he put the pot before them. "You said you were thirsty. Open that and drink."

"It's whey!" said one of the others as he took off the lid. "Give me that bowl!"

"That's right!" said the talkative young man, handing him the bowl. "Drink and finish that whey, and then we'll tell you all the news. It looks as if we've got the trail."

"You've got it?" asked his comrades as one.

"It looks so."

"Let's drink quickly and hear this news," said the one who held the drinking bowl, and he put the bowl down, lifted the large pot and drank directly from it.

The pot passed from one to another quickly, and in no time it was put aside, empty. Then the braves sat up to hear the news. It was the less talkative of the two who told the news. He repeated word for word the whole conversation between his companion and the old woman.

"You've done a great thing, comrades!" said Sidlokolo. "You've got the trail."

"But we could have got more," said the talkative one. "It's this fool here who started nudging me, and then I stopped."

"Yes, I stopped him. He was so excited I feared he was going to blunder and reveal everything. Talkative people like him have to be watched all the time. I cut the conversation short because I wanted us to return here and report, so that we could all discuss and see how to get more from the old woman without making her suspicious. Did I do wrong?"

"No, you did right," said his companion quickly. "I was only teasing you, my equal."

"Yes, he was right," said one of Sidlokolo's chosen ones. "But there's something we must remember. If the old man is there when these pots are returned, the old woman may be afraid to tell us all we want to know. These pots must be returned at once by the two who brought the whey and also a third one to thank the old woman in the name of those of us who didn't meet her. Go with them, So-and-So, and take some meat with you and give it to her to show our thankfulness for her kindness."

The three went immediately, and fortunately they found the old woman still alone. The main speaker was the one who hadn't met her before. He spoke eloquently, thanking her for her kindness, and then he skillfully drifted to the real matter.

"We can see that this home of yours is a home to all strangers, and we are sure that it is both you and your old man who have made it so. We are only sorry we can't stay here to see him and thank him. He doesn't come home till after milking-time?"

"Yes, that is so, my child. He comes home at nightfall."

"Then we shan't see him. Convey our greetings to him."

"Thank you, my child. I'll do so."

"But one thing that is painful is this shadow of sorrow that is cast upon you all by the illness of the child you told my companions about. May she recover."

"I thank you, my child. This is a shadow in truth, a dark shadow. You would understand that even more if you knew whose child she is."

"Whose child is she?"

"This is the child—no longer a child, in fact, but a maiden fit to be married. She is the daughter of great people, very great people, in this land. As I hear from those who knew her before this misfortune, she was a very beautiful girl, beautiful in every way. Then there came this misfortune, this disease that has never been seen before, a disease of the body."

"A disease of the body only?"

"Of the body, that's all. Oh, this young man! Now you're putting me into trouble, asking me to tell things I was warned never to tell anyone. Do you know that I've never seen her with these eyes of mine? I cook for her, but it is someone else, a man, who takes the food to her. I tidy that little hut in which she washes her body. I am the only person who enters there, but I never see her because I enter and leave the hut while she still sleeps in her chamber. Believe me when I tell you that I wouldn't be able to point her out anywhere."

"Why is that?"

"Because she never comes out of that chamber of hers. In fact, if I didn't now and again hear her voice when she speaks to the leader-man who sometimes sits outside her door and speaks to her, I wouldn't believe there's a person in that chamber. But what amazes me is her voice. It's not the voice of a sickly person at all. It's the beautiful voice of a strong, healthy, maiden."

"If that is so, don't you think this illness is not deep after all? Obviously it's not a painful disease."

"I have that feeling too, my child. That's why I haven't given up hope that she will recover."

"May she recover, grandmother, and bring happiness to you all."

"May it be so, my child."

"Grandmother, we must beg for the road now. You have done us a great kindness and if we had the time we would go out of our way to look up your old man and thank him. But I suppose it's rather far?"

"In fact, it's very near and easy to see. When you get over the ridge the way you're going, your path enters a forest on a slope. The outpost faces that forest. It's a big place, standing by itself, on the other side of a stream that borders the bottom edge of the forest. My old man may not be there now, but he will be there at milking time. Do go, if you can. All the people at that place are kind to strangers."

The young men shook hands with the old woman and returned to their comrades. Again it was the quiet one who repeated the conversation, and when he had finished, it was Sidlokolo who spoke:

"Well, comrades! What further evidence do we seek? We've found what we set out to look for. We must move away from this spot at once. Let's climb over the ridge and seek a cave in the forest the old woman spoke about. Maybe we shall

also have time to see something of this outpost before nightfall."

They picked up their luggage and climbed to the ridge.
Even before they entered the forest below them, they saw the
big establishment on the opposite side, and a large stretch of
pastureland on the other side of it. They all stood together for
a moment and looked at the establishment, and then they entered the forest. They had to go fairly deep before they could
find a cave. But when they did, they were delighted to find
that from the roof of the cave the establishment remained in
full view. Quickly they tidied the cave, laid down their luggage, and reclined to rest.

The youths noticed that their leader was troubled in
spirit, and they did everything to cheer him up by recalling
some of the amusing incidents of their journey. For a long
time he did not open his mouth to speak. All he did was to
acknowledge the jokes with a smile. When at last he spoke, he
reminded his comrades that it would be fitting to send runners to let the elderly women at his father's outpost know all
they had found out about the princess.

"Yes, comrades," said one of the two chosen ones. "And
it's obvious who must go. It must be the three who entered
that old woman's house."

"Why so?" protested the talkative one. "Everyone here
knows all there is to report. Anyone can go. Why we three?"

"Because the old woman has seen you closely and will easily recognize you if she sees you again. Then she will wonder
what you're doing here after you had told her that you were
in such a hurry that you couldn't even wait to thank her old
man. The rest of us she wouldn't know. In fact, if she saw us
she would not even know that we don't belong to the land of
Bhakubha." "I understand now," said the talkative one.

The braves could not be sure that no one had seen them
enter the forest. It was therefore decided that by sunrise the
three runners must be as far away from this place as possible,
in order that those people who should see them by daylight
must not be people who might recognize them as three of the

party of eleven that had been seen entering the forest the previous afternoon. Thus it was then that at cockcrow these runners were well out of and away from the forest and had crossed many rivers long before the people stirred in the villages.

Their comrades did not sleep after the runners had gone. They lay tossing about for some time, and then they got up and went to bathe in the falling water of a spring on the mountain-forest slope not far from the cave. When they returned to the cave, none of them felt inclined to enter. They sat on the rocks enjoying the breeze that they found so pleasant on their bodies after their early morning bath. Their eyes were on the other side of the valley. They saw the men at the outpost beginning to stir. They saw the herdsmen drive the cows into the yard. They saw the milkers of the cows coming out with their pails. They saw each one disappearing under a cow and emerging again after a little time. They watched these men as they crossed and recrossed on the way from the cows to the milk-calabash hut and again back to the cows. This went on for a long time, and then the onlookers noticed that the milkers did not carry the pails to the hut any more but seemed to be emptying them into some container in the yard. But what the container could be they could not make out from this distance. They saw the young calves being separated from their mothers, and they saw the herdsmen drive the cows back to the pasture. And now the braves clearly saw the people at the outpost moving about, and all of these were men. Then they rose and went about their assigned duties. Five picked up their spears and shields and went hunting and gathering fruit and firewood. The prince and his two chosen ones remained at the cave, and one of the latter tidied the cave and then came out to join the others.

It was obvious to the prince's companions that he was not happy. He was quiet and thoughtful. He either had his gaze fixed on the homestead across the valley, or his head bent down to his knees. Sometimes he would get up and walk about, and finally go and sit alone on a different rock. But his comrades were doing all they could to keep up his spirits and as far as possible divert his thoughts. So one of them would rise and drift unobtrusively towards him, and finally find a rock close to his and sit on it. Soon after, the other one would follow.

The five companions returned in the afternoon and there was eating of roast meat and wild fruit. Then all eight sat on the rocks and once again watched the movements across the valley. Again the return of the cows, again the milking and crossing of the milkers, again the emptying of milkpails into the unknown container, again the separation of the calves from their mothers, again the return of the cows to the pasture. But the things the braves were watching began to lose their shapes, melting and becoming one with the darkness that was creeping slowly over the landscape. This was the end of the first day, and the occupations of the braves were exactly the same on the second day, and on the third.

Yes, it was the truth, as the old woman over the ridge had said, that the people at the royal outpost had so much milk that they did not know what to do with it. The cattle they had chosen to bring here with them included large oxen and bullocks, many cows in milk, and heifers. Here there was so much rich pastureland that a cow that ordinarily filled one pail of milk now filled two, and very soon the people at this place had much more than they needed. What they did not require they gave to the dogs. But even this did not solve their problem. The dogs could not eat it all. Then since their arrival here, more cows had been calving. The old woman and her old man had more than they required as it was, and no villages were near enough to offer the surplus milk to. At last, the men at the outpost found a way out. They decided to dig a large deep hole and get rid of the surplus milk by pouring it into this hole, and this was the "container" that had puzzled the onlookers in the forest. On the very day of the arrival of the prince and his comrades in these parts, the old woman had seen the men digging this hole, but she had not asked them what its purpose was, for it was not hers to ask any questions about the goings-on at this place. At the very time when she was telling the strangers about the abundance of milk at

this outpost, the milkers were pouring the first pailsful of surplus milk into the hole.

The milkers poured the surplus milk into the hole again
morning and evening on the second and third day after the arrival of the strangers. But on the evening of the third day, they
noticed that the milk was not sucked in by the earth because
it had ripened into curds, and that evening they left the hole
with a feeling that it was not going to get them out of this difficulty of theirs. It was very warm this third night, and after
cockcrow the milk in the hole fermented and bubbled. Then it
rose, and rose, and rose. It levelled with the surface of the
earth, but continued to rise, and rise, and rise until it stood
well above the buildings, overhanging them like a cliff.

The first man to see it in the morning ran back to the
huts, banged the doors and roused his companions. They all
came out and gazed at this wonderful happening. So-Khabazana looked at it once and said, "The princess must see this
wonder before it vanishes! I'll wake her!" He ran to the princess's chamber and banged the door shouting, *"Nkosazana!
Nkosazana!* Get up and come out and see! Here's a wonder of
wonders!"

The princess leaped out of bed and ran out. As soon as
she saw this, she screamed with delight and ran forward with
open arms, and she embraced the wall of milk just as the first
sunbeam of the morning struck it. Thereupon, the wall collapsed and the curds came tumbling down and covered her
body completely. Once more she screamed with delight and
ran back to her chamber and closed the door. She grabbed a
piece of soft leather, but before she used it for removing the
milk, she looked at her body and found that there would be
no need for this, because the milk had vanished. With another
scream of delight she threw the leather away and ran out of
her room. This time it was the men who made exclamations
of surprise and joy, for the girl who came running towards
them with joyful shouts of "Look at me! Look at me!" was
Nomtha-we-Langa, tall and erect, more beautiful than she had
ever been.

Sidlokolo and his comrades had risen early as usual and,

after taking their bath, returned to sit on the rocks. As the
shadows of the night melted, they saw the white wall overhanging the buildings at the outpost and wondered what this
meant. They saw the men standing about or walking around
it, and they thought these men must be constructing something. Then they suddenly saw the wall collapsing and heard
a scream. A piece seemed to have broken away from the white
wall and flown and vanished at the door of one of the buildings. While the rest of the youth were exchanging glances of
surprise, the prince, whose gaze had remained fixed on the wall,
suddenly leaped to his feet and pointed at a female figure that
had just emerged from the same door.

"There she is! There she is!" he shouted, and the next
moment he was running towards the cave, followed by all his
comrades.

Without asking one another what to do, the braves
grabbed their belongings and packed them and swung their
luggage on their shoulders. They ran out of the cave and
down the slope until they reached the valley where the forest
ended. But as they emerged on the other side, they slackened
their pace a little, and approached the royal outpost with the
dignity and respect befitting the occasion.

The princess was still standing in the courtyard, with
all the men around her, rejoicing and congratulating her
on her recovery. Suddenly she disregarded the men's compli-
ments and they saw her looking over their heads, her bosom rising and falling with wonder and delight. They all
turned and looked, and they saw the strangers approaching
the gate.

"Sidlokolo! The prince! The Cub of the Lion of the land
of So-and-So!" whispered the princess.

The prince and his comrades stopped at the gate, waiting
to be invited to come in. So-Khabazana ordered the other men
to attend to the strangers, and he remained alone with the
princess. He watched his men until they reached the gate.
This gave him time to think and the princess to remember
her status and compose herself. When he turned to speak to
the princess, she was all dignity.

"You know each other then—you and this prince?" he asked.

"Yes, we know each other. I met him once, him and two of the others with him."

"That makes my burden light then. It would be a painful thing to have to treat this prince like a stranger after he has done such a great thing for our daughters. Besides, his father and our king are old neighbors and good neighbors too. Return to you chamber and prepare to receive him, *nkosazana*. Meanwhile, I'll go and see that they have some food and drink."

From that moment things began to move very quickly. So-Khabazana called his men together and picked out three to go to the Great Place and tell the news of the princess's recovery. Sidlokolo and his comrades agreed that the remaining five of the eight chosen by lot should precede the prince and his two chosen ones on the way home. But before going to their own homes, these five were to call on the maidens' attendants at the outpost and tell them that the miracle had happened. Then after some feasting and drinking at the men's wing, the seven runners departed together, for they were going to travel part of the way together.

By the time Sidlokolo and his two companions were presented to the princess, they had already been shown in every way that no one regarded them as strangers here, and this made them happy and free. They found the princess lounging on the couch grass at the back of her chamber.

"Here is Nomtha-we-Langa!" said the prince without waiting to be introduced by So-Khabazana. "Do you still remember us, *nkosazana*?"

"I still remember you," said the princess sitting up and stretching out her hand to greet them. "I recognized you far away this very morning—all three of you."

"How far away?"

"As you came up the slope, before you reached the gate."

"We recognized the sunbeam much farther away than that, *nkosazana*, from a cave in the forest yonder, and it guided us to its source. So here we are."

They flung themselves on the grass beside her, and So-Khabazana left them to themselves.

"Do you mean to say you slept in a cave last night?" asked the princess.

"We grew up sleeping in caves, *nkosazana,* whenever it became necessary to do so," replied the prince, laughing. "Even tonight we'll sleep in a cave, and that's why we have to leave very soon."

"You're joking!"

"I'm not joking. We've already begged So-Khabazana for the road."

"Oh, just stop playing! Tell me about the girls of my homeland. How are they? Oh, how I miss them!"

"And that's exactly why we must be on our way home at once, *nkosazana.* My father must know everything now, and he must hear it from me. After I've told him everything, I mean to persuade him to beg your father to forgive the girls of your homeland and your elderly attendants and allow them to return to their homes."

"Oh! You've thought of a great thing. The people of my homeland will be forever grateful to you. I understand now why you want to go so soon."

Sidlokolo and his companions left the outpost late that afternoon. They felt so refreshed that they travelled the whole night without stopping. On the afternoon of the third day they reached the borders of their homeland, but they decided not to approach the Great Place until nightfall, because they did not want to be seen by any and everybody.

Before going to meet his father, Sidlokolo met some of the leading councillors and from them he learned, as he had expected, that all the activities of the braves were known to the king, and that the king was proud of them. This encouraged Sidlokolo to sound the councillors on the matter concerning the elderly women and the maidens, and the councillors asked him to leave the whole matter to them.

On the third day Sidlokolo and all his braves had to appear before the king and councillors and tell the court what had been going on. It was Sidlokolo's two chosen ones who told the whole story. The councillors then wanted to know from Mlindazwe if the maidens were well, and when they had been assured of this, one of the councillors he had sounded asked Sidlokolo directly what he now intended to do about the girls, and it was at this point that Sidlokolo spoke. He addressed himself to the councillors, asking them first to beg the king to forgive the braves for making such far-reaching decisions without saying a word to him, and then to persuade him to beg the king of Bhakubha to forgive the princess's attendants and the maidens of Bhakubha and allow them to return to their homeland. In reply to this, the councillor who had asked the question told the youth that, now that everything had been heard, the king and his inner council would retire to the Great Chamber and decide what judgement to pronouce on these doings, and the youth would have to remain where they were until the king and council returned.

The king and council did not take long to decide what to do. When they returned it was the chief councillor who addressed the youth. In the long eloquent speech that he made, he did not make any attempt to disguise the fact that the whole kingdom was proud of what the youth had done, and in conclusion he said, "All your fathers, grandfathers, and great grandfathers at this meeting envy you this great deed. Even if they don't say it to you, in their hearts they are asking themselves at this very moment if, given such an opportunity, in their youth, any of their age-groups would have been able to display their manhood in such a worthy manner?"

The king then rose to speak, and all he said about the doings of the youth was,"You have heard how your fathers feel about what you have done, and that is enough." Of the request about the women and maidens, he said, "That is a grave matter, especially about the maidens. My neighbor, the king of Bhakubha, is a kind person and may be ready to forgive them and allow them to re-enter their homeland. But even he does not have the power to force individual homes to receive their daughters. Anyway we, your fathers, have heard, and we shall look into this matter. It is possible that we may have to answer difficult questions when we arrive there, and the an-

swers to the questions must be found before we decide
whether to make this attempt or not."

But everything worked out well. The King of Bhakubha
had just welcomed his daughter back home when the deputation came. He very much wanted her to be as happy as possible after what she had gone through, but he knew that she
could not be happy without the other girls. The parents of the
girls too were missing their daughters. So, far from raising any
of the difficult questions that the deputation had anticipated,
the king, his inner council and the parents had nothing but
praise for their neighbors. They thanked the king of the
neighbor kingdom and his people for what they had done for
their maidens and *made a request* that the girls be escorted
back to their homeland, together with the elderly women.

Sidlokolo and his braves received the news with great joy,
but their joy was even greater when they heard that their fathers had decided that Mlindazwe and the ten who had been
guarding the outpost should escort the maidens.

Nomtha-we-Langa had been kept indoors since her return
because her father did not wish to cause the parents of the
other girls pain by giving her her place when all the other
girls were still in exile. The maidens and the elderly women
knew this before they left the outpost. When they approached
the Great Place, the senior attendant said, "Girls! Sing your
song. And don't stop until you see the princess."

People of all ages were gathered at the Great Place to receive the girls, and as soon as their song was heard, all the
youth ran to join their girls and the singing. They entered the
Great Gate singing, calling on Nomtha-we-Langa to come out
and brighten the sky that had been covered by dark shadows
since she had disappeared. They reached the great clearing in
front of the royal chambers and would not stop singing. The
king smiled and looked at his great wife. In response, the
queen disappeared in the Great Chamber, and the next moment Nomtha-we-Langa was standing at the door, smiling
happily.

Mlindazwe and his men remained a number of days as
guests of the Great Place. On the day of their departure, the

parents of the girls brought them many gifts, those who were well-to-do giving them cattle and the less prosperous giving them goats.

The return of the maidens of Bhakubha was followed by what every one, on both sides of the river, expected to happen. The king, Sidlokolo's father, sent representatives to ask the King of Bhakubha to give him his daughter that she might be the wife of his son Sidlokolo and mother of his people. The request was accepted, and after the customary negotiations, Nomtha-we-Langa was accompanied by a large bridal party to her new home where great festivities took place.

During the royal marriage festivities, those who had eyes noted with approval the friendly relations between the maidens of Bhakubha and Sidlokolo's comrades and predicted that many of these maidens would soon rejoin their princess in her new status. The first to do so was Khabazana. Her duties at the outpost as leader of the maidens of Bhakubha had made it necessary for her to meet Mlindazwe very frequently, and the two had grown to like each other very much. They were betrothed before the royal festivities were over. Thus Nomtha-we-Langa and Khabazana opened the ford, and the maidens who had bathed in the dreaded Lulange pool, the maidens who were determined to die fighting for their princess, recrossed the great river, one after another. But this time they did not cross it as shamefaced fugitives begging for asylum. They crossed it as confident future mothers of the sons and daughters of the men who had rescued the name of the lively maidens of Bhakubha.

The Story of Nomxakazo

A respect for humanity and a reverence for custom are the two themes here, the finest narrative in Jordan's collection.* These themes provide the substance for an odyssey which constitutes the broad framework of the story, a pilgrimage which is a rite of purification, a rite of passage which takes the heroine from narcissistic self-indulgence through ordeals that finally purge her of her self-love, which cleanse her until she emerges, at the end, reborn and purified—the Maiden from the Reeds. The odyssey is first a quest for self-knowledge, from which develops a drive for fulfillment. It is a journey which takes Nomxakazo from the center of her grasping world (a child's world, the child shrilly and selfishly demanding, always on sufferance of others) to a recognition that humane actions within a rule of law represent man's best hope not simply for survival, though for that too certainly, but also for those qualities that give life fullness and dignity.

Each of the three major divisions of the narrative represents a parallel situation. The first part, which deals with Dumakude's martial kingdom, details the outrages against humanity committed by the king's men—the ravaging of the countryside and the destruction of scores of people, for no other reason than to fulfill capricious demands for cattle:

---

* Jordan' version of *The Story of Nomxakazo* is very close to that of "Lydia," *Umkxakaza-wakogingqwayo*, in Henry Callaway, *Nursery Tales, Traditions, and Histories of the Zulus* (Natal, 1868), pp. 181–217.

It became a custom of this kingdom that whenever the warriors wanted to increase their herds of cattle, all they had to
do was to tell the leaders of their regiments.

*This wanton slaughter, in the company of gluttonous revelry,
reaches its zenith of vanity and cruelty when the king makes
good his pledge that, on the day Nomxakazo comes of age, he
will darken the sun with cattle.*

*This section of the narrative has its counterpart in the
second, that dealing with the Dlungu-ndlebe, the cannibals.
There is irony in the fact that Nomxakazo's ancestors ostra-
cized the cannibals from the kingdom because of their
wretched habits, and that irony rests in the startling but appropriate correspondence that exists between the barbaric customs of the Dlungu-ndlebe and the destructive customs of Dumakude: they are the same.*

*In the final part of the story, a young, vain prince sends a
sorcerer to capture Nomxakazo and to bring her back to his
kingdom—without considering the customary paths taken
when wooing a young woman. Because the young prince's father had been defeated in a particularly murderous battle by
Dumakude, and because Dumakude's kingdom was now desolate, the prince decides "to disregard custom" because he is
convinced that a "wicked man" like Dumakude deserves "no
human respect." In his own vengeance and arrogance, he du-
plicates the crime of Nomxakazo's father. Both Dumakude
and the prince have their counterpart and reflection in the
subhuman cannibals.*

*Within these three major divisions, the education and the
quest of Nomxakazo unfold. The origins of the girl are woven
tightly into the bloody fabric of her father's military prowess.
Dumakude, at the same time that he supports an invidious
custom which sanctifies human destruction, breaks another: he
goes to war during a time that his wife is pregnant. As Nomxakazo's name mirrors the violence of which her father is
guilty, so her nature comes to reflect that of the king; she
matches his vanity, selfishness and greed, and her infantile demands that he fulfill his vow of darkening the sun when she
comes of age result in destruction and slaughter more mon-*

*strous than any accomplished by Dumakude in the past. She
and her father are partners in selfishness and pride.*

It is in the second part of the narrative that Nomxakazo
begins to deviate from the path of her father. She comes of
age, and starts to undergo the customary rites of purification,
while all about her are the signs of impurity, of decay—
rotting carcasses of animals, which in their putrefaction are
really grim metaphors of the rottenness of the society in which
she lives. In such an atmosphere, purification rites are reduced
to empty mockery, and it is at this point that Maphundu enters and the education of Nomxakazo begins.

At first, her schooling is undertaken by Maphundu himself; Nomxakazo is obviously too much involved in her own
egocentric whims to appreciate the wisdom and necessity of
what is happening. When her sister tells the messengers of Maphundu that the princess is "undergoing custom," they inform
her that "We came here knowing that your sister is undergoing custom"—in fact, that is a primary reason for their coming. Maphundu, a symbol of nature, a mountain containing
the wide range of natural phenomena, prevents her from fulfilling a custom which has lost its relevance and has degener-
ated into hollow ritual; she is not yet ready for purification.

The remainder of the story is in one sense a long, drama-
tized purification rite, as Nomxakazo dies ritually to her past
and is reborn. Custom which has become empty will be given
new meaning. Nomxakazo, still trailing behind her the ornaments which express her vanity, is taken to a cave and there
left alone—with complete freedom to come and go as she
pleases. But she is alone, and "what a bad thing to be alone!"
she laments. As she orients herself to this new life, she experiences fears and recriminations, until she decides that, because
she is after all the king's daughter, she will at least ostensibly
demonstrate her courage. The decision is an important one,
and represents a tentative thrust toward liberation, but it is
still grounded in vanity; her education has only begun. The
Dlungu-ndlebe take her to their chief who, because he is attracted to her, adopts the young girl. She has not yet attained
sufficient insights into herself and the world about her, and

*she accepts the indulgences of the chief, allowing herself to be-
come a pet, spoiled by the chief's attentions much as she was
spoiled by Dumakude's earlier pampering. The chief's solici-
tude feeds Nomxakazo's vanity, and she grows fat—uglier and
uglier. Finally, the chief, repulsed by her beastliness, agrees to
roast her. Three times Maphundu, answering the princess's ap-
peals to the heavens for aid, comes to the rescue, and she finally sets off for home. Some of the vanity has been rubbed off
now; Nomxakazo is no longer interested in taking her ornaments with her.*

*The education of Nomxakazo begins in earnest during
the long trip home, and the contrast between that journey and
her mother's account of the unhappy events that have over-
taken Dumakude's kingdom make a shocking impact on the
girl. She is treated with generosity and pity by people she does
not even know as she makes the grueling trek to her father's
Great Place. When she gets home, she discovers the final result of her father's immense power—desolation, loneliness, and
death. Abruptly, she is led to a recognition of her own crimes
against humanity, and those of her father, that vain man who
is now reduced to mumbling impotence.*

*The queen mother tells Nomxakazo the unhappy tale of
the kingdom's distress. It was none of Maphundu's doing, she
insists. Rather, the misery in the land is the logical result of*
the tears of the thousands and thousands of women whose
men we slaughtered, the tears of the countless numbers of
children we orphaned, the tears of the countless number of
people whose homes we destroyed, whose cattle we looted.

*Hence death comes to the kingdom not as the result of an
external force: death enters the land through the warriors,
through the cattle—that is, through the greed and vanity,
the selfishness and gluttony of the people themselves. And all
are guilty of this, for the women urged their men to fight, and
the entire country must answer for their crimes. The cattle
have become the very means of their destruction; no longer
is the sky darkened by cattle raided from other people: now,
because of the carcasses, the sky is darkened by crows and
vultures, which eat the living and the dead (symbolic, per-*

haps, of Dumakude's own actions when his kingdom was in full blossom). And finally, ironically, death enters through hunger; food is plentiful, but the people cannot survive "because of the rottenness which they saw all around them." This rottenness leads to the decline and dissolution of the kingdom. The youth leave, the old merely await death.

Irony compounds irony, as each incident in the narrative is revealed as the obverse of a previous incident; the operative force is not Maphundu, it is not fate, but an irrevocable chain of events set in motion by greed, uncontrollable until all is destroyed. (Maphundu does not destroy the people, they destroy themselves; Maphundu kills them in the sense that Maphundu is their own nature, or at least represents the fact that they are out of tune with nature.) What seemed positive in the kingdom is turned over, the rank underside exposed, and the frame of values is shown to be a negative one by the very actions that occur within that frame. Logic and irony are shafts of awful light, illuminating the fearful plight of Dumakude and his subjects.

This is the scene and the tale awaiting Nomxakazo on her homecoming, and it is immediately contrasted in her agonized mind with the generous treatment she received at the hands of those very people her father's bands of warriors had ravaged and plundered. Nomxakazo forgets her own suffering, and weeps for her father's people. This is her first act of selflessness. And she asks the inevitable, tormenting questions:

"Why did you let me, Mother? Why did Father allow me to make such a demand, if it meant destroying so many peoples, killing people, making people poor and homeless? What wrong had they done? Had he no pity?"

And she recalls too,

"How numerous the people who pitied me, gave me a place to sleep when I was homeless, gave me food when I was hungry, nursed me when I was ill, in all my wanderings."

It is this recognition that signals the end of the first phase of Nomxakazo's purification rites. Self-knowledge is now hers, with a new respect for the dignity of a human being. This new knowledge now leads her to begin a quest for her own dignity. This princess, who had once been the center of her world, now has no world at all. She is homeless, her land has been destroyed, her parents are indigent. In the past, the question of identity was for Nomxakazo a simple and obvious one: she was the king's daughter. It was this sense of identity which gave her courage when she was first left alone in the cave:

She is a king's daughter. Except for Maphundu, no living man has ever been as powerful as her father. She will be her father's daughter from that moment.

Yet, look at her father. The greatness with which she had identified is now gone; he is perilously close to being "a nobody." Suddenly, her world has been ripped apart; with the decline of her father, she has lost her identity as a person. Being a princess no longer has meaning. And just as the custom of purification had to be invested with new meaning, so also must her own identity as a person be given a new definition. She sets out to find this. It becomes a quest not just for identity, but for self-fulfillment. The first hint of the nature of this quest is provided in Nomxakazo's response to the gifts that the wretched remnants of Dumakude's kingdom bring to the young girl. Her Beauty is restored in full when she realizes, through these gifts, that "she and her parents were still regarded as people." She soon finds that this is not in itself sufficient, that her quest for her identity as a human is not yet complete.

The odyssey again begun, the education of Nomxakazo is in a sense at an end, and the final phase of the purification rites must now be fulfilled: that which will invest Nomxakazo, a woman, a human being, with dignity. In the final part of the story, she symbolizes this purification by washing herself in the various rivers crossed, cleansing herself of past errors and misfortunes, then emerging from the reeds (reeds being a symbol of purity and creation in Xhosa religion).

The selfish quest of the young prince provides the opportunity for the completion of the ritual purification. Disregarding custom, the prince sends a sorcerer to steal the girl and bring her to him. The sorcerer confronts Nomxakazo and makes plain to her that neither she nor her parents are possessed of human dignity. The young woman rebels against this suggestion: "If he wants me to be his wife, doesn't he know the custom? Am I nobody's daughter, that he should want to steal me?" And the sorcerer answers, "But who is Dumakude?" Finally, when he tires of arguing with her, he claims that he will show her that she is "nobody's daughter." He attacks her for her pride, but it is a different kind of pride now. It is not the insensitive and grasping pride of a vain and thoughtless princess; rather, it is the pride of a human being who expects human treatment. When the magician attempts to force her to come with him, Maphundu makes his final entrance: he sends savage animals to save her from the sorcerer, and the experience convinces the prince's emissary that he "did wrong" to try to coerce her.

Nomxakazo then makes her first decision as a mature woman; she decides to go with the sorcerer to the prince. "But when I meet this prince of yours face to face, he will know that I am somebody's daughter." The young woman has learned her lesson well, and even though she faces potential hostility in the village of the prince, she no longer requires the services of Maphundu. Now aware of herself as a person and purified of her past problems, she will teach the prince the same lesson she had to learn. But she is not going to visit the prince as a pedagogue; there is a more compelling reason. Her confrontation with the prince must be successful in that the prince must come to recognize that she is a somebody. This is urgently important to Nomxakazo.

Along the way, she demonstrates again and again her own intimate knowledge of herself, of nature, of other people and their customs. She walks into the village, coming out of the reeds, the purification now symbolically over. She enters the world a mature woman. Deliberately and with determination, she demonstrates to the prince and his councillors that "She has the heart of a human, she has a liver, she is alive in the head." In addition,
she has come here a maiden and means to go back to her

people still a maiden. She has closed all the narrow zigzag paths and left us only the straight road to go by—the road of custom.

She is not a nobody: "she is a maiden of birth and comes from a live home." And the prince agrees: "We thank you," he tells Nomxakazo, "for making humans of us." He treats her with respect, with great dignity. And, finally, the prince and his followers treat her parents and the people of that lonely kingdom as humans.

Her education is complete, her quest fulfilled, her identity as a human (and not simply as the daughter of a king) has been established and affirmed. This has been achieved not through divine intervention but rather through her own efforts, her own wit, her own intelligence. As the destruction of Dumakude's warriors came about because of their own actions and not because of the ire of a supernatural Maphundu, so the salvation of Nomxakazo is found in her character and is not the result of any outside force. Thus, Nomxakazo moves through three situations, each similar; what changes is the girl herself. At first, she is one with her father's selfishness and vanity; second, she learns, and in the process, slowly sheds those things she valued in the past. Finally, she acts as she attempts to affirm her own identity and, in the eyes of the reader, to reaffirm the dignity of mankind. She loses her beauty because of her own vanity, and that beauty is restored when she becomes a humane person.

Nomxakazo's father's might and pride, the sorcerer's magic, the prince's love, the mother's instinct, even Maphundu himself: these are all external and only operate to educate her. They do not magically change her. Merely following the ritual of custom does not purify the girl; she is purified because of what her experiences have done to her. In another sense, Maphundu is symbolic of Nomxakazo's harmony with nature—and her dissonance. The fact that Maphundu refuses to allow her to drink from his streams, to eat from his trees, to sleep in their shade is symbolic of Nomxakazo's state of being with regard to nature—and this includes her own nature. Only when she reestablishes this balance is her education complete. All else is inadequate. The father's might is flaccid when confronted by nature; the queen mother's instinct is insufficient because there must also be understanding, reason, and recognition. The magician's bag of tricks is powerless when confronted by a purified nature. The prince's love is initially selfish, and not until it is genuine and generous does it become a viable form for order and harmony.

Respect for custom is respect for humanity. Inhumanity and custom, distorted and manipulated until it rationalizes destructive activities, provide the initial environment of Nomxakazo. Her odyssey leads her to a respect for custom which has but one purpose: human relations based on respect and made beautiful through love. More broadly, custom provides the path which leads to harmony with nature. In themselves, customs are not inviolate and sacred. Destructive customs, such as those created by Dumakude, must be eradicated, and customs which have become merely empty forms must be given new relevance. This narrative emphasizes not a blind adherence to custom; it celebrates customs which never neglect the people for whom they were fashioned. Properly understood and properly executed, the custom of purification recreates the odyssey which leads to order (just as it is artistically, metaphorically, created in this story). If custom has a suitable relevance to human life, then it can become a rich framework in which men can live in security and with justice; at the same time, it leads to self-knowledge and self-fulfillment. Customs exist, then, not to denigrate humans, but rather to lead them to fullness; they cannot become excuses for inhumanity, for they are at once a rationale for and the foundation of humane activities. This is the lesson Nomxakazo must learn; it is the lesson she must teach the young prince, it is the lesson which destroys her father—and it is the lesson communicated by the ntsomi *to the members of its audience. Man is revealed in the narrative as a frail being given to feelings of antagonisms towards his fellows, but custom develops in him a solid respect for humanity.*

The Story of Nomxakazo

1. "I Still See the Sun"

IT CAME ABOUT ACCORDING TO SOME tale that there
was a great king whose name was Dumakude ("Far-famed").
This king had never been defeated in battle. Wherever he led
his armies, it was certain that he would conquer his enemy,
capture large herds of cattle, and lead his warriors back home
with singing and dancing. On arriving home, he would select
the most beautiful of the loot for himself, and then divide the
rest among his warriors, each one according to his rank and
personal prowess. It became a custom of this kingdom that
whenever the warriors wanted to increase their herds of cattle,
all they had to do was to tell the leaders of the regiments.
These leaders would then come together and agree that on an
appointed day each one of them would march his regiment to
the Great Place, singing war-songs, dancing. There they would
raise their spears high and thunder the royal salute, *Bayethe!*,
which means "Bring them!"—in other words, "Bring the
enemy or lead us where they are, that we may kill them."
Thereupon, the king would have great numbers of fat oxen
slaughtered for his warriors, and after some days of feasting,
he would lead them to any of the neighbouring kingdoms to
kill people, loot as many head of cattle as could be found, and
return to the Great Place to divide the spoils.

There was another powerful king, five days' journey from
Dumakude's Great Place. This king was considered to be as
powerful as Dumakude, because he too had never been de-

feated. It was known that Dumakude's warriors had for a long time been chafing-hot in the reins (straining at the leash) to meet this king and his warriors so that it might be decided by battle which of these two kings was the real bull. So it came about that one day, when his great wife was heavy with child, Dumakude led his warriors against this other king. As they set out, Dumakude's warriors beat their shields with their spears —*xaka! xaka! xaka!*—and they sang the greatest of their war-songs, because they knew that this was the last and greatest battle that many of them would ever fight.

The enemy were taken by surprise, but they fought very bravely, killing thousands of Dumakude's most noted warriors. But Dumakude's warriors killed more thousands of the enemy with spear and club, and there was one sound of *gingqi! gingqi! gingqi!* as the bodies of the slain fell to the hard ground. Eventually, the invaded were routed, and thousands of their cattle were captured and driven away. Amid the praise-songs of the royal bards and the piercing cheers of the women, Dumakude and his warriors entered the gates of the Great Place ten days after the last battle. In eloquent words the leader of the warriors' song related how the enemy were slain, and, with their spears, the rest of the warriors imitated the stabbing of the bodies, and with their clubs, the crushing of the skulls. The thud! thud! thud! of the falling bodies was imitated by the blood-curdling *gingqi! gingqi! gingqi!* of the chorus.

Now the undisputed bull of the world known to him, Dumakude felt very great indeed. But he was even more elated when he discovered that on the very day that he routed the enemy, his great wife had born him a daughter of surpassing beauty. As he held the baby lovingly to his bosom, Dumakude spoke proudly and said, "When I led my warriors out of this Great Place to the land of him who disputed my greatness as a warrior, our spears sounded *xaka! xaka! xaka!* When we met the enemy, their bodies fell *gingqi! gingqi! gingqi!* The great victory I won on the day of the birth of this daughter of mine must be remembered by her name. She shall be called *Nomxakazo wako Gingqwayo*."

After giving his baby daughter this name, the king returned to his warriors and announced the birth of Nomxakazo wako Gingqwayo. When the congratulatory exclamations had died down, the king went on to announce a great vow: "The day this daughter of mine comes of age, the cattle I shall present her will be so numerous that they will darken the sun."

This vow was greeted with acclamation and praises by all those who heard it.

As soon as Nomxakazo reached an age when she could understand things, her father told her the significance of her name, and she felt very proud of this. She was even more delighted when her father went on to tell her the vow he had made after holding her in his arms for the first time. As she grew up, it was impossible to forget her father's great vow. All the people at the Great Place looked forward to the princess's coming of age. They never failed to make mention of it when the opportunity offered itself. If Nomxakazo sneezed, all the elderly women within hearing would exclaim, "May you grow up quickly *nkosazana,* and reach the age when you will receive the herds of cattle that will darken the sun."

The girl's coming of age was marked by her first visit to the moon (menstruation), and the custom was that no matter where this event occurred, the girl concerned was to sit down where she was and await the arrival of the mothers. These would come as soon as the news reached them, cover the girl in bedclothes that had never been used before, and carry her to a bed of reeds prepared in a secluded chamber. There she would remain for days or moons, undergoing purification rites. During this period, only the women and girls were allowed to visit her. On the day of her coming out, there would be great festivities in which everybody could participate, even the passerby from a strange land.

Nomxakazo came of age one day while playing with other girls in the open fields, and at once some of the bigger girls ran home to whisper this news to the mothers. The mothers came promptly, expecting that the princess would readily accept being wrapped and covered in the beautiful bedclothes they had brought with them. But Nomxakazo made it clear

Riding on the animal's back.

that she would not move until her father had brought to the spot the countless numbers of cattle he had promised to present her. When this message was conveyed to the king, he immediately ordered his herdsmen to take five tens of the choicest of his cattle to the princess. But when the cattle arrived, Nomxakazo smiled with contempt and asked, "How do you expect these to darken the sun?"

The king sent a hundred, hundreds, a thousand, thousands of his finest cattle, but every time, his daughter smiled with contempt and shook her head:

I can still see the sun.

The king gave an order that all the remaining thousands of cattle in his kingdom—his own as well as those of his subjects—be gathered together and brought to his daughter, as a present from him. But when the cattle came, the princess looked straight into the sky, smiled with contempt and shook her head:

I still see the sun.

The king summoned his generals and commanded them to lead his armies beyond the borders of his kingdom to capture all the cattle they could find, no matter whose they might be. The order was carried out. Tribes and tribes were attacked, people slaughtered, and their cattle captured and brought to Dumakude's daughter. But she looked up to the sky, smiled with contempt and shook her head:

I still see the sun.

The warriors traversed swamps, jungles, and deserts in search of cattle, but all the human habitations they found were abandoned, and there was no trace of their livestock. The news of these ravages and destruction had travelled to far-away lands, and the people had fled with their livestock. Those who could not go very far hid themselves and their stock in places that could not easily be reached by people who did not know the land. But Dumakude's warriors were too proud to return home empty-handed. They wandered in all directions, many of them dying of hunger, of thirst, and of diseases that had never been known in their native land.

One day, the warriors came to a great fertile valley where myriads of cattle were grazing. Overlooking this valley was an animal of immeasurable size. Its face was a solid rock, its eyes and ears and nostrils like deep red caves. On its body were tall mountains and low hills, large rivers and small streams, big deep lakes and small shallow puddles, large forests and small thickets, fertile lands and barren deserts. In some regions of its body it was summer, and everything was fresh-green and beautiful: in others it was winter, and everything was covered with snow. But the warriors were so greedy for the loot that they took no notice of this object. For all they cared it was nothing more than a mountain forest of extraordinary size and shape. So, with shouts of joy they rounded up the cattle. But just as they were beginning to drive them away, the animal spoke to them in a very deep but calm voice: "Those cattle that you are driving away—do you know whose they are?"

Only then did the warriors realize that this was not a lifeless mountain but a living being, able to speak! But, unaccustomed to being called to account for anything they did, King Dumakude's warriors just gave it one look and answered defiantly, "Ugh! Get away, *Maphundu!* (You-of-the-Nodules")

"Very well!" said Maphundu, as calmly as before. "Take them away."

The cattle from the Great Valley were so numerous that, by the time they reached the princess, the dust they raised had covered the sky and completely darkened the sun. When she saw this, the princess smiled with satisfaction and said to the mothers, "Now, in truth, I cannot see the sun. You can carry me home."

From that day, there was nothing but feasting in the entire kingdom of Dumakude. So many cattle were slaughtered each day that the people and their dogs and also the beasts and birds of prey, had more than enough; and thousands of carcasses lay rotting on the plains. All this time, the princess was in seclusion, and there was no talk of her coming out until a whole year had ended.

When at last it was decided that she must come out, the king made a proclamation that first of all, all the fields must be reaped, in order that the quantities of beer brewed for the final celebrations should be greater than had ever been seen even by the oldest men and women in this kingdom. So, early one morning all the people went to the fields, leaving Nom-xakazo alone with her younger sister, Thubise.

2. *"Bring All Your Spears"*

Some time after the people had gone, the two girls heard the heavens thundering, and the earth shook so violently that even the utensils rattled.

"Thubise!" cried Nomxakazo, "do go outside and see what this means. How can there be thunder when the sky is so bright?"

Thubise ran outside, and when she came in again a moment later, she was terrified by the wonders she had seen. Where the great entrance to the Great Place used to be, she had seen something like a mountain forest. This thing had a face of rock, a beard of tree leaves, ears like tall trees, and body hair that looked like forests. It had broken down the fence completely on one side and was now standing where the great entrance used to be.

While the two girls were talking in low tones, wondering what this could mean, two tiny leaves broke from the face of Maphundu of the Nodules (for this was he), and they floated like feathers in a breeze and entered the princess's chamber without so much as knocking at the door.

"Thubise!" they commanded, "pick up a pitcher and go fetch some water from the river."

"My sister is undergoing custom," protested Thubise. "I can't leave her alone with—with—with things that I don't even know."

"We don't care whether you know us or not," said the leaves. "We came here knowing that your sister is undergoing custom. Do as we bid you!"

Thubise picked up a pitcher and went to the river. But

after filling the pitcher with water, she found that she could not move from where she was. She sat down on the river-bank and sobbed quietly.

Meanwhile, Nomxakazo had her own difficulties with the leaves. They were ordering her to do various things, one after another, that a princess does not ordinarily do because she is not a commoner, and various things, one after another, that a girl may not do during her period of seclusion. When she protested that she could not do this or that because she was a princess or because she was undergoing custom, the leaves answered that they came to the Great Place knowing all that, and they commanded her to do as she was told.

"Make a fire!"

"I am a princess and don't know how to make a fire."

"We came here knowing that you are a princess and don't know how to make a fire. Do as we bid you."

She made the fire.

"Bring a pot and boil some millet."

"I don't know how to cook. I have never cooked since I was born."

"We came here knowing that you don't know how to cook, and that you've never cooked since you were born. Do as we bid you!"

She brought a pot and boiled some millet.

"Kneel at the grindstone and grind the boiled millet."

"I don't know how to grind. I've never been taught to grind."

"We came here knowing that you can't grind, and that you've never been taught to grind. Do as we bid you!"

She knelt at the grindstone and ground the millet.

"Go bring the largest milk-calabash in this house."

"It's too heavy. I can't carry it."

"In that case, come show us where it is, and we'll carry it here."

"I am in seclusion and may not enter the place of the milk-calabashes until custom has been done."

"We came here knowing that you're in seclusion and may not enter the place of the milk-calabashes until custom has been done. Get up on your feet and take us to the place of the milk-calabashes!"

She led the leaves to the place of the milk-calabashes, and they picked up the largest one and carried it between them back to her chamber. Then the leaves set about preparing a meal. One of them brought a large basin and put the *phothulo* (meal from boiled millet) into it. The other leaf lifted the calabash and added *amasi* (fermented milk) to the *mphothulo* to make *mvubo* (dish consisting of meal and fermented milk). The leaves then carried the calabash to Maphundu, and He-of-the-Nodules swallowed the calabash and its contents. Returning to the princess's chamber, the leaves picked out three spoons from a set hanging on the wall, and they ordered the princess to eat with them.

"O, *bawo!* (father) what am I to do about this? I can't eat *mvubo* while in seclusion.

"We came here knowing that you can't eat *mvubo* while in seculusion. Sit down and eat!"

She sat down and ate with the leaves.

After the meal, the leaves left the princess in her chamber and went to the building where the large clay pots of beer were kept. They plunged into the first one, and when they came out again, there was not a drop of beer in the clay pot. They carried the rest of the beer to Maphundu, and he received one clay pot after another, swallowing pot and beer at one gulp.

The leaves returned to the princess and ordered her to prepare some food provisions, collect her belongings, and come with them. Without a word, she took some loaves of bread and put them into a basket. Then she collected her ornaments and put them into a beautiful leather bag. The leaves led the way out of the chamber and floated a little ahead of the princess back to the trees from which they had broken. The princess stopped before Maphundu, not knowing what to do.

"Climb on, *nkosazana*," said Maphundu, calmly. "We're going now."

The princess climbed onto Maphundu's body, and Maphundu moved out of the Great Place, going out the way he had come.

All this time, Thubise had been sitting next to her pitcher on the bank of the river, unable to move. But as soon as He-of-the-Nodules began to move, she found herself able to rise to her feet and pick up the pitcher and put it on her head. She hurried back to the Great Place and arrived there just in time to see Maphundu's tail of trees disappearing over the ridge.

"What's been happening here, Thubise? Where's my child? Where's Nomxakazo?" It was the mother who was speaking. After the crack of thunder and the terrible earthquake, she had felt uneasy, her *nimba* (motherly nature) telling her that all was not well with her daughters at the Great Place. She had therefore hurried home to find out what had happened, and she too arrived just in time to see Maphundu's tail of trees disappearing. Again her *nimba* told her that these strange happenings must be connected with the myriads of cattle brought from the Great Valley. As soon as she heard about the strange visitors, she knew that Nomxakazo had been carried away, and she ran back to the fields, yelling to raise the alarm. The call to arms was immediately taken up by all the women who heard, in the villages and in the fields. Thereupon, King Dumakude and his mighty warriors ran to their homes to fetch their spears and shields.

He-of-the-Nodules could see this commotion, but instead of getting ruffled, he stopped and calmly awaited the arrival of the warriors.

"It's He-of-the-Nodules!" shouted the warriors as they came. It was with blood-curdling war-cries that they surrounded Maphundu and hurled a hailstorm of spears into the mountain forest that was his body. Some spears fell into the lakes and rivers, large and small, some landed in the forests and jungles, some buried themselves in the swamps, some in the snow, some in the sands of the desert. Not a scratch did they make on Maphundu's body.

When every spear had been thrown, He-of-theNodules spoke calmly and said, "Go back to your homes and bring all your spears. I'll wait here until you return."

Every warrior ran to his house and brought his whole pile of spears. More frantic the yells of the women who egged on their men to fight bravely and rescue the princess! More savage the war-cries of the warriors! More furious the hailstorm of spears! But the result was the same as before, and even after the last of the spears in Dumakude's kingdom had been thrown, not a mark was to be seen on Maphundu's body. The warriors stood there, dumbstricken.

Then spoke He-of-the-Nodules, in his deep, calm voice:

"King Dumakude, now that all the spears of your warriors are part of my body, there's nothing more I can wait here for. You will not need the spears, because you have all the cattle you want. Your warriors dispossessed me of all my cattle, and therefore I have the right to take your daughter away."

"I implore you, Nodulated One!" wailed the Great Queen. "Before you take my child away, allow her to come down and shake hands with us."

"I don't refuse that," said Maphundu. *"Nkosazana,* get down and shake hands with your people."

Nomxakazo alighted and went straight to her mother. As mother and daughter embraced each other, clinging to each other, weeping, refusing to separate, the king signalled to his men, and they thronged round mother and daughter, making one last attempt to rescue the princess. Thereupon, the two tiny leaves broke off from their trees and floated into the midst of the throng. The warriors were so overawed at this strange sight that they fell back without being commanded to do so.

"Climb on, *nkosazana!"* commanded the leaves.

Nomxakazo disengaged herself and climbed on, and the two tiny leaves returned to their places. As He-of-the-Nodules began to move, the women raised their voices, wailing and pleading. As for the king and his warriors, they just stood there helpless, speechless.

"I'd rather die!" cried the Great Queen. "I'd rather die than lose my child this way!" And with these words, she ran after Maphundu. But she was just like a hen trying to overtake a hawk that had just grabbed one of her chickens and soared into the sky, its talons sunk deep in the chicken's body. Thubise followed her mother, and when she caught up with her, the two joined hands and ran after Maphundu, wailing, imploring, until He-of-the-Nodules disappeared in the distance. They followed still, now running, now walking, until darkness spread over the earth and they could not see. They spent that night in a cave, huddled together, each one trying to persuade the other not to weep. But both of them continued to weep until daybreak.

As soon as there was enough light, they got up and wandered hand in hand, now this way, now that way, and then over that way, looking for Maphundu's trail. Only then did they realize that, although at the Great Place he had broken down a whole side of the fence just by a push of his body, elsewhere Maphundu had not damaged so much as an antheap, or twig or stalk of grass. It was as if he had floated like the two tiny leaves over all things, except the fence. As for his trail, not a thing! Nevertheless, the Great Queen and her daughter continued to wander in all directions. There they were, looking down into a deep ravine. There they were, crossing the ravine and entering the thick forest on the other side. There they were, climbing the tallest trees and looking in all directions, ever calling Nomxakazo's name. But every call was answered by the echoes of their own voices coming one after another from all sides of the forest. There they were, climbing up a hill, and from its pinnacle shading their eyes and looking every way, calling, calling, calling. No sign of Maphundu, no sound except the echoes of their voices.

Down went the sun, and darkness began to spread over the landscape. Mother and daughter sought a cave and lay down to rest in each other's arms, tired, hungry. They lay there sobbing quietly until sleep descended upon them.

At daybreak they rose again and continued their search, looking down into every ravine, crossing rivers, traversing forests, climbing trees and hills, until it was dark once more and they had to find a cave to rest and sleep. But after this third day, the Great Queen said, "Thubise my child, this doesn't help anything. The only thing we can do now is to seek our way back home and give up ever seeing Nomxakazo again. She's gone. O' my child! My child!"

And so they gave up.

3. Among the Dlungu-ndlebe

Meanwhile there was Nomxakazo, riding on Maphundu, going farther and farther from her people, without the faintest idea where she was, where she was being taken to, or, if perchance she were to be set free, in which direction she would have to go to seek her home. Not a word was spoken between her and Maphundu, except when He-of-the-Nodules asked her if she was not hungry. If she said she was, he would stop immediately and allow her to pick up her food provisions and get down and eat. If she was thirsty, the two tiny leaves would break off from the trees and accompany her to the nearest spring or river where they made her stoop down and drink. The water in the springs and rivers on Maphundu's body was not hers to drink of.

On the tenth day, her food provisions were finished. She felt hungry, but the fruit on the trees on Maphundu's body was not hers to pick of. She was tired of sitting in the same position for so many days and nights, and her eyes were heavy with sleep, but the shades of the big trees on Maphundu's body were not hers to lie down and rest in. At last Maphundu asked her if she was not hungry. She replied that she was hungry, tired, and sleepy.

"Very well," said He-of-the-Nodules, and he stopped in front of a cave. "Pick up all your belongings and get down. In this cave you will find food and water, and a place to rest and sleep. You may eat when you feel hungry, drink when you feel thirsty, lie down and rest when you feel tired, and sleep when you feel sleepy."

The princess alighted and walked hesitatingly towards

The fight.

the entrance to the cave. But on reaching there she stopped
and looked about, fearing to enter.

"Go in, *nkosazana*," said Maphundu, encouragingly.
"You'll not be descended upon by any harm in this cave.
There is a fire of glowing embers in the hearth, and this keeps
the cave bright and warm. You will be able to see everything
inside, and you will not feel cold. The inside is clean and spacious. The floor is polished well with black clay."

Encouraged by these words, the princess walked in. He-
of-the-Nodules waited until she was right inside, and then he
called out to her and said, "May you stay well, *nkosazana*!
The cave is yours, together with everything inside and around
it. You can stay there as long as you please. As for me, I now
return to my Great Valley."

After speaking these words, He-of-the-Nodules went his
way.

The inside of the cave was as described by Maphundu—
spacious, not too warm, not too cool. A fire on the hearth,
with glowing embers. A smooth floor, neatly polished with
black clay. A shapely earthenware cooking pot near the
hearth. Many large earthenware pots full of fresh water along

the walls. A sheaf of ripe-red millet. A bundle of fat, juicy sugarcanes. A neatly made bed of reeds at the far end of the cave.

The princess walked across the floor and laid down her baggage next to the bed. Then she undressed, put all her clothes on the bed, walked to one of the large earthenware pots and sank her whole body in the fresh cold water, bathing. She sat in the pot for a long, long time, enjoying the freshness of the water. On coming out of the water, she buckled on her *nkciyo,* pulled out one sugarcane from the bundle and went to stand by the fire. She peeled the sugarcane with her teeth, one joint at a time, and ate it. While chewing the sugarcane, she turned round and round, very slowly, to dry and warm her body. When she had finished eating, she picked up the rind and refuse from the floor, threw them into the fire, and idly watched these drying up and finally burning to ashes. Then she returned to the bed of reeds, flung herself on it, lay fully stretched out and fell into a deep sleep. She slept until the sun sank and until it was fairly high in the sky the following morning.

She was awakened by two unusually small voices from outside the cave. She listened. These unknown people did not speak as she spoke. They were *tsefula-ing.** She rose quietly, covered her body and crept softly along the wall until she reached the entrance. She listened again. Now she heard clearly what was being said, because the speakers were very close to the entrance.

"There's a thing in this cave today!" said one.

"Yes," said the other. "It's a thing with two legs! Do you see the footprints? They go right up to the entrance, and there are none coming out. This thing must be inside *now!* Who can it be?"

---

* Basically her own language, but *t* for *z, dvu* for *du, dze* for *de.* Thus, they would say *nkosatana (nkosazana), Nomxakato (Nomxakazo), Dvumakudze (Dumakude),* and for *Gingqwayo* they would say *Gingqwako.* These are the Swazi-Bhaca dialects of the Nguni group of Southern African languages to which Xhosa and Zulu belong. When this story is told orally, the one-legged creatures speak their own dialect.

As they spoke, they came closer and closer to the cave, but the princess noted that they were a little frightened. She stretched out her neck and peered out. She saw two creatures in front of the cave. They looked like humans, but they were one-legged. Each one of them carried a bag containing fruit, which must have been gathered from the trees around the cave—from her trees, she thought. That was why they did not seem inclined to come too near.

"Who can this two-legged person be? He mustn't see us stealing his fruit!"

This gave the princess courage. She thrust out her arm without revealing the rest of her body.

"It's a woman! It's a woman!" exclaimed the two voices, and the speakers scampered away.

The princess had looked at these creatures closely enough, and she knew now that they must be of the *Dlungu-ndlebe,* a tribe of one-legged people who had been outlawed as far back as her great great grandfather's days because they had turned cannibals! Will they leave her alone? How many times will she be able to scare them away just by thrusting out her arm, especially since they have discovered that she is a woman? Perhaps they will think there's a man with her and fear to enter the cave? How can she make them think she is not alone? O, what a bad thing to be alone! That she should tremble at the sight of these tiny creatures who would not even be a morsel to her father's warriors! Where's He-of-the-Nodules? Would that he had carried her away with him to his Great Valley. For *he* is not a cannibal, of that she is sure. If he had been a man-eater, he would have swallowed her up long ago, as easily as he had swallowed the large pots of beer at her home. O, where *is* he? Where *is* he? But what does this help? There's nothing going on in the world that Maphundu doesn't know about. He left her here knowing that this is the land of the man-eating *Dlungu-ndlebe* of the mutilated ears. He did this deliberately too. He left her here to be roasted and eaten by those ugly creatures! O, where *is* her father and his warriors? But what can they do, when they have no spears? Her father's warriors without spears! Where is her mother?

"We, mame! We, mame!   O, mother! O, mother!

She collected herself. She is a king's daughter. Except for Maphundu, no living man has ever been as powerful as her father. She will be her father's daughter from this moment. Let not those creatures with mutilated ears think she is afraid of them. Who are *they* to be feared by Dumakude's daughter? She will bathe, roast some millet, eat, take some sugarcanes, and go out to sit in the sun and eat her sugarcanes. These *Dlungu-ndlebe* cowards will never come near her. Never!

She did all these things.

While sitting in the sun, she caught sight of the two *Dlungu-ndlebe,* and she noted that they were coming towards her. There they came—hop! hop! hop! Nomxakazo sat where she was by sheer strength of liver, watching them as they came. She resolved that she would not move away until they were very near, but even then she would walk into the cave quite leisurely, as if she was not in the least concerned about them. They stopped some distance away and regarded her with curiosity. Nomxakazo gazed back at them. They came nearer—hop! hop! hop!—and then they stopped again and gazed at her.

"The beauty of her!" lisped one of them. "I'm sure she's a king's daughter."

Nomxakazo turned and looked away from them, took her time collecting her things, stood up and, without giving them another look, she walked with dignity into the cave.

"The beauty of her!" exclaimed one *Dlungu-ndlebe.*

"The beauty of her figure!" exclaimed the other. "But alas! Two legs!"

The princess was not as fearless as she pretended to be, and this remark about her beauty made her fear that these creatures might come so near that they might even look in and discover that she was alone. So she thrust out her arm, and again the *Dlungu-ndlebe* scampered away.

These two *Dlungu-ndlebe* were scouts. After seeing her footprints earlier in the day, they had run back to report to their chief that there was a two-legged person in the cave.

On being asked questions, they had not been able to say any more, and so the chief had sent them back to look again and bring a fuller report. After their second coming, they were able to tell the chief much more about the princess—her pretty face, her beautiful figure, her height, her grace and dignity of carriage, her complete unconcern about such as they.

"But alas! she has two legs, chief," they said in conclusion.

"There's nothing bad about two legs," said the aged chief, with a smile. "We who have seen some suns know such people very well. They are more beautiful by far than the *Dlungundlebe*."

After saying these words, the chief sent out a regiment to see how many people were in the cave. If the woman was alone, she was to be brought before him unharmed. He exhorted the regiment to approach the cave with calmness and in peace, in order that those inside should not think they were going to be killed.

The regiment carried out these orders so well that Nomxakazo accepted the invitation to come to the chief without fear.

"The beauty of this child!" said the aged chief as Nomxakazo approached him. "The grace of her! The dignity of her! She is the daughter of a great king. She shall not be eaten. She is going to be my own child, the ornament of my house."

So Nomxakazo was received into the house of the chief of the *Dlungu-ndlebe*. She had a special hut assigned to her, a little higher up the slope than the main house. Her food was different from that of the *Dlungu-ndlebe*. It was specially prepared and brought to her hut by one of the women. This was done by order of the chief. This old man was very fond of Nomxakazo. He gave her many ornaments of ivory and brass: a headring, a necklace, armlets, waistbands, anklets. He also gave her beads befitting a princess. He loved to see "the child" moving about the place in her gracful manner, and would not allow her to do any manner of work.

She lived there a year and many moons, doing nothing besides eating the large quantities of food brought to her hut. The result of this eating, eating, eating, and doing nothing else was that she grew fatter and fatter by the day, until she became all fat, and very ugly. This disappointed the aged chief. The councillors, on the other hand, were delighted. They had never been pleased by the chief's ruling that this girl should not be eaten. They watched her growing fatter and fatter, gradually losing all that beauty for which their chief loved her as if she were his own child. They pointed out this ugliness to the chief, as it grew by the day, and they tried to convince him that she might as well be roasted and eaten. For a long time the aged chief rejected this suggestion. But there came a time when Nomxakazo had grown so fat that lumps of fat hung loosely from all parts of her body, and the necklace, armlets, waistband and anklets sank in this fat. She became so helpless that she found it a strenuous task to raise her arm and brush a fly off her face. She could not keep her skin dry. If she sat on a mat, it became wet with sweat. The chief saw all this and at last became so disgusted that one day he suddenly ordered his followers to collect firewood so that they could roast and eat "this fat thing."

Joyfully, the *Dlungu-ndlebe* ran to the woods and collected piles of firewood. This was brought to the chief's place and a great fire was made. As soon as the small twigs had burned out and the big logs caught fire, a very large *lukhamba* (sherd) was placed on the fire. The *Dlungu-ndlebe* watched the *lukhamba* until it was red-hot, and then they carried the princess out of her hut and made her stand by the fire. As soon as she saw the red-hot *lukhamba*, Nomxakazo understood what was happening. In terror, she raised her arms high, looked up to heaven and sang:

We, zulu! We, mimoya yezulu!　　O, heaven! O, winds of heaven!
Zulu lingadumi nokuduma,　　Heaven even though it thunders not,
Lidumel' embilini kuuphela!　　But only rumbles in its belly!
Ma lidume, lidume lisibekele,　　May it rumble, rumble and darken with clouds
Ma line, libuye livelis' ilanga.　　May it rain and then brighten again.

Before this song began, there was not a cloud in the sky. But as soon as Nomxakazo started to sing, the heavens began to rumble, rain clouds darkened the sky, and as soon as she stopped singing, there was a heavy shower of rain. The fire was extinguished, and the *lukhamba* went quite cold. Then the rain stopped and the sky cleared completely.

"Bring firewood and make another fire!" commanded the chief. The wood came, another fire was made, and the *lukhamba* was heated. But as soon as the *lukhamba* was red hot, Nomxakazo raised her arms high, looked up to heaven and sang:

We, zulu! We, mimoya yezulu!	O, heaven! O, winds of heaven!
Zulu lingadumi nokuduma,	Heaven even though it thunders not,
Lidumel' embilini kuuphela!	
Ma lidume, lidume lisibekele,	But only rumbles in its belly!
Line, libuye livelis' ilanga.	May it rumble, rumble and darken with clouds,
	May it rain and then brighten again.

Again the heavens rumbled, rain clouds darkened the sky, and there followed a heavy shower of rain. The fire was extinguished, and the *lukhamba* went quite cold. Then the rain stopped and the sky cleared completely.

"Bring firewood and make another fire!" commanded the chief.

Piles and piles of firewood were brought, and a fire was made, many times greater than the first two. It burned so fiercely that the *lukhamba* became red-hot in a twinkling. But again Nomxakazo raised her arms high, looked up to heaven and sang:

We, zulu! We, mimoya yezulu!	O, heaven! O, winds of heaven!
Zulu lingadumi nokuduma,	Heaven even though it thunders not,
Lidumel' embilini kuuphela!	
Ma lidume, lidume lisibekele,	But only rumbles in its belly!
Line, libuye livelis' ilanga.	May it rumble, rumble and darken with clouds,
	May it rain and then brighten again.

This time there were no low rumblings. The sky was immediately covered with thick black clouds, and the shower that followed was so heavy that a person could not see the one standing next to him. There was one blinding flash of lightning, followed by one deafening crack of thunder. Then the rain stopped abruptly, and the sky cleared. When the *Dlungu-ndlebe* recovered, they discovered that their chief and his senior followers had been struck dead by lightning.

The terror and confusion that followed this sight was so great that if Nomxakazo had been able to, she would have collected all her belongings and departed without anybody knowing. But she was so heavy with fat that in walking back to her hut, she could only take two steps at a time and then stop to rest, panting, then another two steps, and another rest, until she reached her hut. There she sat down and covered her face with her hands.

The *Dlungu-ndlebe* would not even think of touching her again, but they were determined that she must die. Fearing to go anywhere near her, they agreed that the only way to end her life was to starve her by degrees, by giving her less and less food each day until she died of hunger. No one came near her hut except the woman who brought her food and water. This woman would come very cautiously, put the food and water just outside the door, make one loud call to tell the princess, and then run back to her friends. For this reason, the princess had to do all else for herself, tidy her own hut, wash her own clothes, make her own fire when it was cold, and so on. At first this work, though light, so tired her that she had to lie down and rest after finishing. But as she began to lose weight, she found that she could move about without getting tired too soon, and that her sluggishness was lessening and lessening.

One day, when she thought she was not too heavy to travel, Nomxakazo collected her belongings and told the *Dlungu-ndlebe* that she was leaving.

"Your ornaments, and all the other beautiful things that our leader gave you—you are not taking them with you?" asked the leader-regent of the *Dlungu-ndlebe*.

Young man fighting.

"I—I can't carry all those things," she said, hesitatingly.
"They will be too heavy, and I am going far."

"Take them, *nkosazana,*" insisted the regent. "They are
your gifts. The chief was very fond of you. It doesn't bring
luck to throw away the gifts of a person who is no more, if
that person was fond of you."

"They don't fit me any more," pleaded Nomxakazo, looking at her arms.

"Take them even if they don't fit you now. They'll fit you
again some day."

Nomaxkazo said no more, and so the gifts were collected

and brought to her. She carried on her head everything that
was hers and left the land of the *Dlungu-ndlebe.*

4. Going Home

There, then, is the king's daughter, wandering all alone,
now this way, now that, begging for help among people she
does not know, begging for food and a place to rest and sleep
among people whose youthful men have been slaughtered,
people whose homes have been destroyed, people whose cattle
have been looted, by her father's warriors, to satisfy her father's vanity and hers. But these people do not know who this
miserable girl is, because she dares not tell them. Many a time
she loses all strength and falls by the wayside, hungry, tired,
footsore, and she is picked up and cared for by strangers until
she is able to rise again and continue the search for her home.
She loses weight by the day from hunger and fatigue, until she
is as thin as a thread. She is not always sure she is going the
right way, because there is nothing she sees that she remembers ever seeing before. But, because she avoids talking to too
many people lest they find out who she is, many a time she
travels long distances without asking anybody whether she is
travelling in the right direction or not, and so it often happens that when at last she summons up her courage and asks
for help, she is told that she must go back the way she came.
She is told to turn to the left after crossing such-and-such a
river, take this bend and that bend up the river. She is told to
give such-and-such mountains her right arm until she crosses
such-and-such a river. She is told that she will come to a place
where the road by which she has been travelling meets another road going towards the rising sun, and so on, and so on.
It was after six full moons of this manner of travelling
that Nomxakazo entered the borders of her father's kingdom.
But for a number of days she did not realize this, because the
land was so desolate that the only things she recognised were
the mountains and rivers. The great grazing lands were bare,
except for a little flock of goats here, another there, another
over there. Of what used to be cattle—nothing! Very little till-

ing had been done in the fields. Even in the royal fields in the valleys, all she could see were lean stalks of corn on small patches of tilled land. Where there had once been large homesteads, all she could see was just one hut here, another there. Most homes had disappeared altogether. But when what used to be her home—the Great Place—came into view, it was as if she was dreaming. The Great Place of former days had shrunk almost beyond recognition in size. What used to be great buildings were bare, roofless stone walls, all except one, the central one where her parents lived.

When she reached what used to be the great entrance to the Great Place, she saw a shabby-looking, hairy-bodied old man sitting in the shade of a tree. But who was this *ludwayinge* (homeless wanderer) sitting under the tree? Did she know him? He looked like someone she knew, but she could not remember who. She greeted him as she passed, but the old man did not seem to hear or see her. Who was he? Where had she seen him before?

She entered the Great Chamber. There was an old woman inside. Could it be that this was her mother? No! It couldn't be!"

"Greetings, *nkosikazi!*" said Nomxakazo.

The old woman was startled. She dropped what she held in her hand and came towards the girl, her arms open. Then Nomxakazo knew her!

"Mother!" she cried, and she ran into her mother's arms.

"It is you? It is you, Nomxakazo?—O, my child! My child!" said the old woman, and she fondled the girl and pressed her to her breast as if suckling her, and mother and daughter stood there for a long time, weeping to each other.

"Where's father?"

"Didn't you see him outside there in the shade?"

"Mother! Am I to believe that the *ludwayinge* I saw just now is my father?"

"That's your father, my child. He sits under that tree the whole day, whether it's warm or cold, whether it shines or rains. He doesn't want to be spoken to, and if you hear him speak, you can be sure that he is talking to himself."

"What happened, mother?"

"Since you went away, all things have changed and be-come as you see them now."

"Thubise? Where's she?"

"Thubise is married. We gave her in marriage to the son of So-and-so. You know the people of So-and-so, don't you? They offered ten goats as bride-tribute, and we accepted this, because that was all they could offer. As for us, we had noth-ing. Had our shame not been covered by a few people who brought some presents, I don't know what we could have done. We could not even make a proper marriage feast for our child, because it was a period of mourning in every home. We still mourn up to this day."

"Tell me, mother. Tell me everything."

"You're hungry, my child. Sit down. I'll first of all give you something to eat, and then I'll sit down and tell you everything, for it is necessary that you should know all these things."

So saying, she stooped and pulled out a shabby old goat-skin, and she spread it on the floor so that Nomxakazo could sit on it. Then she brought some bread and milk.

"This milk comes from the goats offered by the So-and-so's as Thubise's bride-tribute," she said, as she put the dishes on the floor before her daughter. "That's the only livestock we have now in this home."

After Nomxakazo had eaten and rested a little, the mother brought another shabby old goatskin, spread it on the floor next to her daughter, and sat on it. Then she began her narrative:

"When Maphundu carried you away, I tried to follow, and Thubise came with me. For three days we sought his trail but could not find it. So we gave up and sought the way home. I was tired and found it very difficult to walk. My child, Thubise, found me a long stick to lean upon. But even this was not good enough. Thubise had to support me most of the way. We slept and woke nine days on the way, and arrived here on the afternoon of the tenth. What made us take so long was not only fatigue. We still looked in all directions as we travelled, because it was difficult to give up all hope of catching sight of Maphundu, no matter how far he might be.

"We arrived home to find that death had entered this land. It entered through the warriors. They brought diseases from the lands over which they wandered in search of cattle to loot, diseases that had never been known to anyone living in this our land, and these diseases killed not only the warriors but infected and killed other people as well. They killed old men and old women. They killed middle-aged people. They killed newly married men and their young wives. They killed young men and maidens. They killed children.

"Death entered through the cattle we reared. There were countless numbers of carcasses that lay rotting on the plains, because every person and every dog, every bird and every beast that eats meat had more than enough. Now, the living cattle feared the smells of the rotting carcasses and refused to go grazing. They would crowd near their folds, lowing, lowing all the time. If they were driven by force to the pastures, they would bellow and rave over these carcasses, gore one another most savagely, and then carry their tails high and run in all directions, trampling down the herdsmen, as if driven mad by the stings of swarms of unseen gadflies.

"Death entered through the crows and vultures, through the hyenas and hunting dogs. Even while you were still in seclusion, these birds and beasts of prey started eating the carcasses lying on the plains, but at that time they feared people. When the carcasses were finished, the birds and beasts turned on the living animals, especially the calves. The crows and vultures hovered in the sky above us all day, darkening the sun, ready to devour anything they saw lying on the ground. If a cow lay down to calve, they would hover over it until the calf was born. As soon as they saw this little thing dropping from its mother, they would pounce upon it and tear it to pieces. There were times when the vultures did not even wait for the calf to be born, but swarmed over the cow in labour and devoured her alive. Those birds were more terrifying than the hyenas and hunting dogs, because they did these things during the day, with everybody looking on. They were always ready to devour anything they saw lying on the ground, whether dead or alive, whether human or animal. Some herdsmen over yonder were trampled down by the raving cattle they were herding, broke their backs and legs and couldn't get up. Before they could be rescued, a swarm of vultures had torn their bodies to pieces. In all cases, what was left over by the birds during the day was devoured by the hyenas and hunting dogs at night.

"Death entered through hunger. Even when food was still abundant, people did not want to eat, even young children, because of the rottenness they saw all around them—rotten carcasses all around, swarms of flies that came every morning with a rumbling sound and bussed everywhere until sunset, countless numbers of maggots crawling everywhere, even on our doorsteps. A horror of a thing, my child! A horror of a thing!

"Most people who still had strength left the land. You could have seen fires all around at night, for many of those who decided to leave destroyed their old homes by fire before leaving. These were mostly the younger married people. As for the aged, what could they do? Where were they going to get the strength to travel to far-off lands? When Thubise and her husband told us they wanted to *fuduka* (migrate), we allowed them to go, because there was nothing that strong young people could stay here for. It's only the aged who can remain here and wait for death.

"Such then, my child, were the happenings in the land of your fathers while you were away. Some say it's all Maphundu's doing. As for me, I don't accept that at all. It's none of Maphundu's doing. It's the tears of the thousands and thousands of women whose men we slaughtered, the tears of the countless numbers of children we orphaned, the tears of the countless numbers of people whose homes we destroyed, whose cattle we looted. It's those tears that brought this curse upon us."

There ended the mother.

Nomxakazo had been weeping from the time she saw the condition of her home and parents. She had thought that she herself had suffered over the last two years away from home. But now, when she heard these things, she realized that her own sufferings had been mere play. She forgot her own sorrows and wept for her father's people.

"My father's people!" she cried again and again. "That they should suffer so! Why did you let me, you and father? Why did you let me, mother? Why did father allow me to make such a demand, if it meant destroying so many peoples, killing people, making people poor and homeless? What wrong had they done? Had he no pity? How numerous the people who pitied me, gave me a place to sleep when I was homeless, gave me food when I was hungry, nursed me when I was ill, in all my wanderings! *Me,* his child! Who am I that anybody should pity me? *Me,* the cause of the death of so many many people!" And she threw herself on the ground and wailed pitifully.

Her own story Nomxakazo never told in full to her mother. She told only about the kindness with which she was received everywhere, and she showed her the gifts from the chief of the *Dlungu-ndlebe.*

The news of the return of the princess soon reached the remnants of her father's people, and many of them came to see her. During Nomxakazo's absence, the Great Queen had refused to accept any gifts from the people in their present condition. But the small presents they brought to the princess on her return were accepted very gratefully. Nomxakazo was greatly delighted by the presents. To her they meant everything, because they made her feel that she and her parents were still regarded as people. She brightened up quickly, and her beauty was restored in full.

5. "The Maiden from the Reeds"

The story of Maphundu's visit, the carrying away of Nomxakazo, and the plague that wrought havoc in Dumak-ude's kingdom, was known in every land long before the princess's reappearance. Such happenings had never been heard of before, and all the peoples were horrified.

The news of the return of the princess of famed beauty travelled even faster, crossing over the borders of Dumakude's kingdom and reaching the lands of other princes. One of these princes was the reigning son of the great king whose armies were defeated with great slaughter on the day of Nomxakazo's birth. This prince resolved to have Nomxakazo immediately, but, despising Dumakude in his present condition, and convinced that such a wicked man deserved no human respect, he decided to disregard custom and have the girl stolen and brought to him. He therefore called together his councillors and asked them who amongst them could go and steal Dumakude's beautiful daughter and bring her to him. At once, one of the councillors, a man of magic, assured his prince that he could do this easily.

"Go then," said the prince. "Entice her with your magic and bring her to me. You will have your reward."

"Leave it to me, Child of the Beautiful," said the councillor. "She will be here before you know it."

One day, while Nomxakazo and her mother were conversing with some visitors in the Great Chamber, a beautiful frog suddenly leapt over the doorstep. It stopped near the door and looked at the princess, and the look was so pleasant and so intelligent as to be almost human.

"The beauty of this frog!" exclaimed the princess, rising to her feet.

The frog turned around and leaped out of the chamber. Nomxakazo screamed with delight and followed it. A leap, a leap, a leap, and the frog paused and looked back as if challenging her to overtake it. But as soon as she drew near, a leap, a leap, a leap, then another pause to look back. The princess screamed all the more and followed it, getting more and more excited by the tricks of this beautiful creature. Meanwhile her mother was becoming suspicious. Her *nimba* again!

"What does this portend?" she exclaimed. "Come back, Nomxakazo! Come back!"

But Nomxakazo would not listen. When the frog paused just over the Great Entrance and looked back, she ran past her

Scene for the sun; finally the dust made by the hundreds of cows and oxen shaded by the sun.

father who was sitting in the shade, mumbling as usual. She did not even hear her mother's warning that she was on no account to follow "that thing" beyond the gate. A leap, a leap, a leap, and Nomxakazo ran out of the gate and followed. Her mother gave up and returned to her visitors.

"This must be another of Maphundu's messengers," she said, with resignation.

On and on went the frog along the road, and Nomxakazo followed, her excitement growing and growing. As soon as it was out of sight of the Great Place, the frog took bigger and bigger leaps, no longer making any pause to look back, as if it was now sure that the princess would follow it wherever it might choose to go. And, true enough, she was following it. To her this whole thing was so strange and delightful that she made up her mind not to go back until she had found out where it would end.

"This frog seems to know what it is doing! It seems to know where it is leading me," she said as she tried to keep up with it.

The frog led on until the road entered a great forest. It

led on, faster and faster, until they were very deep in the forest. Then it paused and looked back. The princess came up running and screaming and laughing, but before she came up to it, the frog took a big leap out of the road and into the undergrowth. Then it looked back again. Nomxakazo caught sight of it and followed until it reached a clearing in the forest, and there it stopped and waited for her. It allowed her to come very close, but just as she stretched her hand to grab it, it took a very big leap into a bush and vanished. The princess ran forward and began pushing the branches of the bush this way and that in search of the frog. But the frog was nowhere to be seen. Then suddenly, a tall man emerged from the opposite side of the bush.

She was surprised but not in the least frightened. She looked at the man, and the man looked at her and smiled.

"Who are you?" asked the princess. "Where's my friend?"

"Your friend?" said the man, disregarding the first question. "Who's your friend, *nkosazana?*"

"My friend the frog."

"Your friend the frog!" exclaimed the man. "Where was he? Where did you part with your friend the frog?"

"We were playing, just the two of us, and he vanished in this bush."

"And now, instead of finding your friend the frog, you find *me?* Don't you understand, *nkosazana,* that you'll never see your friend the frog again?"

"No, I don't understand at all. What do you mean?"

"You came all the way from your home, led by your friend the frog, until you reached this bush. Your friend the frog vanished. In his place you see a man. And you still want to know what became of your friend the frog?"

"You mean to say the frog was—you?"

"I wouldn't go so far as to say that, *nkosazana.* If you choose, you can say your friend the frog brought you to me."

"He was sent by you to lead me from my father's house to this place?"

"It may be so."

"You sorcerer!"

"Peace, *nkosazana!* I'm only carrying out the orders of a greater one."

"A greater one! Who are you? And who is this greater one?"

"I am the messenger of a great prince, son of the late king So-and-so. It was he who gave me the orders, and I must carry them out."

"Orders to bring me to this forest? For what purpose?"

"Not to bring you to this forest, *nkosazana,* but to beg you to go to his great place and live with him. He knows you're the most beautiful of all living maidens."

"I don't care what he knows about me. You say he wants me to go and live with him. To live with him as what?"

"As—as—as—"

"As one of his women?" demanded Nomxakazo, now getting angry.

"No, *nkosazana!* Not as a concubine, but as his wife."

"If he wants me to be his wife, doesn't he know the custom? Am I nobody's daughter, that he should want to steal me?"

"Get away, girl!" said the man of magic, with contempt. "I agree you're the most beautiful girl I've ever seen. But who is Dumakude?"

"You dare talk like that about my father? Did this prince of yours send you here to insult me? Who are you to talk to me with such contempt?"

Nomxakazo turned sharply about to leave him.

But the man of magic leaped forward and caught hold of her.

"I'm tired of this talk," he said, with determination. "I see you're still as proud as ever. Now I'm going to show you that you're nobody's daughter. Come with me now, or I'll take you to my prince by force."

Nomxakazo struggled vigorously to free herself, screaming aloud for help as she did. Her cries echoed from all sides of the forest. They were followed by the howls and growls of all kinds of beasts of prey rushing from all directions towards the clearing. As the animals approached, both she and the man of

magic heard the crackling of broken branches and were terrified. Nomxakazo jerked free and climbed up a tall tree just as
the foremost of the beasts of prey appeared. As soon as she
thought she was out of reach, she held fast to one branch with
her hands and stood on another, and looked down. She saw
the beasts of prey crowding the clearing. Some howling, some
growling, they covered the place in a twinkling, sniffing the
ground and the bushes, pushing twigs with their snouts. Then
suddenly they calmed down and disappeared in different
directions.

Nomxakazo stood quite still where she was and listened
until the rustling could be heard no more. Then she looked
around. Where was that man? She wondered. She could not
see him on any of the trees, but she was sure that the animals
had not killed him. Then his calm voice reached her from the
ground.

"They're gone, *nkosazana,*" he said. "You can come down
now."

"Where did you hide, you sorcerer?" she asked, relieved to
hear a human voice. "How did it happen that the beasts
didn't scent you?"

"I climbed up the same tree. I was just below you when
the beasts ran all over this place, sniffing. Come down now,
and let's go. It's getting late, and my companions must be
wondering why I don't return."

"Who are your companions? And where are they waiting
for you?"

"When we left home, we were ten in all. I left my friends
at a village just on the other side of this forest. I was sent by
my prince to come and beg you to come to him. I did wrong
to try to force you, and both of us were nearly killed by the
beasts of prey because of my misdeed. I know you want to go
back to your parents, *nkosazana.* But if you go back alone
now, you may meet with some danger, and the blame will be
laid on me by your parents as well as by my prince. Do come
down, *nkosazana.* Believe me when I tell you that I am the
messenger of a very good man, a man who wants all people to
live happily. All preparations have been made along the way.

Wherever we spend the night, you will have food to eat and your own place to sleep. We took an oath to protect you in every way until you meet our prince face to face."

The princess remained quiet for some time, thinking. Then she spoke with determination.

"All right," she said. "I'll go with you. But when I meet this prince of yours face to face, he will know that I am somebody's daughter." With these words she came down from the tree.

"Let's go," she said.

They walked fast and reached the other side of the forest just before sunset. When the village was in sight, the man of magic pointed out an outstanding homestead and said, "We'll sleep there tonight. That's where my companions are waiting for us."

When they arrived at this place, the princess found the preparations made for her even better than she had expected. She slept well, and when she woke up the next morning, she felt she was fresh enough for the five days' journey before her.

They set out immediately after the morning meal. Five of the men led the way at some distance. The princess and the man of magic followed, and the four remaining men came last. This was done in order that the life of the princess should be guarded from the front as well as from the rear. Nomxakazo showed these men from the start that when it came to travelling, she could keep abreast of the strongest of them. She walked as if she did not even think about walking, because it was no effort to her. She was completely relaxed. That she was alone amongst strangers, and all of them men, did not at all make her feel ill at ease. She conversed all the time. The men discovered in the course of their journey that she knew nature far better than they. She could say beforehand whether or not the day was going to be cool enough for fast travelling. She could tell them if a thunderstorm would be coming in the afternoon. She could tell them if the following morning was going to be misty. Of the wild fruit in the woods they passed as they travelled, she knew a much greater variety than they, and she could tell them which was tasty, which was good for an empty stomach, which could quench a person's thirst. Whenever they halted to rest, they all came together, and she did most of the talking, while the men sat and listened, amazed at her knowledge of peoples and their customs. The company grew to like and respect her very much, and found themselves looking to her for orders. Even the man of magic acceded readily to her suggestion that the company would find the journey less monotonous and tiring if the men changed places now and again, those in front coming to the rear, and those in the rear coming forward to lead the way, and all the men taking turns as her bodyguard. For herself she begged one important concession, namely, that before crossing any of the rivers she had never crossed before, she would like to bathe thoroughly in it, so that whatever misfortunes she might be carrying in her body should be washed down the river, and in that way be left behind. This request impressed the men more than anything else she had suggested, and they accepted it readily. And so they travelled in this happy way, sleeping and waking five days.

When the sun began to slant on the sixth day, the princess's bodyguard pointed out a ridge ahead of them and told the princess that beyond that ridge was the last river they would cross, and also that the Great Place was on the other side of the river, standing alone on a slope facing the ridge. As they approached the ridge, the leaders slackened their pace gradually, and finally halted, laid down their baggage, and reclined on the long grass. On reaching the spot, the rest of the company did the same, except the princess. She remained standing for a while and looked about. Then she walked away from the men in a leisurely manner, looking this way and that. Finally she reached a spot from where she could see the river and everything that lay on the other side of it. She saw the Great Place. It was beautiful, though not so grand as her father's Great Place of former days. She saw the fine dwellings lower down the slope. She saw people at their homes and on the pathways. She saw herds of cattle and flocks of goats on the pastures. She saw beautiful cultivated fields on the riverbed. She liked everything she saw in this place.

While standing there, she saw with the tail of her eye that the man of magic was talking in low tones to two of his companions, aside. She knew at once that he was giving them orders, and she knew what these orders were. These men were to proceed to the Great Place while the rest of the company tarried here till nightfall. These men were going to report to the prince that their mission had been successful. They would return with orders from the prince where to take her at nightfall. She was not going to be taken to the Great Place immediately, but to some outpost. She knew too that for some days and perhaps a whole moon, the only people who would know about this whole affair besides the prince and his council would be the trusted caretaker of the outpost and his wife.

"I'll show them all that I know something about the ways-and-ways of great places," said the daughter of Dumakude, and she smiled and returned to the men, as relaxed as ever. She gracefully declined the food offered her and said she would have a bath first.

"I saw a beautiful river just below, and I want to bathe before I eat. Let one of you please point out to me a suitable bathing place."

"But, *nkosazana*, it is not proper that you should be seen by anyone here besides ourselves until you have been given a place to stay," said the man of magic.

"Of course, I know that!" replied the princess, as if surprised that anyone should point out to her such an obvious matter of custom. "I'm not a child. That's why I request that it should be you who tell me what part of the river is suitable."

The man of magic rose without another word and accompanied her to the summit of the ridge. He pointed out a path by which the princess could reach the river without drawing attention and also a place where she could enjoy her bath in complete privacy. The princess thanked him and promised she would not be long. Then they parted, and she walked quickly down to the river. The two men with whom the man of magic had been conferring had not yet started on their mission, but she was sure they would soon be on their way.

On reaching the river, she stripped and washed herself thoroughly. Then she dressed again, did her hair properly as maidens do, and arranged her ornaments carefully. When she had finished, she went and sat on a rock whence she could see the ford where the two messengers were going to cross the river. Soon she saw them walking briskly towards the ford. All the leisureliness they had shown before she left them had disappeared, and they walked like men who were carrying an important message to one superior to themselves. They stopped at the ford just for a while, to wash their feet and legs. As they moved on, the princess noted that, to reach the Great Place, they would have to pass through one of the villages. She watched them until they reached the outskirts of this village, and she rose to her feet, crossed the river and followed them.

The eight men on the ridge saw this and just did not know what to do. Should they shout and order her to come back? That would be very unseemly. And what would be the use of shouting to her? Would she obey the order? Obviously she was doing this deliberately. Should they run after her and intercept her? That would be a disgrace of a thing, because the whole village would see it. Should they shout to their comrades and tell them to stop her? But then the villagers? Should they. . . .? Should they. . . .? Finally they agreed that the wisest thing to do was to remain where they were and see what she was up to. It might be that she would not go further than the village. If she did, they would leave it to their companions to decide what to do about her. Their eyes were now on the princess and now on their comrades. She reached the outskirts of the village just as they emerged at the other end. She reached the other end just as they reached the main entrance to the Great Place. There could be no doubt now. She was going straight to the Great Place. But what was even more embarrassing was to see the excitement at the village. A large number of women and girls were following her!

The man of magic was puzzled, ashamed, and full of anger, but all these feelings he spoke within himself:

This girl! What is she up to? How can she disgrace him in this manner? To be fooled in this way, and by a mere girl!

And look at those two fools of messengers he sent to the Prince! Why can't they pull him out of this mud? Why won't they look behind and see this girl and stop her? Look at them, the fools! They've entered the Great Gate, and there they go, straight to the Big Tree where the Prince is lounging. There's the girl behind them, almost at the gate now, and they don't even see her! What do they think those women and girls are excited about? Do they think they're excited about them? O, what must he do? How is he going to explain all this to the prince?

By this time things were happening at the Great Place. The two messengers had found the prince sitting in the shade of the Big Tree with some of his leading councillors. No straight report had been made yet. All the messengers had said so far was that they "travelled well," by which they meant that their mission had been successful. The men under the Big Tree noticed that there was a great deal of movement in the women's sector. Evidently something unusual was happening. However, they did not find it necessary to do anything about it until the *njoli* (steward) of the Great Place brought some beer for the two men who had just arrived. After handing over the beer according to custom, the *njoli* reported that there had just arrived a girl, a tall beautiful maiden who said she had been travelling for five days. But she carried no baggage at all, and it was as if she had just come out of the village below. On being asked who she is, she tells the senior women that she is Nomxakazo wako Gingqwayo, first daughter of the House of King Dumakude.

"What do you say?" said the messengers, leaping to their feet. "Where is she? Did she arrive alone?"

"Wait a little, you two," said the oldest of the councillors. "Sit down a little and calm yourselves."

The messengers looked at each other and sat down. Then the old councillor turned to the *njoli,* and said, "Some of us here are getting old, and our ears are rather blunt. Repeat what you have just said, so that we can hear it properly."

The *njoli* repeated what he had said, changing nothing, adding nothing.

"So far that is all you heard, all you saw?" asked the old councillor.

"So far that is all I heard, all I saw, my lords," replied the *njoli*.

"It is good. You can go now. Tell the senior women that the Child of the Beautiful has heard."

As soon as the *njoli* had gone, the old councillor turned to the messengers and said, "Before we were interrupted by the arrival of the *njoli* with this beer, you told us that you travelled well. Here then is what we want to know. You travelled well, up to what point?"

In reply to this, one of the messengers told the story of their mission—their going, up to the point where the man of magic left them in a village and proceeded alone, and then their return, up to the arrival at the ridge yonder, whence he and his companion had been sent ahead to bring the news of their return. Asked if everything had happened as now reported by his companion, the second messenger confirmed everything, and then went on to say that none of those who had remained at the village this side of the forest knew what magic had been used to make the princess come so willingly with them, because it was not theirs to ask a man of magic how he worked such things.

"We understand," said the old councillor. Then he turned to the other councillors and said, "Unless some of you have further questions, I think we had better allow these men to drink their beer. As for us, it is fitting that we pay heed to this matter. Two of you had better go right now to the women and dig us the truth about this tale brought to us by the *njoli*."

At once two of the other councillors nodded at each other and rose to go. As for the prince, he had not uttered a word up to this time. Even after the two councillors had gone, he just sat there quiet, his eyes on the ground. But everyone knew that he was taking in everything that was being said and done.

The councillors were away for some time, and when they

returned, both of them looked puzzled and amused by what they had heard and seen.

"Yes, my lords," reported one of them. "Things are exactly as we have already heard from the *njoli*. We report what we heard and what we saw with our own eyes. The women from the village say they saw a maiden suddenly emerging from the reeds on the water's edge. The maiden did not look this way or that, but looked straight ahead and came up the road, through the village and into the Great Place. The women and girls followed, asking one another who she could be, but the maiden seemed not even to know that she was being followed until she was within the gates of this House. She waited just inside the gate until the village people came, and then she turned round, smiled, and greeted them with great affection. But before they could ask her any questions, she turned away from them and walked straight to the women's sector of this House. The women and girls stood there looking at her and exclaiming with wonder and admiration, *INtombi yase Mhlangeni! INtombi yase Mhlangeni!* (The Maiden from the Reeds! The Maiden from the Reeds)

"It was to the senior women that she showed she was willing to speak. She told them she came from far away, that she went to play in a forest near her home. There she met a man who told her that he was coming to this place, together with nine companions who were waiting for him on the other side of the forest. Because she had always desired to visit this place and meet the princesses, she decided to come with these men, without even telling her parents. So she travelled with the men, sleeping and waking five days on the way, and finally reached the ridge over there this afternoon.

"She left the men resting on the ridge and went to bathe in the river, as she had been doing all the way during this journey. Before leaving the men, she told them she would return soon, but after bathing, she suddenly felt a longing to proceed to this place at once, because she was missing the company of other girls after travelling for five days with no one to talk to except those men.

"While she was telling her story, the senior women could hear the chanting about the 'Maiden from the Reeds,' but they could not understand what it meant until this maiden told them about the bathing. When she had finished, they asked who she was and whose child she was, and when she told them, the women decided that the prince and council must be told at once.

"Yes, my lords! The daughter of Dumakude is within the gates of this House. As I am speaking now, she is with the maidens of this Royal House, relaxed, reclining, and very happy among other maidens."

"Let her relax and recline," said the old councillor. "She has the heart of a human, she has a liver, she is alive in the head. As I see it, she has come here a maiden and means to go back to her people still a maiden. She has closed all the narrow zigzag paths and left us only the straight road to go by— the road of custom. This maiden has not come here a homeless fugitive to be succored and even married off by strangers. She is a maiden of birth and comes from a live home. She comes here visiting as a maiden, and it is our duty to protect her until she decides to return to her parents. When that time comes, it will be necessary that she be escorted, in order that she may meet her parents still the maiden she was the day she came to our midst. That's how I see this matter, my lords."

The prince and the councillors during this speech indicated by nodding and nodding that they too saw this matter as the old councillor saw it. For the first time the prince opened his mouth to speak. He wanted to know from the councillors who had brought the report from the women if they had any idea how long this maiden intended to stay here, and one of them replied, "Three moons, Child of the Beautiful." On hearing this, all the men exchanged glances and smiled.

"I said to you that maiden is alive in the head," said the old councillor.

That same evening, after the prince and his council had been conferring for a long time, the two senior princesses of this House—both of them sisters of the prince—brought "the

Taking the young girl back to her family.

Maiden from the Reeds" to the Great Chamber to greet the prince. On entering this chamber, Nomxakazo stood for a moment, tall and proud, before the prince and his council. Then she walked gracefully across the chamber to the far end, and she knelt with dignity at the prince's feet. The prince stretched out his hand to greet her, and she received this hand gracefully with both hands and kissed it. Then she rose and stood erect, and she moved backwards, one step at a time and then a bow to the prince, until she reached the two princesses of this House and sat down between them on a beautiful carpet of lionskins that had been brought from the princesses' quarters for this purpose.

After a brief pause, the prince spoke as follows:

"*Nkosazana,* we thank you for making humans of us by visiting us at this little home of ours. We have already heard that your parents don't know that you are here. We have heard too that you don't intend to stay more than three moons in our midst. We have therefore decided to send runners to let your people know that you are here in our midst, visiting, and that you are to be expected when the third moon is dying.

"We hear also that when our people saw you, they liked you so much that they gave you a name—'the Maiden from the Reeds.' It's a beautiful name, a very beautiful name, and while you are in this House you will be known by that name. And up to the day when you meet your parents again, you will still be the Maiden from the Reeds."

Nomxakazo understood clearly what this meant, and her heart warmed up with joy and happiness. She rose with a graceful smile and once again she walked across the chamber to kneel at the prince's feet and kiss his hand in gratitude.

After another brief pause, the old councillor inquired in general after the health of Nomxakazo's people. This was followed by general conversation. The man of magic was here too, but Nomxakazo had not noticed him. When their eyes met in the course of the conversation, the man of magic smiled, looked down, and shook his head.

On the third day, ten runners set out for Nomxakazo's home. Besides the news of Nomxakazo's visit, they carried presents for her parents. Another three days passed, and two tens of men were picked to drive five tens of cattle to Nomxakazo's home—"a little gift from our prince and his people to our beautiful guest, the princess of this House." But it was decided that "the Maiden from the Reeds" must not know about this gift until she returned to her people. Nomxakazo knew, of course, that there must be some such goings-on, but she knew that these were kept secret even from her closest friends, the princesses of this House. She carried herself as "a child of this House," and all the people grew very fond of her. She visited the village frequently and loved to hear the people call her "the Maiden from the Reeds." She grew to like the prince very much, especially when she noticed that he was careful never to meet her alone, but always made it a point to invite her together with his sisters when he desired to meet her.

One evening when the third moon was dying, Nomxakazo asked the two senior princesses to accompany her to the Great Chamber. Here she thanked the prince for the kindness that had been bestowed upon her by all the people she had met during her stay. Then she went on to ask to be allowed to beg for the road (to take her leave). In reply, the prince thanked her for coming such a long distance to make all his people so happy, especially his sisters. As to her begging for the road, he assured her that as far as the Great Place was concerned, everything was ready. Two tens of men had been picked to escort her.

As soon as it became known that "the Maiden from the Reeds" had begged for the road, gifts came from all sides. When the day of departure came, crowds of people came from the neighboring villages to wish "the Maiden from the Reeds" a pleasant journey.

On the way home, Nomxakazo found that all along the route the preparations for her coming were as pleasing as they had been on the occasion of her forward journey. They stopped for the night at the same places as before, and at every stop, she slept in the same chamber and the same bed as before. On the fifth day, they approached the village at the edge of the forest where she had slept the first night of her journey out. The pasture between them and the village was covered with large herds of cattle tended by armed men. The leader of her escort broke from the company and went to confer with the leader of the herdsmen. On returning, he told the princess that the whole company, except five men, would stop and rest at the village for a few days. The five men would be sent as runners to let her people know that she was on the way, in order that preparations could be made for her.

Before the messengers returned from her home, the princess discovered many things, some of which she had never suspected. She discovered that the large herds of cattle she had seen on the pasture outside the village came from the prince's kingdom and had been on the way a whole moon before her return. They had travelled steadily all the time, tended by the armed men. Were these large herds of cattle a gift to her, or were they something else? she wondered. A day before the messengers returned, the prince arrived with an unusually large retinue. He had left his Great Place only two days after her departure, to visit the parents of "the Maiden from the Reeds." Then the princess was filled with happiness. She knew now that the five messengers had been commissioned to go and tell her people that the prince was on his way to her home, to beg the House of Dumakude to grant him blood relationship by giving him their daughter Nomxakazo in marriage. She knew also that the large herds of cattle were going to be offered to her people as bride-tribute.

Five days after the return of the runners, the armed herdsmen gathered the cattle and led the way to Nomxakazo's home. They sang appropriate songs as they drove the cattle. The prince and Nomxakazo followed with their retinue. The songs of the herdsmen were heard at the Great Place long before the party appeared, and the remnants of Dumakude's people hurried to the Great Place to await the arrival of the princess. There were cheers and shouts of joy when Nomxakazo entered her home with the prince to whom she was going to be given in marriage.

There was much feasting and rejoicing for some days while the marriage negotiations went on between the representatives of the two royal houses. The prince's followers mingled in a friendly manner with Dumakude's people, eating and drinking with them, competing with them in song and dance. When the negotiations were over, Nomxakazo was ceremonially handed over to her in-laws, and as she departed, her father's people cheered, saying, "May you go well, *nkosazana*. May you make us, your people, a good name by serving your in-laws, by opening your arms and being a mother to all homeless wanderers who enter the gates of your home."

COMMENTARY TO
Nomabhadi
and the Mbulu-Makhasana

The themes of this narrative can be outlined as follows:

1. Out of a dying society comes life, beauty, and purity.

2. But it is the purity of childish innocence, an easy prey to temptations and the machinations of evil.

3. The innocent nature of this girl and the education her mother has given her are not sufficient to keep her from falling into the grasp of the mbulu-makhasana, a subhuman creature (suggested by its lisp and tail) which represents evil.

4. Thus subverted, she loses everything, including her identity as a human being.

5. She suffers; she wishes that she could die, but her parents return from the dead with a reminder that she must live.

6. She now recognizes what has gone wrong, and has insights into her own character for the first time, and she is then prepared to meet the challenge of the mbulu.

7. But she cannot do this alone. All of society is involved in the battle. The evil being is destroyed by her mother's people and in the presence of the entire village.

8. But evil persists, and it must be destroyed again, and again.

9. The evil being is finally destroyed, and the heroine's purification rites can be completed. Marriage is the next step, and her entrance into womanhood.

Thus is the hope of her parents realized: the girl, product of a dying society, now lives and will produce offspring who will maintain and increase the beauty and sustain the hopes invested in the girl. The narrative is an affirmation of humanity in the face of constant threats of disharmony.

From the time the girl leaves the dying village until the time of her marriage, she is undergoing a dramatization of the intonjane *(female purification) ceremony similar to that experience by Nomxakazo (in the preceding narrative). Alone, she must face the* mbulu; *alone, she must come to an understanding of her own nature and the evil that has taken possession of it and which has destroyed her innocence—thus, the loss of identity. Her parents return to her, perhaps in her mind only, and she is reminded of her roots, of her goals, her education. With recognition comes a desire to purge herself of this evil: she has been wrapped in the ugly garment of the* mbulu, *and now she bathes to cleanse herself. She no longer wants to die, and in order to destroy this evil creature, she will don the clothing of evil again, but now with full knowledge of what she is and what she must do. With the assistance of her mother's people, and then alone, she triumphs over the* mbulu: *her identity and beauty are restored, and she takes her rightful place among her people. She has been purified.*

Nomabhadi and the Mbulu-Makhasana

IT CAME ABOUT, ACCORDING TO SOME tale, that a certain village was visited by drought and famine. There were no crops in the fields and very little water in the springs and rivers, and no grass for the cattle and goats. The cattle died in large and small numbers in every homestead until there were none left in the whole village. Then followed the goats. These died one by one until only one she-goat was left. This goat belonged to the home of a beautiful young girl named Nomabhadi, and she and her two brothers fed on its milk. The names of the brothers were Ngubendala, the first-born, and Sihele, the last-born.

As the spell of drought continued, things became worse and worse. The food stores in the corn-pits were running low, and there was no milk for the young children. To have any soup, the people had to boil the skins of the dead domestic animals, cutting off a tiny bit at a time in order that the skins should last as long as possible. When these were finished and the corn-pits gone quite empty, the children began to die of hunger. They died in twos and threes and fours until the only children left in the whole village were Nomabhadi and her two brothers, and they were saved by the milk of the family goat. This calamity so hit the village that all the grown-ups except Nomabhadi's parents, seemed unable to speak. They walked about silently with bowed heads, and the only thing

that seemed to brighten them at any time was to see Nomabhadi and her brothers running about and to hear their little
voices. But Nomabhadi's parents were worried too. The goat
was running dry, and very soon their children might go the
way the rest of the village children had gone.

At last, a light shower of rain fell, and Nomabhadi's parents immediately set about getting their hoes ready so that
they could plant some corn. They were the only people in the
village who had any spirit left in them for such work. The rest
were so weak in body and so broken in spirit that they seemed
to be looking forward to the day when they would be carried
away to the land of the shades to join their children. But
when they saw Nomabhadi's parents hoeing their field one
morning, all the people of the village took their hoes and
went to help them. No one said a word to anyone else during the hoeing. Men and women came and hoed away in the
hot sun from morning to sunset, and then they carried their
hoes home, to return again the following day and work as
hard as ever without speaking.

Nomabhadi's parents felt so grateful to their neighbors
that one evening they sat and considered how to show their
gratitude. The goat had now gone quite dry and there was no
point in keeping it alive any longer. So they agreed that they
had better slaughter it and invite all their helpers to a modest
feast at the end of the next day's work. This was carried out,
and the following morning Nomabhadi's mother stayed home
to prepare the feast. At the end of the day's work, all the villagers came and feasted in silence. They then went to their
several homes to sleep and rest, so that they could rise early
the next morning and continue the hoeing.

For some days, Nomabhadi's parents fed themselves and
their children on the tripe of the goat, and when that was finished, on bits of the skin. Occasionally, the mother produced a
tiny bit of dry bread and made the children share it. It was
clear now that the children were starving. Quarrels arose
among them at meal time, especially between the two brothers. Ngubendala grumbled because his younger brother got
the biggest share of anything they were given. He just would

not accept the view that because Sihele was the youngest, he should therefore have more to eat than anyone else in the family.

One morning, after the parents had gone to the fields, Nomabhadi brought out some soup which the mother had left ready for the children to drink as soon as they got up. There was very very little indeed, but as usual, Sihele had a little more than the others. As soon as the little bowls were put in front of them, Ngubendala looked at his share and looked at his younger brother's. Then he seized his bowl, drank the soup at one gulp and then grabbed his younger brother's. Sihele held on, protesting aloud, and in the struggle, all the soup spilled on the ground. In his rage, Ngubendala struck his younger brother on the head with the empty bowl and killed him.

Things had happened so quickly that Nomabhadi hadn't time to come between her brothers. When she saw what had happened, she buried her face in her hands and sobbed. Meanwhile Ngubendala looked around in alarm, carried his brother's body to the edge of the enclosure, dug a shallow grave, and buried it.

He came back and sat sullenly next to his sister. Then after a little while he turned around and asked her, "Why are you crying, Nomabhadi?"

Silence.

Again, rather sharply, "Nomabhadi, why are you crying?"

"Because, because I—I'm hungry," she replied.

"Did you see anything?"

Silence.

"Nomabhadi, I'm asking you did you see anything?" This sharply and threateningly.

"N-no! I didn't see anything."

"All right, my sister. Stop crying now."

Ngubendala was sitting in a coiled-up position, his arms rested on his knees crosswise, and his head rested on his arms. He was silent.

Nomabhadi slipped out of the courtyard quietly and walked towards the fields, As she walked she sang sadly:

U-Sihelan' ubulewe   Little Sihele has been killed
Ngu-Ngubendala,   By Ngubendala,
Ngu-Ngubendala.   By Ngubendala

Suddenly, Ngubendala overtook her and demanded sharply:

"What's that you're singing, Nomabhadi? What's that you're singing?"

Nomabhadi replied, "I'm only singing:

Awu! Awu! Mhm!   O! O! Alas!
Awu! Awu! Mhm!   O! O! Alas!

"O, good! Go on then, my sister."

Nomabhadi went on a little, and then sang her sad song again. Ngubendala, who had been following at some distance, overtook her again and wanted to know what she was singing, and again she told him she was only singing: *"Awu! Awu! Mhm!"* Again Ngubendala was satisfied and allowed her to proceed. This went on for a long time until Ngubendala decided to go back home.

As Nomabhadi drew nearer and nearer, her voice reached the hoers in the field. Without saying a word to one another, they stopped hoeing and strained their ears to catch the words of her song. The first one to catch the words exclaimed: "Do you hear what she sings? Ngubendala has killed his younger brother!"

Thereupon, the one next to him exclaimed in horror, *"Hayi, suka!"* (Oh, No!) and struck his neighbor dead with his hoe.

The rest listened again, and then a second hearer exclaimed, "Yes! She says Ngubendala has killed his younger brother!" He met with the same fate as the first reporter from the hoer next to him. This went on and on. Each one who caught the words and reported was killed by the one next to him. Man killed woman and woman killed man in this way until only Nomabhadi's parents were left to hear the whole story.

As soon as Nomabhadi had finished telling them what had happened, they shouldered their hoes and went home

without saying a word. Nomabhadi followed behind, still sobbing. On reaching home, the parents caught Ngubendala,
killed him, and buried him next to his brother without saying
a word to him or to each other.

The mother then took out a piece of dry bread—the last
piece of food they had in the house—and gave it to her
daughter.

"My child," she said, "If you remain in this village any
longer, you will die of hunger. You've been to my brother's
village over yonder mountains many times, and you can get
there alone easily, can't you?"

"Yes, I can, mother."

"Good! Now, as you know very well, they have plenty to
eat over there because they have plenty of rain. My brother
has more cows, more goats, more corn, more pumpkins than
anyone else in his village. He has many children. They are
healthy and happy and kind. You will play with them the
whole day. My brother's wife is a very kind person. She will
look very well after you. If you go at once, you'll reach there
before nightfall. When you feel hungry, just eat a little of your
bread, and don't wander off your way to look for berries in
the thicket."

As her parents embraced her, Nomabhadi began to sob
again.

"Don't cry now, my child," said the mother, trying to
look cheerful. "If you cry along the way, the *Mbulu* will hear
you, overtake you and rob you of your bread. Remember, you
are to look straight ahead all the time. Don't look to the right
or to the left. Above all, my child, don't look back. Do you
hear? Don't look back at all!"

Nomabhadi set out for her mother's brother's village. It
was a fairly long stretch to the foot of the mountains, but she
walked on bravely and took the winding path up the slope
steadily. But before she disappeared over the ridge, the desire
to take one last look at her old home was too strong. She
looked back. What she saw made her cry out in pain. The
whole homestead was in flames. She knew at once what this
meant. Her parents had burned everything in the courtyard,

set fire to each and every one of the smaller huts, and then shut themselves in their own great hut and set fire to it from the inside. She would never see her father and mother again.

As she turned to resume her journey, she remembered her mother's warning that she was not to cry, and she quickly checked her sobs. But her first cry of pain had been heard, for she heard a strange voice calling to her in a lisp, "Sister! Sister! Why are you crying? Wait for me."

With a start, Nomabhadi wiped away her tears and, before she knew what she was doing, she had looked left and right to see where the voice came from. A strange creature had just emerged from the thicket and was running to overtake her. It was half-human, half-beast. It was walking on its hind-limbs but could not hold its body up. Its body was wrapped in the skin of some animal resembling the baboon, but much bigger. What she could see of its face was human, but all the facial bones were sticking out, and the cheeks were hollow, as if they had been sucked in. Its body was hard and dry, as if drained of all blood and water. Its hands were coarse and bony, and its nails long and ugly. It had a long, lively tail that contrasted with the tail of the baboon-like animal whose skin this creature was wearing.

"Don't be afraid of me," it said as it overtook her. "I am your sister. Stop crying and tell me your name."

Nomabhadi had heard descriptions of the *Mbulu* many times, and the appearance of this creature, its manner of speech and its voice tallied so well with these descriptions that she knew at once that this was one. But this *Mbulu* was kind and called her "sister." So why should she fear it?

"My name is Nomabhadi," she replied, trying to smile.

"Nomabhadi, Nomabhadi," the *Mbulu* said repeatedly. "It's a nice name, a very nice name indeed."

"And what's *your* name?" asked Nomabhadi.

"Oh, just call me 'sister.' I'll tell you what. Let's just call each other 'sister.' I'll call you 'sister' too, though I like the name Nomabhadi very much. Nomabhadi, Nomabhadi." the *Mbulu* repeated the name over and over again as they went along, but all the time with the lisp that Nomabhadi had already noted.

Then the *Mbulu* noticed the small bundle on Nomabhadi's head.

"Sister," it called, "what have you got in that bundle? Is there any bread or meat? I'm very hungry. I haven't had anything to eat for many many days."

There could be no doubt that this was true, and Nomabhadi, knowing what it was to be hungry and used to sharing with others, readily replied, "Oh, yes, I have some bread, sister. It's little enough, but I'll share it with you."

But as soon as the bread was produced, the *Mbulu* stretched out its bony hand greedily and protested, "No, sister, this is too small to share. I'm sure you can't be as hungry as I am."

"It's all right, my sister. You can have it all." And she handed it over.

The *Mbulu* grabbed it, devoured it greedily and noisily, and disappeared in the thicket without even thanking her. Nomabhadi had seen many a hungry child grab greedily at any kind of food it came across in her famished village, but she had never seen anything so disgusting. As she went on her way, she began to feel the pangs of hunger, and she remembered how her mother had warned her about the *Mbulu*. She did not cry, but as she went, she sang sadly:

Wayetshil' umama	My mother did warn me
Mpanga-mpa!	*Mpanga-mpa!*
Wayetshil' umama	My mother did warn me
Mpanga-mpa!	*Mpanga-mpa!*
Ndosukelwa yimbulu	That a *Mbulu* would chase me
Mpanga-mpa	*Mpanga-mpa!*
Ihluth' isonka sami	And rob me of my bread
Mpanga-mpa!	*Mpanga-mpa!*

Suddenly, she became aware that she was surrounded by beauty. She was travelling through forestland. It was a long time since she had last heard so many little birds twittering and chirruping, or seen so many beautiful, bright-colored but-

terflies flying from one beautiful flower to another. She forgot
her mother's warning altogether and gazed with delight at this
gay new world. Her eye was arrested by one particularly
bright-colored butterfly that crossed her path and landed on
what first seemed to be a shrub but turned out, to her delight,
to be *msobosobo*. Screaming with excitement, she ran across
the road, grabbed the plant by its stem and pulled it out by
its roots, and then went on her way, plucking the berries and
eating them so greedily that in a short while not only her
tongue but also her lips and cheeks were stained purple by the
sweet juice of her favorite *msobosobo*.

"Sister! Sister!" came a voice from the thicket. "Here I am
again. Oh, don't eat all the berries before I come. Leave some
for me."

It was the *Mbulu,* as gaunt and greedy as ever. Nomabhadi was very hungry now and therefore not prepared to give
over all her *msobosobo* to this creature. But on catching up
with her, the *Mbulu* protested, "Oh, you've almost finished it"
and, wrenching the plant from her hands, it devoured the
msobosobo without even plucking the fruit.

This time the *Mbulu* did not run back to the thicket but
went along with her, gazing in admiration at her clothes.
After some time it asked her to tell it all about herself, her
people, her village and its people. Nomabhadi told the story
of her life fully, and the *Mbulu* paid the closest attention to
every little detail. When she had finished, the *Mbulu* seemed
deeply moved.

"I weep for you, my sister," it said, covering its face with
its hands as people do when they weep. "I must go along with
you so that no harm may befall you. I'll take you right into
your mother's people's house."

Nomabhadi felt very thankful, for indeed the *Mbulu*
proved a wonderful travelling companion. It taught her many
games which they played together as they travelled, and she
found these so amusing that she forgot her hunger and fatigue.

They came to a river.

"I'll teach you another game, sister," said the *Mbulu.*

"We're going to compete. Let's see which one of us will be able to get to the other bank of the river without getting any part of her body wet. You hop from one stone to another, like this, like this. Whoever touches the water before reaching the other bank has to take off her clothes and bathe her whole body. Do you think you can try?"

"I've crossed our river many times like that without getting wet," said Nomabhadi brightly, "and I'm sure I'll reach the other bank of this one quite dry."

"You lead the way then, my sister," said the *Mbulu*, smiling.

As it followed her into the water, the *Mbulu* felt quite sure that Nomabhadi would miss her footing, by jumping too short or too long, before reaching the other bank. But Nomabhadi hopped from one flat rock to another with such skill that the *Mbulu* realized that she was going to reach the other bank quite dry. So, just as she made the last rock before reaching the bank, it dipped its tail in the water and splashed it on her legs.

"You've touched the water!" it shouted. "Look at your legs! Come, take off your clothes and bathe your whole body."

Nomabhadi looked at her legs and, true enough, they were wet. She was greatly puzzled at this, because she was quite sure that she had not touched the water at all, but as she could not explain how her legs got wet, she decided not to argue. She was not at all averse to bathing as such. She loved bathing and was a good swimmer. Quickly she took off her clothes and, with only her *nkciyo* (waist-apron) on, she plunged into the deepest part of the river, swimming delightfully first from one bank to the other, then down stream, up stream, now face down, now on her back. It was most refreshing.

Meanwhile, the *Mbulu* was watching her closely, and as soon as it noticed that she was really carried away by the rhythm of her own swimming, it threw off its covering, wound its tail carefully round its waist and put on Nomabhadi's clothes. The swimmer did not notice this until the *Mbulu* called out, "Come out now, sister. It's time to go."

Looking up and seeing the *Mbulu* in her clothes, Nomab-hadi was horrified, and she swam quickly up to the bank.

"My clothes, please! My clothes!" she said, rather curtly.

"Oh, just wait a little, sister," said the *Mbulu.* "I'm only trying them on."

"No! I want my clothes. Take them off at once."

"Oh, how pretty I look in these clothes," said the *Mbulu,* paying no heed to Nomabhadi but gazing in admiration at its own image in the water. Then it turned and looked at her ap-pealingly, and said, "Sister, don't be so unkind to me. I've been very kind to you, coming with you all this way and teaching you delightful games. I'm not going to run away in your clothes. I'm not asking you to give them to me to keep either. I just want to walk a little distance in them and feel how it is to walk in pretty clothes. I've never had such clothes. My parents are poor. It will make me happy to be in nice clothes for once. Come, sister, let me wrap you in my garment and we'll continue our journey."

And without waiting for a reply, the *Mbulu* picked up its garment and proceeded to wrap Nomabhadi in it, covering her whole body except the eyes and fore-arms and lower parts of the legs, and knotting it very carefully.

As they continued their journey, the *Mbulu* kept Nomab-hadi's mind away from the new situation by teaching her one game after another, and by the time they reached the river, she was quite happy again. But when she reminded the *Mbulu* about her clothes, it said, "Wait until we cross the third and last river, sister. It's not far."

When they reached the last river, they were in full view of Nomabhadi's mother's people's house.

"Give me my clothes quickly," she said. "My mother's people mustn't see me dressed in this thing of yours." And in her impatience she tried to take it off. But it was so cunningly knotted at so many points that she could not undo any of the knots.

"But your mother's people's home is not in sight yet?"

"Yes, it is."

"Which one is it?"

"That one over there." And she pointed it out.

"That big one with many beautiful huts fenced in with wood?"

"That's the one."

"And do all those fat cattle and goats belong to your mother's brother?"

"Yes," replied Nomabhadi with pride. "You can come with me. I'll tell them you've been very kind to me. They'll give you meat, milk, and bread and pumpkin, and you'll be full before you leave. My mother's people are very generous. They'll even give you a leg of mutton to carry home to your mother, because you've been so kind to me."

"All right, sister. I'll come with you. But just let me wear these pretty clothes a little longer. Do you see that big ant-heap over there? I'll give back your clothes when we reach it."

So they went on. But when they reached the ant-heap, the *Mbulu* said, "Do you see that tall tree just outside the entrance? I'll give you back your clothes when we reach it."

By the time they reached the tree, Nomabhadi was already struggling impatiently to get the loathsome garment off her body, but she could not undo the knots. Then suddenly the *Mbulu* turned round and, with the most savage look in its face it said, "Look here! From this moment onwards, I am Nomabhadi and you are '*Msila-wanja*' and my dog. These are *my* mother's people. If you ever open your mouth in this house, I'll kill you."

Nomabhadi was so terrified by the look on the *Mbula's* face that it took her a little time to take in what was happening, and when she did, the *Mbulu* was inside the enclosure and making for the Great Hut. She caught up with it near the door. It turned round to give her another savage look to warn her, and then knocked at the door.

"Greetings, *malume!* (uncle, mother's brother)" it said to the head of the house. "Greetings *malumekazi!*" (feminine of *malume*) this to the mistress of the house. "Why? Don't you know me? I'm Nomabhadi, your sister's daughter."

The people were stunned. They had heard accounts of the happenings in Nomabhadi's home village, but they had never thought that their sister's child would be in such a state. Nomabhadi, once so full and beautiful, now so emaciated and ugly! Nomabhadi's voice, once so sweet and refined, now so husky and coarse!" Nomabhadi's whole personality, once so pleasant, now so distasteful! A curse must have come upon her home village. And this ugly creature that followed her into the house! What was it?

The *Mbulu* glanced over its shoulder to give Nomabhadi a warning look and then proceeded to tell the story of Nomabhadi's home village to the last detail.

"I myself," concluded the *Mbulu,* "was very ill, so ill that for many moons after I had recovered I was unable to speak. That's why I can't speak properly now. The muscles of my tongue are stiff and the tongue itself feels shorter."

After hearing what "the poor child" had gone through, the people could understand why she should be in such a state.

"And your companion? Who is she?" asked the head of the house, pointing at Nomabhadi.

"Companion!" exclaimed the *Mbulu* with a coarse laugh. "No, *malume,* this is only a strange animal that overtook me on my way here. I don't know what animal it is, but it's very intelligent and understands me when I speak to it. I gave all my food to it because it was very hungry, and after that it kept on following me, and so I decided to keep it as my dog and have given it the name '*Msila-wanja*' (dog's tail) because of its tail."

By this time, the evening meal was ready. The people were disgusted by the "nieces" manner of eating. Her skinny hands went from one dish to another as if she feared someone would snatch the food away from her. She grabbed huge chunks of meat, biting off large pieces and chewing noisily, crunching the bones. She grabbed the bowl of *amasi* (curds) and, instead of filling her cup from it, she held the bowl between her hands and drank noisily out of it.

Meanwhile Nomabhadi, who had been ordered to have her scraps of food outside the hut, had made friends with the dogs. She had given all the scraps to the dogs, for she felt she would rather die of hunger than eat scraps in her own mother's brother's house while the *Mbulu* enjoyed all the privileges that were rightfully hers. She spent that night in the company of the dogs, her only friends in this great house.

The following morning, the girls of the house had to go to the fields and stay there the whole day keeping the birds away from the corn. The *Mbulu,* in order to keep Nomabhadi as far away from her *malume* and *malumekazi* as possible, ordered her to go and help the girls. Ordinarily, the girls used to take turns in their work. One would take her position in the middle of the field and the rest would sit or stand in a group outside the field, but in such a position that they could see the birds coming and tell the one in the middle of the field which way to go to scare them away. They enjoyed this occupation because it offered them plenty of time to play in the open air. So they used to carry plenty of food with them, eat when they felt like doing so, play games, lounge about, and so on.

On this occasion things were better than ever, for they had *Msila-wanja* with them, and they would make her take her position in the middle of the field and remain there the whole day while they enjoyed themselves on the slope, only now and again calling out to the "dog," *"Nanzo, Msila-wanja"* (There they come, *Msila-wanja!*).

Whereupon Nomabhadi would run across the field, waving her long stick and shouting:

Tayi! Tayi bo!	Tayi! Tayi bo!
Ezo ntaka zidl' amabele kamalume,	Three birds are eating my mother's brother's corn,
Noko angemalume wenene,	No mother's brother in truth,
Kuba mna se ndingumsila-wanja,	For today I am a mere msila-wanja,
Kanti eneneni ndandingu No-mabhadi.	Whereas in truth I was Nomabhadi.

This then was Nomabhadi's occupation on her first day with her mother's people while the *Mbulu* gobbled and gobbled at the house. She had to run from one end of the field to the other according to the directions of the guard on the slope above the cornfields.

By midday she could not bear the *Mbulu's* garment any more. It was suffocating her. So she sat down, sought all the knots so cunningly tied by the *Mbulu,* untied them and hung it on a tree to scare the birds away. Then, with nothing on except her *nkciyo,* she went to a stream at the edge of the cornfield and bathed.

On returning to her position in the field, she did not feel inclined to put on the *Mbulu's* garment again. She picked up the long stick that she had been using to scare the birds, returned to the bank of the stream and sat on a rock. The bathing had certainly refreshed her, but it had also made her feel very hungry. What was she to do? She would never, never live on scraps in her own mother's brother's house. She had thrown away the scraps that the other girls had given her when they ordered her to take up her position in the field. She would rather die than pick up those scraps again. In despair she sang:

Wayetshil' umama	My mother did warn
Mpanga-mpa!	Mpanga-mpa!
Wayetshil' umama	My mother did warn
Mpanga-mpa!	Mpanga-mpa!
Ndosukelwa yimbulu	That a Mbulu would chase me
Mpanga-mpa!	Mpanga-mpa!
Ihluth' isonka sami	And take away my bread
Mpanga-mpa!	Mpanga-mpa!

"If only I had been strong enough not to look back to my old home before climbing over that hill, I would never have cried out, and the *Mbulu* would never have known that I was there. And now my weakness has brought so many troubles upon me. The *Mbulu* robbed me not only of the last piece of bread my mother ever gave me but also of my clothes and my rightful place with my mother's people. This creature has fooled me all the way, calling me sister, begging for food, borrowing my clothes. I could bear all this. But to rob me of my name and to say to my own mother's people that I am its dog! *I* the *Mbulu's* dog! My own mother's people to treat me like a dog—the *Mbulu's* dog! I'd rather die than bear this any longer!"

She sang again:

Gantshi! Gantshi-ntshi!	Gantshi! Gantshi-ntshi!
Yimbulukazana!	It's a little female Mbulu!
Gantshi! Gantshi-ntshi!	Gantshi! Gantshi-ntshi!
Yimbulukazana!	It's a little female Mbulu!
Ndenzwe sidengazana, yoho!	A fool she made of me, yoho!
Yimbulukazana!	That little female Mbulu!
Ndenziwe sidengazana, yoho!	A fool she made of me, yoho!
Yimbulukazana!	That little female Mbulu!

Then she seized the scaring-stick and struck the ground hard with it, calling out aloud: "Open, O Earth, and swallow me, for I've no mother and no father!" Thereupon the ground began to shake where she had struck it, then it opened, and behold! There were the shades of her parents standing in an open grave. They had brought her plenty of food, clothes and beautiful ornaments, and without saying a word, they held these up to their daughter. She received them with great joy, first the food, which she laid aside on the green grass, and then the clothes and ornaments, which she put on immediately. Then she settled down to eat while the shades of her parents watched silently.

As soon as she had finished eating, the shades held up their arms, indicating that everything was to be handed back to them. Nomabhadi took off the clothes and ornaments, packed them and handed them back to the shades together with the mats and bowls and cups in which the food had been served up to her. Then the shades vanished and the grave closed and everything was as it had been before.

This made Nomabhadi very happy. She no longer wished to die, for now she knew that her parents wanted her to live. If they had wanted her to die, they would have received her into the open grave and carried her to the land of the shades. She knew also that it was their wish that she should continue wearing the *Mbulu's* garment, otherwise they wouldn't have taken those beautiful clothes and ornaments back to the land of the shades. She would live! She would live! And all this would be corrected sooner or later. She ran back to her post and put on the *Mbulu's* garment.

"It's time to go home, *Msila-wanja!*" shouted one of the girls on guard. For the first time, the name *Msila-wanja* amused rather than hurt Nomabhadi. She smiled, collected her belongings and went back to the house as calmly as if nothing had happened and as inobtrusively as was expected of her in her position as *Msila-wanja*.

In her misery that afternoon, Nomabhadi had been quite forgetful of her surroundings, forgetful of her cousins on guard, forgetful of the women who were working in the neighbouring fields. Her songs had not been heard by her cousins, because these girls had been running about, laughing and shouting the whole day. But the women in the neighboring fields had heard her songs and wondered, for they had never heard such a beautiful voice in that neighborhood. They could not catch the words, but they could make out that the songs were full of meaning. They had gone on working, hoping that sooner or later the singer would emerge from the stream, but the only living thing that came out of the fields a little later was the *Msila-wanja* about whom the whole village had heard by now.

On the following day, Nomabhadi went to the fields again. Early in the afternoon she did exactly what she had done on the previous day, throwing off the *Mbulu's* garment, bathing, singing her songs and striking the ground with her scaring-stick. This time the village women came softly, each from her field, listened to the beautiful singing and catching and noting every word. They saw the ground opening and the food and clothes coming out of the earth, but they did not see the shades. Each one of them was stricken with fear and concluded that something very deep was happening.

That night, the women of the village came together to discuss the situation, for what they had seen was such a wonderful thing that each one of them wanted to know if the others had seen exactly what she had seen. When they were satisfied that they had all seen the same thing, they decided to tell Nomabhadi's mother's people that same night.

Her mother's brother was astounded when he heard the story. He immediately called his most trusted neighbor and made the women repeat the story in his presence. Then they decided that this matter must not be known to anyone outside of the Great Hut until the men had satisfied themselves that there really were such goings-on in the fields. The women were asked not to go anywhere near the stream on the following day.

Early the next morning, the head of the house and his trusted neighbor went to hide themselves near the spot as described by the women and waited to see what would happen. Things happened exactly as on the two previous days. The men watched until everything was over, and just as Nomabhadi was putting on the *Mbulu's* garment, they came out of their hiding-place. Her mother's brother immediately took the garment off her body, handed it to his neighbor and, without saying a word, took his sister's child into his arms and carried her tenderly to his house. The trusted neighbor followed with the *Mbulu's* garment. Without being seen by any of the people of the house, they took Nomabhadi into a private hut and then called the mistress of the house to come and hear the story. Then for the first time they heard the voice of their true *mtshana* (sister's child) who told them all that had happened to her.

When they had heard the story, they all agreed that this evil must be exposed and destroyed in the presence of all their neighbors. They knew the habits of the *Mbulu*. Its tail could not resist sour corn and milk. The test on sour corn would be carried out that same night. The "Thing" would be made to sleep in a hut where there was sour corn, and some elderly women would spend the night in that same hut and watch what happened. If the results pointed out that this was really a *Mbulu*, they would carry out the milk test and destroy the "Thing" thereby. Meanwhile, everybody was to continue being as kind and indulgent to the *Mbulu* as ever, so that it might not suspect anything.

So the mistress of the house saw to it that a hut was prepared for the *Mbulu* and three elderly women. Then, unknown to the girls who prepared the hut, she herself put some sour corn in a hidden place inside. After the evening meal, the *Mbulu* was told that since she was of marriageable age and would soon be asked for by one of the wealthy families in the village, it was necessary that she should spend at least one night in the exclusive company of three elderly women who would tell her all she had to know about marriage and married life.

When the *Mbulu* entered the hut, she found the three elderly women there. These had been warned strictly that at least one of them must be awake at a time throughout the night in order that every little thing that happened that night might be noted. So when the *Mbulu* came in, they had already decided to take turns in watching. For some time they spoke freely and openly about marriage. But they noticed that the *Mbulu* was not paying attention to their teaching. Instead, it kept on adjusting its skirt. The women noted this and exchanged significant glances. The tail of the *Mbulu* had smelled the sour corn and was unfolding itself. The *Mbulu* was anxious that the light be put out partly because it feared that its restlessness would be detected and suspected, and partly because it wanted these women to fall asleep so that its tail could trace the sour corn. This suited the women, and they put out the light at once and very soon they pretended to snore. Then the tail became very lively, brushing the faces of the women as it flew all round the hut hunting for the sour corn. None of the women slept a wink that night. At one time one of them jumped up and called out, "What's this brushing against my face? I can't sleep at all!" Whereupon the *Mbulu* answered immediately, "It must be a rat, grandma! It must be a rat! Please lie down and sleep." Then it folded its tail and wound it round its waist as tightly as it could so that there should be no movement until the old woman had fallen asleep. But the tail had got completely out of control. It unwound itself immediately and made such a noise that the women could no longer pretend to be asleep.

"There's evil in this house!" said the shrewdest of them. "Unless the head of this family does something at once, this niece of his will die unmarried. Why is it that we hear such noises in this hut as soon as preparations begin for her marriage? My child, you are in danger. We must tell your *malume* to take steps at once to avert the evil that is threatening you."

The *Mbulu* was flattered by this, and when the elderly women left the hut at daybreak, it felt relieved because it thought they were on its side, and it folded its tail and fell asleep.

It was awakened by an announcement that was shouted at every door just a little after sunrise. The announcement was that it had been discovered that there was an evil person in this house; that the head of the family had therefore invited the whole village to come and see him and the clean people of his house expose the evil person: that no one was to leave the house without the permission of the head; that a deep pit was at that very moment being dug and a bowl of milk was going to be put at the bottom of this pit: that every single person who had spent the previous night in this house was going to be made to jump over this pit, and the evil one would be exposed by the clean milk at the bottom: that the head of the house was going to slaughter an ox so that the clean people of the village might not leave his house hungry after his house had been cleansed of evil.

The *Mbulu* was horrified at this announcement, so horrified that for once it did not go to the cooking hut first thing in the morning to look for food. It went from one end of the household to the other to see if there was no way of escape. But whichever way it turned, there was a young man on guard who told it that no one was to leave the house. In despair it went into the pumpkin garden, sat on a flat rock, unwound its tail and began to plead with it to break off.

"Oh, my tail! My beautiful tail! Can you be unkind to me after I have done so many good things for you? Why won't you break off? I beg you, my tail, to break off just for today. I am going to hide you here so that no one may find you, and I promise you that as soon as this jumping is over, I shall return here, pick you up and restore you to your place. Help me! Please help me, my beautiful tail!"

Because the tail would not break off of its own, the *Mbulu* tried to bite it off, but became so sore that it had to give it up. Then it found a stone, laid the tail flat on the rock on which it was sitting, and tried to break the tail by hitting it with the stone in its hand, but it could not summon up courage to hit hard enough. After each blow it jumped up writhing with pain and exclaimed, "Shu! Shu! Shu!" At last it had to give up this also. So the only thing the *Mbulu* could do was to wind its tail round its waist and fasten it tighter than ever before. This also was very sore, but it had to be done.

The villagers arrived early in the afternoon, and the whole household was ordered to repair to the pit. *Msila-wanja* was there too, all covered with the *Mbulu's* garment. When the *Mbulu* saw her, it drew the attention of the head of the house to her, protesting that a mere dog could not compete with people."

"It is by my orders," said the head of the house and turned away.

Then all those who had spent the previous night in this house were made to stand in a line. The head and mistress of the house were in this line too, and so were the elderly women who had spent the night in the company of the *Mbulu*. The trusted neighbor was in charge of affairs, while the most reliable of his sons took command of the guard to see that no one who had spent the night in that house escaped the test. Each person was allowed to take any position in the line of jumpers. The *Mbulu* chose to be right at the back, in the hope that by some lucky chance some other person might be exposed by the milk before its turn came. *Msila-wanja* was somewhere in the middle.

Then one by one the people of the household jumped over the pit while the rest of the villagers watched. One after another they cleared the pit until only the *Mbulu* was left. Summoning up its courage, the creature took a wild leap, reckoning that it might reach the other side before the tail betrayed it. But the tail broke loose right in the air, and shot straight down to the center of the milk bowl in the pit, dragging the *Mbulu* down with it. Immediately some men, who had been given orders beforehand, quickly filled the pit with earth and buried the *Mbulu* alive. The head of the house removed the hateful garment from his niece and burned it over the *Mbulu's* grave.

A big fat ox had been driven into the cattlefold before the test, and now the head of the house ordered that as his house had been cleansed of evil, this ox be slaughtered in honor of his sister's daughter. By the time the ox had been flayed and the meat prepared for the feast, Nomabhadi was dressed in beautiful clothes and ornaments. Before the feasting, her *malumekazi* brought her out of the girls' hut, and her *malume* presented her to the villagers, relating her whole story and thanking those neighbors' wives who had heard her song and told him what they had heard and seen.

From that moment, Nomabhadi took her rightful place in the house of her mother's people and became very happy. Her body filled up quickly, her pleasant personality was restored, and she developed into a beautiful young woman.

It soon became known throughout the village that the trusted neighbor had visited Nomabhadi's uncle to make a request that she become his daughter-in-law and the wife of his handsome son, but that this request would not be considered until Nomabhadi had undergone her initiation.

So one day Nomabhadi was removed to a secluded hut. Here she was going to be in the company of elderly women who would teach her all the things that a girl must know about marriage and married life before she goes into it. They would also bathe her with the sweet-scented *mthombothi* and feed her well, so that at the end of the period of seclusion she would be refined and beautiful in body as well as in spirit. During the period of seclusion she would be known as the *ntonjane*. She might not leave her hut until the period was over, but other women might visit her. The instructresses, on the other hand, could leave the hut occasionally and go to other parts of the household.

On the evening of the first day of seclusion, Nomabhadi was lying peacefully and calmly in her hut when she suddenly heard a "thud-thud" coming towards the hut. She listened wondering, and then she heard a faint voice calling, *"Nton jane,* who are you with in there?"

"I'm alone," she replied.

Thereupon a huge melon came leaping into the hut.

"I'm going to kill you!" shouted the melon.

"You'll never kill me!" shouted Nomabhadi, leaping to her feet. For in the few words uttered by the melon she had detected the lisp of the *Mbulu!*

She had hardly uttered her defiant reply when the melon made a leap at her face, hitting her so hard that she fell on her back and all but bumped her head against the wall. But in a twinkling she was on her feet again, determined to fight back. When the melon flung itself at her a second time, she caught it and threw it hard on the ground, trying to crush it. Nothing happened to the melon. But apparently it sensed that someone was approaching, for instead of charging a third time, it made for the door.

"You'll never kill me. Never!" shouted Nomabhadi, panting but determined.

"Who are you talking to?" asked one of the elderly women returning. She was alarmed to find the *ntonjane* on her feet, agitated, and shouting to the air, when she should have been lying calm and quiet on her bed of reeds behind the curtain. Had something gone wrong with the ntonjane's mind? she wondered.

When she heard Nomabhadi's story, the old woman was troubled.

"Something must be done at once" she said quietly. "It is clear that the evil has not been destroyed altogether. I must see your *malume* at once. But I can't leave you alone again. If you had come to any harm just now, all of us who are looking after you would have been in trouble."

"You can leave me alone. I'm sure I'll come to no harm. That thing will never kill me. Never!"

"No, my child's child. These things are not done that way. It is your mother's people, your *malume,* who must rid you of this thing."

The old woman went to the doorway, called one of the

girls, and ordered her to tell one of the women to come at once. As soon as this woman came, the elderly woman went to see the head of the house, leaving Nomabhadi to tell what had just happened.

It was only when the elderly woman reported this incident that it became known, through the young boys in the house, that a wild melon plant had sprung out of the *Mbulu's* grave during the last few days. As soon as he heard this, the head of the house took an axe, went to examine the spot, and true enough, there was a wild melon plant and a huge melon attached to the stem. He broke off the stem chopped the melon to pieces and left it there for the animals to eat overnight.

At daybreak he went to the spot expecting to find the melon gone. But, far from being eaten by the animals, the melon had gathered together overnight and became one solid mass once again attached to the stem. He went straight back to the house, took a firebrand from the hearth, collected some firewood and returned to the *Mbulu's* grave. He pulled out the wild melon by its roots, chopped the stem, the leaves and the melon into tiny pieces. Then he made a big fire on exactly the same spot where he had burned the garment, and he burned the melon, seeing to it that every tiny bit, whether root or pip, was reduced to ashes. Then he brought some soil and covered everything.

This was the last ever heard of the *Mbulu*. The women were now able to go ahead with the purification rites that Nomabhadi had to undergo, and at the end of the set period, she came out of the hut lovelier than ever. The whole village turned up for the great feast held in her honor on the day of her coming out, and there was singing and dancing by all people according to their age groups.

Soon after this, the trusted neighbor's request was listened to, and the marriage negotiations went apace. Then one day, when the moon was full for the third time after her coming out, Nomabhadi set out for her new home, accompanied by a very large bridal party that carried presents for her in-laws, and, amid great rejoicing, she was given in marriage to the handsome son of the trusted friend of her mother's brother.

The King of the Waters

Tfulako, a young prince, brings evil into his society by promising his sister to a monster, which keeps the parched warrior from drinking water. The narrative deals with the princess's efforts to rid herself of this unseemly suitor, which coils itself about her body. Further symbolic of its destructive nature is the fact that when the King of the Waters initially comes to the princess, it comes in the form of a terrible cyclone, nature at its most disordered and most destructive.

The princess leaves her village and goes to the home of her mother's people where her uncle and aunt assist her and become involved in her destiny. Her uncle charts a plan whereby the monster may be killed, but it is important to note that the final confrontation with evil must be between the princess, alone, and the snake. Society can assist the individual to a point, but the ntsomi *tradition insists that just as the individual is not a pawn of society, neither must he become wholly reliant on society. There is room, indeed there is encouragement, in Xhosa society for the development of individual traits of bravery and initiative—there is room for the hero. This performance fits into the* epic matrix *of the Xhosa* ntsomi *tradition, that dealing with the exploits of Sikhuluma.*

This version of the narrative comes from the Bhaca language group in the Transkei.

The King of the Waters

IT CAME ABOUT, ACCORDING TO SOME tale, that Tfulako, renowned hunter and son of a great chief, was returning
home with his youthful comrades after a hunt that had lasted
many days. On a misty night, they lost their way in the forests,
and when the next day dawned, they found they were travelling on a wide plain of bare, barren land that they had never
seen before. As the days strengthened towards midday, it became very hot. The youth had plenty of baggage—skins and
skulls of big game, carcasses of smaller game as well as their
clothes and hunting equipment. They felt hungry and thirsty,
but there was no point in camping where there were no trees,
no firewood, and no water. So they walked on wearily, their
baggage becoming heavier and heavier, their stomachs feeling
emptier, their lips dry, and their throats burning hot with
thirst.

At last, just as the sun was beginning to slant towards the
west, they suddenly came upon a fertile stretch of low land
lying between two mountains. At the foot of the mountains
there was a grove of big tall trees surrounding a beautiful
fountain of icy-cold water. With shouts of joy the youthful
hunters laid down their baggage on the green grass in the
shade and made for the fountain. They took turns stooping
and drinking in groups. Tfulako was in the last group, together with his immediate subordinates. When he knelt and
bent down to drink, the fountain suddenly dried up, and so
did the stream flowing from the fountain. All the youths fell
back, startled. They exchanged glances but said nothing. Tfu-

lako stood a little while gazing at the fountain, and then he motioned his subordinates to come forward, kneel and bend down again. They obeyed his order, and the fountain filled and the water began to flow as before. Tfulako stepped forward, knelt beside them, but as soon as he bent down to drink, the water vanished. He withdrew, and the water appeared again, and his comrades drank their fill. Tfulako walked silently back to his place in the shade, and from there he gave a signal that all must draw near.

"Comrades," he said, "you all saw what happened just now. I assure you I don't know what it means. You all know me well. I've never practiced sorcery. I don't remember doing any evil before or during or after this hunt. Therefore I've nothing to confess to you, my comrades. It looks as if this matter has its own depth, a depth that cannot be known to any of our age group here. However, I charge you to go about your duties in preparation for our day's feast—wood-gathering, lighting of fires, flaying of carcasses, and roasting—as if nothing had happened. We'll feast and enjoy ourselves, but before I leave this fountain, I must drink, for we don't know where and when we'll find water again in this strange land."

The youths went about their assigned duties, some flaying the wild game, some collecting wood, some kindling the fires, some cutting off tidbits from the half-flayed carcasses and roasting them, so that while the main feast was preparing the company could remove the immediate hunger from their eyes, and stop the mouths watering. Tfulako tried to eat some tidbits too, but this aggravated his thirst. So he went to stand some distance away from his comrades and watched the fountain. It had filled again, and the water was streaming down the valley as it had been doing when they first came upon this strange place.

When the main feast was ready, he joined his comrades as he had promised, but found it impossible to eat because of his burning throat. So he just sat there and joined in the chat, trying to share in all the youthful jokes that accompanied feasting. The meat naturally made all of them thirsty again. So once more they took turns drinking from the fountain. Once more Tfulako came forward with his own group, but once more the fountain dried up as soon as he bent down to drink.

There could be no doubt now. It was he and he alone who must not drink, he alone who must die of thirst and hunger, he, son of the great chief. But what power was it that controlled this fountain? He moved away from the fountain and thought deeply. He had heard tales of the King of the Waters who could make rivers flow or dry at will. He concluded that the King of the Waters, whoever he was and whatever he looked like, must be in this fountain, that this King must have recognized him as the son of the great chief, that this King must have resolved that the son of the great chief must either pay a great price for the water from this fountain or die of thirst. What price was he expected to pay? Then suddenly he turned about, walked up to the brink of the fountain, and, in sheer desperation, called out aloud:

"King of the Waters! I die of thirst. Allow me to drink, and I will give you the most beautiful of my sisters to be your wife."

At once the fountain filled, and Tfulako bent down and quenched his thirst while all his comrades looked on in silence. Then he had his share of meat.

After this the whole company felt relaxed, and the youths stripped and bathed in the cool stream to refresh themselves for the long journey before them. Tfulako took part in all this and enjoyed himself as if he had forgotten what had just happened. Towards sunset, they filled their gourds with water from the fountain, picked up their baggage and resumed their journey home. On the afternoon of the fourth day, they were within the domain of their great chief and, to announce their approach, they chanted their favorite hunting-song:

Ye ha he! e ha he!
A mighty whirlwind, the buffalo!
Make for your homes, ye who fear him.
They chase them far! They chase them near!

As for us, we smite the lively ones
And we leave the wounded alone.
Ye ha he! Ye ha he!
A mighty whirlwind, the buffalo!

So Tfulako and his comrades entered the gates of the Royal Place, amid the praises of the bards and the cheering of the women.

Tfulako took the first opportunity, when the excitement over the return of the hunters had died down, to report to his people what had happened at the fountain. No one, not even the oldest councillors, had any idea what the King of the Waters looked like. Most of them thought that since he lived in the water, he might look like a giant otter or giant reptile, while others expressed the hope that he was a man-like spirit. But everybody, including the beautiful princess, felt that this was the only offer Tfulako could have made in the circumstances. So they awaited the coming of the King of the Waters.

One afternoon, after many moons had died, a terrible cyclone approached the Royal Place. On seeing it, the people ran quickly into their huts and fastened the doors. As it drew nearer, the cyclone narrowed itself and made straight for the girls' hut where the beautiful princess and the other girls were, but instead of sweeping the hut before it, as cyclones usually do, this one folded itself and vanished at the door.

When calm was restored, the girls discovered that they were in the company of a snake of enormous length. Its girth was greater than the thigh of a very big man. They had never seen a snake of such size before. This then, they concluded, must be *Nkanyamba*, King of the Waters, come to claim his bride. One by one the girls left the hut, until the princess was left alone with the bridegroom. She decided to follow the other girls, but as soon as she rose to go, the King of the Waters unfolded quickly, coiled himself round her body, rested his head on her breasts and gazed hungrily into her eyes.

The princess ran out of the hut with her burden round her body, and, without stopping to speak to anybody at the Royal Place, she set out on a long, long journey to her mother's people, far over the mountains. As she went, she sang in a high-pitched, wailing voice:

| *Ndingatsi   ndihumntfan'   abo Tfulako,* | Can I, a daughter of Tfulako's people, |

Ndingatsi   ndihumntfan'   abo Can I, a daughter of Tfulako's
Tfulako, people,
Ndilale   nesibitwa   ngokutsiwa Sleep with that which is called
hinyoka, nyoka? a snake, snake?

In reply, the King of the Waters sang in a deep voice:

Ndingatsi   ndimlelelele   ndinje, Long and graceful that I am, so
ndinje, graceful,
Ndingatsi   ndimlelelele   ndinje, Long and graceful that I am, so
ndinje, graceful,
Ndingalali   nesibitwa   ngokut- May I not sleep with that
siwa humfati, fati lo? which is called a woman, a
 mere woman?

And so they travelled through forest and ravine, the whole night and the following day, singing pride at each other.

At nightfall they reached the home of the princess's mother's people. But the princess decided to wait in the shadows for a while. When she was sure that there was no one in the girls' hut, she entered there unnoticed and closed the door. Then for the first time she addressed herself directly to her burden:

King of the Waters, mighty Savior of the lives of thirsty
one! hunters!
Sole possessor of the staff of Thou that comest borne on the
life! wings of mighty storms!
Thou that makest the rivers Thou of many coils, long and
flow or dry at will! graceful!

By this time, the King of the Waters had raised his head from its pillowed position and was listening. So the princess went on:

"I am tired, covered with the dust of the road and ugly. I pray you, undo yourself and rest here while I go announce the great news of your royal visit to my mother's people. Then I shall also take a little time to wash and dress myself in a manner befitting the hostess of the greatest of kings, *Nkanyamba* the Mighty, Nkanyamba the King of the Waters."

Without a word, the King of the Waters unwound himself and slithered to the far end of the hut where he coiled himself into a great heap that almost reached the thatch roof.

The princess went straight to the Great Hut and there, weeping, she told the whole story to her uncle and his wife. They comforted her and assured her that they would rid her of the *Nkanyamba* that same night, if only she would be brave and intelligent. She brushed away her tears immediately and assured them that she would be brave and determined. Thereupon, her mother's brother told his wife to give orders that large quantities of water be boiled so that the princess could have a bath. While these preparations were going on, he took out some ointment and mixed it with some powders that the princess had never seen before. These he gave to his wife and instructed her to anoint the whole of the princess's body as soon as she had had her bath. Then the princess and her aunt disappeared, leaving the head of the family sitting there alone, grim and determined.

When they returned, the princess looked fresh and lovely in her *nkciyo*. She had stripped herself of most of her ornaments. All she had were her glittering brass headring, a necklace whose pendant hung delicately between her breasts, a pair of armlets, and a pair of anklets.

"Your aunt has told you everything you are to do when you get there?" asked her mother's brother, rising to his feet as they came in.

"Everything, *malume*," replied the princess, smiling brightly.

"You're sure you will not make any mistake—doing things too hastily and so on?"

"I'm quite cool now, *malume*. You can be sure that I'll do everything at the right moment."

Then the head of the family produced a beautiful kaross, all made of leopardskins, unfolded it, and covered his sister's daughter with it. "Go now, my sister's child. I'm sure you'll be more than a match for this—this snake!"

The princess walked briskly back to the girls' hut. Once inside, she threw off the kaross and addressed the King of the Waters:

"King of the Waters! Here I stand, I, daughter of the people of Tfulako, ready for the embrace of *Nkanyamba,* the tall and graceful."

As she said these words, she stretched out her beautiful arms invitingly to the King of the Waters.

This invitation was accepted eagerly, but when the King of the Waters tried to hold her in his coils, he slipped down and fell with a thud on the floor. Smiling and chiding him, the princess once more stretched out her arms and invited him to have another try. He tried again, but again he fell on the floor with a thud. Once again the princess stretched out her arms encouragingly, but again the King of the Waters found her body so slippery that for all his coils and scales he could not hold her. This time he slipped down and fell with such a heavy thud on the floor that he seemed to have lost all strength. He could hardly move his body, and all he could do in response to the princess's invitation was to feast his eyes on her beautiful body.

"It's my mistake, graceful one," said the princess, lowering her arms. "In my eagerness to make myself beautiful for the King of the Waters. I put too much ointment on my body. I'll go back to the Great Hut and remove it immediately, then I shall return and claim the embrace I so desire."

With these words, she picked up her kaross, stepped over the threshold, and fastened the door securely from outside. Her uncle and aunt were ready with a blazing firebrand, and as soon as she had fastened the door, they handed it to her without saying a word. She grabbed it and ran round the hut, setting the grass thatch alight at many points, and finally she thrust the firebrand into the thatch just above the door. The grass caught fire at once, and the flames lit the entire homestead.

No sound of any struggle on the part of the King of the Waters in the burning hut. He had lost all power. No power to lift his body from the ground. No power to summon the wings of mighty storms to bear him away from the scorching flames. The King of the Waters was burned to death.

Everything happened so quickly that by the time the neighbors came, nothing was left except the crackling wood.

"What happened? What happened?" asked one neighbor after another.

"It's only one of those things that happen because we are in this world."

"Is everybody safe in your household?" they asked.

"Everybody is safe. It's a pleasant event, my neighbors. Go and sleep in peace. When the present moon dies, I'll invite you all to a great feast in honor of my sister's beautiful daughter here. Then will I tell you all there is to tell about the evil we've just destroyed."

The following morning, the head of the family rose up early and went to examine the scene of the fire very carefully. He found that although the body of the *Nkanyamba,* had been reduced to ashes, bones and all, the skull was intact. He picked it up and examined it. Then he collected some wood, piled it on the ashes and set fire to it. He then picked out the brains of the *Nkanyamba* from every little cranny, and let them fall on the fire. Then he scraped the inside of the skull, removing every little projection and making it as smooth as a clay pot. All the matter removed fell onto the fire and burned out completely. He took the skull indoors and washed it thoroughly with boiling-hot water, and then rubbed it thoroughly with the remnants of the grease and powder that had been used by the princess on the previous night.

Meanwhile the princess was in a deep sleep, nor did she wake up at all until the early afternoon. Her aunt had given orders that no one was to go into the hut where she was sleeping, except herself, for a whole day and night. So, after putting the *Nkanyamba's* skull away, the head of the family went about his daily duties and kept away from his niece's hut. But on the following morning, as soon as he knew that the princess was awake, he went to see her, taking the skull with him. The princess shuddered a little when she saw it.

"Touch it, child of my sister," said her uncle. "Touch it, and all fear of it will go."

The princess touched it, but noticing that she still shuddered, her uncle withdrew it, sat beside her and chatted a little.

Later in the day, the head and mistress of the house discussed the condition of the princess. They agreed that her cousins could enter her hut and sit and chat with her as long as they wished, but that she must remain in bed until all signs of fear had disappeared. So every morning, her uncle took the skull to her and made her handle it. When he was quite satisfied that she did not shudder any more, he told his wife that the princess was now ready to get up and live normally with the rest of the family.

One day, the head and mistress of the family were sitting and chatting with the princess in the Great Hut, when the princess casually rose and walked across the floor, took the *Nkanyamba's* skull down from its place on the wall and turned it over and over in her hands, while all the time she carried on with the conversation as if not thinking about the skull at all. The two elderly people exchanged glances, nodded to each other and smiled.

"Now I can see she's ready to go back to her parents," said the head of the family as soon as he and his wife were alone. "She doesn't fear that skull any more now. It's just like any other vessel in the house. So we can proceed with the preparations."

Two-three days passed, and a great feast was held in honor of the princess. All the neighbors came, and the head of the family told them the whole story of Tfulako's promise to the King of the Waters, and what happened thereafter. The neighbors praised the princess for her bravery and thanked their neighbor on behalf of the parents and brother of the girl. The uncle then pointed out five head of cattle that he was giving to his sister's child to take home. Then one after another, his well-to-do friends and neighbors rose to make little speeches, thanking him for the gift to his sister's child, and adding their own "little calves to accompany their neighbor's gift," until there were well over two tens of cattle in all. After each gift of a "little calf," the princess kissed the right hand of the giver. Then it was the uncle's turn to thank his neighbors for making him a somebody by enriching so much the gift that his sister's child would take home with her.

The village mothers had withdrawn to a separate part of the homestead, and while the men were making gifts in cattle, the women were making a joint present consisting of mats, pots, bowls, and ornaments of all kinds. When these had been collected, the head of the family was asked to accompany the princess to come and see them. Some of the elderly mothers made little speeches, presented the "small gift" to the princess on behalf of the whole motherhood, and wished her a happy journey back home. Both the head and the mistress of the family thanked the mothers.

Before the festivities came to an end, the young men of the village sent spokesmen to their fathers, reminding them that the princess would need an escort.

"We know that very well," said one of the elderly men, with a smile. "But you can't all go. And let me remind you that those of you who are going will have not only to drive the cattle but also to carry all those pots and other things that your mothers have loaded the princess with."

"We understand, father," replied the chief spokesman. "We are ready to carry everything. We have already agreed too that it would be fitting that the princess be escorted by those of the age-group of her brother, Tfulako."

"You've done well," murmured some of the men.

A few days later, while the princess was being helped by her aunt to pack her belongings, the head of the family brought the beautiful kaross that the princess had worn on the night of the killing of the *Nkanyamba*. The princess accepted it very gratefully and embraced her uncle for the wonderful gift. Then he produced the *Nkanyamba's* skull and would hand it over to her.

"What am I to do with this thing, *malume?*" asked the princess, much surprised.

"It's yours," replied her uncle. "It was you who carried the King of the Waters all the way from your home-village so that you could destroy him here."

The princess received the skull with both hands, thanked her uncle, looked at it for a little while and smiled.

"I know what I'll do with this," she said as she packed it away.

"Aren't we going to be told this great secret?" asked her uncle.

"In truth it's no secret to you two," replied the princess. "Some day, some day when my brother Tfulako becomes the chief of our people, I'll give this to him to use as a vessel for washing."

"You have a mind, child of my sister," remarked her uncle.

"Why do you say that, *malume?*"

"Because that was exactly what I hoped you would do with it."

It was a pleasant journey for the princess and her male cousins and other young men of her brother's age-group. They did not take their journey hurriedly, for they must allow the cattle to graze as they went along. They themselves camped and rested whenever they came to a particularly beautiful place. They sang as they travelled and, among other songs, the princess taught them the songs that she and the King of the Waters had sung to each other in these same forests and ravines. She sang her high-pitched song, and the young men sang the song of the King of the Waters in a chorus.

When they approached the Royal Place on the afternoon of the third day of their journey, they started to sing this song aloud. The song was heard and immediately recognized by all those villagers who had heard it on the day of the cyclone. The princess's voice was recognized as hers, but the many deep voices remained a puzzle.

No one had seen Tfulako run into his hut to grab his spears and shield, but there he was, standing alone near the gate, shading his eyes in order to have the first glimpse of the singers who were about to appear on the horizon.

When the singers and the herd of cattle came in sight, he concluded that his sister was in the company of the *Nkan-*

yamba she loathed, together with a whole troop of followers driving the customary bride-tribute of cattle.

"What!" he exclaimed, blazing with anger. "Does this mean that my sister has been burdened with this hateful snake all this time? I'm going to get my sister free!" And he took one leap over the closed gate.

"Wait, Son of the Beautiful!" shouted the councillors. "You're going into danger. Wait until they get here."

"I'll never allow those snakes to enter this gate. I don't want any of their cattle in the folds of my fathers. If no one will come with me, I'll fight them alone. Let him bring all the *nkanyambas* in the world, I'll die fighting for my sister."

And he ran to meet the singers.

Before he had reached them, however, all the hunters of his age-group were with him. For the women of the Royal Place had raised the alarm, and it had been taken up by other women throughout the village, and from one village to another, so that in no time all the youths had grabbed their spears and shields and followed the direction indicated in the cries of the womenfolk.

The singing suddenly stopped, and there were bursts of laughter from the princess' escort.

"Withold your spears!" shouted one of them. "The enemy you're looking for is not here. That which was he is now ashes at Tfulako's mother's people. Here's Tfulako's sister, beautiful as the rising sun."

And the princess stepped forward to meet her brother who had already leapt forward to meet her. They embraced with affection.

"Forgive me, my father's child," said Tfulako, deeply moved.

But the princess would not allow her brother to shed a tear in the presence of other young men. She laughed, disengaged herself and stepped away from him.

"Forgive you what?" she asked. "Forgive you for giving me a chance to prove that I am the worthy sister of Tfulako, killer of buffaloes?"

Before Tfulako could reply, she started to sing his favourite hunting-song, altering the words to suit the event. By this time, the youths of the two groups had mingled together in a friendly manner. As soon as they took up the song, she pulled out the *Nkanyamba's* skull and, holding it high, she led the march into the village and through the gates of the Royal Place:

Ye ha he! e ha he!
A mighty whirlwind, the Nkanyamba!
Fasten your doors, ye who fear
him.
They chase them far! They
chase them near!

As for us, we scorch the cy-
clone-borne
And we carry their skulls aloft.
Ye ha he! e ha he!
A mighty whirlwind, the Nkan-
yamba!

COMMENTARY TO

Sonyangaza and the Ogres

The hero is a young man whose strength and courage are so envied by the cannibals that they conspire to obtain his head and liver, seats of his wit and valor. They fear and admire him, but they can do no more: they can never emulate him. They can kidnap his twin sister, father children by her, but they cannot approximate his power and intelligence. The hero's feats are superhuman at times; he knocks a single buck down with his club, and by so doing destroys the entire herd.

His strength is matched by the gentleness of his sister, yet each of the twins possesses something of the other. The hero is strong, but he is also kind; the heroine is gentle, but she also has something of her brother's strength. The two cannot be separated, together they represent honored Xhosa qualities. Thus, when the gentleness of the sister is endangered, then strength in the form of the brother emerges from the reeds and the quality of gentleness is defended and restored. Thanks to the wit of the hero, the evil that threatens the gentle maiden is eliminated when the cannibals are drowned in the purifying river. Sonyangaza has proven himself a man, and he can now undergo initiation.

Narratives about Xhosa heroes usually dramatize the activities of the perfect member of the society, that citizen who destroys evil through his own bravery and cleverness and by accepting the customs of his society and fulfilling himself.

Sonyangaza and the Ogres

IT CAME ABOUT ACCORDING TO SOME tale, that to a certain household there were born twin babies—a boy and a girl. Each baby had a birthmark on its chest. The boy was therefore named Bala (birthmark) and the girl Balakazi (*kazi* is a feminine suffix). The birthmarks resembled the moon. From early childhood, Bala and Balakazi were proud of their birthmarks. First thing in the morning, Bala used to seek Kazi and show her the birthmark on his chest, and she would smile and show him hers. Then they would laugh, embrace each other, hold each other's hand and run to play in the open fields, now chasing bright-colored butterflies, now listening to the birds and imitating their calls, now climbing trees to look for eggs in birds' nests, now running after a hare, now dabbling in the river shoals, learning to swim, now looking for beehives and getting stung by bees.

These children grew up like that, very fond of each other, full of health and vigor of mind and body. In their knowledge of plants and animal habits, they far surpassed other children of their age group. Long before his equals knew anything about hunting, Bala could trap any bird or small animal, and, with stick or stone, he could hit any bird within reach, on the ground or in the sky. He could hit any running hare or buck with his club, and he did this with such skill that he amazed the greatest hunters of his homeland. If he saw an otter basking in the sun on the opposite bank of the river, he would pick up a stone and hit it right on the forehead, and then plunge into the deep dark pool, swim to the opposite bank and bring the dead animal home. He used to climb fearful cliffs to hunt rock-rabbits, and if anyone warned him about "the huge, rabbit-hunting snake whose head is like a rock-rabbit's," he used to say, "In truth I would be glad to meet him, for someone must bring him home one day, so that all the young people may know what he looks like." For in his adventures, Bala had encountered many a big, poisonous snake, which he had killed and skinned in order to make armbands and waist-belts for himself and his sister.

On being initiated into manhood, Bala had to assume a new name, according to custom. He was renamed Mbengu. In manhood, he became the most skillful and most daring cattle-raider. His exploits earned him the nickname *Sonyangaza* (Wizard Chief of Raiders), and he became known as *Mbengu Sonyangaza*. He was so strong that those who saw his deeds of valor said, "Truly his ribs are made of iron. He is not Mbengu Sonyangaza but *Mbambo ze Nyangane* (Ribs of Iron)." In the hunt he had no equal. If his hunting party surrounded a herd of buck, he would aim his club at one buck only, but he would hit this buck with such skill and force that the whole herd would come tumbling and falling at his feet, all dead.

One day in autumn, while Mbengu was away on a great hunt, Balakazi went to the cornfields to watch the birds (that is, to keep the birds away from the corn). She was seen by a band of ogres, and they chased and caught her. Balakazi fought and struggled hard to free herself, but eventually the ogres overcame her. Although the ogres had such greed for human flesh, they were so impressed by this girl's beauty and strength of body that they decided not to eat her, but to carry her to their land so that she might become the head wife of their king.

When this news reached him, Mbengu gave up the hunt and set out at once in search of his sister, swearing that he would never return without her. He had no idea where these particular ogres lived, but he was determined to go from one ogre territory to another in search of her, no matter how long it took him. Moons came to life and died again, the *Silimela* (the Pleiades or "seven sisters") appeared in the sky and disappeared again, and still Mbengu wandered. He traversed wide plains and thick jungles, waded or swam many noted mighty rivers, all alone, in search of his sister. He would not beg anyone for food or shelter. He lived on honey, wild fruit, sweet reed, and on the meat of the wild game he could kill so easily. If the night was cold, he slept in a cave; if it was warm, he slept under the stars.

One day, he came to a big river that bordered the land of the fiercest of known ogre kings. From his side of the river, he could see the Great Village where the king of the ogres had his Great Place. It was on the slope of a hill. He could see many footpaths leading from various points of the village. He noticed that many of these paths ended at one point at the river. He therefore concluded that he must be very near the place where the ogresses drew their water, and he decided to wait as near that place as possible. The river was very deep where he was, but he would not look for a ford, lest he be seen. So he swam to the opposite bank and found a place to hide among the tall reeds.

Very soon he saw a group of ogre "girls" coming to draw some water. They were followed by a little human girl with a small pitcher on her head. He was startled. The little girl looked just like his sister Balakazi. This must be his sister's child. Mbengu noted with delight that this child was not one with the ogresses. She was much younger than they, but she was quite independent of them. She ignored them, and they ignored her. After filling their pitchers, the ogresses put them in a row and began playing about. When the little girl came, she filled her own little pitcher, and though it was a little too heavy for her, no one offered to help her as she climbed the river-bank with the pitcher on her head. As she took it off her head, she spilt some of the water onto her body, but this did not startle her at all. She put her pitcher all by itself, some distance from those of the ogresses, and, instead of joining the other "girls" in their games, she began to look for birds' nests among the reeds.

The little girl's movements finally brought her very near

Mbengu's hiding-place and he managed to draw her attention. First she looked at him, rather startled, but when she saw him smile at her, she smiled too. He beckoned her, and she walked quietly to him. As she drew near, Mbengu noticed that she had a moon on her chest.

"Who are you?" asked the little girl, eyeing him with curiosity. "You don't look like these ugly things, these ogres. You look like me and mama."

"Who's your mama?" he asked.

"She is the *nkosikazi*."

"She has never told you her real name—what she was called when she was a little girl like you?"

"Oh, yes. I know her name. She was called Balakazi, but no one calls her that here. All the ogres call her *nkosikazi*."

"Your mama swears * by whom?"

"She swears by Mbengu Sonyangaza."

"She ends there?"

"No, she doesn't end there. She goes on."

"Well, go on. I'm listening."

Umbengu Sonyangaza' onen-yang' esifubeni,	Mbengu Sonyangaza who has a moon on his chest.
Inkosi yase Mbo nase buNguni,	Warrior-leader of the land of the Mbo and Nguni,
Obeth' inyamazan' ibe nye ngegqudu	Who smites one buck with his club
Zonke zizo/kufel' ezinyaweni zakhe.	But brings all to die at his feet.

"Well done, little girl! Well done!" said Mbengu, delighted because in singing his praises, the child imitated her mother so well not only in voice but also in carriage.

"But tell me," he went on after a pause. "Who is this Mbengu Sonyangaza?"

"That's my mama's brother—my *malume*."

"What does he look like?"

"He's a big tall man, stronger than the ogres."

"Have you ever seen him? Is he here too?"

"No. He hasn't come yet. But one day he'll come and take us away from these ogres."

* Women swear by their brothers, and men by their sisters.

Hunting.

"How do you know that he'll come?"

"Mama says so. She tells the ogres that her brother will come, and when they hear that, they tremble all of them. The king too. He trembles and the water runs down his face and washes away his paint."

"Your mother's brother has a moon on his chest?"

"Yes, he has. It's like this one of mine." And the child pointed at her moon just as proudly as Balakazi used to point at hers. "Mama has a moon too. It looks just like mine, but hers is big."

Without another word, Mbengu rose to his full height, bared his chest, bent low so that the child could see the moon on which he laid his pointing finger. Thereupon, the little girl flung her arms around his neck.

"You're mama's brother!" she cried with joy. "You've come to take us away."

"Sh!Sh!" warned Mbengu, closing her mouth with his big

hand. "Don't speak so high. The ogre girls will hear us and tell."

"Oh, but their king is afraid of you. He'll run away if they tell him you're here."

"Wait, little one. This thing is not as easy as that. Let me think."

A pause. Then he stretched out his arm and pulled out a handful of reeds.

"Do you want your mother to see me?" he asked.

"Yes, I do. Aren't you coming home with me then?"

"I must see your mother alone first, and that's why I'm going to give you these reeds. Listen carefully. You are to carry these reeds home. When you get to the door, lay them across the threshold, and then ask mama to help you take the pitcher off your head. If anyone else offers to help you, you are to refuse. It must be mama and no one else. When she takes the pitcher off your head, she is sure to tread on the reeds and break them. Then you must cry and insist that she replaces them at once. Tell her you went to a lot of trouble looking for the finest reeds on the river bank, and that she must go to the exact spot where you got these and bring you a bundle just as fine as this one."

The little girl saw the point at once and jumped about with excitement.

"And if she doesn't break them, I'll break them myself and say she did it," she said brightly.

"You're a clever girl—. By the way, you forgot to tell me your name!"

"I am *Nomavukazi*, (Mother-of-the-evening-dews) but mama just calls me Vukazi."

"It is well then, Vukazi. Take your reeds and go now. The ogresses are already on their way. Try to overtake them before they reach the village."

The plan worked out well. Just as Mbengu had calculated, his sister trod on the reeds and broke a number of them. Thereupon, Nomavukazi threw herself on the ground and cried aloud.

"I want my reeds!" she wailed. "Mama must go and get me fresh reeds now, now, now."

"I didn't see the reeds, my child," said the mother, begging for peace. "Stop crying now. Mama will send some one to get you nice reeds."

"No. No. No!" protested Nomayukazi. "Go and get them yourself. It was you who broke my reeds. I won't accept reeds from anyone else."

"All right, my child. I'll go tomorrow morning."

"No! I want them *now*. And you must go to the exact place where I found these."

"Oh, Vukazi! But can't you see that mama is tired? Why can't you wait until tomorrow morning?"

"Because I want to play now. That's why I went to that place to get them. If you don't go now, I'll cry the whole night."

"All right, Vukazi. I'll go."

Balakazi did not want her child ever to cry, and the child knew this. As she left the house, Nomavukazi shouted after her, "Go to the exact place, mama. If you bring me reeds from any other place, I'll know at once that you've cheated me."

"It's enough, Vukazi. I've heard."

When he saw his sister coming, Mbengu sharpened his eyes lest she was being followed, and when he was satisfied that she was not, he hid among the reeds and waited. As soon as she was close enough to hear, he made a bird call. Balakazi paused a little. When she started to move on, he made another call, imitating a different bird. This time Balakazi stopped sharply and looked quickly this way and that. Mbengu made a third call, and Balakazi came straight to his hiding place.

Mbengu rose to his feet and pointed at the moon on his chest. Balakazi smiled, bared her chest, and showed him hers. Then they embraced each other, silent.

"Five whole years you've been wandering, looking for me," said Balakazi as she disengaged herself and looked her brother up and down.

"It will be five years when this moon dies. There isn't a river that I don't know now in the whole of the land of the Mbo and the Nguni peoples."

"I can see by your kaross, child of my people," replied Ba-

lakazi, still looking her brother up and down. "Many are the
suns that have scorched it, many the night dews that have
slept on it, many the rains that have drenched it, many the
snows that have fallen like feathers on it. But you—it is now
that you are strong. You're just sinews the whole of you. Say,
how did you and Vukazi meet?"

"She discovered me hiding here," he replied, smiling.
"She has a mind, that child."

"And when she got home, she did it well, so well that I
didn't suspect anything until I heard your bird calls."

"Oh, I was sure she'd do it well. She's full of news too.
She told me how mama frightens the ogres by telling them
that her brother will come; how the king trembles until he
perspires: how the sweat runs down his face and washes off his
paint."

They looked at each other and laughed softly.

"You understood from her talk that she doesn't know that
the king is her father?" asked Balakazi.

"That I understood, and I was delighted, Kazi."

"There's another thing she doesn't know?"

"And what is that?"

"She doesn't know that every year in autumn, the king of
the ogres sends a band of his followers to hunt you, kill you,
and bring your head and liver to him."

"You must have fought very hard before they could carry
you away, Kazi. If they want your brother's head and liver,
that means you've impressed them with your strength and
bravery."

"Of course, I did fight. I broke the wrist of one with my
hands, and I crushed the thumb of a second with my teeth before they overpowered me."

"I thought so!"

"But that's not the reason why they want your head and
liver. They wanted these things long before they'd ever seen
me. It appears that they've known you by sight for a long
time. From their hiding places in the jungles, they've watched
you hunting, many a time, but they've never had the liver to
come close to you. In fact, when they found me in the corn-

fields, they were looking for you. It was only after I began singing your praises that they realized I'm your sister. Well, that pleased them in one way, but terrified them in another."

"I understand, Kazi. I understand. It is well then! The head and the liver have come. Let the ogres have them, if they can."

"They'll have neither head nor liver!" said Balakazi, gazing at her brother's build with pride. "We must plan to leave at once. Let me go and fetch the child."

"No, Kazi! We can't do it that way. If these ogres know me by sight, they'll continue to hunt me. And how can I be sure that they'll always be afraid to come close to me? Once you know that a man is after your head and liver, you must act."

"But you can't kill the king, Bala. He's too closely guarded for you. Rather let *me* kill him."

"No, child of my father!" said Mbengu, smiling with affection. "Things won't go well that way. I must get to the Great Place and plan out everything myself. I can only know how to plan when I've seen the place. If you hadn't told me that they're after my head and liver, I would have said, 'Go fetch the child and let's be off!' But now that I know, I must blot out his name before I cross this river again."

"I hear you, child of my people. If that is so then, I must make you my *vavunge*."

"*Vavunge!* What's that?"

Balakazi laughed, and then she explained: "Any human who strays into the land of the ogres is called a *vavunge,* and he is chased and caught and eaten up. But a *vavunge* brought by a person of my rank, brought by a *nkosikazi,* may not be eaten up if the person who brought him has decided to make him her chopper of wood and lighter of fires."

Mbengu smiled, but said nothing.

"I must smear you with mud," proceeded Balakazi, smiling back, "and make you look like a worn-out old man. Not only your face! Your legs and arms must also be smeared to hide your iron muscles."

She brought some mud and clay, and worked so skillfully

over her brother's body that he looked like a wrinkled old man. She also bespattered his kaross and turban and sandals.

"Now I want some reeds for my daughter. Only you and she know where you got the ones I broke, so bring me some."

Smiling at his sister, Bala stretched his hand without even looking at the reeds and pulled out a whole bundle at one go. He chopped off the root ends with his broad-bladed spear, thrust the spear into the bundle, and handed the bundle to his sister. Balakazi put it on her head immediately and, without speaking, pointed at her brother's heavy club which was lying on the ground.

In reply, Mbengu picked up the club by its knob-end, covered the knob with his big right hand and leaned on the club as heavily as a worn-out old man leans on his staff, his waist bent and his left hand holding painfully to its side.

"Now I must go ahead of you," said Balakazi, approvingly. "When I reach the top of the hill, I'll stop and watch you coming. As soon as I notice that some of the ogres have seen you, I'll shout and say, 'There comes the *vavunge* of the *nkosikazi!*' Then they will know that they're not to touch you. And don't forget to limp as you come up the hill, Bala!"

"Leave that to me, Kazi. I'm going to be the weakest *vavunge* they've ever seen."

And so they went.

When Balakazi reached the top of the hill, she turned to look back. There was her brother, far behind, limping painfully as he climbed slowly up the hill. Some ogres noticed that the *nkosikazi* was watching something, and they came to look.

"There comes the *vavunge* of the *nkosikazi!*" shouted Balakazi, pointing at the sorry figure coming up the hill.

"Not to be eaten then, nkosikazi?" asked the ogres, disappointed.

"Not to be eaten!" replied Balakazi in a commanding voice. "He's going to chop the wood and light the fire for me."

There was excitement in the village as Balakazi led her *vavunge* to the Great Place. Crowds of ogres followed them, their mouths watering.

"*Uvavunge! Uvavunge!*" they kept shouting.

"Not to be eaten!" Balakazi commanded. "No one must touch him."

The ogres lost interest, the crowds thinning down by degrees until, by the time Balakazi and her *vavunge* reached home, they were not being followed by anyone. There the *vavunge* was given food and told what his duties were going to be. So for the next two days Mbengu served his own sister as her attendant.

On the third day, the king of the ogres came to Balakazi's Great Hut, and for the first time Mbengu came face to face with him. The king had come to see this *vavunge* that his "people" were talking about, to find out where he came from, and if by any chance he knew a famous raider and hunter of the land of the Mbo and Nguni, a very tall man of great strength named Mbengu Sonyangaza.

"I often heard of him in past years," replied the *vavunge* in a croaking voice, "I myself never saw him with my own eyes, but the young men of my homeland saw him often, and told us stories about him. But I think he is dead now, because —"

"He's dead?" interrupted the king. "What makes you think he's dead?"

"I say so because our young men don't see him any more, and they don't ever talk about him. A man lives and lives and dies, Great One."

"But he was not an old man!"

"You knew him then, Great One?"

"I heard great things about him, but I never saw him. When a man does things that are amazing, there's much talk about him everywhere."

"Where did you hear the talk about him?"

"From my hunters."

"They hunted with him?"

"Not even once! They used to watch him hunting, and they never forget the man's liver."

"When was this? When last did your hunters see him?"

"There have rolled by many years since they last saw him. His trail is not known. But I refuse to believe that he's dead.

My own feeling is that he's looking for something—something of his that was taken away by my hunters."

"And what may that thing be? Is it a secret?"

"It's not a secret so much. You'll soon know it now that you're here."

"It is the thing that makes him the greatest raider and hunter?"

"It's something he loves very much. My hunters were sent to get me the thing that makes him the greatest hunter, but they brought me the thing he loves above all things, and I think he's looking for it."

"You fear him, Great One?"

"If my bravest hunters fear him, he's a man to be feared. A *dlaligwavuma* (headhunter) is brave. If he fears to go near a man after watching him kill buffaloes and wild boar, you must know that that is a man to be feared."

After saying these words, the king of the ogres rose to go. He stretched himself and yawned, opening his cave of a mouth very wide.

"Oh, I don't know who it is that can find me Mbengu Sonyangaza, warrior-leader of the land of the Mbo and Nguni!" he said aloud as he bent low and squeezed his huge body through the doorway.

Mbengu had held himself back throughout this conversation, but as he watched this big-bellied thing walk away, all his sinews became so taut that the clay that covered his body cracked audibly. His sister had been watching him with anxiety during the conversation, and she was pleased to mark that he was so able to control himself. She gave him a warning look when she saw the frowning eyebrows, the clenched fists, the clenched teeth, and the expanding chest.

"Be calm, child of my people," she said. "You did well in that conversation. Now you've heard with your own ears. He even said *dlaligwavuma!*"

"That's what makes me blaze with anger, Kazi. That he should say it with such coolness, as if a man's head is like a buck's!"

"Be calm nevertheless, Bala. Let me tell you something.

Woman being carried away by an animal.

His headhunters have just returned from the yearly autumn hunt, and they've told him that your trail is not known. On hearing that there had just arrived a *vavunge* here, the leader *dlaligwavuma* said, 'It may be that this *vavunge* knows Mbengu Sonyangaza! Let him be asked.' That's why the king came here."

"I hear you, Kazi. In fact, this ogre is not as stupid as ogres are said to be. He feels it in his own body that this Mbengu Sonyangaza isn't dead."

While they were still talking, they heard the footsteps of some ogres coming towards the enclosure, and they stopped talking. Mbengu sat down and became the worn-out old man it was necessary that he should be. The ogres entered. They had come to invite the *vavunge* to come and watch them hunt on the following day.

"Come, *vavunge*," they said. "You must be lonely here.

You were a hunter yourself in your days of youth. You'll just sit on the slope and look on. When you want to come back, come back, even if we are still hunting."

Mbengu agreed.

So on the following morning, Mbengu leaned heavily on his staff and followed like a lame man far behind the hunter-ogres. He felt suspicious and would not go deep into the jungle with them. Calling out to the hindmost ogre, he asked in a croaking voice to be shown the place where the hunting was going to be. When it was pointed out to him, he said he would find himself a place on the hillslope whence he could watch the hunt.

On the top of the hill there sat a wrinkled old ogress. From where she sat, she could see the whole of the hunting field. As soon as the hunters reached the jungle, she shouted to them, telling them which way the herds of buck were running, and they followed her directions. Her eyes were surprisingly sharp, and her voice so powerful that it echoed from one hill to another.

Mbengu was listening to all this and watching with excitement as the hunters ran from one direction to another in response to the shouts of the old ogress. Then a great herd of panic-stricken bucks emerged from the bushes and came leaping and bounding towards him. Before he knew what he was doing, Mbengu Sonyangaza had leaped to his feet, let fly his club and hit one of the bucks, whereupon all the bucks came tumbling over one another and fell dead at his feet!

There were shouts of admiration from the approaching hunter-ogres. The killer, however, was already cursing himself for having been so carried away with excitement. There could be no doubt that he had given himself away, for while the younger hunters continued their exclamations of praise as they greedily collected the dead bucks, the more experienced hunters stood in groups, heads together, speaking low and continually glancing and pointing at him. He had picked up his club and was now leaning heavily on it as before, some distance away from the ogres. He looked unconcerned, but he was watching and interpreting every gesture made by the ex-

perienced hunters. There was no doubt that they were overawed. Even if they were convinced that he was the famous
raider and hunter for whose head and liver they had long
been hunting, they would not attack him immediately. For if
by hitting only one of a herd of bucks he could bring the
whole herd falling dead at his feet, how could they be sure
that with that same club he could not bring the whole of the
hunting party falling dead at his feet? Mbengu waited until
they had picked up all the dead animals and were on their
way home. Then he followed slowly limping.

He knows what must follow. He is going to be invited to
go hunting soon. He is going to be killed in the jungle. His
head is going to be cut off, his body torn open and his liver
cut out carefully. The head and the liver will be taken to the
king of the ogres, who will be waiting for this great prize
somewhere in the jungle. The rest of the body will be devoured by the hunters. At the end of the day, the ogres will
come home, and one of them will be sent to go and tell the
nkosikazi that her *vavunge* was killed "by accident" or "by a
wild boar" in the jungle. His life is in danger now, and he
must abandon the idea of staying here to kill the king of the
ogres. The safest thing to do, while planning to escape with
his sister and her child, is to stick to his sister's Great Hut and
never let her out of his sight. For he knows one thing at least,
that if his head and liver are going to be used for ritual purposes, the ogres will not kill him openly anywhere in their village, least of all in the presence of females. So went his
thoughts.

True enough, that same evening three of the senior ogres
came to his sister's Great Hut. First they praised the *vavunge*
for the wonderful hunting skill he had shown, then they told
him that there would be another hunt on the following day, a
hunt much bigger than that day's, for the king himself would
be present, together with the greatest hunters in their land.

"Headhunters and liverhunters," thought Mbengu, but he
remained quiet to allow the spokesman of the ogres to finish
what he had to say.

"You will come then, *vavunge?*" asked the spokesman, his

mouth watering already at the thought of the feast he would have. "This time we want you to hunt too. You can't sit there on the slope like a woman while other men are hunting. You've still plenty of strength, much more than any of your age amongst us here. This land that you come from must be a land of strong men, if one of your age can do such wonderful things."

"It is well," replied the *vavunge*. "I'll come with you tomorrow. But I can't run about as you do. I'm worn out with age. I'd rather sit again where I can see everything, and if any game come near me, I'll try to hit. But I can't be sure that I'll have luck such as I had today. Fortunes don't heap on each other."

"It is the truth," said the spokesman, nodding many times. "We rejoice that you will come." And so the ogres left.

Mbengu never closed his eyes that night. He was thinking out his plans. It is good that this hunt is tomorrow. He knows that tonight his hut is being watched closely, and that those who are guarding it will not go until daybreak. Since the aim is to kill him tomorrow, and since the ogres are all afraid of him, all the strong and swift ogres will go hunting, and only the worn-out old men and the women and the children will be left in the village. Once they know who he is, none of these old ogres will come out of their huts. But then there is that old ogress with sharp eyes and a powerful voice. It is she alone who is a danger to him. Her eyes are useless without her voice. They will reach all places and see all things, but if she has no voice to tell the hunters what she sees, she is like any of the other cronies in the village. That voice! That voice! He must remove it!

He rose before the sun had risen and went to gather wood for the *nkosikazi*. He had a digging rod hidden under his dress of skin. When he returned, he had some salty earth and some herbs under his armpit. He was walking very slowly, as if in great pain. The look on his face was that of a sick man.

When the ogres came to remind him about the hunt, they

found him grinding the salty earth and mixing it with the herb.

"Come, *vavunge!*" said their spokesman. "Just leave these things of the women and come with other men."

"I can't come," said the *vavunge* in a weak voice. "Sleep never descended on me last night. I have a bad stomach. This that I am preparing is a cure that old people use in my homeland when they have a bad stomach. I'm going to boil it, cool it, and drink it. If I feel better as the day proceeds, I'll come and watch the hunt. I'll drink my cure and lie down awhile, perhaps sleep even. But I promise you I'll come and see your great hunters."

The ogres believed, and they left.

Mbengu went on grinding his mixture until his sister came to the cooking hut where he was. Without looking at her, without any change of expression, without stopping what he was doing, he spoke to her saying, "Kazi, everything stands well. We leave today. The shades of our people are with us."

"Why do you say that, Bala?"

"I've been to the river. The river is filling up. When the day strengthens towards midday, it will be right over its banks. That suits us well. Prepare yourself and the child something to eat. When you have finished eating, go both of you and wait for me by the deep pool that I swam to get to this side of the river."

Balakazi girded her skirt high (worked with energy and speed) at once, and by the time Mbengu finished his grinding, mother and child were having their morning meal. As soon as they had finished eating, Balakazi took a small pitcher and held it out to her daughter.

"Where are we going, mama?" asked Vukazi.

"We are going to draw some water, and also to get you some reeds—the most beautiful reeds on the river-bank."

Vukazi smiled very brightly, grabbed the pitcher and placed it on her head, and mother and daughter set out for the river.

Left alone, Mbengu put his mixture into a clay pot, filled

up the pot with gravy, and put it on the fire to boil. When the mixture was ready, he took it off the fire, cooled it quickly, and poured it all into a large drinking bowl. Then he leaned heavily on his staff and carried the drink to the ogress on the hilltop.

"You have brought me some beer, *vavunge?*" asked the ogress, greedily.

"I've brought you something more tasty than beer, old mother—the kind of brew that we make for aged people in my homeland. It will be very good for you who have to keep shouting the whole day."

Then he knelt in front of her and took the customary sip to assure her that the drink was not poisoned.

"You can have it all," he said as he handed her the bowl. "I've plenty left for myself at the house."

But there was, in fact, no need to make this offer, for the ogress's mouth was already watering at the smell of the gravy. She grabbed the bowl greedily, threw her head back, opened her mouth very wide, and gurgle! gurgle, gurgle! went the mixture down her throat.

When she raised her head again, there stood in front of her, not the wrinkled old *vavunge* who had offered her the tasty drink, but a sinewy giant of a man with a moon on his chest, a weighty club in his right hand, and a broad-bladed spear in his left.

"Who are you?" she asked in awe. "Where's the *vavunge?*"

"This is Mbengu Sonyangaza, warrior-leader of the land of the Mbo and the Nguni people, now *vavunge* no more."

"What! You're not going to kill me?" she asked in a voice whose hoarseness startled her.

"Hear me before you try to shout. It is not my custom to kill women. Even men I don't kill unless they hunt me, as your king has been doing. I'm taking my sister and her child away. I'm not going to steal them in the night, like a thief. I'm going to take them away like a man, while the sun pierces the earth. I meant to kill your king before I left. I can't do that now, because of some foolish thing that I did yesterday. Nevertheless —I swear by Balakazi!—if I can't kill him, I'm going to do something that will always remind you ogres that Mbengu Sonyangaza once came to this land of yours. You see those herds of cattle spread over the pasture? By the time today's sun goes to its mother, they'll all be far away from here, on the way to my homeland. If you still have a voice, you can shout as loud as you can and tell your ogre-king and his head-hunters to come and rescue their cattle, if they are men."

He sped down the hill and made for the pasture. He raised his club and spear, waving them vigorously and shouting, and in no time he had rounded up the cattle. They carried their tails high and galloped towards the river. There was a moo, moo, of lowing cattle, a crash! crash! of breaking reeds, and a splash! splash! splash! as Mbengu ran from one end of the herd to the other, forcing the cattle across the flood. Balakazi was helping him, but she was handicapped by the child, whom she had to carry on her shoulders at this critical moment. As the number of cattle on the other side grew larger and larger, it became easier and easier to manage the rest.

"Here! Take hold of the child!" shouted Balakazi over the din. And just as the last big ox plunged into the water, she leaped forward, caught hold of its tail and held on to it with both hands. Mbengu held his teeth tight as he watched his sister and the ox approach the middle of the river where the current was strongest. But Balakazi held on, and when she had passed it, Mbengu smiled with pride and plunged into the flood with the child in his arms. In no time all three were safe on the other side.

Where are the ogres? The ogress tried to raise the alarm as soon as Mbengu had left her, but the drink he has given her has made her voice so weak and hoarse that it does not reach the hunters. She sees him rounding up the cattle with amazing ease, and she tries to announce this to the hunters. But one hunter says, "She says the buck are running towards the setting sun!" thereupon the whole hunting party runs towards the setting sun. She shouts again, but another hunter says, "She says the buck are running towards the rising sun!" Thereupon, the hunting party runs towards the rising sun. This goes on and on until the hunters realize that there is something crooked. Some of them run up the hill until they are close enough to hear. Then at last one of these says, "She says our cattle are being raided by Mbengu Sonyangaza!" Then the ogres set up a hue and cry that makes a person feel cold in the stomach.

"I-i-i-wu!" they shout from all sides. "I-i-i-wu! The Wizard Chief of Raiders! Cut him off! Cut him off and tear him to pieces! I-i-i-i-i-iwu!"

The hunter-ogres ran with such speed as had never been seen. They leaped over rocks and bushes with ease, carrying their shields high, so that they seemed to be flying rather than running. And all the time they kept up their blood-freezing hue and cry. The king was not able to keep up with the swiftest headhunters. When he reached the river, they were all standing on the bank, talking and pointing, partly in awe and partly in admiration, at a tall figure on the opposite bank.

"It's the very man!" those who had seen Mbengu in action were saying. "That deep broad chest! Those ribs of iron! That moon on the chest! The very man! The Wizard Chief of Raiders himself! The liver of him! The liver of him, to raid in the daylight like that, unaided!"

The king of the ogres saw and was satisfied. Yes, this must be the man whose wonders he has been told about. He has the skill to round up and drive all their cattle across a flooded river as if into a fold, and he has the liver to stop and wait on the other side until the ogres, who are so feared by other men, can see him. There he stands facing them all, the last traces of the mud that made him look like a wrinkled old man completely washed away by the flood, and in their place now sinews hard as iron.

"You are speaking?" demanded Mbengu, in a deep voice but cool.

"Yes, we are speaking, *Mkhwe* (brother-in-law)," answered the king in person. "What is this bad thing that you do to us?"

"*Mkhwe?* You dare call me your mkhwe when you so despised my people that you carried my sister away, as if she was nobody's daughter?"

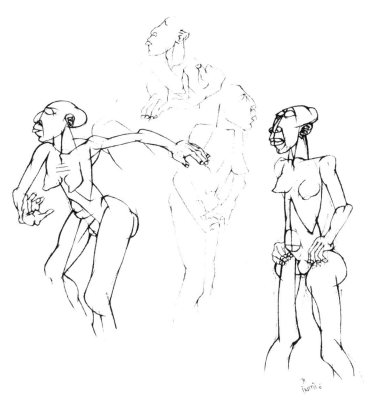

Scene between the reeds.

"Peace, Wizard Chief of Raiders!" begged the king of the
ogres. "I know I made a mistake. But when you did come, you
should have proceeded according to custom."

"There's still time even now," replied Mbengu, smiling.
"If you want to talk custom, here I am, I, brother of Balakazi.
You can cross the river and sit down, and then we talk."

"But the river is full!" complained the king.

"I thought I was talking to men," replied Mbengu, with
scorn. Then his mood suddenly changed, "Or is it because a
river always gets full when kings refuse to talk custom about
the daughters of people they despise? If that is so, then come
over and take your cattle by force, or you'll never milk again."

The ogres looked at one another and at the flood. The
herds of cattle had crushed the reeds and laid them flat over a
large area, and the flood had now covered this area, so that

the river looked even broader than it really was. The ogres were standing knee-deep in a pool—a mixture of mud and the dung dropped by their own cattle as they were being forced across the river. The king and his leading followers stood heads together and talked.

"No, Wizard Chief of Raiders!" pleaded the king after some time. "Who could ever, ever despise a man like you? We are willing to come over and talk custom with you, but none of us can go into this flood. Can't you wait until the river goes down?"

"Wait? Do you know how many *zilimela* (years, reckoned by the appearance of the Pleiades) I've been wandering, looking for my sister? If you're afraid to swim—a shame of a thing for men to fear water!—weave a long, thick rope and I'll show you how to get across by means of it."

The ogres quickly divided themselves into groups, and each group pulled out piles and piles of grass and wove its own portion of the rope. The various portions were then joined together very tightly and became a long rope that could easily reach the other side.

"Now, take a stone that can be thrown by the strongest of you across the river and tie it to one end of the rope. Then give it to the strongest to throw across to me."

The ogres did this, and Mbengu caught the end that was thrown to him in the air. He removed the stone and threw it into the river, and then he directed the ogres, saying, "Now, I am going to hold this end. Those of you who are not in the first group to cross will hold your end. When the rope is tight, let those who are coming in the first group take hold of it, one behind the other. You are to swim with the help of the rope, arm over arm, like this, like this. Do you know how to swim that way?"

"Oh, yes! We've been doing that since we were mere boys, Wizard Chief of Raiders," answered the ogres.

Then the king divided his followers into two groups. In accordance with custom, he himself would, of course, not be in the first group.

The rope tightened, and they came, arm, over arm, arm

over arm, arm over arm, until the leading one was past the center, and the last one was well off the bank. Then suddenly, it looked as if Mbengu was finding the weight too heavy. He made grimaces as he seemed to strive hard to hold his position. Then, with a cry of feigned horror, he let go his end. Screams of horror from the on-lookers on the other bank. Yells and gurgles from the rope swimmers, and the veteran head-hunters were carried away by the flood.

"The current was too strong for me!" cried Mbengu. "I lost my grip! I lost my grip! We should have foreseen this and fastened the rope to the trees instead of holding it in our hands. Come! Fasten your end to the thickest tree and then throw my end to me so that I can do the same. In any case, you're all coming into the next group and there's no one to hold your end."

The ogres quickly found a suitable tree on their bank, and they fastened their end of the rope as tightly as they could. Mbengu's end was thrown to him as before, and he chose the thickest tree he could find. The ogres could see every muscle of his body taut as he fastened the rope and tightened the knots. He tested the knots a number of times until he was satisfied. He shouted to the ogres and insisted that they do the same at their end. The ogres tried the knots, making tighter and tighter any that seemed doubtful. The king himself checked up carefully before ordering the first half of the group to lead the way.

Then the ogres came on, the king right in the middle. Mbengu was standing near the tree, as if watching very carefully in case the rope loosened. Hand over hand, hand over hand, hand over hand the ogres came, and just as the king reached the strongest current, Mbengu pulled out his broad-bladed spear and cut the rope asunder with one blow. Yells! Yells! Yells! Gurgles! Gurgles! A yell! A gurgle! A yell! A gurgle! A gurgle! . . . A gurgle!. . . . A gurgle!. . . . Silence!

Mbengu turned away from the river and walked up to his sister, his finger pointing at the moon on his chest. Balakazi bared her chest and showed him hers. They exchanged a smile of pride and embraced with affection.

"Mine too, malume! Mine too! Said Vukazi, pointing at the moon on her chest.

"Yes, Yours too, Vukazi!" said Mbengu as he picked up his sister's daughter. "And yours is the prettiest of all, because it is small, just as mama's and mine used to be when we were pretty little children like you."

And all three flung their arms round one another's neck and embraced again.

Then Mbengu put his sister's child on his shoulder, and the three, with all the cattle of the ogres driven before them, set out on their long journey home.

COMMENTARY TO
Siganda and Sigandana

Like other tales in this collection, this story centers about a rite of passage—this time the initiation of two boys into manhood. The elder brother, Siganda, waits to be initiated until his younger brother, Sigandana, is old enough, and after their education at the secluded place of initiation is complete, they go off to seek their fortunes.

The elder brother's initiation has not been as successful as that of the younger: he is first stricken by laziness and fear in turning over the pots, then by fear when they come to the bamboo grove, and then by jealousy and greed when the younger brother finds the magnificent cow. Meantime the younger brother rescues an old woman who tells him, "You're a man!" Because of his thoughtfulness and humaneness, the woman leads him to a treasure grove. The younger brother is generous; he offers his brother thirty head of his cattle. And the younger brother is generous later too when he is abandoned in the ravine—he cannot believe that his brother did this deliberately.

The younger brother is a man; he has fulfilled the purpose of the initiation ceremony and has become a thoughtful and considerate adult member of his society. He left his childish ways behind when the suthu lodge was burned down.

But the elder brother is not so purified, his love turns to jealousy and hatred, and he attempts to murder his younger brother. He fails the responsibilities of manhood, the communal traditions he should uphold and respect as a man. He fails himself and his people. His assault on his brother is an *assault on the harmony of the society, a harmony which seemed to be perfectly achieved in the brotherly love earlier expressed. Now this love is shattered by the greed of the elder brother. But he cannot succeed. Nature, his own people and that broader natural force in which Xhosa artists see the metaphorical perfection of their own halting efforts to build a society, will not allow the crime and deception to go unpunished. It is in the nature of man and his society to seek balance, a sense of harmony. To right the disturbed equilibrium, nature again steps in, this time in the form of a cow and a honeybird.*

Evil has entered the family through the elder son, and this evil must be purged. Nature helps, and the father leaves it to the village to determine Siganda's fate. Children can be forgiven much, but once they have undergone initiation, then they must forego the things of childhood; these are "beneath the dignity of manhood." Initiation has prepared the children to go out and, in the words of their father, seek wealth and *wisdom. Siganda, however, seeks wealth only.*

Siganda and Sigandana

IT CAME ABOUT, ACCORDING TO SOME tale, that there were two brothers, Siganda the elder, and Sigandana the younger. From early childhood they loved each other very much. They used to play together all kinds of games the whole day, climbing trees, riding goats and calves, setting bird traps, molding clay cattle and, when they were biggish boys, hunting wild game together. They always preferred each other's company to that of other boys of their respective age groups. Even their parents could never separate them for daily duties at home. If one was sent on an errand, the other would insist on going with his brother. Their father noted all this very early in the boys' life and felt very proud of it.

The time came when Siganda had to be initiated into manhood, and the father was greatly worried because this meant that socially the two boys must be separated for some years. As the first stage in the initiation process, Siganda would have to go with other boys of his own age group to a *suthu* (secluded establishment for novices), far away from home, and remain there for about six moons. During that period, he and his colleagues would receive rigorous training in physical endurance and self-control. They would also be instructed in matters relating to sex and marriage, on the responsibilities of manhood, and on all the communal traditions they would be expected to respect and uphold as men. Until this period was over, only initiated men could visit the novices. This meant that of the members of this family, only the father could visit Siganda. At the end of the training period, the establishment that had been erected for this purpose would be burned to ashes, with all the initiates looking away from it, as a sign that all the things of boyhood they had left behind were destroyed forever with the establishment. The father knew also that Sigandana would be disappointed when his brother returned, because Siganda would be changed. All the things they used to enjoy together as boys would be beneath the dignity of manhood, and Siganda would not be expected to participate in them. On the other hand, Sigandana would not be able to participate in most of the things Siganda would be doing until after his own initiation, and the time for this would be about two summers after his brothers' initiation.

The father did not like the idea of separating his sons for such a long time. For many days he pondered over this problem, and at last he decided that it had better be the boys themselves who told him what to do. So one day he called them to him and said, "My sons, you have never been separated since you were born. You have always done everything together, and you have never quarreled over anything. But now the time has come when Siganda must go with his equals to the *suthu*. This means you must be separated. I've been thinking how this separation can be avoided. I would not like you to be separated at any time, for any purpose, but my difficulty is that Sigandana is yet too young to be initiated into manhood. Were it not for that, I would have both of you initiated now. What then must I do? Answer, Siganda."

Siganda answered promptly and said, "We thank you, father, for seeking our advice on this matter. We thought about it and discussed it between ourselves in these past moons, and we agreed that I should wait until my younger brother comes of age."

"You realize that this means you will be two summers behind your equals?"

"Yes, I understand that, father, but that does not trouble me at all. There are many others who have waited for their younger brothers, and two summers is not such a long time."

"You've spoken well, my son. I did consider that myself, but I thought you might not like to be left behind by your

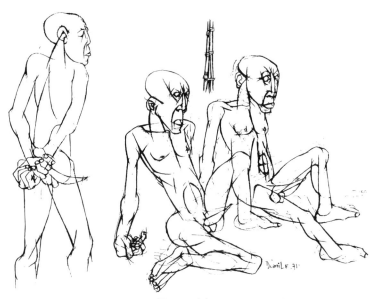

Circumcision.

equals. That's why I asked you to answer. You've answered me then, and I accept your answer."

So Siganda and Sigandana remained boys for another two years, and they continued to love each other until they were fully initiated.

One day, two moons after the initiation festivities, the father called his sons to him and said, "My sons, you are men now. You see the livestock of this home? Some of it belongs to the stock that was left by my grandfather to my father, and by my father to me. The rest comes from these hands of mine. I left home to seek wealth and wisdom in other lands before my father died. I brought the stock home, and my father saw it before he died. He died happy because he knew that I knew how to work, because he knew that there was a man left behind to look after the house of his fathers. I too then want to die happy. I want you to show me that when I am dead, this house of my fathers will not be a house of poverty. Go out and seek wealth and wisdom."

A few days after this, the two young men picked up their spears and shields, slung over their shoulders the large food provisions that their mother had prepared for them, called their dogs, and set out to seek wealth and wisdom. They travelled for many days, sleeping and waking in the wilds, but finding nothing to take back home.

One day, they came upon a large number of clay pots of unusually great size, all standing upside down in a circle. At once, Sigandana became curious and excited.

"Elder brother," he said, "whose pots can these be? Why are they upside down? What's there under them?"

"How can I know that?" asked Siganda.

"Elder brother, we've travelled for days and found nothing. We may travel more days and still find nothing. It won't kill us if we spend this day pushing those pots over to see what it is that they cover."

"No, son of my father," said Siganda. "You can do that alone if you want to. As for me, I'm tired. I want to lie down and rest. To tell you the truth, I'm afraid to touch these pots. I don't want to bring harm upon myself by touching pots whose owner I don't know. What are they doing here? What's under them?"

"That's exactly what I am determined to know before today's sun goes down," replied Sigandana.

"If there's nothing under them?"

"Then I'll know there's nothing under them."

"Won't you have eaten up your strength for nothing?"

"I won't have eaten it up for nothing. I'll know there's nothing under the pots. Elder brother, we've been travelling for days and days, eating up our strength. But we haven't eaten it up for nothing. We know now that over the area we've covered there's no wealth to be found, and that's why we are travelling farther and farther away from home, not even knowing where we are going. It may happen that we'll travel and travel and travel until we feel so tired that we give up and decide to return home empty-handed. When that day comes, we'll hate ourselves for not looking under these pots. I won't sleep until I've pushed over every one of them."

So saying, Sigandana tightened his waistband and set to work. He pushed over the first pot and found nothing, the second one, nothing, the third one, nothing. But he did not give up. He went on and on until he came to the last one. This was the largest and heaviest of all. He tried and tried and tried, now and again stopping to rest, panting, dripping-wet with sweat. At last the pot began to move, up, up, up, and with one last tremendous effort he pushed it over.

There was a little old woman sitting under the clay pot. But as soon as it had been pushed over, she rose to her feet and looked the young men up and down, amazed but grateful.

"You're a man!" she said. "I've been a prisoner under this clay pot for a long long time. If you hadn't come to my help, I don't know what would have happened to me in the end. Follow me."

So saying, she led the way, travelling towards the rising sun. Sigandana picked up his luggage, called his brother and the dogs, and followed. Siganda got up and followed too, but at a distance, because the sight of this little old woman made him more fearful that he and his brother were going straight into a trap.

On and on went the old woman, never looking this way or that, never resting, until she came to a big, big forest. She stopped at the edge to wait for the brothers, but even now she did not look behind to see how far behind they were. As soon as they came up, she moved on without looking at them, going deeper and deeper and deeper into the forest. The deeper she went, the taller the trees she passed, and the greater Sigandana's excitement grew.

In the depths of the forest there was a large pool of deep dark water. It was surrounded by bamboos of extraordinary height and thickness. The old woman stopped at the edge of the pool and waited. Sigandana, who had been following close behind, soon came up and looked at the old woman questioningly. But she seemed not to be thinking about him at all. She was looking longingly at the water. When at last Siganda arrived, the little old woman spoke, without looking at the young men. Pointing to a thick little bush nearby she said, "Whoever thrusts his hand into that bush will find something of great help."

Immediately, Sigandana walked to the bush, but before

doing anything, he turned and looked at his brother. Siganda shook his head and turned away. Then Sigandana thrust his hand into the bush and pulled out two sharp axes. Excited, he brought these to the little old woman. But, without touching the axes, without looking at the young man, the little old woman pointed to the thick bamboos that surrounded the pool and said, "Whoever hews down these bamboos will find what he came out to look for."

Having said these words, the little old woman went into the pool and disappeared under the water without a sound.

For a moment Sigandana stood looking where the little old woman had disappeared, and then he turned to his brother and offered him one of the axes. But Siganda refused to take it.

"No, son of my father!" he said. "I refuse. I refuse altogether. A terrible thing may happen to us here. Who is this little old woman? Where has she gone now? Whose are these bamboos? What's hidden in them? If the owner of this pool should come out and find us hewing them down, what will happen?"

"Elder brother," said Sigandana, "if these things that you fear do come, we shall see what to do about them at the time when they come. Let's get to work!"

But Siganda shook his head and retreated without accepting the axe offered to him.

Once again, Sigandana worked alone. He hewed and hewed at the first bamboo with great energy. Then the bamboo crackled and fell over into the pool and sank to the bottom. In the hollow of the stump left behind there was a beautiful cow with its young calf. The cow jumped out of the stump, followed by its calf. The cow looked around, mooed, and then it bent its neck to the ground and grazed. The calf sought its mother's udder and began to suck greedily. Sigandana shouted joyfully and began to fell the next bamboo. When this one fell over, out came a beautiful heifer. The heifer looked around, mooed, joined the cow, and grazed. The next bamboo produced a young ox, the next a large ox. So Sigandana went on felling one bamboo after another, and every

Hunting together.

one produced one or more head of cattle. All this time, Siganda stood aloof, full of fear. After he had been watching the beautiful cattle coming out of the bamboos, he concluded that the danger was hidden in the last one, which was the thickest and tallest of all. As his brother came nearer and nearer to it. Siganda fixed his gaze on this bamboo.

At last, Sigandana reached it. But before trying to fell it, he walked round and round it many times. He thought he would have to work at it many times as hard as he had worked at any other one, and this excited him. It must be hiding the greatest prize, he thought. He reminded himself that when he pushed the clay pots over, the last one was the largest and heaviest of all. Then he started. But he struck only once and the bamboo began to crackle. Before it fell over, he heard the moo! moo! of a cow. He struck a second time, and the bamboo fell over. What came out was a cow of such beauty as he had never even dreamt of—a beautiful white cow of great size, with shapely horns that tapered to a point.

While Sigandana was still gazing at her with delight, the white cow looked around, emitted a succession of beautiful resonant moos, so resonant that they seemed to come from all sides of the forest. Then she tripped gracefully and went to join the large herd of cattle grazing round the pool.

Siganda had been watching his younger brother very

closely at the last bamboo, and when the beautiful white cow came out, his chest heaved with wonder.

"Son of my father!" he exclaimed. "Such a beautiful animal has never been seen by human eyes before! What does this mean?"

"I agree with you, elder brother. This in truth is an animal of wondrous beauty. Here before us is a large herd of cattle, beautiful cattle all of them. But while all the others gladden the eye, this white cow satisfies the very soul.

The young men rounded up the cattle and began to drive them towards the edge of the forest. As they went, Sigandana noted the color-markings and the shape of the horns of each one of them. But Siganda fixed his gaze on the white cow, hearing none of his brother's excited comments on the bright color-markings and shapely horns of the cattle, and too amazed at the beauty of the cow to express his feelings in words.

At the edge of the forest was a beautiful valley, all covered with rich-green pasture grass. Here the brothers sat down to rest and eat their provisions while the cattle grazed with relish.

After the meal, the young men reclined on the grass, watching the cattle as they grazed. Then suddenly the beautiful white cow emitted a moo! that filled the valley and echoed from hill to hill. This brought such delight to Sigandana that he leapt to his feet and called to the cow:

"Kha uphind' ubize, mhlotshazana!" "Call again, beautiful white cow!"

As if it understood what he said, the cow turned and looked towards him and mooed again. Sigandana grabbed one of his sticks and held it high and once more called to his cow:

"Kha uphind' ubize de kusabele nabasekhaya" "Call again till even those way back home respond."

The cow mooed again, its face still turned towards him. There could be no doubt now that the cow understood that he was complimenting it. Sigandana could not contain himself anymore. He ran around in semicircles and a song of praise broke through spontaneously:

Kha uphind' ubize, mhlotshazana! Kha uphind' ubize!
Kha uphind' ubize, 'de kuve nabasekhaya, basabele!
Wena lusatshazana lumhlophe ngathi yingqaka,
Ngathi yingqaka yeemazi zaseMbo apho kwavel' oomawokhulu,
Kodwa koba yini na kwe lakowethu mini wagaleleka,
Unkqenkqeza phambi kwalo mhlambikazi weziziba,
Wezizib' ezimnyama kwezo nzulu zamahlathi,
Apho sithi sigawul' uqalo 'suke kuvel' iinzwana nenzwakazi?
Amaxheg' olibal' imisimelelo, yoluk' imisipha,
Akhuphuk' ezigcakin' ebizwa lizwi lomhlotshazana,
Amadod' olahl' amazembe, abafazi balahl' amagaba,
Iintombi zowis' imiphanda be ziba ziqhel' ukuyingcekelela!
                    Heyii-i-i-i-i-i-i-i-i-i-i-i!

Call again, beautiful white cow! Call again!
Call again, till even those 'way back home hear you and re-
spond,
O, lovely maiden, white as the rich milk curds,
As the curds from the cows of Embo whence came our fore-
bears,
What strange things will happen the day you reach my home,
Tripping gracefully 'fore this mighty herd from the pools,
From the deep dark pools in the depths of the forests
Where we fell the bamboos to harvest handsome males and fe-
males?
The aged shall forget their crutches, their muscles renewed,
They shall rise from their cosy shelters at the sound of the
voice of
          the white cow;
Men shall abandon their axes, and women their hoes,
And maidens shall drop the pitchers they were wont to keep
          safely poised on their heads!
                    Heyii-i-i-i-i-i-i-i-i-i-i-i-i-i-i-i!

By this time, Siganda was on his feet too. He was still gazing at the white cow, but at the same time listening to the
praises inspired by her beauty. He walked up to his brother
and said, "Son of my father, I beg you to give me that white
cow."

Sigandana stared at him unbelievingly, but quickly collected himself and said, "My elder brother, there are many cattle here, all of them exceedingly beautiful. You can choose any
ten of the very best—heifers, cows, oxen, just as you like. But

don't even dream that I could ever give away that white cow."

"My younger brother, son of my father, I beg you beg you. Give me the white cow, the white cow only."

"My elder brother, I have told you not even to dream that I shall ever give away that white cow. I have offered you any ten of your own choice. If you think that offer is too small, I'll increase it to two tens, and even to three tens. I make this offer with a white heart."

"Younger brother, I beg for the white cow. I want no other."

"Well, elder brother, I thought it was *ubuntu* (human kindness) on my part to cover you by offering you so many head of cattle without father knowing that you got them from me. If you can't accept my gift, you either have to remain here and continue to seek for wealth or go home empty-handed. Make your choice. As for me, I'm going home now."

"I can't let you go home alone. You are my younger brother. I must help you drive the cattle home. We left home together, and we must reach home together, even if one of us has nothing to present."

So the young men gathered the cattle and set out on their journey home. They travelled steadily, allowing the cattle to graze as much as possible where there was plenty of pasture grass. During the journey, Siganda said nothing more either about the white cow or the three tens of cattle he was offered. He seemed reconciled to the fact that he must arrive home empty-handed.

The last day of the journey was very hot, and the stretch of land the young men had to traverse was quite dry. Both men and cattle were very thirsty, but for a long time no water was to be found anywhere. While travelling along the edge of a deep ravine, Sigandana happened to look down the precipice, and right at the bottom of the ravine he espied running water. He called his brother and showed him.

"Oh, yes!" said Siganda. "That's water, and it looks very sweet. But how are we to get there? This precipice is too steep. It would be death to try to scale down."

"That's true," said Sigandana. "But I have a plan. Let's

The two brothers growing up.

weave a rope. I'll tie it round you and lower you gently to the bottom. When you've drunk to your satisfaction, you'll tug the rope and I'll pull you up. Then it will be my turn to go down."

They cut piles of *msingizane* (a kind of grass) and wove a rope as thick as a man's arm. Sigandana then tied one end firmly round his brother's body, and he held the other end and lowered Siganda gently till he reached the bottom. Siganda drank till he was satisfied. Having finished drinking, he removed his kilt and splashed his whole body with water to cool himself. Then he tugged the rope. Sigandana pulled him up, hand over hand, hand over hand, hand over hand, until he brought him to the top.

Then Siganda tied the rope round his younger brother's body and lowered him as gently as he had been lowered till he reached the bottom. As soon as Sigandana stooped to drink, Siganda looked around. From the bottom, he had examined the terrain and come to the conclusion that for anybody at the place where the running water was, there was no way of coming out again without being pulled up from the top as he had been. He looked at the white cow as it lay in the shade of a tree, calmly chewing the cud. He looked at his brother at the bottom of the ravine, and he dropped the rope. A moment's pause, and then he collected his baggage, rounded up the cattle and continued his journey home.

He had the white cow now, and all the other cattle, but he was palpitating all the time:

The white cow! The beauty of the white cow! She's mine now, and all these other cattle are mine too. But oh, the cruelty of me! My younger brother! My father's child! My mother's child! Does he know that I did it deliberately? He loved me so much. But I loved him too. I still love him even though he refused to give me the white cow. But why did he refuse to give it to me? I begged him so much. He has never refused me anything before. But why did I refuse to accept his offer? Three tens of fine cattle! How pleasant it would have been to arrive home together, each having cattle to his name. Yes, even if mine were fewer than his! The white cow! There she is, leading the herd just as my brother predicted when he praised her. I love that cow. I can't help it. Who doesn't love her? Every living thing loves the white cow. Look at that tiny bird perching on the sharp point of her horn right now! What bird is it? A honeybird? Oh, where is it now? It's gone! Ah, there it is! It's fluttering round and round the body of the white cow. There it perches on the horn again! The same horn. It's off the horn now, and again it's fluttering round the cow. It's on the horn again. No, it's still fluttering. Ah, on the horn now! What a wonderful thing it would be if it would continue to do that till we reach home! To see the tiny bird fluttering about the beautiful body of the cow, now on the horn, now off, now fluttering about her, now on the horn again! They'd all marvel at this sight. Now it's off the horn! Where is it? Where has it gone? I can't see it any more! No, it's gone now. It's gone for good. For good. For good.

The white cow continued to trip lightly in front of the herd, but the tiny bird whose comings and goings had captivated Siganda's mind was nowhere to be seen. By the time his home village was in view, Siganda had forgotten all about the bird. As if she knew that this was the village to which they were going, the white cow began to moo repeatedly, and her resonant voice echoed and echoed from one hill to another. Now, in every village, it was the oldest men who used to sing the praises of the celebrated mooing cows, and it was the oldest men who knew the voices of these cows better than anyone else. So when the white cow mooed, the oldest men in the village were the first to detect that the cow they heard had never been in this neighborhood before. When the villagers came out of their houses to listen to the mooing of the cow, they saw the large number of cattle going towards Siganda's people's, and all the men abandoned whatever they were doing and went to this homestead. Old men shuffled along, not caring how long it would take them to reach there. Middle-aged men held their sticks high and hurried to get there before the cattle arrived, so that they could have a good look at them. As for the young men, they raced to meet the cattle, and by the time he reached home, Siganda had a large number of equals and near-equals congratulating him and helping him drive the cattle. The white cow continued its mooing until it entered the gate. The women cheered and the old men sang the traditional praises of the ancestry of this house.

After the men had admired the cattle as a whole, noting the color-markings of each one, they crowded round the white cow that had so fittingly announced its arrival in their midst. They were all amazed at its beauty, and the oldest men swore they had never seen such a beautiful animal before. After the excited shouting had subsided, Siganda was asked, "Where's your younger brother? Where and when did you part with him?"

"Isn't he home yet?" asked Siganda, pretending to be astonished at this question. "It's some time since we parted. After wandering in all directions for days and finding nothing, we came to a place where two roads meet, one from the rising sun, one from the setting sun. We decided to part there, one to take the road towards the rising sun, one to take the road towards the setting sun. But before we parted, we agreed that it would be a good thing to come and meet again at the place where we parted and return home together. I took the road towards the setting sun, and as soon as I had found these cattle, I returned to the place where we had parted. I waited and waited and waited there, but my younger brother never turned up. Then I thought it might be that he had had to travel so far towards the rising sun that, after getting his wealth, he decided to come straight home by some other way."

"But you two boys have never, never been separated before," said the father, greatly troubled. "What came between you two on this day, that you should turn your backs on each other and go different ways? Did you quarrel?

"No, we didn't quarrel, father. When we parted, we were the brothers that we have always been."

Before the father could say anything more, the tiny bird came. It fluttered about the white cow till all the men saw it, and then it perched on the cow's horn and sang sadly:

Tsiyo-tsiyo! Tsiyo-tsiyo?
Phants' emwonyweni, phants'
emwonyweni,
Ulaph' uSigandana, uhlel' ulin-
dile;
Asemnand' amanz'omfula-mhle,
Isaqinil' intamb' esinqeni;
Kodw' ukhala ngoncedo, ngon-
cedo, ngoncedo,
Kuba ngekhe abuy'aphume.
Tsiyo-tsiyo! Tsiyo-tsiyo!
Phants' emwonyweni, phants'
emwonyweni,
Ulaph' uSingandana, uhlel'
ulindile.
Tsiyo-tsiyo! Tsiyo-tsiyo!

Down in the ravine, down in the ravine,
There Sigandana is, alive and waiting;
Still sweet is the water of the beautiful stream,
Still tight is the rope around his waist;
But he cries for help, for help, for help,
For he cannot come out again.
Tsiyo-tsiyo! Tsiyo-tsiyo!
Down in the ravine, down in the ravine,
There Sigandana is, alive and waiting.

"What does this tiny bird say? In the ravine?" asked many people, startled.

But the bird did not sing again. It fluttered around the white cow and then retreated, flying low, and perched on one of the gateposts. The white cow carried her tail high and followed. As soon as the cow came up to it, the bird fluttered, still flying low, going back the way Siganda and the cattle had come.

Two brothers playing together.

"Follow, all those who still have manly strides!" shouted an old man. "Follow that bird and that cow."

The father started to run after the bird and the cow immediately, and he was followed by all the strong men of the village. The tiny bird led the way, and the white cow followed the bird, and the men followed the white cow.

"*Tsiyo-tsiyo! Tsiyo-tsiyo!*" cried the tiny bird, now fluttering about the white cow, now perching on her horn, now flying so low as almost to touch the ground. *Tsiyo-tsiyo! Tsiyo-tsiyo!* The men could hear the tiny bird's call even when they could not see the bird, but they kept their eyes on the cow.

The tiny bird led them straight to the spot from which Sigandana had been lowered, and when the cow came up, it perched on her horn. As the men came up, the white cow lowered its tail. "*Tsiyo-tsiyo! Tsiyo-tsiyo!,*" and the tiny bird flew off the white cow's horn and fluttered straight down the way Sigandana had been lowered. The white cow looked the way the tiny bird was going, raised her head high and mooed and mooed. Sigandana recognized her voice immediately and leapt to his feet and praised her:

> "Call again, beautiful white
> cow! call again!
> Call again, till even those at
> home hear you and respond!"

"That's my child's voice!" cried his father. Then he ran to the very edge of the precipice and called out, "Sigandana! Sigandana! What happened? How can we get down there to help you?"

"No one can get down here without being lowered by a rope, father," Sigandana shouted back. "I have a strong rope tied around my waist. Weave another rope and lower one end of it to me. I'll join the two together, and then you can pull me up. Who are you with up there, father?"

"I am with other men, my neighbours."

"Where's my elder brother."

But the father did not hear this question, because he and his neighbors were busy. Some were cutting grass, some were collecting the cut grass and piling it before a third group who were weaving a thick strong rope as fast as they could. When the rope was long enough, one end of it was tied round a stone and lowered to Sigandana. Sigandana received it, removed the stone, and wove the two ropes together very skillfully. The tiny bird was fluttering round him all the time. As soon as Sigandana called out to tell the men he was ready, almost all of them seized their end of the rope and pulled. As he went up, up, up, the tiny bird fluttered about him and chirruped cheerfully. In no time Sigandana was landed on top of the precipice, panting, but smiling gratefully. The tiny bird vanished and was never seen again.

The men crowded round Sigandana and greeted him, all thankful that they had been able to save the life of their child.

Brothers.

"But how did all this happen?" asked his father. "Who lowered you there?"

"I was lowered by my elder brother."

"By your elder brother? When?"

"At midday."

"Today?"

"Yes, today. I don't know what happened to him. Haven't you seen him?"

The father looked down and did not reply.

"This matter has its own depth," said one of the elderly neighbors. "I request that we all sit down so that we can calm ourselves and hear all this from the beginning."

They all sat down, and Sigandana told the whole story, from the day he and his brother left home to the moment when he was lowered by his brother. In conclusion he said, "After I had quenched my thirst, I tugged the rope, but there was no response from the other end. I tugged a second time, but again there was no response. I called aloud to my elder brother and tugged the rope with strength. Then I saw the rope coming down the precipice and piling at my feet. I was horrified. I thought my elder brother had been dragged down the precipice, and I expected to hear the thud of his body as he reached the bottom. But there was no thud. So I called out again. Silence. Although there was no reply, I felt that my elder brother was still alive. I thought perhaps he had had to drop the rope and attend to the cattle, and that on returning and finding the rope gone, he had decided to cut some more grass and weave another rope. But I wondered why he didn't call to tell me this. Now, when I heard my father's voice, I concluded that my brother must have run home to seek help."

Throughout the story, the men exclaimed and exchanged so many looks of surprise that Sigandana believed that they had not yet met his brother. When he had finished, they all looked down, and there was a long pause.

At last, his father cleared his throat and, in a low voice, told him about his brother's arrival at home, and all the lies he had told them when asked where his younger brother was. In conclusion, the father said, "My son, I know that you and your elder brother loved each other. But now I must point out something to you, and you will just have to accept it, painful though it is. Your brother ceased to love you the day you acquired those cattle, and especially when you refused to give him this beautiful white cow. When he left you in this ravine, his intention was that you should never come out again. If he didn't kill you with his own hands, it was because he had left it to others to do the evil deed. Deep in his heart, your elder brother murdered you himself at the moment when he left you there to die."

Then he turned to his neighbors and thanked them for rescuing his son. He further reminded them that, as they were witnesses to this evil of evils, it would be the duty of them all to open the way to a decision as to what the community should do about Siganda.

"As for me, his father, I know what I must do," he concluded.

Two of the elderly neighbors spoke, one after the other. To console the father of these two young men in the great grief he suffered, they commended Sigandana very eloquently for his manhood and generosity, and they congratulated the father on his great blessing in having such a son. After this, they all rose to return to the village. Sigandana put his white cow on the road, and she led the party all the way, just as she had led them to the rescue. They reached the village late in the evening, to find that Siganda had disappeared. What became of him no one ever knew, for he never returned to that neighborhood.

The Woman and the Mighty Bird

Essentially, this narrative details the testing of a person's response to the dictates of her society. There has been a long cold spell, and the women of the village need wood, but they are having more and more difficulty finding it. For a reason not given on the strictly narrative level of the story, they are forbidden to penetrate the forest, in the center of which is a thick grove of trees that shuts out the sun. As the temptation to enter the forest to seek firewood grows, the prohibition is again stressed. But the heroine of the narrative, a headstrong young woman not particularly given to tedious labor, goes into the forest. There, in the depths, she confronts a mighty bird, a symbol of masculinity and authority, parts of the male body and parts of the body of a bull being used to describe the bird. But these metaphors do more than merely describe the creature: they also point again to the rule of the society, the rule laid down by the men of the community, and the bird becomes a symbol of that authority and restriction.

The temptation is heightened when the woman sees that the bird is sitting on bundles of firewood and is surrounded by such bundles—the very things she lacks, the very things she wants. The symbolism of the bird deepens and broadens to include the girl's own conscience; for that reason, she is initially terrified of the bird, as the conflict between her needs and the external forbidding authority rages within her. The bird grows many times its former size, it makes her explain—rationalize—her actions, makes her repeat again the prohibition that women are not to enter the forest. The conflict

within the young woman is thus embodied in this confronta-
tion with the bird. She promises the creature (i.e., herself)
never to tell anyone, and certainly not her husband, what she
has done.

This is a crisis, and in the ntsomi *tradition, in a crisis,*
characters turn to song, the core-cliché that is the basic struc-
ture of the narrative's surface movement, and the words of the
song summarize her plight. She sings sadly at first, because she
is yielding to temptation, she is breaking the prohibition. The
bird becomes the more fearful each time it repeats the song,
fearful because she is more keenly aware of the punishment for
her indiscretion. She goes home, and she lies to her husband
who is nevertheless suspicious when she arrives with a giant
bundle of firewood. Then she goes to the forest again, and
again she finds the mighty bird and the firewood. This time,
the girl finds it easier to break the prohibition, and this is re-
flected in the way she sings the song: sweetly now, and more
brightly than before. (Note too how the repeated singing of
the cliché moves the plot of the performance closer and closer
to its climax.) The more menacing the bird gets, the ore as-
sured she is. She is not as frightened as before, she assures her-
self, she got away with it once. When the bird deflates and is
calm, she is calm. When the bird says not to tell her husband,
it is she who is reminding herself of that. The husband is even
more suspicious on this occasion. And the third time that she
goes to the forest, she is wholly self-confident, an old hand
now at such criminal activity. As menacing as the bird (her
conscience) might be, she is completely assured. She takes the
bundle and goes home. This time, her husband confronts her,
and threatens to kill her unless she tells him the truth. The
woman falters, then tells. But she is not destroyed at this
point. It is when she confesses that she got the wood from the
mighty bird that the bird moves in from the forest and kills
her, swallows her up. The man faints, and is thus out of the
way: he is not to be destroyed, for he has broken no law.

But it is not simply the breaking of the law that destroys
the young woman; she is eliminated because she has broken a
promise to a mightier power. It is not the fetching of the

wood that causes her destruction, though the society might have punished her for this. The "mighty bird" actually gives her the wood. What destroys her is the revelation that she got it from the mighty bird. There are two loyalties here: first, to her husband and presumably to the society, and second, to the mighty bird (that is, to herself). Society says, "Don't go to the depths of the forest." The bird says that it is all right to come to the depths, but she is to tell no one that she has seen the mighty bird. She is swallowed up because she revealed her relationship with the bird. The conflict is finally not between the girl and her husband, it is between her and the bird. Her husband was going to take her life for lying to him; the bird does take her life for betraying it.

Either way, she would have been killed. Her lies get her so enmeshed that the only outcome must be her death. She is lazy, curious, and arrogant. She gets caught between society's restrictions and the restrictions of the bird. She has committed a crime of conscience, and she must suffer for this. Her conscience is a higher power than the society, it is more demanding because it represents the internalization of the laws of that society. It is not the breaking of the prohibition per se that destroys her; it is the idea that she has broken the prohibition —this idea has become so embedded in her conscience that when she breaks it, when she goes against the dictates of her society, she must of necessity be punished—if not by the society, then by her own conscience. The bird seeks the harmony of a society at peace with itself, and the bird represents nature —but in this narrative, it represents the girl's own nature. Her crime has upset her own natural equilibrium, which is a reflection of the social equilibrium, and she is destroyed. Thus is the balance reachieved.

The Woman and the Mighty Bird

IT CAME ABOUT, ACCORDING TO SOME tale, that there
was a beautiful young woman who lived with her husband
close to a very big forest where all the women used to gather
firewood. In the depths of the forest there were very tall trees
that cast fearful shadows all around. The depths were greatly
feared by the whole community, and though no one ever gave
the reason why, the women were constantly warned by the
men never to go anywhere near the tall trees.

It so happened at one time that there was a long spell of
cold, and the women had to go more frequently into the forest, bringing home much bigger bundles of firewood on their
heads. Moons rolled by, and the cold spell did not pass. Wood
became scarcer and scarcer, and the women took longer and
longer to gather, and the bundles they brought home became
smaller each day. What was to be done? The women were to
be seen standing in small groups in the forest, talking in low
tones and pointing towards the depths. The beautiful young
woman never voiced her own opinion in these talks but always stood close and listened with interest while the older
women talked at length and reminded every woman that none
of them was ever to venture into the depths.

One day, when the women had scattered in all directions,
each one picking up a twig here and a twig there in order to
make up her bundle, the young woman stole quietly away
and, holding her skirt daintily just above her knees, she tip-

toed towards the depths. She went on and on, crossing streams and streamlets, until she came to the grove of tall trees that hid the sun, making day look like night. She paused and looked around, her heart beating wild.

Then suddenly, deep in the dark shadows of the great trees she saw two red lights, as big as a man's head. Looking more closely, she saw a big red beak, a big long neck as big and long as the trunk of a big tall man, many sizes that of a great bull. It was a giant bird on whose red throat was fold upon fold of flesh that hung loosely like the dewlap of a giant bull. The woman was seized with terror and would have turned and fled, but she found herself unable to move from where she was. Then, his eyes fixed on hers, the giant bird beckoned her with his wing. It was then that she noticed that the tips of the winds were white and the rest of the body black. She hesitated. He beckoned again, his red eyes still fixed on hers. She let down her skirt and walked slowly towards him.

He was sitting on a huge bundle of firewood, like a hen sitting on its brood, and all around him were bundles and bundles of firewood of all sizes, ready to pick up and carry away on one's head. As she drew nearer and nearer, the bird puffed himself until he was many times his former size, and his eyes and beak and throat became a deeper and deeper red. The woman came to a stop in front of him.

"Be not afraid," he said in a deep voice. "Come closer!"

The woman came closer.

"You are the woman whose homestead is at the edge of this forest?"

"Yes."

"You are married to the Ndelas?"

"Yes."

"What have you come here for?"

"I—I'm looking for firewood."

"Is there no more where you usually gather?"

"There are only small twigs left, and they are so scarce that it takes a whole day to make up just a small bundle. It tires one."

"I understand. Where are the other women now?"

"They are scattered all over the usual area, picking up those small twigs."

"Do they know that you're here?"

"No. I—I stole away."

"Weren't all the women told never to come near this place?"

"Yes, we have been told many times never to come here. But as for me, I get tired of walking over that same place every day, picking up thin little twigs that do not make a good fire. And—it's so cold. So I came."

"You speak well! Now, if I give you a bundle of wood to carry home, do you promise never to tell anybody?"

"I promise."

"You will not tell the other women?"

"I promise."

"Your husband?"

"I'll never tell him."

Thereupon the giant bird puffed himself to a huge size, rolled his deep-red eyes and boomed:

Ungaz' utsho kwabakwa Ndela	You're never to say to those of Ndela
U'b' ukhe wayibon' intak' enk-ulu	That you've ever seen the mighty bird
Eqeba-liqeba lubilo-bilo!	Of manifold windpipe and manifold dewlap.

In reply, the woman sang sweetly but sadly:

Soze nditsho kwa bakwa Ndela	I'll never say to those of Ndela
Ukuba ndikhe ndayibona intak' enkulu	That I've ever seen the mighty bird
Eqeba-liqeba lubilo-bilo.	Of manifold windpipe and manifold dewlap.

The bird puffed himself to a yet greater size and boomed again:

"You're never to say to those of Ndela" etc.

The woman sang again:

"I'll never say to those of Ndela" etc.

The bird puffed himself still greater and more fearful, his rolling eyes and beak and throat a deeper red than ever, and he boomed a third time:

"You're never to say to those of Ndela" etc.

The woman sang a third time:

"I'll never say to those of Ndela" etc.

"Very well!" said the bird. "Pick up any bundle you like and carry it home. Remember! You are not tell your husband."

The woman picked up a bundle of firewood, put it on her head and went home, taking a round-about way in order not to be seen by the other women.

Her husband was surprised to see her come home so early and with such a big bundle of good firewood.

"How does it happen that you come home so early, and with such a big bundle on your head?" he asked.

"I—I've been very lucky," she replied. "I found plenty of wood in a place that the other women don't know about."

"Where's this place?" asked the husband sharply.

"In the forest."

"I know *that*. But whereabouts?"

"Somewhere—not very far from the place where we usually gather wood."

"Where are the other women now?"

"They're still gathering twigs in the usual place."

The husband said no more, but he followed the woman with his eyes as she moved about the home preparing the evening meal.

When the time came to go to the forest again, the young woman joined the other women of the community, and as soon as they had scattered, she stole away and made for the depths. She found the bird sitting on the pile of wood as if he had never moved. He beckoned her, and she came up to him. As soon as she was close enough, he puffed himself and boomed:

Ungabo'b' utshilo kwabakwa Ndela	Woe to you if you've said to those of Ndela
U'b' ukhe wayibon' intak' enkulu	That you've ever seen the mighty bird

Eqeba-liqeba lubilo-bilo!	Of manifold windpipe and manifold dewlap.

In reply, the woman sang sweetly and more brightly than before:

Mn' anditshongo kwa bakwa Ndela	I did not say to those of Ndela
Ukuba ndikhe ndayibona intak' enkulu	That I ever saw the mighty bird
Eqeba-liqeba lubilo-bilo.	Of manifold windpipe and manifold dewlap.

The bird puffed himself greater and boomed louder:

"Woe to you if you have said to those of Ndela" etc.

The woman sang sweetly and assuringly in reply:

"I did not say to those of Ndela" etc.

The bird puffed himself and boomed yet louder and more menacingly:

"Woe to you if you have said to those of Ndela" etc.

The woman sang sweetly and more reassuringly:

"I did not say to those of Ndela" etc.

Then the bird deflated and calmed himself and told her to pick up a bundle of wood and go. She cast her eye over the bundles, taking her own time, and then picked up a much larger one than before. As she turned to go, the bird again gave the warning: "Remember! You are not to tell your husband!"

When she reached home, her husband was more startled than surprised because she had returned much earlier and her bundle was noticeably bigger. Again he asked her, and again she gave the same explanation as before. He said no more, but looked more troubled than ever.

When the pile of wood was almost finished, the woman went to the forest again, and again she stole away as soon as she knew that the other women were far enough. This time she went close up to the bird without waiting to be asked, and when the bird boomed three times, "Woe to you . . ." each time more menacingly than before, she sang sweetly in reply, "I did not say . . .," each time more brightly and reassuringly than before. Then she picked up the best bundle next to the one on which the bird was brooding, and turned to go.

"Remember! You are not to tell your husband!"

On reaching home, she threw down the bundle on the usual spot and was just turning to go to the cooking hut, when her husband appeared at the door of the Great Hut and beckoned her. She walked up to him, noting that he was agitated, but not letting him see that she had noted this.

He stood aside to let her go in, and as soon as she had entered, he grabbed a pile of spears with his left hand and one glittering long-bladed one with his right, turned and faced her.

"Woman!" he said. "Twice you have told me lies. This time you're going to tell me the truth or I'm going to stab you to death. Where do you *alone* get this wood?"

And he raised his long-bladed spear threateningly.

"But what are you asking me, my husband? I told you before that I found—"

"You told me, but you told me a lie. I want the truth!"

He stepped towards her, his long-bladed spear held high in his right hand. The woman tried to run this way and that along the wall, but he caught up with her, pressed her to the wall with the blades of the spears in his left hand, and then lowered the spear in the right hand and held it close to her heart.

"Will you tell the truth or shall I kill you? Where did you get this wood?"

"Wait! Don't kill me! O, don't kill me! I'll tell the truth!"

"Speak!"

"I got it from the depths."

"From the depths!! Who gave it to you?"

"O! Mhm! O!"

"Speak!"

"It was given to me by—by—by—the mighty bird."

No sooner had she uttered these words than the great trees moved from the depths of the forest, surrounded the en-

tire homestead and cast their dark shadows over it. The great
bird emerged from the shadows and made straight for the
Great Hut. His eyes and beak and throat were a terrifyingly
deep red, and as he approached, he grew bigger and bigger
until, by the time he reached the doorway, he was many sizes
bigger than the hut itself. The man was so terrified that his
spears dropped from his hands, and he fell senseless near the
hearth. The woman crouched at the far end of the hut, clutch-
ing her chest with her right hand and shielding her face with
her left, as if she was being blinded by the light of the big red
eyes that glared at her from the doorway.

The great bird thundered:

> Woe to you if you have said to
> those of Ndela
> That you ever saw the mighty
> bird
> Of manifold windpipe and
> manifold dewlap.

The woman sang weakly, a little out of tune:

> I did not say to those of Ndela
> That I ever saw the mighty
> bird
> Of manifold windpipe and
> manifold dewlap.

The great bird interrupted her, thundering more fiercely:

> Woe to you if you have said to
> those of Ndela
> That you ever saw the mighty
> bird
> Of manifold windpipe and
> manifold dewlap.

The woman sang more weakly, much more out of tune:

> I did not say to those of Ndela
> That I ever saw the mighty
> bird
> Of—

The great bird interrupted her, thundering most fiercely:

> Woe to you if you have said to
> those of Ndela
> That you ever saw the mighty
> bird
> Of manifold windpipe and
> manifold dewlap.

The woman sang very weakly, completely out of tune:

> I did not say to those of Ndela
> That I ever saw—

Like lightning the great bird stretched out his long red neck right over the prostrate man, opened his great red mouth very wide and—gulp!—he swallowed the woman alive. Then turning sharply about, he vanished in the grove, and the great trees and their shadows receded to the depths of the forest.

COMMENTARY TO
Sikhamba-nge-nyanga

The beauty of Sikhamba-nge-nyanga, *"She-who-walks-by-moonlight" involves her whole community. She becomes identified with nature and becomes abstracted as the people see the similarities between the beauty of nature and the beauty of the human female. She is a blessing for all of society, and all may delight in her loveliness. Such beauty must therefore be protected. To abuse it is to negate it, and the happiness engendered by that beauty is thereby lost. It is a man's privilege to gaze on* Sikhamba-nge-nyanga, *but the people are punished when they attempt to consign the wrong* function *to the girl, i.e., to beauty; when they violate the customs that protect and nourish her. She returns to nature, whence she came, and she cannot be restored until a sacrifice is offered, until the people recognize their guilt and make reparations. Nature does not destroy her, it merely reclaims her from those who have treated her in an uncustomary fashion, who have attempted to force upon her an unwanted function. Beauty is fragile, elusive, evanescent, and it fulfills its own function; when made to serve another function, beauty dies. That which created it (nature and a love of beauty—in this narrative, represented respectively by the doves and the pool on the one hand and the mother on the other) is alone able to restore it.*

Barrenness plagues her mother during the first years of her marriage. Initially favored by her husband, she must first endure the jealousy of her co-wives·and then the disgust and indifference of her husband when it is discovered that she is barren. She is alienated; the mother's beauty dies, and the husband visits her very seldom. Finally, nature takes a hand in the miserable life of the woman; two doves give her pellets which make her pregnant. A girl of exceptional beauty is born, Sikhamba-nge-nyanga, *and the birth of this child causes a number of changes in the life of the mother: her former beauty is restored, she becomes very happy, and her husband is reconciled to her.*

As for Sikhamba, *people can only gaze at her—men do not go hunting, women do not hoe in the fields, girls do not go to draw water, herdboys do not tend to the cattle and goats. Even the animals do not graze. All living things are stricken by the beauty of this girl, so much so that the mother must bring her inside so that the people and animals may go about their business. So awe-stricken is the father by the beauty of this girl that he does not question her paternity. He begs his wife's forgiveness and promises to make up for his cruelty to her. Such is the influence for goodness and kindness exerted by* Sikhamba. *But there is a time and a place for all activities, and the fact that* Sikhamba's *beauty stops people from carrying out their duties creates a problem. The community must therefore create a new law:* Sikhamba *can come out only by moonlight—hence, her name. There is thus an association between the beauty of the moon and* Sikhamba's *beauty.* Everyone *can see the moon and marvel at its beauty. This is a privilege for all men; all can enjoy it. And no one will become jealous of someone else.*

She marries and has a child of her own. Then, one day, when all the others are in the fields, Sikhamba *is in the house with a withered woman, and two customs clash. The old woman demands that* Sikhamba, *being the only other adult around, go to the stream and bring her water. When* Sikhamba *reminds the woman of the custom, the crone says, "I can't die of thirst when there is a grown-up woman in the house. . . ." And so* Sikhamba *is forced because of one custom to violate another. She is unused to the sunlight, she stumbles and gropes—this is not her accustomed role, she is being forced to do something she does not normally do. Because of this, some unseen power draws her into and under the water. But this is no evil force. When the* mpelesi *brings Sikhamba's child to the water, Sikhamba comes out and nurses the child. When the in-laws attempt to carry her back home, the river follows them to the village and turns blood-red. Until the people realize what they have done, until restitution is made for the broken custom, nature will not give her up. Had the river remained red, the people would have died, it would have been the end of life itself. And so, in their fear, they release her again to the water.*

When the people are at a loss as to what to do, the doves again appear and offer to fly and tell Sikhamba's *parents. At the suggestion of those parents, a sacrifice is made, and the waters (nature) releases* Sikhamba-nge-nyanga. *And again, men may gaze on her beauty, as always. It will never die, never end.*

Sikhamba-Nge-Nyanga

IT CAME ABOUT, ACCORDING TO SOME tale, that there was a wealthy man who had many wives. Among these women was one very beautiful one. At the beginning, she was her husband's favorite, and this made the co-wives very jealous of her. Unfortunately, she did not bear any children, and this disappointed her husband greatly, and after some time he neglected her altogether, despising her. Then she became the laughing-stock of the co-wives. Hardly any of them spoke to her, and even the children were told never to set foot in her house or run any errands for her. The co-wives were in the habit of forming themselves into groups and working together, hoeing their fields together, cutting grass together, weaving mats together, and so on. But none of them would work with her. So she used to do all her work by herself. She could be seen hoeing her field alone, cutting grass alone, sitting on her stoop and weaving her own mats alone. Moons used to roll by without her ever seeing her husband, and when he did come, he used to spend just a day or two with her and then go back to the houses of the wives who bore him children. This made her so sad that she was nearly always in tears.

One day, she picked up her hoe and went to hoe her field as usual. She hoed and hoed and hoed until she was tired. Then she went to sit in the shade of a tree in the middle of the field. There her sorrows overcame her, tears flowed down her cheeks and she wept silently.

"Why are you crying *nkosikazi* (madam)? What makes you so sad?"

The speaker was one of two doves that had come unnoticed and perched on one of the boughs of the tree under which she was sitting. "I'm crying because I am sad. I am sad because my husband doesn't love me any more. He doesn't love me any more because I don't bear him any children. I don't bear him any children because I cannot."

The doves flew away, but soon returned, each of them with a pellet in its beak.

"Take these pellets and swallow them immediately, and very soon you will be heavy with child," they said.

The woman took the pellets eagerly and swallowed them at once. She felt so grateful to the doves that she offered them some corn, but the doves would not accept this.

"No," they said, "we don't want any reward for what we've done for you. We'll be satisfied if you give us a pebble each."

So the woman picked up two pebbles from the ground and gave them to the doves.

True enough, after a few moons she discovered that she was heavy. She was delighted at this, but she made up her mind that she would tell neither her husband nor any of her co-wives about this. And she knew that they cared so little about her that none of them would notice anything until the child was born.

When her time came, she gave birth to a girl of exceptional beauty. This brought her great joy. She gave the child the name *Thanga-limlibo* (Budding Little Pumpkin), and she felt so bitter against her husband that she could not persuade herself to let him know. If he ever came, he would make the discovery then, but as for her, she would never go out of her house to seek him in the houses of her co-wives. She was so determined about this that she would not take her child into the light of day, lest some one might see it and carry the news to her husband. So she kept the child indoors during the day and only after nightfall would she allow her to come out to drink the evening air. This went on for years until Thanga-limlibo sprouted (reached the age of puberty). It was only at that age that her mother occasionally made her do something or other in the courtyard during the daytime. They were very happy together, and the mother's former beauty was restored. One morning, Thanga-limlibo came out into the courtyard and began to tidy the clearing in front of the huts. For the first time the people saw her. Her beauty was so amazing that they all stood there gazing at her. The men would not go hunting; the women would not go to hoe the fields; the girls would not go and draw water from the spring; the herd-boys would not drive the cattle and goats to the pastures; the animals too would not go grazing. All living things flocked round the courtyard of her home and gazed at her, feasting their eyes on her beauty. It was not until her mother noticed this and ordered her to come in, that the people and the animals could move away.

The head of the family was not present at this gathering, but the news of the girl of extraordinary beauty reached his ears that same morning. He set out immediately to find out what it meant. He found his neglected wife in the courtyard and was amazed to see her so happy and beautiful. Embracing her warmly, he asked her what had restored her beauty. She smiled and invited him to come in. There for the first time he came face to face with his daughter and with such beauty as he had never seen even in his dreams. With joy he embraced his daughter and then his wife and then his daughter again and then his wife again, begging forgiveness, and making a solemn vow that he would more than make up for his cruelty to her. Then he set about making preparations for a great feast in honor of his daughter.

Now that Thanga-limlibo had been seen by her father, the mother felt that it was not necessary to keep her indoors any more. But as soon as Thanga-limlibo stepped into the light of day, all living things flocked where she was. If she went to draw water from the spring, they all followed her. If she was working about the house, they stood there gazing at her and would not move until she went indoors. So the community decided that she was not to come out during the daytime: she was to come out by moonlight, go to the fields by moonlight, go to draw water from the spring or river by moonlight, when the people had finished their day's work and could gaze at her beauty. She therefore became known to the community as *Sikhamba-ngenyanga* (She-who-walks-by-moonlight).

By the time the great feast came, the fame of the beauty of the girl who walked by moonlight had spread to all the neighbouring villages, and all the people, young and old, made up their minds that they would come. The feast was going to take place in the moonlight, and this unusual arrangement made the occasion even more attractive. It was not surprising therefore that when the day came, the village saw the greatest gathering that had ever been seen even by the oldest men and women in that community. When Sikhamba-ngenyanga came out, the people were so amazed at her beauty that they all stood there gazing at her. The young people who were seeing her for the first time flocked round her, and the grown-ups who should have left her to those of her own age-group and gone about their feasting found it difficult to tear themselves away from the young people. In any case the celebrations went on until daybreak, when Sikhamba-ngenyanga had to go indoors to make it possible for the people to go.

Soon after this, it was known that Sikhamba-ngenyanga was going to be married to a handsome young man who had met her at the great feast. All the young men had, of course, fallen in love with her, but she had fallen in love with this particular one, the son of a wealthy man whose home was three days' journey from her home-village. When the day came, she was accompanied by the largest bridal party that had ever been seen, and amongst the cattle given as her *nqakhwe* (dowry) was a beautiful dun-coloured ox, the most beautiful ox over a very large area. The wedding took place in the moonlight, and before leaving Sikhamba-ngenyanga at her new home, her people warned the in-laws that this young woman was not to go out during the day-time, and they stressed that this custom must be observed very strictly.

The in-laws observed the custom. Sikhamba-ngenyanga stayed indoors during the day-time and came out at moonrise to hoe the fields or draw water from the river. The people knew this and would come out and gaze at her as she passed by. Everything went well until a baby was born, and her parents immediately sent her a *mpelesi* (young girl sent specially to nurse the baby).

One day all the people of the house went out to work in the fields, leaving the young mother with her baby and the *mpelesi*. The only other person in the house was a withered old woman, the mother of Sikhamba-ngenyanga's father-in-law. She was so worn out with old age that she could not help herself in any way, and whoever remained in the house with her had to help her with everything. In the middle of the day, the old woman felt very thirsty. Sikhamba-ngenyanga brought her some water, but the old woman complained that it was sour and she demanded fresh water at once. In vain Sikhamba-ngenyanga tried to coax her to drink the stale water, reminding her that there was no one to bring fresh water as the river was rather far and the *mpelesi* too young to go there alone.

"I can't die of thirst when there is a grown-up woman in the house," said the old woman. "Go and fetch me fresh water at once!"

So She-who-walks-by-moonlight was forced to pick up her water pot and ladle, step into the light of day and go to draw water from the river. She knew her way very well in the moonlight, but as she had never gone to the river during the day, the light was too strong for her eyes. As she tried to pick her way down the slope, through the bushes and reeds she stumbled several times and fell. She scratched her arms, her face, her legs. But at last she reached the deep pool where she had drawn water many times in the moonlight. She tried to draw water with the calabash ladle, but this was pulled out of her hand by some unseen power, and it disappeared under the water. She tried to draw with the water-pot, but this too was pulled out of her hands and disappeared. She took off her leather mantle and tried to draw water with it, but this was also pulled out of her hands and disappeared. She took off her head-cover and dipped it in the water so that she could run back home and let the thirsty old woman suck the water from it, but this too disappeared. In despair, she cupped her hands in order to draw just sufficient water to wet the throat of the old woman. Then the unseen power drew her under the water.

When her husband and in-laws returned from the fields and found that she had been away for some time, they sent the *mpelesi* to look for her. The little girl went to the pool, looked around, called out, but received no reply. Then she went back to report. The grown-ups went to the pool, saw her footmarks at the water's edge, and concluded that she was drowned. They did all they could to recover her body, but they could not find it. Meanwhile the baby was hungry and crying for its mother.

At moonrise the *mpelesi* picked up the baby, put it on her back and, without saying a word to the in-laws, she walked quietly to the edge of the pool where the mother had disappeared. There she sang sadly, calling on the mother to come out and suckle her baby:

Uyalila, uyalila, Sikhamba-ngenyanga *Uyalila umntan' akho. Uyalila.* *Kha uphume umanyise, Sikhamba-ngenyanga.*	It is crying, it is crying, Sikhamba-ngenyanga It is crying. Your baby is crying. Do come out and suckle it, Sikhamba-ngenyanga

Thereupon there was a disturbance on the surface of the deep pool, and the mother's head and face appeared. Standing breast-high in the water, Sikhamba-ngenyanga sang:

Yinto yangabom! Yinto yanga-bom, *Yenziwe ngabagama ndingalibi-ziyo,* *Ukuthi ma ndikhe amanzi emini;* *Ndaba kukha ngomcephe, wat-shona;* *Ndaba kukha ngomphanda, watshona;*	It was intentional! It was inten-tional On the part of those whose name I may not utter; To send me to draw water dur-ing the day-time; I tried to draw with the ladle, and it sank; I tried the pot, and it sank;

Ndaba kukha nge ngubo, yatshona;	I tried the mantle, and it sank;
Ndaba kukha ngeqhiya yatshona;	I tried the head-cover, and it sank;
Ndathi ndakukha ngezandla, ndatshona.	And when I drew with my hands, I sank.

After singing her song, Sikhamba-ngenyanga came out of the water, took her baby into her arms, suckled and fondled it, and without saying a word, she handed it back to the *mpelesi* and disappeared under the water. The *mpelesi* carried the baby home and put it to bed. She did this again the following night and the night after. Then the in-laws discovered it and questioned her. When she told them what had been happening, the men decided to waylay the mother. They hid themselves in the reeds near the pool some time before moonrise. They saw the *mpelesi* coming with the baby on her back. They heard her sing her sad song. They saw the mother standing breast-high in the water. They heard her song and saw her come out, suckle and fondle the baby. And just as she was handing the baby back to the *mpelesi*, they sprang upon her, seized her and would carry her home. But the river followed them, followed them beyond the reeds, followed them through the woods, beyond the woods, up the slope, right up to the village, and there the water turned blood-red! Then the in-laws were seized with fear and they put her down. The river immediately received her, resumed its normal colour and receded to its place.

When the people were at a loss what to do, two doves appeared and offered to fly immediately to Sikhamba-ngenyanga's own people, report what had happened and seek advice. On reaching the village, the doves perched in the gate-posts of the cattlefold. The herdboys saw them and were just about to throw sticks at them and kill and roast them when the doves sang:

Asingo mahotyazan' okubethwa,	We are not doves that may be killed,
Size kubika Sikhamba-ngenyanga;	For we come to tell of Sikhamba-ngenyanga;

Ube kukha ngomcephe, wat-shona,	She dipped the ladle, and it sank,
Waba kukha ngompanda, wat-shona,	She dipped the pot, and it sank,
Waba kukha ngengubo, yatshona,	She dipped the mantle, and it sank,
Waba kukha ngeqhiya, yat-shona,	She dipped the head-cover, and it sank,
Waba kukha ngezandla, wat-shona.	She dipped her hands, and she sank.

Sikhamba-ngenyanga's parents gave the doves some corn to eat, and then asked them to fly back swiftly and tell her in-laws to slaughter and flay the dun-coloured ox and throw its carcass into the pool after nightfall. The doves flew back swiftly, delivered their message, and the order was carried out immediately.

At moonrise that night, when the *mpelesi* carried the baby to the water's edge, all the people of the village followed her. They heard her sing her sad song, they saw Sikhamba-ngenyanga stand breast-high in the water and heard her sing her song. They saw her come out of the pool and suckle and fondle her baby. But this time, after the baby had been fed, the mother did not hand it back to the *mpelesi*. Instead, she carried it lovingly in her own arms. And as she walked quietly back to the village, the people gazed and gazed and gazed at her beauty in the moonlight.

Why the Cock
Crows at Dawn

IT CAME ABOUT, ACCORDING TO SOME tale, that Hawk visited his cousins, the family of Cock. The little ones of the House of Cock were always glad when Father Hawk came, because he never forgot to bring them nice toys. On this day, however, they were disappointed because Father Hawk had not brought any gifts of any kind. When he saw that the little ones were disappointed, Hawk asked them to forgive him and promised that he would bring them many toys on his next visit. He then took out the key of his house and gave it to them to play with. The chickens took the key and ran to the ash heap to play. But after some time they forgot the key and ran all over the courtyard, playing some other games. Meanwhile, Hawk was inside the house, conversing with Cock and his wife.

Towards the end of the day, Hawk said to his cousins, "My cousins, it's rather late. Let me beg for the road now. Where are these little ones? They must bring my key."

"Little ones! Little ones!" shouted Hen, flapping her wings. "Bring the key now. Father Hawk wants to go home."

The little ones ran to the ash heap to look for the key. They sought for a long time, arguing among themselves, this one here saying to that one, "You had it last," and that one saying to another one, "No, he had it last. I saw him." The grown-ups in the house noticed that there was something wrong, and they all came out to help in the search, but the key could not be found.

At last it became clear that Hawk must go home without his key. Cock and Hen were very sorry about this, and they begged their cousin's peace for this thing that had happened. Hawk replied and said, "Oh, don't be troubled, my cousins. Little ones are little ones after all. I'm sure that one of them will sooner or later remember were they left the key. In any case, the blame is mine. I shouldn't have forgotten to bring them toys."

Having said this, Hawk flew away, leaving the family of Cock scratching, scratching, scratching and scattering the ashes in all directions to find the key.

Then suddenly, the family of Cock heard a whiff and saw a shadow flitting past, then they heard a painful cry high up in the sky. Hen knew that cry immediately. One of her little ones had been pounced upon, grabbed and carried away in Hawk's talons!

"Bring back my little one!" she implored. "My little one! O!"

Hawk spoke to Cock and Hen and said, "My cousins, I'm sorry to do such a painful thing. But I can't help it. On my way home, I remembered that all my food is locked up in my house. I shall not be able to enter without my key. In order that I may not die of hunger, I shall be compelled to live on these your little ones until my key has been restored. If you want me to stop taking away your little ones, look for that key until you find it." So saying, he flew away with the little one.

And from that day, Hawk has been living on the little ones of the House of Cock. Whenever he feels hungry, he comes swooping down and carries away one of them. As for Cock and his family, they go on scratching, scratching, to find the key. From the moment that it comes out of the egg, the first thing that a young chicken has to learn is to peck and scratch the ground, looking for the key. Every dawning day, you can hear Cock calling out aloud:

"Vukani nonke lusa-a-pho! Ma sifune isitshi-i-i-ixo!"   Wake up, all of you, my family! Let us look for the key!

At once, you will see Hen leading her little ones to the ash heap, scratching, scratching, scratching with her claws, pecking, pecking, pecking with her beak, picking up this little thing here, then throwing it away, picking up that little thing, then throwing it away. You will see the little ones running after their mother, learning to do what she is doing. You will see Cock strutting about, now scolding this little one, now scolding that one, now scolding that one over there. Sometimes you will see him turning round sharply and scolding the mother herself. But all the time, he is watching every little shadow that flits by so that he can give the alarm, because he knows that any moment, Hawk may swoop down, grab and carry away another little one. There will never be rest, there will never be peace in the House of Cock until Hawk's key has been found and restored.

Why the Hippo
Has a Stumpy Tail

IT CAME ABOUT, ACCORDING TO SOME tale, that the Hare one day took a long rope and went with it to the Elephant.

"Elephant", he said, "today I want to show you that I am stronger than you. Let's pull each other by means of this rope."

"Who are you, Little Hare, to think of such a thing?" said the Elephant, laughing.

"I know that I am smaller than you, but I know that I am stronger. Come! Here's the rope. I'm going to show you now." The Elephant laughed again, but agreed to pull.

"You see then," said the Hare, "you are going to stand here at the top end, and I will go and stand at the bottom end, on the bank of the river. Take hold of this end of the rope, but you are not to pull until I give you the signal. I am going to hold the other end of the rope. When I get to the bank of the river, I'll tug the rope twice. When you feel the rope go tug! tug!, then you are to begin to pull!

Then the Hare took hold of his end of the rope and ran to the bank of the river. Arriving there, he called out, "Hippo! Hippo! Where are you?"

When the Hippo appeared (on the surface of the water), the Hare said, "You think you are a very strong animal. But today I want to show that though you are so big, you are not as strong as I am. Just take hold of this end of the rope. I am going to hold the other end up there, and you and I are going to pull each other."

The Hippo laughed at this, just as the Elephant had done, but eventually agreed to pull.

Then the Hare said, "You are going to stand here in the water and hold this end until I give you the signal to pull. When the rope goes tug! tug! you had better pull with all your strength."

Having said this, the Hare went to the center and tugged the rope twice. Immediately, the Elephant pulled at the top end, and the Hippo pulled at the bottom end. Then the Hare sat down in the shade and watched.

Soon the Elephant was to be heard exclaiming, "What! Is the Hare so strong then? Can it be that he has asked some other animals to help him? I'll soon find out." The Hippo too at the bottom end was amazed to discover that the Hare was so strong, and he put out all his strength and pulled. But very soon he found himself being dragged right out of the water.

"Pulled out of my place by the Hare! I'm sure he is not alone. But I'll not leave off pulling until we come face to face. And if I find that he's tricking me, I'll deal with him."

The pulling went on and on, and the Elephant, who never shifted from his original position, brought the Hippo nearer and nearer, and the coils of the rope heaped higher and higher in front of him. At last the Hippo lost all his strength and found himself being drawn faster and faster until he came face to face with the Elephant! Both were startled on seeing each other.

The Elephant was the first to speak. "Oh!" he said. "So it's you! You tricked me into this in order to try my strength?"

"Mercy, O great one! implored the Hippo. "I didn't know that I was pulling against you. The Hare challenged me to pull, and all this time, I thought I was pulling *him*."

"You thought you were pulling the Hare!" said the Elephant, blazing with anger. "Do you understand what you're saying?"

"Believe me, great one. In truth, in truth, I didn't know that I was pulling *you*. The Hare said to me that *he* would hold the other end. In fact, I myself was wondering where he got so much strength."

"Do you think I'm going to believe that tale? I'll not be tricked a second time. What is more, I'm going to teach you a lesson. Choose between two things—that I kill you, or that I cut off your tail!"

"O, great one! I implore you neither to kill me nor to cut off my tail. Believe me when I say that . . ."

But the Elephant would not listen any more. Instead, he pulled out a sharp crude *assegai* and took long strides coming close to the Hippo. Seeing this, the Hippo retreated and then turned sharply about trying to run away. But the Elephant sprang forward, caught him smartly by his tail and chopped it off with his assegai.

"O!" cried the Hippo. "How can I return to my family in such disgrace, without my tail?" And hanging his head with shame, he walked slowly back to the river.

On reaching there, he called the whole House of Hippo before him and made a decree that all Hippos must immediately cut off their tails. This decree was carried out, and so it is that today the Hippo has a stumpy tail.

Choosing a King

IT CAME ABOUT, ACCORDING TO SOME tale, that the birds decided to come together and choose from amongst themselves a bird who would be king of all the birds—those in the sky as well as those on the ground.

The birds arrived punctually on the appointed day, and, before the assembly opened, groups of them were to be seen putting their heads together, whispering, whispering, whispering. In all these groups the name "Ostrich" could easily be heard, because it was mentioned with a great deal of excitement, and it became clear that the majority of the birds felt that since Ostrich was the biggest of them all, the Seat of Chieftainship sould be awarded to him.

Silence was at last requested, and the groups broke up, the birds taking their proper places in huge concentric circles so that every one should be able to see everybody else. They left a clearing in the center. As soon as the business of the meeting was announced, one bird immediately raised the name of Ostrich. This proposal was greeted with much chirruping, twittering, and flapping of wings, and it looked as if the meeting was one in spirit.

Amidst the cheering, however, Ostrich rose to his feet and spoke, saying:

"My countrymen, although I am thankful that so many of you think that I am worthy of the Seat of Chieftainship, I feel unable to accept it. This seat is too exalted for me.

"Allow me to place my finger on something that you seem to be overlooking. And it is this. There is one gift of nature which makes the birds different from all other creatures on earth, and that is the gift to rise from the ground and soar into the sky. As you all know, I am one of the few who have been denied this gift. For that reason I am not worthy of this seat. We have assembled here today to choose a king who will be king of all the birds—those in the sky as well as those on the ground. A king must be able to see all his followers. A bird that cannot fly is obviously unable to see the birds in the sky. On the other hand, a bird that can fly is able to see all the birds he wants to see—those in the sky as well as those on the ground. According to my (way of) seeing (things), the only bird who is worthy of this seat is the bird who can soar higher than any other bird into the sky. If such a bird is king, he will be able to see every bird he wants to see in the sky. If he wants to see those on the ground, he can fly low and, if necessary, even land on the ground."

At this point, there were chirrupings and twitterings and flappings of approval, and Ostrich had to pause. When silence was restored, he continued with confidence and said, "If this assembly goes along with me in what I have said, as it seems to, allow me to put forward a proposal. Let us disperse now, but assemble again early tomorrow in order that every bird who can fly may participate in a contest. Let him who soars highest and remains longest in the sky, no mater who he is, be immediately hailed as 'King of all the Birds—those in the sky and those on the ground. 'I vanish, my countrymen."

The assembly accepted the motion unanimously and proceeded to elect Ostrich to be chief steward of the contest.

Very early on the following morning, the birds were to be seen coming from all directions, and by the time the morning sun had left the mountains behind it, the birds had covered the whole field. Ostrich was to be seen striding up and down, giving orders to his subordinates—Domestic Fowl, Guinea Fowl, and other birds that could not join the contest.

When everything was ready, Ostrich begged for silence. Then he spoke and said, "My countrymen, I, your servant, greet you all in the name of the House of Bird. We are now going to hold our contest. In order that there may be no complaints or disputes when the results are announced, I am going to give you the pith of our resolution. Yesterday we agreed that the bird who soared the highest and remained longest in the sky, no matter who, would immediately be hailed as 'King of all the Birds—those in the sky and those on the ground.' Am I on the track?"

"Yes, you are on the track!" chorused the birds.

"Now, if you are all ready, I am ready to give the order to fly."

"We are ready, all of us!" came the chorus.

"Hookoo!" shouted Ostrich, flapping his wings as if he himself were trying to fly.

The birds rose as one, and in a moment, they had hidden the sun. Up, up, up, they went. Then suddenly, in large and small numbers, they came down again. First Quail and then many others came dropping, dropping, dropping faster and faster on the ground, until only one bird was to be seen in the sky. It was Eagle, high up in the clouds.

As soon as they saw this, the stewards arranged the birds in the customary concentric circles, and Ostrich gave the order to salute. Then all the birds, in big voices and small, gave the royal salute:

Bayethe, lukhozi!	Hail, Eagle!
Kumkani wazo zonke iintaka—	King of all the Birds—
Ezisezulwini nezisemhlabeni!	Those in the sky and those on the ground!

Then, beckoning with his wings, Ostrich called out in a very loud voice: "Come down, Great One! You have won the Seat of Chieftainship." But just as he was beginning to come down, Eagle suddenly heard "ting-ting! ting-ting!" Glancing up quickly, he saw Grass Warbler, the tiniest of the birds, in the sky well above him.

"You little thing!" thundered the Eagle, blazing with anger. "How dare you! What are you doing up there?"

"You ask me what am I doing!" piped Grass Warbler. "Can't you see I am contesting the Seat of Chieftainship? Look here, Eagle. It's no use trying to bully me. I know the resolution of the birds as well as you do."

Eagle felt angrier than ever, but thought it wise to say no more. So he continued his downward flight and landed on the clearing in the center. But this landing was hardly noticed, for almost every bird was gazing at the sky, straining his shaded eyes to make out what that tiny moving speck was, and exclamations of "Unbelievable! Unbelievable!" came from all sides.

"Impossible! How did it happen? shouted Hawk.

How, indeed, did it happen? Grass Warbler had thought out his whole plan overnight, and just when the birds were taking their places for the flight, he had woven his way nnoticed, creeping between the legs of the big birds until he stood next to Eagle. As soon as the order to take off was given, he leaped up and settled on Eagle's back. He had calculated, correctly, that on such an exciting occasion Eagle would not notice the weightless body on his back. Grass Werbler had sat there quite still, breathless with excitement, until the moment when Eagle was listening to the birds sing his praises. Only then he hopped off, and, from a safe distance, drew the attention of Eagle with his "ting-ting!" Now, Eagle's decision to fly straight down after the exchange of words gave Grass Warbler a splendid opportunity to demonstrate that he had succeeded not only in soaring higher than any other bird but also in remaining longer than any other bird in the sky. He performed all sorts of stunts while the other birds gazed at him in silence and astonishment. First he came straight down as if he was preparing to land, but suddenly he checked his flight, jerking once or twice. Then he veered and sailed swiftly to one end of the field, then wheeling round, he came whiffing over the assembly right across to the other end:

> Ting-ting!   Ting-ting!   Ntyilo-
> ntyilo!

Then he made a curving upward turn and, arching gracefully, came sweeping over the assembly, diving as if he were landing.

Then he soared again into the sky and, poised delicately right above the clearing, he fluttered his little wings triumphantly:

> *Ting-ting!   Ting-ting!   Ntilo-*
> *Ntyilo!*
> *Ting-ting!   Ting-ting!   Ntilo-*
> *ntyilo!*

Then he came straight down and landed right in the center, next to Eagle.

The spell was immediately broken, and a hot dispute began. Nor was this an orderly discussion at the beginning. First one bird turned and addressed himself to those immediately around him. One of those who heard him replied in opposition. Then a fourth one came up in support of the second, and so on. This happened at several points, so that in a short time there were groups all over the field, some large, some small. These groups, however, consisted mainly of the smaller birds, for the chief steward had communicated to the bigger ones, not in words but in his attitude, that their proper place was the official center where he was. So the groups gradually thinned down, and finally all the birds had resumed their places at the assembly.

A great dispute was raging here. The big birds were divided in opinion. One group, led by Blue Crane, argued that Eagle could not be king because, as Eagle himself admitted, Grass Warbler had outsoared him, and because, as every bird had seen, Grass Warbler had remained in the sky longer than any other bird. It was noticeable, however, that Blue Crane was not prepared to go so far as to say that Grass Warbler should be king. Another group urged that since the assembly had already hailed Eagle as king, nothing more could be done.

"We cannot fool our worthy countryman in this manner," said Vulture Baldhead, leader of this group. "We cannot hail Eagle as king while he is in the clouds, and deny him the Seat of Chieftainship the moment he lands on the ground."

"On the other hand," replied Bittern, leader of a third group, "we cannot disgrace the whole House of Bird by trampling underfoot a resolution that we accepted in one spirit only yesterday, a resolution that was renewed before we took off this morning. It is the truth that when we hailed Eagle as king, we all thought that he had outsoared us all and remained in the sky longer than any other bird. If we made a mistake, because we did not know the facts, let us admit that we made a mistake. I am sure that our worthy countryman will not think that we are fooling him, for he himself bears witness that he saw Grass Warbler well above him and even exchanged words with him."

This speech made an impression on the birds, and many of them made side glances at Eagle, obviously expecting him to say something at this stage. But Eagle would not utter a word.

Suddenly Raven Whiteneck leaped forward:

"Countrymen, this is unbearable! Granted that Grass Warbler outsoared Eagle, granted that Grass Warbler remained in the sky longer than Eagle, is the great House of Bird going to be ruled by this little thing here?" So demanded Raven Whiteneck, waving his left wing scornfully at Grass Warbler and almost blowing him over with the whiff of it.

"The reins! The reins, chief steward!" protested many of the birds, demanding that order be restored. "This is an assembly of grown-ups. We cannot allow such behavior."

Thereupon Ostrich reproved Raven Whiteneck and ordered him to go back to his place.

"Countrymen," said Stork, stepping calmly into the clearing, "we began this argument at the strengthening of day. Our shadows have now shrunk until they have almost disappeared under our bodies, and it is almost noon. Before the sun begins to slant, let us be clear where we are facing. Up to now the chief steward has not been given an opportunity to voice his own opinion on this matter. I beg that the assembly grant him that opportunity at this stage."

"You have spoken, son of Stork!" murmured a large section, approvingly.

Ostrich felt embarrassed. He had hoped that he would be able to take advantage of his position as chief steward and hide his head (conceal his own opinion) on this issue till the end.

He looked around uneasily, hemmed and hawed, cleared his throat twice or three times, and then began:

"Countrymen, it's a heavy day this, for all of us who belong to the House of Bird. To most of those in this assembly, it seems a fact that cannot be disputed that Grass Warbler outsoared Eagle the Most Beautiful."

"The reins! The reins! interrupted Bittern. "Let everyone be called by his name until we've reached a decision. There's no Most Beautiful one yet in this House. That's exactly what we're trying to settle."

"Peace, countrymen!" said Ostrich, withdrawing. "I mean Eagle. Yes, countrymen, we've been arguing the whole morning, and if we're not going to remain here till nightfall, there's one question that we've got to answer, and it is this: Just how did Grass Warbler manage to outsoar us all, including—er— Eagle? Only the answer to this question will enable us to . . ."

At this point Grass Warbler could restrain himself no longer.

"Don't hide your head, Ostrich!" he piped. "You know the resolution of this assembly. It was you who put it forward, and it was you who renewed it this morning. There's no 'how' in that resolution. None at all. I've been watching you since yesterday, Ostrich. For all your seeming modesty—declining the Seat of Chieftainship, offering your services as runner and what not—you're not honest."

"How dare you insult the chief steward of this assembly?" demanded a sharp voice from one of the outer rings, and·in a twinkle Hawk came swooping in an attempt to blot out the name of Grass Warbler. But Grass Warbler dodged neatly, dived, and disappeared in a hole.

Meanwhile Hawk, unable to check his own flight, went bumping and crashing into several of the respected big birds in the inmost ring. This caused another row. The insult to Ostrich was forgotten, for all the great ones were now concerned about the offense to their dignity.

"These little bullies!" said Vulture Baldhead in anger. "Who invited him to take this matter into his hands? Is this an assembly of youngsters?"

"Where's Grass Warbler?" demanded Bittern.

"Gone into that hole," answered several birds together, pointing at the hole with their wings.

Bittern, Vulture Baldhead, Blue Crane, and Stork strode with dignity to the mouth of the hole.

"Come out, Grass Warbler!" shouted Vulture Baldhead. No reply.

"Come out, Warbler!" shouted another of the great ones. "None of these bullies is going to touch you again, not while we're here."

No reply.

"Why doesn't he speak? What's happened to him?"

"Frightened to death, I assure you," said Raven White-neck with contempt. "There is a king for you!"

"Silence!" thundered Bittern, swinging round and glaring at Raven Whiteneck.

Not only Raven Whiteneck but all the birds were so startled by this voice that they shrank back in terror.

Ostrich was the first to recover. He reminded Bittern and the other great ones by the look he gave them that he was still in charge of affairs, and they went silently back to their places. Then he spoke:

"My countrymen, sons of the House of Bird, I beg you all to listen to what your servant is going to say. It seems to me we chose an unlucky field for this assembly, for since the dawning of this day, not a single thing has gone the right way. I beg therefore that we move from this place now and seek another field where we shall be able to hold a meeting worthy of the House of Bird. I make this proposal in the hope that when we resume, each one of us will have had time to calm and collect himself, remind himself whose son he is and what is expected of him."

All the smaller birds cheered, and all the big ones nodded with dignity.

"But what about Grass Warbler?" asked one of the smaller ones.

"Yes! Something must be done about him," replied Ostrich. "Who will make a suggestion?"

"Yes, I have a suggestion," said Butcher-bird, speaking for

the first time. "It would not be proper to let Grass Warbler have his own way just because of the little mistake made by Hawk. If Grass Warbler will not come out of that hole, let us choose someone here to stand over the hole so that he does not slip out while we are away. I agree with the chief steward that we have to answer the question just how Grass Warbler managed to outsoar Eagle. Until we have found the answer to that question, we shall not be able to decide what to do with him. Therefore, he must be watched until we have decided what to do."

"Does the assembly agree?" asked Ostrich.

"We agree!" answered the majority, but a considerable number did not reply either way.

"Allow me to propose, countrymen," continued Butcherbird. "Grass Warbler is very small, and we must therefore choose a bird with very big eyes to watch this hole. The bird who has the biggest eyes here is Owl, and I therefore raise his name."

The proposal was accepted in one spirit. So Owl immediately took his position at the mouth of the hole while the other birds went to seek a fresh field.

After jumping into the hole, Grass Warbler had made up his mind that he was not going to risk his life again, in spite of the assurances of Bittern and the other great ones. Sitting very still, he listened carefully and heard every word, and when the decision was made that Owl was going to watch him, he began to think how he was going to affect his escape. He found a way, but he decided to wait until he was sure that Owl was left all alone above the hole.

When he reckoned that the other birds had found a new field, he dug some clay, molded it carefully, and then very skillfully modelled a tiny little mouse. Then gently and slowly he pushed this "mouse" up, up, up, towards the mouth of the hole. As soon as the mouse appeared, Owl pounced upon it. The clay broke into many many tiny fragments, some going into his eyes, some into his nose, some down his throat. Owl choked and sneezed and coughed, his eyes and nose running. He took some time to recover, but when he did, he quickly cleaned his face and, remembering his duty, he resumed his position and stared into the hole without winking or blinking.

Late in the afternoon the birds returned. The first to arrive was Hawk and close behind him was Butcher-bird.

"What's the news, countrymen?" asked Owl. "Who is king?"

"We have not decided who is going to be king," replied Hawk. "This matter is very difficult. Eagle didn't win, and therefore he cannot be king. That one thing is clear to all of us now. As for Grass Warbler, it was decided that he must be hanged at once."

"Hanged?"

"Yes, hanged," replied Butcher-bird. "Take him out at once. Where is he? Take him out!"

Owl shook his head doubtfully, but there wasn't time to ask how this decision was arrived at, for most of the birds had returned by now, some looking quite ashamed, but the majority chirruping aloud with excitement.

"Take him out!" many of them shouted. "We're going to hang him, that insolent little thing who insulted our worthy chief steward. Make haste, Owl!"

Owl went into the hole without saying a word. He looked into every corner, but he could not find Grass Warbler. Meanwhile the birds on the surface were shouting impatiently, "What's keeping him so long? Make haste, Owl! The sun is setting and we're getting drowsy."

Raven Whiteneck, Hawk and Butcher-bird went into the hole to try and hurry things up, but after a long search they returned to the surface. Owl was the last to come out.

"Where's Grass Warbler?" demanded the birds.

"My countrymen, I beg you to forgive me for what has happened. I can't explain it, but it is a fact that Grass Warbler has escaped."

"Escaped? Where were you when he escaped? Then you are going to die."

Then a large number of birds fell upon Owl. But Owl fought very bravely and skillfully, warding off many blows with his wings, pecking with his beak, scratching with his talons, and sometimes beating off with his wings. And all the time he kept retreating, until he squeezed into the hole.

"Come out, Owl!" shouted some of the birds into the hole. "Come out and find Grass Warbler at once, or we'll surely come into the hole and kill you."

Now, Owl was not a coward, and in his whole life he had never been so shabbily treated before. When he heard these threats, some of them coming from birds who knew that ordinarily they were no match for him, he bristled.

"Come in and kill me if you want to," he said defiantly. "But remember that you won't get another chance to swarm upon me as you did just now. You'll have to come in one by one."

The assailants paused and exchanged glances. The mouth of the hole was just big enough for birds of the size of Hawk and Crow to go in. The great ones couldn't have gone in even if they had not felt it beneath their dignity to do so.

"There's your opportunity, Hawk and Crow," said Vulture Baldhead, smiling scornfully. "You were very eager to show your bravery earlier in the day. We give you authority now to go in and kill Owl for letting Grass Warbler escape."

No bird moved. Meanwhile the sun was fast going home to its mother, and many of the birds began to look about uneasily. Then a large section, consisting of those birds who had been looking ashamed since the return and had taken no part in the attack on Owl, were seen to whisper together, and then they rose as one and started their flight home.

"Come back!" shouted many of those who still kept to their places. The meeting is not over."

"It is not the custom of the House of Bird to hold meetings after sundown," was the reply.

Then the rest of the birds, in ones and twos, in small groups and large groups, began to wing their way home, and when darkness fell, not one was left at the place of assembly.

Down in the hole, Owl began to consider his position. Going home was out of the question. But then, must he die of hunger in that hole? Certainly not! For the first time in his life, he would have to go out hunting at night, while the other birds were sleeping, and then return before dawn to spend the rest of the day in this same hole. It was very difficult at first, and he bumped against trees and other hard objects. But after some time his eyes became used to the darkness, and he was able to find enough food.

So Owl resolved to live this way, sleeping by day and hunting by night. He has never been forgiven by the other birds. If they surprise him anywhere during the day, they swarm round him, reviling him and trying to scratch him, but he has always succeeded in keeping them at bay. He is used to hunting by night now and sees far more clearly in the night than in the day. But he has never been happy since he was separated from the rest of the House of Bird. In the silence of the night he may often be heard crying out pitifully: "*Isizungu! O, Isizungu!*" (Loneliness! O, Loneliness!)

The birds have never assembled since, nor are there any signs that they ever will, for they fear even to refer to that contest. Grass Warbler is at large. For the first few days after his escape he had to hide in the grass, for he knew that birds like Hawk and Raven Whiteneck would certainly kill him if they found him. Indeed, these two have not forgiven him up to this day. But among the rest of the birds, there seems to be some understanding that Grass Warbler is to be left alone, for, after all, he is a harmless little fellow and, should the matter of the Seat of Chieftainship be raised again, it is hardly likely that he will want to contest.